JUL -- 2023

BY SUSAN ELIA MacNEAL

Mother Daughter Traitor Spy

MOTHER
DAUGHTER
TRAITOR
SPY

Bantam Books
New York

MOTHER
DAUGHTER
TRAITOR
SPY

A Novel

SUSAN ELIA MacNEAL

Mother Daughter Traitor Spy is a work of fiction. All incidents and dialogue, and all characters with the exception of some well-known historical figures, are products of the author's imagination and are not to be construed as real. Where real-life historical persons appear, the situations, incidents, and dialogues concerning those persons are entirely fictional and are not intended to depict actual events or to change the entirely fictional nature of the work. In all other respects, any resemblance to persons living or dead is entirely coincidental.

Published in the United States by Bantam Books, an imprint of Random House, a division of Penguin Random House LLC, New York.

BANTAM BOOKS is a registered trademark and the B colophon is a trademark of Penguin Random House LLC.

LIBRARY OF CONGRESS CATALOGING–IN–PUBLICATION DATA
Names: MacNeal, Susan Elia, author.
Title: Mother daughter traitor spy: a novel / Susan Elia MacNeal.
Description: New York: Bantam Books, [2022]
Identifiers: LCCN 2022012165 (print) | LCCN 2022012166 (ebook) |
ISBN 9780593156957 (hardcover) | ISBN 9780593156964 (ebook)
Classification: LCC PS3613.A2774 M33 2022 (print) |
LCC PS3613.A2774 (ebook) | DDC 813/.6—dc23
LC record available at https://lccn.loc.gov/2022012165
LC ebook record available at https://lccn.loc.gov/2022012166

PRINTED IN THE UNITED STATES OF AMERICA ON ACID–FREE PAPER

randomhousebooks.com

2 4 6 8 9 7 5 3 1

First Edition

Title page art by Adobe Stock/rangizzz

To the real Los Angeles spies and spymasters
of the 1930s and '40s

We Americans . . . are characters in this living book of democracy.

But we are also its author. It falls upon us now to say whether the chapters that are to come will tell a story of retreat or a story of continued advance.

—*President Franklin D. Roosevelt's final campaign speech of 1940*

INSPIRED BY REAL PEOPLE AND TRUE EVENTS

Violet and Veronica Grace are fictional. However, they're inspired by two very real people: Grace and Sylvia Comfort, a mother and daughter who both became spies in 1940 and infiltrated various isolationist and Nazi organizations in Los Angeles. Little is known about their personal lives, save for the basic facts. Records of the undercover work they did to fight American Nazis in the early 1940s in Los Angeles are held at the University Library at California State University, Northridge.

Ari Lewis is also a fictional character. Like Veronica and Vi, he's also inspired by a real person: Leon L. Lewis, an American attorney and World War I veteran who became the first national secretary of the Anti-Defamation League, a national director of B'nai B'rith, and founder and first executive director of the Community Relations Committee of the Jewish Federation Council of Greater Los Angeles. He also created and led a spy operation that infiltrated numerous American Nazi groups in the 1930s and early 1940s. The Nazis referred to him as "the most dangerous Jew in Los Angeles."

Jonah Rose is based on Lewis's then assistant, Joseph Roos. Roos was a journalist as well as an activist and spy, trained by Admiral George C. Marshall and his men. He was an executive director of the Community Relations Committee of the Jewish Federation Council of Greater Los Angeles and vice president of the American Jewish Congress. Like Lewis, he's best known for his anti-Nazi spying activities in the 1930s and 1940s, which resulted in the successful arrest, deportation, and prosecution of Nazis in the United States and the prevention of acts of sabotage, murder, and assassination. Lewis's and Roos's files from the 1930s and 1940s are also kept at the University Library at California State University, Northridge, and Roos's later files are at the University of Southern California.

All the German and American Nazis are based on real people as well. Their names have been changed, except for Hermann Schwinn.

MOTHER
DAUGHTER
TRAITOR
SPY

PROLOGUE

"Imagine—it's a year from now, 1941, or maybe even '42—and Germany and the Axis have won the war," Hermann Schwinn was saying in a thick accent. "A long black limousine drives along the Pacific Coast Highway. Palm trees sway in the warm breeze, as sunlight glitters on the blue ocean."

Schwinn, a Frankfurt-born insurance salesman in his forties, was a member of the Bund, a German American organization, established in 1936 as a successor to the Friends of New Germany. The Bund was comprised of only Americans of German descent, and its goal was to promote a favorable view of Nazi Germany and recruit new members.

Schwinn was the Bund's Los Angeles regional commander. A naturalized American citizen, Schwinn was a devoted National Socialist, five feet nine inches and slim as a knife, a small mustache beneath his nose, a pipe stuck in his mouth at a jaunty angle. At his feet slept his dog, a large German shepherd, who Schwinn bragged would attack any Jews in biting distance.

"The limo turns right onto a small dusty road," Schwinn continued, "lined with tall sycamore trees. It approaches large black iron gates, opened by armed guards in uniform. They give the *Sieg heil!* salute as the limo passes."

Schwinn was sitting at a corner booth in the restaurant at Deutsches Haus, a German social club in downtown Los Angeles and home to the Bund. The restaurant had a bar running the long length of the room. Dining tables covered in red-checked cloths were piled high with the white-fleshed veal schnitzel, rich wursts, and sweet pastries German ex-pats craved, accompanied by draft beer and dark coffee. The air was fragrant with the scent of hops and fried meat. Cigar and cigarette smoke curled up to the ceiling, covered in plaster swastikas. Along the walls ran hand-hammered bronze plates flourished with the hooked cross.

A man in the booth next to them was reading the *Los Angeles Times;* the headline declared: "Germans March into Paris: French Are in Full Retreat." A black-and-white photograph showed Nazis raising the swastika flag.

He continued: "It follows a road winding through orchards and vegetable gardens—you can see red barns with horses and cows. The air smells of eucalyptus."

Across the table was another of the Haus's members, Wilhelm Wagner. Wagner was not impressed. "How poetic," he said with a Viennese accent. Wagner was the owner of the Continental Bookstore, screened German movies downtown, and was Schwinn's lieutenant. It was rumored he answered directly to Joseph Goebbels. Wagner looked more like the Aryan ideal: taller and younger, tanned and well muscled. His center-parted hair was so blond it appeared almost white and his eyes were an arresting silver.

Schwinn took a swig of dark bock beer and laughed. "Well, this might please you then," he countered easily. "Just out of view there's a water storage tank, with its own water supply from springs, along with a double-generator power station and a twenty-thousand-gallon fuel oil tank. Terraces have been leveled and planted with fruit trees, all supplied with copper pipes and a watering outlet for each tree. A culvert's been built for the stream and there's a cold storage locker for storing food." He beamed with pride. "It's completely self-sustaining! Is that practical enough for you?"

Wagner grunted as an oompah band began the stirring notes of the military parade song "Bayerischer Defiliermarsch." It was almost midnight; the regulars remained, drinking steins of beer and glasses of schnapps, celebrating the news of the fall of France. Hitler's triumphant taking of Paris was theirs to applaud—and the noninterference by the rest of Europe or America reassured them no one and nothing could stop the new Nazi world order. In a dark corner, two men in their eighties played *kriegspiel,* the Prussian version of chess.

"Like a military bunker?"

"Exactly!" Schwinn exclaimed. "Underneath, it's a bunker. We could fight a war, considering all the weapons we'll have stocked in the armory." He frowned, annoyed to be thrown off. "Where was I? Oh, yes—finally, the limo comes to a stop in front of a gorgeous four-story, twenty-two-bedroom ranch." He unrolled translucent tracing paper: an architect's plan showing scaled drawings of buildings. "Complete with servants' quarters, a garden, a tower, a swimming pool, an enormous garage. On one flagpole is the American flag. On the other is the swastika. More armed guards salute and open the passenger door.

"And . . . a man emerges. It's our führer, of course, who's come to meet with General Tojo and his men, and to praise us personally for the work we've done in his name, here in America. What do you think?"

Wagner's reply was a sarcastic slow clap. "And how much does all this cost?"

Schwinn considered. "About four million. Maybe more. Oh, what am I saying? Definitely more."

"And who's paying?"

"Our friends from the Silver Shirts—one generous couple in particular."

Wagner nodded. "How much has been built?"

"More than you'd imagine."

A waitress with thick yellow braids, wearing a frothy lace blouse and ankle-length dirndl, carrying a tray of drained beer mugs and dirty plates, passed a bald man gesturing wildly. She lost her balance and tripped. The tray fell to the floor with a loud crash, glasses shattering. Everyone turned and froze, while Schwinn and Wagner reached for their pistols. There was a long moment of silence. A man's voice rang out: "Paris has fallen! To Hitler in Paris!"

The sound of relieved laughter filled the room as those in the crowd raised glasses yet again, echoing, "Hitler in Paris!" Schwinn and Wagner relaxed as the waitress struggled to her feet and another brought out a broom and dustpan.

Schwinn gestured to a waiter, dressed in lederhosen, knee socks, and a small hat, for another round of beer. The waiter nodded, then fetched and carried over a fresh pitcher. Adam Haber, short and stout with a round face and prominent belly, grinned affably at the two men as he approached with the foaming beer. "What's this?" he asked, indicating the architect's plan, as he carefully refilled the men's mugs.

"Nothing you need to concern yourself with," Schwinn replied easily as he rolled up the architect's plan. He and Wagner exchanged a glance.

"It's a glorious day for the fatherland, my friends," Haber offered as he set down the pitcher. "On the house. Will there be a public celebration of the victory?"

"Yes, of course! A huge party!" Schwinn motioned for Haber to join them. "You hear anything new about infiltrators?" he asked with a genial smile.

A muscle under Haber's eye twitched as he slid into the booth next to Wagner. "No—nothing."

Schwinn nodded as a passing waitress set down a plate heaped with freshly baked pretzels, golden brown and flecked with sea salt. "You know," he said, leaning forward, "I always wondered how you pay for those two expensive kids of yours." Schwinn reached for a hot pretzel. "Your daughter's wedding was quite large, no? I hear you had the reception at the Biltmore."

Haber laughed. "You know women. They must have their dresses and flowers and pretty things, or else there'll be hell to pay."

"And your son's college tuition?" Schwinn pressed, tearing the pretzel in half. "USC isn't a state school."

"He has a scholarship."

"A lot of people," Schwinn said mildly, taking a bite, "wonder where you and your wife get all your money. You work here as a waiter . . ."

Wagner nodded. "Even as a Navy vet, you can't get much of a pension, what with Franklin Delano Jewsevelt meddling."

Haber smiled blandly. "We're doing fine."

"I have to ask," Schwinn continued, "because the boss is paranoid about infiltrators. What's your view? Surely you must look around at meetings and wonder sometimes."

"I do," Haber replied evenly. "But when I don't see any hooked-nose Heebs sniffing around anywhere, I relax."

"Not all spies look like Jews," Wagner said. "Hell, not even all Jews look like Jews." He leaned in toward Haber. "What's the best way to prevent it, do you think? Infiltration, that is."

"What we're already doing," Haber said. "Background checks. Making sure all the paperwork's in order. I know I had to go through quite the process before I was accepted to the Bund."

Wagner frowned and sipped his beer. "People can forge anything these days."

"You call around," Haber offered. "Check references. Clarify people really are who they say they are."

Schwinn sniffed and put down the pretzel. "People can fix those things."

Wagner leaned back against the back of the booth and spread his legs wide. "Some of the *jugend* told us they saw you taking down license plates in a notebook after last night's meeting here."

"Ah, yes," Haber said, laughing nervously. "That was nothing. A misunderstanding with some overenthusiastic young men. I've already told you—I was writing a note to myself to pick up milk and eggs." He blanched. "Hermann, I would never—ever— You know how loyal to the cause I am . . ."

Schwinn nodded. "Good to know, good to know. It's just—we can't be too careful these days. Germany's taken France, Britain's next—and things are about to get serious here. The war here's already begun, even if most Americans don't realize it yet."

Haber grinned widely, revealing square white teeth. "You *know* I'm loyal." He placed a hand to his throat, rubbing it.

"Are you okay?" Wagner asked the waiter. "You look a little pale, my friend."

"Just tired. Almost the end of my shift—and it's been a long day of celebration." Haber rose. "Excuse me, gentlemen—I gotta see a man about a horse."

* * *

HABER WENT DOWN the long back hall to the staff men's room. Inside one of the stalls, he took a deep breath. When his hands finally stopped shaking, he went outside and walked down the darkened street to the pay phone. Inside the illuminated booth, he lifted the black receiver and dialed a series of numbers. The line crackled and hissed as a voice on the other end answered. He said without preamble, "They know."

Despite the booth's closed doors, Haber could still hear the hum of traffic, the shouts of the newsboys, and a siren in the far distance. "They *know*," he repeated, his voice rising in pitch. "They don't trust me." There was a long pause as he listened. "Do you know what a 'necktie' party is? Do you? Because they mean nooses!"

He shifted his weight and leaned against the glass. "This is my last shift here. It's not safe anymore. After tonight, we're done. I'm out. You're never gonna see me again." He slammed down the receiver so hard the telephone's bells jangled, and went back to work.

When his shift was over, Haber walked to Deutsches Haus's parking lot, to his dented Ford V8, which displayed the bumper sticker KEEP U.S. NEUTRAL next to BUY AND VOTE GENTILE. He saw shadows move from the corner of one eye. "Damn coyotes," he muttered, trying not to panic. He'd already taken his car key from his pocket when he heard something behind him. But before he could reach the footboard and open the door, his head smashed into the driver's side window. The tempered glass broke but held, creating a radial crack pattern like a silvery spiderweb.

As Haber's body slid to the ground, the man who'd assaulted him knelt to take his pulse. He was a hulk of a man in a long black leather trench coat, with a shaved scalp and a face as creased as a balled fist. "Damn it, he's still breathing," he said to his companion. The waiter's skin was turning waxy; but even with a smashed skull, his face was intact.

"Can you hear me?" the other one asked, shorter and thinner but also in leather, shaking Haber by the shoulder.

Haber tried to speak, a drop of red sliding from his ear, but could only moan. Around his head, blood began to pool. He panted for air, then gasped. He was dead.

"Finally," the attacker muttered as he rose, giving the body a final kick in the midsection with his dusty thick-soled boot.

The smaller man began pouring a bottle of whiskey over Haber's body. "Let's make it look like he was blotto drunk."

"Or maybe an epileptic fit?"

"How about both?"

They laughed as he smashed the emptied bottle on the pavement. The harsh scent of alcohol rose, while down an alley, a stray dog barked.

"*Ding-dong, the spy is dead,*" the assailant said. "Now let's get outta here."

CHAPTER ONE

June 19, 1940
New York City

"And now, may I introduce to you our very own Lois Lane, the intrepid editor of the award-winning *Hunter Envoy,* and the winner of the prestigious National Pacemaker Award for excellence in American student journalism: Veronica Grace!"

A wave of warm applause flowed through the audience in the majestic cream-and-gold auditorium of Carnegie Hall as Veronica stepped onto the stage. She was tall for a woman and slim, with pale blond waves of hair, intelligent deep blue eyes, a strong nose, and a pointed chin. As she approached the podium in her purple cap and gown, she wobbled on her new high heels, stumbled, and nearly fell. "Watch yourself, Miss Grace!" Hunter College's president called.

Veronica laughed, a full-bellied guffaw, righted herself, and shook his hand. Emotions—pride, embarrassment, amusement, and stoicism—played across her face. "Thank you, sir," she said, flashing a grin. Then, in an aside to the audience in an exaggerated Brooklyn accent, "Good thing I'm gonna be a journalist, not a ballerina, right?"

The members of the audience chuckled as they fanned themselves with their paper programs. The day was hot and humid, with rain in the forecast; inside the auditorium, it was warm and sticky. Veronica took a moment to search the audience for her mother, who she knew would be sitting in the middle of the orchestra section, wearing a green-and-gold straw hat festooned with yellow poppies. *Found her,* she thought, seeing the beloved face, so like her own. The two women's eyes met, and they nodded, recognizing the enormity of the moment.

Veronica again addressed the crowd: "Thank you, distinguished faculty, ladies and gentlemen, and my fellow graduates," she began in a low voice, surprisingly husky from a childhood illness. She looked to her classmates, in their purple caps and gowns, sitting in the first three rows. "Well, girls—we did it!"

There was a rousing cheer from the assembled graduates.

"We're now graduates of Hunter College, the inheritors of a radical idea: that educating women can change, well, everything. And education for *all* women, not just the daughters of the elite. Yes, we may have a couple of those . . ." She pointed to a tall young woman in the front row. "Priss, we see you!"

Priss waved back good-naturedly, and the audience laughed.

"But most of us standing before you today are the daughters of immigrants, of factory workers, of former slaves. We're the strivers and the seekers. Many of us are the first generation in our families to graduate from college. And our success is a testament to the persistence and power of the American dream. Of democracy."

How I love this country, Veronica thought, catching sight of the American flag on the podium. *This glorious beacon of hope and promise.*

Every woman in the class of 1940 was following her dreams: Veronica's best friend and co-editor of the *Envoy* was going to be student-teaching at the Little Red Schoolhouse while earning her degree from Teachers College. The star of all the school's plays was headed to the Bellevue School of Nursing, focusing on a new specialty: postpartum care for mothers. A leggy alto who also tap-danced was joining the chorus of *Pal Joey* on Broadway. And the class valedictorian would be studying child welfare at the newly opened Columbia University School of Social Work.

There was more applause as Veronica looked out over the crowd. "And we'll need strong shoulders. France has fallen to the Nazis, and the battle for Britain will begin soon. The war's getting closer to the U.S. every day. It's easy to think what happened in France could never happen here. But let's not forget: on February twentieth last year, our own Madison Square Garden was filled with twenty thousand chanting, stomping, shouting Americans rallying in support of Nazi Germany." Veronica hadn't just read about it; she'd been there in person. She'd gone undercover at the rally to research her prize-winning story about the rise of Nazism in New York City for the *Hunter Envoy*.

She swallowed, remembering. "That's right—*twenty thousand* Nazis and Nazi sympathizers. Right here, in the heart of New York City. It's a warning America's not immune from the authoritarianism running rampant across Europe. And it's a call to arms to those who believe the United States is the last, best hope for freedom and democracy.

"What gives me joy and courage is how furious the Nazis would be to see all of us here today." She met the gazes of her fellow graduates. "Colored, Asian, and white. Jewish and Gentile. All social classes. This incredible, diverse, brilliant class of 1940 stands tall and proud, even during this challenging year." She smiled. "And that, my friends, is the real America!"

There was more applause and even a few cheers.

"Our Hunter motto is 'The care of the future is mine,'" she said, wrapping things up. "So, let's take it as our charge—it's up to all of us." She grinned. "Hunter class of 1940, congratulations—and good luck to us all!"

Still beaming, Veronica took her seat alongside the rest of her class as the ceremony ended with a rendition of "America the Beautiful," a benediction from the rabbi, and, finally, the recessional to Edward Elgar's "Pomp and Circumstance."

As the last notes of music faded and the crowd dispersed, Veronica hung back with Izzy Horowitz, her co-editor. The two had worked together for four years on the *Envoy*, with deadlines, late nights, strong coffee, and all the stress and pride of seeing each new issue printed. Veronica adjusted Izzy's cap and fixed her friend's hair. "I can't believe this is it," she said.

"I'm just so glad we're both staying in New York," Izzy replied. Although many of their friends were content to listen to Frank Sinatra and read the comics, Veronica and Izzy—who read every newspaper their school library carried, especially Drew Pearson's syndicated column "Washington Merry-Go-Round"—knew things were bleak, the world was growing darker each day. There was a sense of bated breath as Europe's leaders, like chess players, plotted their next moves.

Veronica's face darkened. "If people don't wake up, we're all going to be goose-stepping a year or two from now."

Another of the graduates, wearing pearl earrings and an orchid corsage, rolled her eyes. "Oh, here she goes again—Veronica Grace and her 'Nazis are evil' schtick."

"They are—just ask the folks in France. Or maybe you haven't heard the latest?"

"I have, and the Germans have promised to be respectful in France. Pétain's in charge now, in Vichy. It'll all be fine."

"It's not 'fine,'" Veronica told her. "Don't you see what Hitler's going to do to them? Just wait."

"Ugh, you're always assuming the worst."

"But the worst keeps happening." Veronica tried not to roll her eyes. Germany was protected by its alliance with Russia to the east and by a neutral America to the west. The Nazis had marched across Holland at lightning speed and taken Belgium, Holland, and Luxembourg easily. France had fallen in six weeks. Now the *Luftschlacht um England,* the air invasion of England, was about to begin.

But why aren't *they angry?* Veronica bit her lip. *A madman's conquering the world, and no one can be bothered. When the fight comes, you need to fight back, not back down like the British fool calling for "peace for our time."*

She took a deep breath and remembered what her late father used to say: *Illegitimi non carborundum—don't let the bastards get you down.*

✷ ✷ ✷

VERONICA'S MOTHER, Violet Engel Grace, better known as Vi, was already at the concert hall's bar, holding a cocktail coupe beaded with condensation. She looked at her tiny gold watch and squinted, counting down the seconds until the hands stood at exactly twelve noon—what she considered the earliest civilized moment of the day to drink. "Here's mud in your eye," she said, toasting the bartender. She took a sip of her gimlet and savored the gin's burn as it ran down her throat. "A few of these and I just might be able to deal with today," she told him as he poured a beer for the man in the double-breasted suit behind her.

Like Veronica, Vi was tall and pale blond—aided by the salon, where she had the grays covered—with the same strong nose and intense blue eyes, surrounded by fine lines and age spots. Her voice was higher and clearer than Veronica's, almost bell-like, and her pronunciation more precise, a product of her German American upbringing in Manhattan's Yorkville. She was the daughter of a butcher from Munich and his wife, who had immigrated in the 1880s. Where Veronica had sharp angles, she had curves—a softening of the jawline, rounded breasts, and plump upper arms. She'd recently begun calling herself "stout," although Veronica had laughed and told her, "You're hardly Winnie-the-Pooh, Mother!"

And although she hadn't officially reached the dreaded "change" yet, Vi was aware she didn't sleep as well as she used to, her temper was shorter, and she had a new propensity for headaches. She was wearing what appeared to be a wheat-colored crepe suit from the Elsa Schiaparelli spring collection, but actually one she'd sewn herself, on her old Singer sewing machine at home. She'd even hand-embroidered the silk collar with the yellow poppies she'd always loved. Her only jewelry was the gold wedding band she never took off and a small engraved cross at her neck.

A Black man in a navy chalk stripe suit approached as she took another sip. "Hello, Mrs. Grace." She recognized him: the father of Veronica's friend who'd sung "America the Beautiful" at the ceremony.

"It's Vi, please." She shifted her weight; her shoes were pinching her toes.

"Call me Louis." He had large brown eyes with shaggy eyebrows and a shiny bald spot circled by graying hair. "The children really are flying the nest, aren't they?"

"Yes," she said with a sigh. "They're hardly children anymore, are they? They're grown women now." She added, unable to stop herself, "It's also my birthday."

"Happy birthday!" he exclaimed. "Twenty-five?"

"Yes—for the twenty-fifth time," she joked. "Fifty," she said in a softer voice. "I'm turning fifty."

"Well, you certainly don't look it." He raised his glass to her. "And Veronica gave a great speech—you must be proud."

Vi took another sip of her drink. "I just wish her father could be here to see it." Navy commander Thomas Grace had died at his desk at the Brooklyn Navy Yard from a heart attack six years previous, at the age of forty-seven. Vi held up her left hand, still wearing her gold wedding band. It still didn't seem possible he was really gone.

"I wish my late wife could be here to see this as well," Louis was saying. "I've taken mine off," he said, looking at the finger where his ring used to be. "It's been eight years for me. Decided it's time to walk among the living again."

"I prefer to wear mine." She took another sip.

"What are Veronica's plans after graduation?"

"She won *Mademoiselle* magazine's Guest Editor competition," Vi told him proudly. *Mademoiselle* was an American magazine for literary yet stylish young ladies. "Very prestigious. She'll be working in Manhattan—they're putting her up at the Barbizon." She pictured it as something incredibly glamorous: young women in the latest fashions, striding across the marble lobby floor, typing up brilliant stories, then leaving in the evening for cocktails at the Oak Bar at the Plaza with men from Harvard and Yale.

"Congratulations."

"And what's your daughter doing? Singing, I hope!"

"She's going to be studying voice privately while she picks up a few waitressing shifts at Le Jardin Creole—our restaurant up in Harlem. But may I ask, what are *your* plans, Mrs. Grace—er, Vi? Now that the nest is almost empty?"

Vi took another sip of her gimlet. "Oh," she said vaguely, "I'll . . . think of something." She felt embarrassed. Here she was, surrounded by so many bright and ambitious young women, her daughter included, and all she had to show was being a wife and a mother. *I'm not a wife anymore—and barely needed as a mother.*

She spotted her daughter in the crowd of emerging graduates with a sigh of relief. "Veronica!" She waved with a white-gloved hand. "Over here! Let me give you a hug, sweetie!"

Louis exited as Veronica swooped in to kiss her mother's cheek. "Mother! I couldn't have done any of this without you." Veronica and Vi held each other, forehead against forehead. "You're my North Star, my partner in crime, my guiding light—you know that, right?"

"Don't forget bridge partner," Vi said, her voice thick with emotion. They both played a mean game of bridge with the other Navy wives and daughters in Wallabout, Brooklyn.

"I could *never* forget my intrepid bridge partner."

Vi smoothed back a strand of Veronica's loose hair. "I only wish your father . . ."

Veronica blinked back tears. "I miss Daddy."

"I know, sweetie," Vi said, kissing Veronica's forehead. "I miss him, too."

Veronica looked around. "Where's Uncle Wally?" Walter Engel, Vi's older brother, had gone to Columbia on scholarship and was now an oncologist in Pasadena. He'd made the trip across the country to see his niece graduate and to celebrate his sister's fiftieth birthday.

"Couldn't stand the crowd," Vi told her. "Or the humidity—California's made him soft. Said he'll meet us at the Heidelberg." She gave Veronica an up-and-down look and whispered, "Are you even wearing a girdle?"

"It's hot, Mother. Be glad I'm at least wearing a brassiere."

Vi pulled a face, and Veronica gave another of her big laughs.

"Speaking of clothes, I need to get the gown and cap back to the rental company." She unbuttoned the graduation gown, revealing her outfit underneath. She wore Katharine Hepburn–inspired wide-legged, cream-colored trousers, paired with an open-necked spring-green silk shirt with satiny pink cherry blossoms on the collar, which her mother had painstakingly hand-embroidered just for the occasion. Three wooden bangles slid up and down each wrist. The hook of the gown's clasp had caught on the threads near the collar and pulled, causing a snag in the satin stitches. "Oh no!" Veronica said, reaching for it, her fingers worrying at the broken thread. The blossom would be ruined.

"It's nothing, sweetie—don't worry," her mother told her. "I'll fix it for you when we get home."

* * *

WALTER ENGEL WAS waiting for them at a back table at the Heidelberg Restaurant in Yorkville, the Grace family's longtime favorite place for celebrations large and small. When they arrived, he pulled out chairs for both women, saying, "Happy graduation to my favorite niece!" to Veronica with a kiss on the cheek. "And happy birthday to my favorite sister!" to Vi with a peck on hers. Ceiling fans spun, moving hot air fragrant with onions, fried schnitzel, and beer.

"I'm your *only* niece."

"And I'm your *only* sister."

He smiled. "You two just missed the rain," he said, looking out the window as the skies exploded into showers, raindrops pelting the plate glass. As a plump and jolly waitress took their order, Walter cleared his throat. "Your mother tells me you're going to be a journalist," he said to Veronica. "This *Mademoiselle* gig sounds pretty exciting. Lots of stories about lipstick and hats, isn't that right?"

"I know it's a women's magazine, Uncle Wally," Veronica told him patiently, "but it's a great place to start a journalism career. The magazine's helped launch any number of famous writers."

Among young women with literary ambitions, the magazine was best known for its guest editor program. The "Millies," as they were called, formed an unofficial sorority as they worked and ate and lived together at the Barbizon Hotel, an "elite fortress for single girls" located eight blocks from the magazine's Madison Avenue office.

"Lipstick and literature—I could write about that!" Walter teased, not unkindly. "By the way, you do know you're unraveling, right?" He pointed to the pink embroidered flower on her collar; it was even more frayed than before.

"It's all right, I'll fix it later," Vi told them.

"Listen," Veronica said to Walter, "everyone would be qualified to be a reporter if journalism was just the act of writing, editing, and publishing information. But it goes beyond that. The best journalist is guided by ethical standards—to help readers make decisions about their lives, their societies, and their governments."

"And their lipstick," Walter added.

Veronica did her best not to roll her eyes as the waitress arrived with glasses on a tray: another gimlet for Vi, a glass of Coca-Cola for Veronica, and a mug of beer for Walter. "More like . . . women who want to write the next Great American Novel—and *also* want to have boyfriends and go to parties and have fun. Yes, while wearing lipstick." She tilted her head. "Because being smart and being stylish aren't mutually exclusive you know, dear Uncle Wally."

"Oh, still so serious! Just like when you were a little girl!" Walter locked blue eyes with his sister. "Wonder where she gets that from?"

"I wonder." Vi smiled as she patted Veronica's hand.

"Happened to pick up a copy of the June issue of *Mademoiselle* at the newsstand on Eighty-Sixth," Walter said, reaching down and placing a magazine on the table. On the cover, a young woman in a striped two-piece bathing suit, sunglasses, and a large straw hat stared back at them. "And there's also a delightful story about wedding dresses, if you're interested."

"Not in the slightest," Veronica replied. And she wasn't—she had no interest in marriage. She'd wanted to be a writer since she'd first been able to read the newspaper. When she'd originally told her parents, they'd laughed, thinking the phase would soon pass— she'd ultimately become a nurse or teacher, before getting married and raising a family, of course. But she'd created her own newsletter in elementary school, began a school paper in middle school, and ultimately became editor in chief and yearbook editor at Boys and Girls High School in Brooklyn. Before her father had died, he had always told her how proud he was of her and her ambitions—and how her investigations and words made the world a better place. He'd even given her a book by the famous young journalist Martha Gellhorn, *What Mad Pursuit,* right before he'd died.

"But what about love?" Walter asked. "Marriage, babies? A house with a white picket fence?"

She did have a boyfriend—or, more specifically, a lover too old to be called a boyfriend. But she had no illusions of marriage. "Maybe." She'd already received five wedding invitations from her classmates, and it was just the beginning, she knew. "But I'd rather be like Martha Gellhorn—stay single, travel to Europe, cover the war."

She took a sip of Coca-Cola. "Gellhorn's completely changing war reporting—Dorothy Thompson, too." Since war reporting was still an uncodified profession, the social climate allowed for women to work: Margaret Bourke-White, Virginia Cowles, Helen Kirkpatrick, Sigrid Schultz, and Betty Wason had all, like Gellhorn, become top-ranked journalists.

"I'm more a fan of Mrs. Roosevelt's writing," Vi offered. "I love 'My Day.'"

"Did you know Mrs. Roosevelt has a weekly press conference for female journalists? And she's written about Gellhorn before, you know—about her novel on the German-Jewish refugee crisis in Prague. Did you read her most recent column?" Veronica asked. "It's about supposed fifth columnists here in the U.S. The paranoia about them changing our attitudes toward civil liberties."

"Well, she has a point," Vi said. "Although as the daughter of German immigrants and a Navy widow, I'm a bit offended."

"Do you really think there aren't any Nazi agents here in the U.S.? Do you really think there aren't true-blue Americans following Hitler and cheering him on? I saw those people, up close, in person, at the rally at Madison Square Garden." She looked out the thick, mottled window at the tree-lined street. "Yorkville's probably a hotbed of spies. That's why the U.S. needs to declare war."

"Oh, ye gods and little fishes, Veronica, you're so *dramatic!*" Her mother sighed. "You didn't live through the last war, and you wouldn't be so quick to speak that way if you had. War is ugly and brutal and horrible—and it's better if the U.S. stays out of it and keeps her husbands and sons alive. I want America first to be healed, to be protected, to be set on its own glorious path to the future. Not destroyed in a war that has nothing to do with us."

"Ladies!" Walter interjected. "The war might be here before much longer, you know," he said. "New York might not be the safest place to wait it out."

"Things aren't looking good for England," Veronica added glumly. She took another sip of her Coca-Cola. "Churchill might think they'll fight the Nazis 'on the beaches,' but if they can't hold back the inevitable invasion, Mosley's Blackshirts and Diana and Unity Mitford'll have Edward and Mrs. Simpson on the throne and a swastika hanging from Buckingham Palace in no time flat."

As Vi prepared to respond, Walter cut in, "Today, let's celebrate." He raised his glass. "To Hunter's class of '40!" he toasted. "Go forth and set the world on fire, Veronica. I can't wait to see what you'll do with your life and your talents."

Vi added, "We're so happy for you, sweetie."

They all drank.

"Veronica, I really am proud of you. And thrilled." She took a deep breath. "And maybe now I need to make some plans of my own, for this next chapter of my life."

"Yes, happy birthday, baby sis!" Walter toasted.

Veronica also raised her glass to her mother. "It's never too late to set the world on fire."

Mother's changed, she realized, *before my very eyes. Maybe it was Daddy's death and widowhood, maybe it's my graduation. Maybe it's turning fifty. But she seems tired—older. Sadder.* Under the table, she took hold of her mother's hand and squeezed it tightly. *She needs something new.*

They finished their celebratory late lunch of Veronica's favorite, sauerbraten with pickled cabbage and mashed potatoes. Dessert was Black Forest cake, dark with chocolate and covered in red maraschino cherries, with a candle for Vi and a round of "Happy Birthday" with the waitstaff.

Afterward, they stood under the restaurant's awning to avoid the driving rain as Uncle Walter hailed a taxi. Somewhere on the Manhattan Bridge, high over the East River, Veronica looked down to realize the pink cherry blossom on her collar had completely unraveled.

CHAPTER TWO

The Wallabout neighborhood of Brooklyn sloped from Myrtle Avenue to the fortress of the Brooklyn Navy Yard. Veronica and Vi lived there, in a single-family brick row house, surrounded by other Navy families. It was tranquil, removed from the hustle and bustle of Manhattan and downtown Brooklyn, the streets lined with modest brownstones and shaded by lindens and maples. It had been the only place Veronica had ever lived; to her it felt permanent, solid, unchanging.

It was still raining as they arrived, the cool, damp breeze causing the leafy branches to sway as they reached Vanderbilt Avenue. Once inside, they all took off their hats and the women their gloves in the dim interior, and Vi made her way to the kitchen. "I'll make us some coffee!" she called to Veronica and Walter. "We had a big lunch, so I'm thinking cream cheese sandwiches for dinner later, or maybe just cake . . . ?"

Veronica looked around the parlor, the furniture plain and worn, then up at the gray-and-blue painting of a nineteenth-century ship caught in a storm, fighting to stay upright. It hung above the fireplace that hadn't worked in years, a tin pot in the hearth plinking with dripping rain. Still, she felt great affection for the painting, the room, the house, and thought of how soon she'd be leaving with a bittersweet mixture of nostalgia and anticipation.

When the telephone rang, Walter called, "I've got it!" and picked up the receiver in the front hall. "Veronica, it's for you."

"Thanks, Uncle Wally—I'll take it upstairs!" She scrambled up the steep carpeted steps and took the monstrous hall phone from the table on the landing into her bedroom. It smelled of Elizabeth Arden's Blue Grass; Veronica had left the bottle open in her hurry to dress for the ceremony earlier. On the floor were piles of newspapers—the New York *Daily News,* which Vi had agreed to, but also the *New York Times,* the *Post,* the *Herald Tribune,* the *Sun,* the *Advocate,* the *Daily Mirror,* and the *Morning Telegraph,* all donated by neighbors, as well as a stack of *New Yorker, Collier's,* and *Life* magazines from the library.

Veronica picked up the Bakelite receiver, heavy and cool against her cheek. "Hello?" She heard her uncle hang up the telephone downstairs as the line crackled.

A young woman's voice asked, "Is this Veronica Grace?"

"This is she." Veronica turned to look out the window; she'd left it open, and the sill was wet. Still, the cord didn't reach far enough for Veronica to close it. Rain-soaked light hit a black-and-white photograph in a silver frame on the dresser of baby Veronica after her christening, held by proud parents. Outside, there was the patter of rain in the trees and the distant sound of a siren.

"Please hold for Miss Blackwell."

There was a pause and the click of the call being transferred, then: "Miss Grace, this is Betsy Blackwell."

Veronica, of course, knew who Betsy Blackwell was— *Mademoiselle*'s legendary editor in chief. She cleared her throat. "Miss Blackwell, hello." *Why would Betsy Blackwell be calling me?*

"I'm afraid I have bad news, my dear."

Veronica felt cold, even in the warm, humid air. "Bad news?" she managed.

"I've been in contact with a woman named Mrs. Maxwell Applebaum—Evelyn Feldman Applebaum. Do you know her?"

Evelyn Applebaum was Veronica's lover's wife. "I—I don't," she answered truthfully, even as every part of her turned cold. She had, in fact, never met Max's wife. Although early on in their affair, one afternoon in a hotel room, she'd gone through his wallet when he'd gotten up to take a shower and seen pictures of a wide-eyed brunette, with hair coiffed in the latest style and a tiny gap between her two front teeth. Veronica sat on the candlewick bedspread. "What's this about?" Her fingers twitched, aching to hold a cigarette. *Surely this can't be real.*

"I'm a freethinker, Miss Grace, and not one to indulge in gossip. However, I met in person with Mrs. Applebaum today. She alleges you're having an affair with her husband. Now," Blackwell continued, "I don't think it's any of my business who our new guest editor's sleeping with. However, having a distraught wife drop by the office is another matter entirely. You may remember we have a morals clause here at *Mademoiselle.*"

"Yes." Veronica swallowed, feeling the blood drain from her face, remembering the contract she'd signed. A high-pitched ringing went through her ears.

"You understand—when Mrs. Applebaum came forward with her accusations, we had to take them seriously."

"I—" Veronica felt suddenly light-headed.

"Before you say anything, please know Mrs. Applebaum had a private investigator take photographs of you and Mr. Applebaum leaving the Plaza Hotel together. On the one hand, the two of you are quite photogenic and obviously have great affection for each other. On the other, leaving a hotel together isn't the smartest thing to do . . ."

Veronica swallowed. She'd met Max Applebaum—an immaculate, unruffled, excessively good-looking, and very married *New York Times* war correspondent—when she'd won the National Pacemaker Award, known as the "Pulitzer Prize of student journalism." He'd presented the award onstage at Hunter, and taken her out to the Oak Bar to celebrate. Then to bed, in one of the rooms upstairs. It had all happened so quickly Veronica didn't give herself enough time or space to ask questions or even form an opinion.

She didn't know he was married at first, and she'd felt intrigued, dazzled by his experience as an international reporter, by his lust, by his sophistication. When she found out, he swore to her it was nothing but a marriage of convenience between two old families. More than once, Veronica called things off and refused to see him. But he'd always send flowers, make wheedling telephone calls and empty promises, and soon enough their affair always resumed. She believed she was in love. And that he loved her, as well.

"Mrs. Applebaum is the daughter of Saul Feldman." Saul Feldman was a titan of New York City publishing. "She told me to let you know you won't find employment in publishing, at least in this city."

Veronica clutched the telephone receiver, her knuckles white. *This can't be happening.*

"And so, Miss Grace, we must terminate our contract with you. We can't have you working for *Mademoiselle*. I'm sorry, but . . ."

Veronica listened but heard nothing except the increasingly high-pitched keen in her ears. "Thank you, Miss Blackwell," she said by rote. She replaced the receiver in the handset to cut the connection, only to raise it again. She dialed a number and waited, biting her lip, curling the metal telephone cord around a finger.

A woman answered the telephone; Veronica wasn't expecting that. But she plunged ahead anyway. "Hello, may I speak to Max?"

There was a silence. "You must be Veronica."

"Excuse me?"

"I'm Mrs. Applebaum. I'm assuming you heard from Betsy at *Mademoiselle*."

Veronica blanched again. "Yes."

"You see, dear, there's a baby on the way." Veronica's mouth dropped open. "And that changes things."

"I'm—I—" Veronica instinctively wanted to say congratulations, but it was just too awkward.

"Ah, he didn't tell you. Of course." Veronica heard the strike of a match and an inhale. "Look, dear, you're young and beautiful. Max says you're smart and come from a nice family. You have everything to look forward to. Just start over. Somewhere else." It sounded more like a threat than a suggestion. "Find your own way, your own man—and leave me to mine."

"I didn't know he was married," Veronica managed, "when we started." She'd known and she hadn't stopped. Shame, hot and poisonous, began to seep in past her defenses. She'd behaved badly, and now she was caught. *Daddy would be so ashamed.*

"I understand. Few of his girls do."

His girls? Veronica thought. She felt she might be ill and looked in vain for the wastepaper basket, under her desk and too far away to reach.

"But regardless, I still need you out of our life—and out of New York. The city isn't as big as people think, especially in publishing. For the sake of the baby. You understand."

Veronica heard the click on the other end of the line, then the phone slipped from her hand and dropped to the floor.

*   *   *

IT WAS WELL past midnight: Veronica, Vi, and Walter were still seated in mismatched wooden chairs at a table with a faded flowered oilcloth. The pot of coffee Vi had made when Veronica had told them the news had long since grown cold, and none of the three had even thought about dinner—although a box with the remainder of the Black Forest cake from the Heidelberg sat untouched in the center of the table. Vi had stopped crying, but her eyes and nose were red. "How *could* you?" she said to Veronica, her voice quieter now, but still knife-edged. "With a married man? I'm just glad your father isn't alive to see this."

Veronica recoiled. "I didn't know Max was married, for the longest time." At first, Max had helped her with her stories, suggesting a few cuts and changes, facilitating interviews with people who wouldn't take her phone calls. And—just like that—she'd slipped into a life that seemed to belong to someone else. "He was a champion for me—for my work."

"Your *work*," Vi snorted.

"We talked about important things—journalism, yes, but also books, the war . . ."

"Where did you do it? Some little fleabag hotel in Times Square?"

Walter looked over sharply. "Vi!"

Veronica stiffened. "If you must know, the Plaza."

Vi raised her eyes from her glass of gin. "Oh my stars."

"He told me he lived in Philadelphia, and he was in New York to file stories with the *Times*." She swallowed. "That's how he explained the hotel."

"And then what did you do?" Vi asked. "I'll tell you what you did—you kept sleeping with him. Kept sleeping with a married man!"

"I just didn't . . . see. And he said he would leave her. He just . . . never did."

"Isn't a journalist supposed to see? Observe? Note?" Vi shook her head. "And a woman who doesn't see—and acknowledge—what's right in front of her is a stupid woman. Stupid!"

"Mama . . ."

"You deserve it. You deserve this." She took a deep breath. "You. Are. A. Stupid. Woman. No—a stupid, silly little girl! Your future—gone! Everything I did for you, sacrificed for you—gone!"

Veronica had listened to her mother for hours and had had enough. She looked up, blue eyes flashing. "I love him! *Loved* him," she corrected herself, trying not to think about the other girls. "At least I'm still alive. You—you're dead inside! You died when Daddy did, and now you're just dried up, shriveled, and pickled in alcohol!" A wave of rage washed over Veronica. She picked up the empty gin bottle and threw it against the icebox, where it smashed into a hundred pieces.

Vi stood to reach across the table and slap Veronica across the face, but Walter caught her hand. "Stop it, you two! Stop it! Right now!" He looked to Veronica. "Go and clean that up."

"Yes, sir," she said in a low voice.

"And you," he said to Vi. "No more booze for you. You've had enough—more than enough—for tonight." He picked up her glass and dumped it out in the sink, next to Veronica, who was on her hands and knees, gingerly picking up the larger pieces of broken glass. "Can this woman really blackball you?"

"Yes," Veronica said without looking up. "She's a Feldman. Her father is Saul Feldman. One of the Feldmans. He pretty much *is* New York publishing."

Walter raised both hands, palms out. "Okay, so you can't stay in New York. Vi, you were going to find a new place anyway. So I have a suggestion . . ." He looked at each of them. "Why don't you both move out to Los Angeles with me?"

Vi and Veronica both stared at him, speechless.

"Look, it's a lot less expensive out there than New York. The food's cheap and fresh. And I've got that summer house in Santa Monica you can use. So you've got a place to live, rent-free." He turned to Veronica. "We've got the *Los Angeles Times,* the *Los Angeles Examiner, Hollywood Citizen-News*, all those showbiz rags, you name it! Plenty of places to write for. You can't beat the weather! Paradise on earth. Sunshine, oranges, blue skies . . . It's the Elysian Fields! Well, except during the Santa Ana winds in October, and the two weeks of straight rain in January. But I digress . . ."

"That's insane," Veronica said, blinking. "We can't just . . . *go* west. It's crazy." It was all so sudden. "I don't *want* to move to Los Angeles," she added, almost petulantly.

Vi threw back, "As if I do!"

"You can get another job, right?" Walter asked Veronica.

"Y-yes. Yes, of course."

"And you can get a job, too," Wally added to Vi.

Vi snorted. "Doing what? I've only ever been a wife and a mother."

"You're more than that, little sis. You went to Barnard on scholarship. Remember the marches?"

"Marches?" Veronica asked.

"Before I married your father, I was a suffragist."

For a moment, Veronica's surprise clouded everything else. "You were?"

"There's more to your mother than you know, Veronica." Walter cleared his throat. "Now, about the place in Santa Monica—"

"What place in Santa Monica?" Veronica asked. "I didn't know you had one." As far as she knew, her uncle had always lived in Pasadena.

"Greta and I had a summer bungalow there. 'Cottage' you New Yorkers would say." Walter and his wife, Greta, had lost their only son, Walter Jr., to polio in 1935. They'd divorced not long after his death. "Well, I still have it. Just closed it up after . . . You know."

Vi went to the icebox and pulled out a bottle of club soda. "It's probably falling apart." She took out three glasses, and began to pour.

"I do have people come in and clean," Walter stated as he accepted his glass. "I just don't go anymore. Too many memories." He turned to Veronica. "You could write a book there. Like—who's it again? That girl journalist you adore? Martha Gellman?"

"Gellhorn," she corrected him gently. "Martha Gellhorn."

Vi took a sip. "I do have my widow's pension . . ." She looked hard at the soda in her hand as if wishing it would somehow turn into gin. There was a long silence. "We would pay you rent," Vi said to Walter finally.

"No, you won't—"

"Yes, we will." She turned to Veronica. "We can make it work, sweetie. We can start over. Both of us."

"The air out west will do you good," Walter told them. "No more cold and damp. No allergies."

Veronica knew her mother was disappointed in her. She was disappointed in herself. She'd been with a married man. A man who now had a baby on the way—with his wife. A man who collected young women like her as if they were ties or hats. *This was not supposed to be my story,* she thought. As a girl she'd written in a journal every day, documenting her life, dreaming of literary glory. Now there was nothing. *No, this will not be my story.*

"I'd like for us to stay together," Vi said to Veronica in gentle tones. "At least for a little while longer." She laughed. "That's selfish of me, I know. But, just maybe, you still need me."

Veronica's eyes filled with tears. "You've never been selfish a day in your life. And of course I still need you. I'll always need you."

"I've put some money by," Vi continued. "It's not much, but it's enough to start."

Vi and Wally looked to her and waited for her reply. "All right," Veronica said finally, exhausted. "All right."

"It's a generous offer," Vi said to her brother, rising and wrapping her arms around him. "Thank you."

"You're doing me the favor."

Vi broke from the embrace, took a deep breath, and addressed them both, blinking hard. "Time for bed now, what do you say? Tomorrow's another day."

She's being brave, Veronica thought, *as brave as she can be. Daddy was Mama's North Star, just as Mama's always been mine.* The young woman's heart cracked. She went to her mother, who smelled of rose talcum powder and gin, and took her in her arms.

After the embrace, Veronica left, climbing the stairs quietly, fighting the flicker of panic threatening to burn out of control. *My life,* she kept thinking. *I've ruined my life.* And *my mother's.*

In her pink bedroom, she looked around—at her writing desk, at the snug twin bed with her one-eyed, one-armed Steiff teddy bear, Bear. At the bookshelves filled with childhood favorites: *The*

Secret Garden, Little Women, Anne of Green Gables. On one wall, covering a water stain, there was a Cab Calloway poster she'd tacked up, from last fall's performance at the Cotton Club in Harlem. Above the desk was her favorite quote from Hemingway's *A Farewell to Arms:* "Nothing ever happens to the brave"—the epigraph in Martha Gellhorn's debut novel, *What Mad Pursuit.*

My room, she realized. *My room, in the house of my childhood.* She changed into her white cotton nightgown. *I've spent my entire life working hard, studying hard, preparing myself—and now for what?* She didn't want to run away from New York. She didn't want to go to Los Angeles, tail between her legs. Yet it seemed like the only way out. Her world was like France—one minute beautiful; the next, invaded and completely ruined. *Well, hardly that,* she thought, the voice of reason cutting in, sounding a lot like her mother. *You're not in a war-torn country now, are you? Be grateful for what you have.*

But as she slid under the sheets and reached for Bear, she thought, *What happens now?*

CHAPTER THREE

7:04 A.M., on Kensington Avenue in Wilshire Park, Los Angeles: Ari Lewis was already awake, washed, shaved, dressed, and on his way downstairs to the kitchen. He'd left his wife asleep in their bed, and he could hear his two daughters, ages twelve and eight, getting ready for school. They were arguing in the bathroom, loudly. He knocked at the door. "Girls," he said in a low voice, "Mama's still asleep."

"Sorry, Papa!" they replied in tandem, then resumed bickering more quietly.

As Ari made his way down the stairs, he heard his wife slam her bathroom door. "Ah, *boker tov,*" he muttered. He was in his late forties with large shadowed brown eyes and the face of a sad clown—part basset hound, part Renaissance cherub. A veteran of the Great War who'd worked in Naval Intelligence, he was now a well-respected lawyer in Los Angeles.

In the front hall, he straightened his bow tie in the mirror. He was dressed in a white linen shirt the housekeeper had freshly washed, starched, and ironed and a well-made but conservatively cut dark blue suit, including an old-fashioned vest. He sniffed the cool morning air—his maternal aunt, the eighty-two-year-old Bella Gottlieb, was cooking. The scent of fresh herbs and orange zest perfumed the air, and he could hear the sizzle of eggs hitting the pan.

"Look what I'm making you, *bubala*," she said as he walked in. Ari saw sautéed green onions, fresh chives, and a dollop of cream cheese melting into the scrambled eggs in the cast-iron frying pan she'd brought with her when she'd fled Berlin in 1933. She was cooking *shakshuka,* one of those onomatopoeic Hebrew and North African words, meaning "all mixed up." It was his favorite.

"Thank you, Tanta," he replied. "Did you take your pills this morning?" She didn't reply. He asked again, this time a little louder, "Did you take your pills?"

"I'm old, *bubala,* not deaf," she said, pushing eggs around the pan with a wooden spoon. "And I don't need those pills." She was already dressed in a blue linen blouse and khaki skirt, thick white hair pulled back into a bun. Despite her age, her movements in the kitchen were deft and graceful.

He took a pitcher from the icebox and poured a glass of freshly squeezed orange juice, then found the bottle of prescription medication on the counter and took out two pills. He placed them on a napkin next to the glass of juice. "Here you go."

She sniffed loudly and continued to watch the eggs cook. Ari sat at the table, already set. It was covered with plates of sliced cheeses and meats; raspberry, Concord grape, and fig jams; a pot of honey; a bowl of freshly sliced fruit; a platter of smoked fish; and Tanta's homemade seeded bread. She slid a plate of eggs in front of him and set down a cup of black coffee.

"Thank you," he said, beginning to eat.

"I made you a chopped liver sandwich to take to the office."

He sighed. "Tanta, I don't like chopped liver."

"I went to a new butcher," she told him. "Try it."

"Fine." Then softer, "Thank you."

As he sipped his coffee, she stared at the juice. Finally, she took her pills. "I miss Berlin."

Ari looked up. She was gazing out the window, in the direction of the goldfinches pecking at the birdfeeder, but he knew she was seeing something else, a scene from long ago and far away. "I know you do."

"I miss *Königsberger klopse.*"

"I know, Tanta. But there's so much wonderful food here."

"It doesn't taste as good." She threw her hands in the air. "And lemons! Too many lemons!"

"But you don't miss the Nazis."

"No! *Fa! Diese bastarde!*"

"Well, there you have it." Ari rose and put his empty plate in the sink.

Neither of them recognized the Germany they'd once loved—democratic. Now the Fatherland was all about fascism, invasion, and violence. Breaking the law. Targeting Jews. As a lawyer, this ate away at Ari—that Germany, whose legal system was once considered the greatest in the world, which had once stood for justice, was now blackened. He hated reading about the Brownshirt thugs now patroling the streets, about the broken glass and roundups. *Damn Hitler, Himmler, and Heydrich and all the others. I will never let the same happen here in the U.S.* Everything he did, he hid from Tanta and his daughters. Only his wife knew the truth.

"I'm proud of you, *bubala*. Our big shot lawyer." She pointed a finger up into the air. "Wait!" On the kitchen counter was a chessboard. "You almost forgot—it's your turn."

"I'm proud of you, too," he said as he moved his knight into position. *There, that'll give her something to think about besides the old country today.* "I'll see you tonight for dinner."

"Don't be late. I'm roasting chicken with potatoes and rosemary, just the way you like." She handed him a brown paper bag. "Your liver sandwich—you almost forgot."

He reluctantly accepted the bag, clapped his hat on his head, and picked up the briefcase waiting by the door. "Thank you, Tanta." He kissed her soft, wrinkled cheek. *"Yom tov."*

* * *

ARI'S OFFICE WAS located on the fourth floor of the off-white terra-cotta Roosevelt Building, on the corner of Seventh at Flower Street. He took the elevator up and greeted his secretary. She could take dictation and type 130 words per minute; she was also curvy, grace-ful, and glamorous, with perfectly painted coral nails that matched her lipstick exactly. Wednesday nights, she was a jazz singer at the Club Alabam, next door to the Dunbar Hotel in South Central.

"Morning, Mr. L," she said with a bright smile. "This just arrived for you." She handed him a manila envelope with no return address.

"Thank you," he said, going straight to his office and closing the door. Inside was controlled chaos. Files were stacked neatly on a side table, while cardboard boxes of documents took up space on the worn brown leather sofa. A reproduction of *Washington Crossing the Delaware* hung over the modest wooden desk.

Ari dropped his briefcase, sat in his swivel chair, opened the envelope, and slid out the papers. Squinting and sighing in exas-peration because he couldn't read the tiny print, he reached in his suit's breast pocket for his rimless eyeglasses and put them on. It was a coroner's report for Adam Haber, the spy he called "S4." Reading it over, certain words popped: "Deutsches Haus parking lot," "basal skull fracture," "softening of the brain," "alcohol," "epileptic fit," and then, finally, "DECEASED."

"My God," he said, dropping the papers. Adam Haber was dead. Adam Haber, one of the first agents he'd taken on when he'd started his spy operation in 1933, was dead. Adam Haber, who'd feared for his life because he'd committed the unspeakably stupid sin of copying down license plate numbers in the Deutsches Haus park-ing lot and had gotten caught, was dead. Ari took off his glasses and pinched the bridge of his nose.

He looked up at silver-framed pictures of his wife and daugh-ters, laughing in front of their cabin on the shore of Lake Arrow-head. He took a deep breath, folded the report, and slipped it neatly into his briefcase.

"Please call A-Two," he said to his secretary as he headed back out the door. "And cancel all my morning appointments." He clapped his hat back on. "Tell him to meet me at the Hollywood office as soon as possible."

* * *

JONAH ROSE HATED Los Angeles. He thought about it as he stirred his first morning coffee: Nescafé and hot water from the sink in a cracked mug. Jonah had no kitchen per se and usually took his meals at the diner down the street, where the portions were hearty, the waitresses motherly, and the java refills free. But this morning, he was still in his studio apartment.

He took a sip without tasting. He hated Los Angeles's relentless, glaring sun. He hated the monotonous weather. He hated what he saw as the absence of history and culture. He missed the snow in Buffalo, New York, where he'd grown up. He missed the four seasons in Chicago, where he'd studied history at the University of Chicago, then gone to journalism school at Northwestern and started his career at the *Chicago Tribune*. Most of all, he hated the people of Los Angeles—their untested optimism, their naive good cheer, and their too-wide gummy grins.

Taking the mug to the apartment's sole armchair, Jonah sat, gazing at the horizontal stripes of thin morning sunlight seeping through Venetian blinds. *Another sunny day in Los Angeles—shocking.* He'd never meant to live in Los Angeles. But after seeing the Nazis and what they were doing to Germany in Berlin in 1936, he and his uncle, Fred Klein, assessed the local Nazi threat in Chicago and found it volatile. Together, they founded the anti-Nazi newspaper the *National Free Press* in order to publish a continual stream of documentation of Nazi activity in the United States. And Jonah's reporting of local Nazi groups eventually caught the attention of General George C. Marshall, who'd mentored him, training him in espionage. But it didn't mean he liked L.A. any more now than when he'd arrived three years ago.

He drained the mug and leaned back. He was in his late twenties, tall and lanky, with uncombed straight brown hair flopping down over his eyes. While most of his friends were married, comfortable with their wives and young children, working as doctors or lawyers or teachers in Buffalo, Chicago, or New York, Jonah lived in a small studio at the Gaylord Apartments on Wilshire, around the corner from the Brown Derby and across the street from the famed Ambassador Hotel and Cocoanut Grove. Not that he ever went to those places. He didn't have the time. Or the inclination.

He looked around—his apartment was nearly as bare as when he'd first moved in. There were elegant high ceilings and moldings, but the room was tiny, furnished with a seedy leather sofa he used as a bed. In a corner was a battered wooden desk and an old Royal typewriter. Tacked on the wall above was a postcard of Picasso's *Guernica*. Jonah had seen the actual painting in person on its American tour, which had raised funds for refugees fleeing the Spanish Civil War. The only other personal items were a baseball he'd caught at a White Sox game in Cominsky Park and a silver-framed wedding photograph of his parents.

The one good thing about his room was that it was on a high floor. Not only could he keep a careful watch on the street below, but there was a doorman on duty who refused to let strangers in. Still, he had three dead bolts on his door.

The jangle of his telephone broke his reverie. He picked up the receiver. "Yes?"

It was Ari Lewis's secretary. "Meet A-One at VF," she told him, then hung up before the call could be traced.

*   *   *

"WHAT'S WRONG?" JONAH asked as he walked into the office in Hollywood he and Ari nicknamed "Valley Forge." Jonah, A2 to Ari's A1, was wearing a worn leather jacket over his wrinkled button-down shirt, khaki trousers, and a black fedora.

Jonah had been referred to Ari by General Marshall; he and Ari had been working together for two years. The men had moved their operation from a small office downtown to this larger space on Hollywood Boulevard, between La Brea and Highland, only three months ago. They'd needed more room to accommodate Jonah's expanding metal filing cabinets, crammed with all the information their spies had gathered over the past seven years. The walls were covered in corkboards pinned with photographs, newspaper clippings, and handwritten notes.

"Did Haber ever show up for his debrief?" Ari asked from the conference table at the center of the room. He was wearing his glasses and had various papers in front of him.

"No, he didn't make it—I figured I'd catch him later this week."

Ari's face was grim. "I think you should sit."

Jonah took off his jacket and lowered his long frame into a wooden chair.

"Haber was working a shift at Deutsches Haus on Friday."

"Right," Jonah said, steepling his fingers and stretching out his long legs. He took off his hat. "They were celebrating the Nazis taking Paris."

"He called me from the pay phone outside that night. Thought he'd been made."

"Because of the business with him copying down the license plate numbers?" Jonah asked. "I thought he talked his way out of it."

"It didn't work—they didn't believe him. I'm sorry," Ari said gently. "Adam's dead."

Jonah sat up straight, his eyes as big as those on a Lewis chess piece. "What happened?"

Ari took the papers from his breast pocket and handed them over. "This is the police report." As Jonah began to read, face inscrutable, Ari watched him with concern. "This isn't your fault."

"I told him to stay the course," Jonah said in a rough voice, throwing down the papers on the table and putting his head in his hands. "We needed tabs on Schwinn and Wagner. I didn't listen to him."

There was a small kitchen in one corner of the office. "Why don't I make us some coffee?" Ari said.

As Ari went to make a pot, Jonah picked the folder back up and continued to read. "The coroner ruled Haber had been drinking," he said without looking up. "Adam *never* drank. He was a Yoo-hoo kinda guy." He read further. "And the injury happened in the parking lot of Deutsches Haus during an epileptic fit?" Jonah looked to Ari. "Did he ever mention anything to you about epilepsy?"

"No," Ari replied as he measured ground coffee.

"Me either." Jonah went to the long wall of metal filing cabinets, organized by his own baroque principles, and pulled out Agent S4's file. He ran one finger down a page. "According to this, Adam was in perfect health—only a history of childhood asthma and allergies to hay, grass, dogs, and shrimp. Do you really think he told us about shrimp—and forgot to mention he had epilepsy?"

The coffee began to percolate; Ari watched as the brown liquid gurgled up into the transparent top knob. "No, I don't."

"They killed him," Jonah said, replacing the file. "The Nazi bastards killed him." He looked out the window, his eyes blank. "And I *made* him go . . ."

"You didn't make him do anything."

"I did, though. I thought it was so important we get more information about the bunker, the airplane factories . . ."

Ari poured the steaming fragrant coffee into two mugs and walked to the younger man, setting one down in front of him. "It's not your fault," he said, taking off his glasses.

"What about his family?"

"I'll find out when the funeral is. Ask his wife about the epilepsy."

Jonah looked up to the pinned maps on the corkboard: all of Los

Angeles and the California coast, up to San Francisco and down to Mexico. "They're planning something. Something big."

"I'll send flowers once I get the details of the service."

Jonah continued as if he hadn't heard. "We're going to need more people at Deutsches Haus. New people. Patriotic Christians. Germans or German descent, preferably. Willing to go undercover. We need to get them in as soon as possible."

"We don't exactly have folks like that lining up."

"'Folks like that'—you mean pale, snub-nosed Heinies who love bacon and know the lyrics to all the Christmas carols?"

"Brave Americans, fighting with us for democracy," Ari corrected.

Jonah sighed. "Sorry. Still upset about Haber." He shook his head. "He loved his bologna and mayonnaise sandwiches, didn't he? On white bread." He shook his head, "What about the Big Guy?" That was their nickname for their contact at the FBI. Despite Big Guy's lack of interest in the Los Angeles Nazis, preferring to focus on the threat of communism, Ari and Jonah kept Big Guy updated on everything that happened, also sending the carbon copies of their typed documents to Agent Doolin at the Los Angeles Bureau of Investigation.

Ari sighed. "Big Guy doesn't care—unless the Reds are involved."

"We at least have to keep the damn paper trail going," Jonah muttered as he went to his desk.

He took the cover off his typewriter, inserted a fresh sheet of paper, rolled it up, and began typing:

J. Edgar Hoover, Director
Federal Bureau of Investigations
United States Department of Justice
Washington, D.C.

Dear Mr. Hoover . . .

CHAPTER FOUR

It had been a long journey for Veronica and Violet—two days to Chicago and a change of trains, then three more across the west. The narrow bunks in the sleeping car had allowed only minimal rest, and over the five days Veronica had examined her failures and found herself wanting on many counts. *But I can't go to pieces just because I made a mistake,* she thought. *I'll never do anything like it again. And,* she promised herself, *maybe in Los Angeles, I can find somewhere to belong, something that needs me to do it. And in the meantime I can go everywhere, see everything, and write about it.*

She stepped out of Union station and into the outrageously bright California sunshine, which reflected off the pavement. It warmed her instantly. Maybe, just maybe, the sun could melt her shame, worry, and heartbreak and make her feel alive again. Vi, behind her, pulled the brim of her straw hat down farther over her face. She tugged on cotton gloves, muttering about sunspots. "Are you all right, Mother?" Veronica asked, concerned.

Vi's face and chest were red and sweaty. "I feel like I'm burning up."

Walter looked over. "Do you think it's a fever?"

"No!" Vi exclaimed. She whispered in her daughter's ear: "It's a . . . a . . . hot flash." Veronica had never heard her mother mention anything about them before. "And I have a pimple—smack dab in the middle of my frown lines! You know, if anyone had told me about the 'change,' I would have just said no thank you."

"Let's see if we can get you a cool drink," Veronica told her.

On Alameda Street, there was even more dust, as well as cars, buses, and the occasional horse-pulled cart. Veronica could barely hear herself think over the shouts of the paperboys: "BRITISH BOMB ITALIAN FLEET," one headline read. "Battle Wrecks Musso's Ships—British Coup Stirs Anger of Italians and Germans." *Good for them,* she thought, although she realized they'd pay dearly.

Veronica shielded her eyes from the sun's glare with a hand. *What do I really know about Los Angeles?* she thought. Only what she knew from the movies and magazines about the movies. She tried to think: the Navy, with ports up and down the coast. Airplanes— she'd read about Howard Hughes and his work with aviation. And Hollywood, of course. Movie stars. Oranges . . .

She approached a street vendor, a middle-aged woman with her black hair in a bun, wearing a dress covered in colorful Otomi embroidery, selling grilled corn and tamales. *"Cuánto cuesta una bebida?"* Veronica attempted in the beginner's Spanish she'd taught herself on the train.

The woman broke out laughing. "Are you trying to ask how much for a drink?"

My accent must be truly awful, Veronica realized. She blushed. *"Sí.* Er, I mean, yes."

"I have sodas, but this one is the best," the woman said, handing Veronica an icy cup.

"What is it?" Veronica asked as she passed over a few coins.

"Chamango," the woman told her. "Mango and ice, drizzled with *chamoy* sauce."

"Perfect, thank you." Veronica brought it back to her mother, who accepted it gratefully.

"We need to get a map," Vi was saying to Walter. "Where's the trolley stop?" She took the icy beverage and pressed it to her forehead.

"I think you're supposed to drink it, Mother."

Vi took a sip. "Delicious." She put the cup back to her forehead.

"We're taking a taxi, Vi," Walter replied. He'd changed the date of his return trip to travel with them, promoting Los Angeles the entire way. "This isn't New York."

As they walked to the taxi queue, Veronica lagged behind, listening to a busking musician playing the guitar and singing "Poor Wayfaring Stranger." He smiled, revealing a few teeth, and tipped his cap.

"We can't afford a taxi, Walter," Vi was saying. "Surely there's a cheaper way to get to Santa Monica."

"Taxi's on me."

Vi rolled back her shoulders and frowned at her brother. "We can't."

"You can and will. Look," Walter told her, setting down the suitcases. "My wish to take a taxi isn't out of some sense of pity. In case you haven't noticed, *I'll* have to carry your bags, and even though you've shipped the rest of your things, these"—he indicated the suitcases—"are heavy. *Heavy.* So, really, the taxi's for me."

"Thank you, Uncle Wally," Veronica said, realizing he was right.

"Well, you don't have to come with us," Vi was saying. "I may be new here, but I know Pasadena's in the other direction. You're going far, far out of your way . . ."

"I want to let you in—and make sure the house is still standing."

"Why wouldn't it be standing?"

"Vi!" he cried in exasperation.

Vi allowed herself and Veronica to be bundled into a taxi's back seat, while Walter sat in front. They rode west, into the glare of the hot citrus sun.

Vi blotted her sweating forehead with a cotton handkerchief and sipped her drink, while Veronica looked out the window. There were palm trees—impossible-looking things, seemingly defying the laws of physics. There were dry, cocoa-powdered mountains to the east. They passed tiny houses covered in flowers of dazzling colors and roadside stands offering rainbows of fruits and vegetables, often with ominous biblical quotes painted on the wooden crates: AND THERE WILL BE STRANGE EVENTS IN THE SKIES— SIGNS IN THE SUN, MOON, AND STARS, she read while they stopped at a red light. AND DOWN HERE ON EARTH THE NATIONS WILL BE IN TURMOIL, PERPLEXED BY THE ROARING SEAS AND STRANGE TIDES . . . It was both disconcerting and intoxicating.

The driver, a sixty-something man with graying black hair, eyed them in the rearview mirror. "Where you folks from?" he asked.

"New York," Veronica answered, as she rolled down her window. The air was warm and smelled fresh.

"Ah, the Yankees! I'm an Angels fan myself."

"Who?" Veronica and Vi asked in tandem.

"Minor league Los Angeles team—for now," he explained.

"We root for the Dodgers," Vi told him, finishing her drink.

"I'm sorry," he said without missing a beat. "How long're you staying?"

Veronica's and Vi's eyes met. "This . . . is our home now," Vi said finally.

"Well, welcome to Los Angeles," he said, gesturing. "You've got your baseball, beaches, and Beverly Hills. Plenty of transplants, just like you—lots of 'em trying to make it in Hollywood. Me? Born and raised here, in Little Tokyo."

"Please take the scenic route," Walter instructed the driver as they reached Santa Monica. To Veronica and Vi, he said, "Welcome to the 'Pearl of the Pacific'! This way you get the lay of the land. Or the beach, as you'll see." Before them was the ocean, with its indigo water, blue sky, gleaming sand, and small fishing boats. The air was cooler, and a soft, salty breeze was blowing.

"Lots of ex–New Yorkers here," the driver added. "Lots of people from *everywhere,* really. Looking to start over here in Los Angeles. We're the land of dreams and new beginnings, you know."

"Started with the gold rush and never really stopped," Walter mused.

"Sounds perfect for us," Vi said, placing her hand over Veronica's.

At the ramp leading to the pier was a spectacular sign spelling out SANTA MONICA in bright red letters. They could see signs for sport fishing, cafés, and a yellow building that looked like a castle with a pointy dome. Through the open windows, they could hear organ music. "That's the carousel," Walter told them.

"Honky-tonk," Vi whispered to Veronica, winking.

Veronica was thrilled. "Look, there's music and dancing!" she said, pointing to a ballroom at the end of the pier. "They've got their own orchestra!"

"La Monica, the largest dance hall on the West Coast," Walter told them proudly.

"Louis Armstrong's playing this weekend!" Veronica exclaimed.

Walter pointed to a grand house overlooking the ocean: "The vacation home of Mary Pickford."

"Well, la-di-and-da," Vi said, leaning back.

They drove along Ocean Avenue, lined with tall, thin palm trees, the blue waves sparkling in the sun. Veronica was overwhelmed with an unexpected feeling of exhilaration. This might not be what she'd planned, but she'd now traveled far beyond her old sphere and former dreams. The world had widened before her and she was finding it thrilling.

They passed beautiful, bronzed people playing volleyball in the sand, bodysurfing on waves, racing on paddleboats. "Ye gods and little fishes, they've all gone native," Vi murmured, eyes wide.

Veronica tried not to roll her eyes. "Well, I for one can't wait to work on my tan."

"The men need haircuts," Vi noted tartly, noticing a group of young men in rainbow-colored shirts smoking on a street corner. "And they need to tuck in their shirts."

Veronica noticed her mother's face was turning red and she was beginning to perspire again. *Uh-oh,* she thought. *Another hot flash.*

"Those are called island shirts," Walter explained. "They're from Hawaii. You're supposed to wear them untucked."

Vi was undeterred. "The women need shawls," she muttered darkly, as they passed a woman in a skimpy flowered sundress, barely covering a strapless bathing suit. "They must be cold." She murmured something unintelligible, ending in "all catch pneumonia" as she dug a fresh handkerchief from her purse and began blotting the sweat on the back of her neck.

"Mother, it's 1940—and you sound Victorian. Think how wonderful it'll be not to have to wear heavy overcoats and galoshes!"

Vi was silent.

They turned up Wilshire Boulevard, through a neighborhood of modest beach houses. "These were built as vacation homes after the turn of the century," Walter told them. "For people from Pasadena and the San Fernando Valley—gets hot inland in the summer. Nowadays, a lot of people live here year-round."

Veronica saw a young woman wearing a strappy, sheer sundress, eating a bright red snow cone. "I bet she's not wearing a girdle *or* brassiere," Veronica teased.

"Hmm" was all Vi would say as she rolled down the window for more air.

* * *

"AND HERE SHE IS!" Walter declared as the driver turned right from Wilshire onto Eleventh Street. It was lined with bungalows in eclectic styles—Victorian, Swiss cottage, Spanish Colonial Revival—all side by side. Once the taxi parked in the gravel driveway, Veronica got out and stretched. She could smell jasmine, warmed by the sun.

A small plane buzzed by in the blue-gold sky overhead, and finches twittered in the jacaranda trees. Theirs was a Craftsman, painted white with navy shutters, with a white picket fence around the yard. Walter thanked and paid the driver, then led them to the backyard; it was filled with overgrown grass and a tangle of un-pruned pink roses. There were avocado, lemon, and pomegranate trees, thick with flowers and fruit.

"I'll have a gardener come by," Walter said as he pulled a brass key from the crook of the pomegranate tree near the back door. He struggled with the lock for a moment, but finally the bolt shifted. *"Voilà!"* he announced. "Welcome to your new home!"

The door creaked open, and Vi and Veronica followed him in-side. The dim interior was stuffy and warm, smelling of dust and mothballs. "Let's just open these windows," Walter said.

Light flooded in as he pulled back the curtains. He removed sheets to reveal plain rattan furniture. Veronica saw the walls were covered in faded wallpaper with wheat sheaves, and there was a modest brick fireplace. Vi nodded in approval, then went to inspect the kitchen, while Veronica was drawn to the framed photograph on the wooden mantel. It was of Walter, his ex-wife, and their son, Walter Jr. *Must have been taken right before he died from polio,* Veronica realized.

"Come on, come on!" Walter was saying to both the women. "I'll show you the rest!"

Veronica wondered if his joviality was forced. *Must be hard, to come back to this place with so many memories,* she realized. *And he's doing it just for us.*

"The bathroom!" he announced. It had green and yellow glazed tiles and a pink sink and bathtub. He led them upstairs, where there were two bedrooms and another bath off the hall.

Veronica wandered into what must have been Walter Jr.'s bed-room. The shelves were full of books of Greek myths, as well as various translations of the *Odyssey* and the *Iliad,* alongside models of ships he must have built and a framed reproduction of Rem-brandt's *Rape of Proserpina,* with the goddess of spring clawing at Pluto's face as his carriage carries her from the world of light into the dark land of the dead.

She took the sheet covering off the bed and sat on the patch-work quilt. Walter followed her in; she noted the tightening of his face. "I can sleep downstairs," she said, immediately standing.

"No, he'd want you to have it. It's good," he assured her. Then, to himself, "It's good." He opened the curtains and let sunshine stream in, and threw up the sash. "Air it out," he told her. "Pick some fresh flowers from the backyard and put them in a vase. You might appreciate some of his books." He gave a crooked smile. "He was deep into his Greek and Roman phase."

"Thank you." Veronica went to him and kissed his cheek. As he left to show Vi the master bedroom, she looked around the room, thinking of her cousin, whom she'd never met. He would have been twenty-seven now, if he'd lived. *I have the opportunity to start over,* she realized. *He didn't get that.* She looked around. *I can't waste this chance.*

There was a scream from the other bedroom. "What? What is it?" Veronica said, bursting in, picturing the worst.

"It's all right," Walter said, placing one hand on Vi's shoulder. She was unable to speak. All Vi could do was point at the bottom drawer of a dresser, which had been left slightly open. Inside, on a folded blanket, was a cat. A brown-and-gray tabby, with a white ruff, stomach, and paws. The cat blinked up at them with luminous green eyes as heavily lined as Cleopatra's. She began to purr, a low rumble filling the room.

"I want it out!" Vi said in a barely controlled whisper. "I don't like cats. I'm not a critter person." Veronica noted the beads of sweat were back.

"Mother, she might not have anywhere else to live," Veronica said, feeling an instant kinship with the feline. She knelt and offered her hand. The cat rubbed her cheek against it, the low rumble in-creasing to a dull roar. "What's wrong with cats?" She'd always loved her friends' pets.

"They hiss, they bite, they scratch!" Vi exploded, while the cat slowly blinked its large green eyes. "They . . . *urinate* on things!"

"Only if they can't go outside," Walter said mildly. He did a cursory examination of the cat, who remained docile. "I'm a doctor, not a vet, but I'd say our little squatter here's about to become a mama. Her belly's distended, and she's made herself a nice nest." The cat looked on, still purring.

Veronica went to the window. It had been left open a crack. The cat could easily have climbed from any of the trees onto the roof and then found her way in.

"'Mama'? You mean she's going to have kittens?" Vi whispered.

"No, hummingbirds," Walter teased.

"Ye gods and little fishes, this is supposed to be a respectable house. Not some"—she lowered her voice—"*cat house!*"

Veronica and Walter tried not to laugh. "I don't think you need to whisper, Mother. She can still hear you."

"She's settled in," Walter told them. "It means the birth should be soon."

"A birth!" exclaimed Veronica. "It's a good omen!"

"She should really stay indoors until the kittens are weaned," Walter told them.

"You know what our father would have done," Vi said to Walter in ominous tones. Veronica could only imagine various scenarios, none of them good.

"Well, he's not here—and we are," retorted Walter. "And I think we have some sardines in the pantry . . ."

"I'll go look!" Veronica flew downstairs and searched until she found a tin of sardines. She put the oily fish in a bowl, filled another with water, and brought both upstairs, placing them in the cat's drawer. The cat rose and began to eat hungrily.

Walter considered. "We have some time, since mama cats stop eating twenty-four hours before the birth."

"I'll take care of all this," Veronica said with a wave of one arm, "and bring her to my room. Mother, why don't you go downstairs? Have a sit-down? Maybe a glass of water?"

"I'll make you some coffee," Walter said. "We have some instant, I think. Come on, Vi."

"I'll pick you up more food from the store later," Veronica told the cat as she pulled out the drawer and lifted. The cat was heavier than she looked. "And find some more old towels and blankets." The cat blinked up at Veronica and began to purr again.

"Don't mind Mother," she whispered. "She'll come around, just you wait and see."

* * *

WHEN THE CAT was settled, Veronica realized she should help her mother clean and unpack, but she'd been cramped in a train for five days and needed to get out. She pulled a bathing suit out of her suitcase—blue ribbed rayon jersey lined with cotton—and put it on. She slipped her bare feet into faded tennis sneakers and topped it all off with a pink-flowered sleeveless linen sundress, a bright green scarf in her hair, and round tortoiseshell sunglasses.

Downstairs, Walter was instructing Vi on life in the cabin. She was seated at the kitchen table, fanning herself with an old magazine. "If you want ice," he was saying, "you'll need to put a sign in the window for the ice man."

"Ice," she said, fanning faster, "yes, we'll definitely want ice."

"And there's a wringer washing machine you can attach to the kitchen sink. The clothesline's still up in the backyard—there should be pins around here somewhere . . ."

Vi sipped her instant coffee. "It sounds wonderful, Walter, thank"—but before she could finish her sentence, one of the blue shutters outside fell with a loud and ominous crash—"you."

"It's just cosmetic," Walter hastened to reassure her. "Everything's structurally intact, Vi. I'll come back next weekend to see how you girls are getting along. Make a few repairs."

Veronica entered in her swimsuit and dress, and Vi and Walter looked up. "You're going to the beach?" Vi asked.

"No, I'm going to build a snowman."

"In my day, ladies avoided the sun."

"Coco Chanel put an end to that more than a decade ago, Mother. It's fashionable to be tan now. Which you'd know if you ever opened a magazine."

The name *Mademoiselle* hung unsaid as Walter placed a stack of junk mail on the counter. Veronica went through the pile. She stopped at a red, white, and blue printed leaflet from the American Nationalist Party, opened it, and began reading:

Whenever a people or nation discovers existing within a body politic any factors or elements of a nature inimical to its welfare and to its very life, it is a right inherent in such a People or Nation, and indeed a duty if means are available to such an end, to curb and eliminate all such dangerous elements. Jews, through their closely unified banking interests, have constituted themselves as a menace to our free institutions, our Christian Civilization, and our Aryan culture.

We call upon citizens to prepare the way for the ultimate solution of "the Jewish problem" now unattainable through any legislative enactment. Asking all Gentile working people to boycott Jewish merchants and the perfidious movie industry . . .

She dropped it on the counter as if it had burned her fingers. *Ugh, I thought we'd left this mess behind in New York,* she thought, then crumpled it up and put it in the trash can.

Vi looked to Veronica. "Do you have everything?"

"Sunglasses, tanning oil, and Martha Gellhorn's newest."

"Well, while that sounds fun," Vi replied, "I mean, do you have a hat, change for a telephone call, your wallet, a key . . ."

"We don't have a telephone yet, have my wallet, and the key's in the pomegranate tree."

"Go and have fun, sweetie. I need to go to the bank," Vi told

Walter, "set up an account, get all the utilities switched to our name, get the telephone line reactivated, file a change of address . . ."

"That's what tomorrow's for," Walter told her.

"I'm going to pick up a newspaper and look through the want ads, too. And"—Veronica fixed a look on Vi—"get some cat food."

Her mother pretended not to hear.

"Well, I'll be heading back to Pasadena now, ladies," Walter told them. "There's a pay phone at the corner of Wilshire and Ocean, if you need to get hold of me before your telephone's working."

"Of course," Vi said, rising. "Sorry we've taken up so much of your time."

"Nonsense! I'm so grateful to you—finally, to have family nearby again!" He and Vi hugged, and she left tearstains on his shirt.

Walter and Veronica walked out together. "You know where you're going?" he asked.

She laughed. "I think I can follow the sound of the surf to the beach." She wrapped her arms around his neck and kissed his cheek, which smelled of sandalwood cologne. "Thank you for everything, Uncle Wally."

He looked concerned. "Is your mother all right?"

"It's just the 'change,' I think," Veronica told him. "Don't worry, I'll look after her."

"Ah," he said, realizing. "Yes, our mother went through it around fifty, too. Be kind," he told his niece. "Even if she's being difficult. You'll go through it someday yourself."

"I think we just need to get settled in," Veronica told him. "Once she gets her sea legs, she'll be fine."

"Just wait for those kittens to be born," he told her. "Your mother loved cats when she was a little girl and always wanted one of her own. She'll come around. You'll see."

CHAPTER FIVE

At the beach, Veronica spread her towel by the tall wooden life-guard station. The soft, salty breeze smelled of roasted peanuts, cotton candy, and baby oil—unlike the pervasive scent of Nathan's hot dogs at Coney Island. Beautiful blue-green waves topped with foaming whitecaps rolled onto the shore and she could hear the surf, children laughing, and the occasional shriek of a gull. Not far from her, toddlers built sandcastles with tin pails and shovels, while their mothers looked on from folding chairs beneath fluttering beach umbrellas. Older kids used the playground and swings, and teenagers played volleyball in the sand. Farther down the shore, a few bare-chested men in rolled-up dungarees dug for clams as a lone hawk hung in the sky.

Veronica watched it hover for a few moments before taking out her book. She opened it and began to read: "The young Jew, sitting next to the American, stirred and noticed where he was when he heard them laugh. 'You are English?' he said. 'No, American. A journalist,' she said, as if you would have to explain why you were coming to Prague this October."

A young boy holding a toy plane ran by her towel, kicking sand in her face. "I'm Germany!" he shouted, knocking over a little friend's sandcastle. "I declare war on England!"

Veronica put down her book and brushed off the sand, looking out over the ocean, facing the "wrong" way—at least for her. Far out, somewhere in the distance, was Japan. According to the news, war between the United States and Japan was inevitable, just as inevitable as war with Germany and Italy.

In the United States, there were immigrants from Germany, Italy, and Japan, of course. But in the event of war, Veronica feared most for the Japanese. She'd known a few Japanese and Nisei, or second-generation Japanese, students at Hunter. The young women's patriotism and love for America was unmistakable, and they often spoke of how they disagreed with Japan's military actions in China. *They have nothing to do with the war,* Veronica knew. *They're good citizens. But not everyone will see them and their families like that if and when we go to war.*

She stripped off her dress and left it, her bag, and her sneakers on the towel, and walked down to the shoreline. Knee-deep in cold, salty seawater, she held her left hand with a ring on her middle finger in the light. It had been a "promise" ring from Max— although a promise of what, exactly, he'd never specified. She examined it closely. How many other girls had won a similar ring from him? How many were still wearing them? While it once had looked golden and shiny, she could now see it was starting to tarnish. With one quick movement, she took it off then threw it into the sea. "Goodbye, Max!" she called into the breaking waves as a gull screeched overhead. "And good riddance," she muttered, thrusting both middle fingers up into the air as a final farewell.

Back at her towel, she took out a pack of cigarettes and lit one; it took a few tries because of the wind. Taking a long pull, she looked up, turning her attention to a parade of broad-shouldered Herculean lifeguards in tiny red swimsuits running down the beach. *Oh my,* she thought, flicking ashes into the sand. *Max who?*

Veronica closed her eyes and wondered what her father would make of the beach, the Pacific, their living in Uncle Wally's bungalow. In her memory, her father was forever young and handsome, tall and lean, with kind eyes and a strong jaw. They'd talked about everything—Army versus Navy games, politics, movies, and jazz—over chocolate egg creams made with U–Bet syrup at the counter of the local diner. *Made with neither egg nor cream,* he'd always say with a wink, *but absolutely delicious.* He rooted for the Dodgers and hated the Yankees with a passion.

At the thought of egg creams, Veronica's stomach growled and her eyes blinked open. She ground out her cigarette in the sand and went through her bag to assess exactly how much she had left in her wallet after the train journey and realized Walter had slipped her a few crisp green bills. *Thank you, Uncle Wally.* She stood and smoothed back her blond hair. *There might not be egg creams, but who knows what else Los Angeles has to offer?*

* * *

WHILE VERONICA WAS at the beach, Vi put her hair up in a scarf, wrapped an apron around herself, and turned on the radio to the sounds of Bach's Brandenburg Concerto no. 3. First, she opened all the windows and the front and back doors and then took the sheets off the rest of the furniture. She dusted and swept and mopped the floors. There was an enormous spider in the bathroom sink, and instead of cleaning, she just backed away. "All right, Arachne," she muttered. "When I come back in here, you'll be long gone—and I'm going to put the plug in the drain. Do we have an understanding?"

When the cabin sparkled to her German mother's standards, she went out to the backyard and picked some of the golden poppies. She found an iridescent Depression-glass vase and plopped them in with some water, placing it just so on the kitchen table. Then she went upstairs, to her new room. It was cozy and sweet, with green floral wallpaper and a double bed with a colorful patchwork quilt.

Vi opened her suitcase and took out one of her most cherished possessions, a heart of woven wheat sheaves. It had been her mother's, and her mother's before her, brought from Munich. Having it meant there would always be bread in the house, she'd been told. She also found two photos she'd brought from Brooklyn, wrapped up in newspapers. One was of her and her husband on their wedding day, and the other a tiny silver-framed photograph of Veronica as a chubby baby with Bear, when he was still new.

She went downstairs to arrange them on the fireplace mantel and stepped back to judge her handiwork, twisting her wedding ring. *I can't believe we did it. Made it all the way across the country.* Vi looked around. *What would Tom make of this, I wonder? I suppose he'd be glad we're still by the ocean, even if he'd think it's the wrong one.*

Realizing she was hungry, she went through the pantry, taking stock and throwing out any cans that had swollen over time. There was, she noted, no gin—or alcohol of any sort. *Well, we'll have to fix that now, won't we?* she thought, mentally preparing a shopping list.

When, finally, she took a moment to sit and drink a glass of water, she felt a wave of homesickness wash through her. She missed New York; she missed Brooklyn. She'd taken the comforting racket of the city around her and the presence of her neighbors for granted. Some things you never knew you loved until you missed them.

* * *

THE BLACK FOREST Inn on Wilshire and Ocean Avenue offered the heavy, comforting food of southern Germany. To celebrate their first night in Santa Monica, Vi and Veronica both ordered the day's special, *kaesespaetzle*—noodles and cheese—which came with a cup of vegetable soup and a small cucumber and sour cream salad. "And a gimlet," Vi told the waitress. "With Rose's, please, not the other stuff." She glanced at Veronica, who was trying not to pass judgment. "Come on, it's a celebration!" Vi said. "Our first night!"

"You're right," Veronica said, taking out the *Los Angeles Times* she'd bought on the walk over and placing it on the table next to her. "But we have a lot more nights ahead of us." She changed the subject. "I checked a bulletin board at Tommy's Diner earlier—it was full of help wanted flyers. Mostly for waitresses, babysitters, that kind of thing. The ads for secretary jobs will be in the *Times,*" she said, putting a hand down on the paper. "As well as leads for reporter jobs. I'm not looking for anything fancy—streetcar crashes or fires would be fine . . ." *If only I could swallow the world around me and have it come out in words . . . and then have people read them!* "Work will heal all wounds."

Vi nodded, accepted her gimlet from the waitress and took a sip. Her eyes closed in relief.

"Maybe . . ." Veronica tried to broach the subject to her mother delicately, "it's time for a beau? Work off some of that"—she raised her eyebrows suggestively—"excess energy?"

"Absolutely not!" Vi twisted her glinting wedding ring. "That door's closed."

"You could always open a window."

"Veronica Rose!" Vi exclaimed, and Veronica laughed. "Sweetie, I loved your father with all my heart, and I'm just not ready to date yet. If ever." She looked around the restaurant, at the shelves of colorfully painted ceramic and pewter beer steins from different regions of Germany lining the walls. "And I like this place already." Then, a gasp. "Oh, ye gods and little fishes! Don't look now . . . but is that"—she dropped her voice to a whisper—"Clark Gable?"

Veronica used the reflective surface of a knife to look behind her. "It does look like him," she whispered back. She intentionally dropped her napkin, and snuck a look when she retrieved it. "Not positive, though."

A woman at the table next to them smiled. She was in her late fifties, with a gray Dutch boy haircut and hazel eyes behind silver-framed glasses. She leaned over toward them when the man had passed out of hearing range: "Clark Gable's stunt double, actually—he lives in town. Funny thing is he fell in love with Vivien Leigh's stunt double on *Gone with the Wind*. And they got married! So don't be surprised if you see them around town, our own 'Clark and Viv.' Here's the thing, though—the *real* Rita Hayworth actually does come to town sometimes."

Veronica quite liked Rita Hayworth. Not as much as Katharine Hepburn, but still. "Why's that?"

"She grew up here—her family owns a restaurant here. We old-timers know her as Margarita Carmen Cansino."

"We'll keep a lookout," Vi told the woman.

"Are you German?" the woman asked them.

"We are," Vi replied proudly. "My parents were originally from Munich. My daughter here's German, and English on her father's side—a true American."

"A true American!" The woman raised her half-pint of beer in a toast. "With beautiful blond hair and blue eyes!"

The waitress arrived with their soup, rolls and butter, and salads. The woman saw their surprised look. "East Coast?"

They nodded.

"Salad," she told them, "is served first in California. Don't ask me why."

"Anything?" Vi asked as Veronica went back to the paper.

"According to Drew Pearson in the 'Washington Merry-Go-Round,' Roosevelt might seek a third term, but Farley's lips are sealed," Veronica said. "So far, the Royal Air Force is holding off attacks from the Luftwaffe—oh, and they have two clues as to who's responsible for the bombings at the World's Fair. No suspects yet," Veronica said, skimming the article. "Someone called in an anonymous threat for the gas tanks at Con Ed at West End and Sixty-Fifth."

"My stars, I don't know what this world is coming to," Vi said, looking at her roll, looking away, finally breaking off a small piece and buttering it. "Anything in the want ads?"

Veronica flipped through the pages, scanning the columns. "They all want reporters with at *least* two years of experience." She raised her eyebrows. "Even for the mortuary beat."

"You have experience."

I do have experience, Veronica thought. She knew how to observe, ask questions, come forward when it was necessary, disappear into the background when it was not—but without the clips to back it up, she was just another hopeful. And a female, at that. "They mean professional experience, not just a college paper. I want to get a job around here first, even if it's just a few shifts. Make some money while I'm going to actual reporting-job interviews."

"What are you thinking of?" Vi asked.

"Well, Tommy's looks neat and clean, and they need waitresses. But since I have shorthand and typing skills—thank heavens for Katie Gibbs—I'd like to go for something secretarial. I can make better money and won't have to carry plates."

"I hope you don't mind my saying," the woman with the Dutch boy said, leaning over again, "but my brother-in-law's looking for a typist—a nice American girl like you would be perfect. I don't think it's anything fancy, just mailing labels or something like that. But he's a good man and he has a small publishing company. Here . . ." As the waiter cleared away her plate, she reached into her purse and took out a pen and a scrap of paper. "His name's Donald Pierce McDonnell. Tell him you talked to Mrs. Florence Conant." She put a hand to her bosom. "That's me."

Veronica asked, "What's the name of his business?"

"The Educational Services Bureau," Florence said. "He writes about current events and politics. Readership's growing!"

"Thank you," said Veronica as she took the slip of paper, feeling the glow of something that might be hope. "Thank you very, very much."

*   *   *

AS THEY LEFT the restaurant, Veronica cajoled her mother into going for a walk to see their new neighborhood. They strolled along under the rainbow-colored lights as a neon sign blinked OCEAN PARK PIER RIDES AND FUN, the salty scent of the ocean mixing with the strong odor of fish from the day's catch.

"Well, this isn't what we expected," Vi said, taking Veronica's arm as they eyed a row of penny arcade games. "But we'll find a way. And who knows?" As they passed an aging Hollywood beauty queen with leathery brown skin, bleached hair, and red lips and fingernails holding hands with a short, potbellied man in an island shirt, she bit her lip. Veronica smiled as she saw her mother fight the urge to say the woman needed a shawl. "You've never failed if you try, sweetie."

They stopped to look out over the water. Veronica leaned against her. "Daddy would like it here, I think," she said. "Although everyone walks too slow and talks too slow."

"I noticed that, too—they wouldn't last a day in Brooklyn, let alone Manhattan." Vi laughed. "He'd say we're on the wrong ocean, but yes, I think he'd secretly like it. Probably would have bought a boat and taken up fishing." She rubbed her cheek against Veronica's silky golden hair. "As long as we don't start rooting for the Angels, we'll be all right."

"I don't think he'd mind the Angels—just as long as it's not the Yankees."

"*Never* the Yankees." Vi shuddered. "Now if only the Dodgers would move out here."

"Thank you, Mother." Veronica kissed Vi's cheek. "For everything. For picking up and moving to a new place. I love you. You're my North Star."

"I love you, too, sweetie."

"We're going to make it here, you know. Really make a difference." *I can still put everything I see and hear into words. I can still write terrible and glorious things that can change the world.*

"I sure hope so."

They watched as the sun disappeared in a flaming red burst, the trailing clouds looking like puffs of pink cotton candy. "So strange to see the sun *setting* over the ocean, isn't it?" Veronica asked. "Everything's upside down here."

She fought a moment of homesickness. She wished she were back in Brooklyn, with the comforting presence of neighbors sitting out on the stoops. She missed the tree-lined, cobbled streets. She even missed her view of rooftops, patrolled by pigeons, with water pipes extending down the backs of brownstones and washing hung on clotheslines criss-crossing the small backyards.

"I know," Vi said, squeezing her daughter's hand. "I feel a bit upside down myself. But we have each other."

Without the sun, the air cooled rapidly, and Veronica felt chilled. She swallowed to get rid of the lump in her throat.

Vi took her daughter's arm. "We'd best be going, sweetie. Big day tomorrow."

CHAPTER SIX

To Veronica's dismay, getting a job as a journalist at a newspaper in Los Angeles turned out to be next to impossible. After a few weeks of taking the Red Car to downtown L.A. and going on multiple interviews, she felt disoriented and discouraged.

None of the places wanted her—they wanted men. If they hired her, they explained patiently, she'd only get married and leave them in the lurch. When she protested, they came back with, "But when there's a baby in the picture, you just won't be able to keep up!"

Or she was too young or too inexperienced. She'd gotten an interview with the *Malibu Bee,* but it hadn't gone well. She didn't know enough about local politics—the ongoing argument between the school board and the crossing guards, as well as the petition for a new stoplight. "But I can learn," she'd told them. "I'm a fast learner!" It made no difference.

A small press in the Hollywood Hills had almost hired her, but the job required a car. "I'm sure I can get around on the trolleys and buses," she told them, but they just didn't think it right or safe for a young woman to do that, especially with the late hours. Nothing came of any of her meetings, and she was conscious of all the money she was spending on fare. Her oxfords had begun to wear at the heels, and Vi took them to the cobbler to be resoled. Her only solace was time spent at the beach in the early morning or evenings.

They had bills coming in, and Vi's widow's pension hadn't trans-ferred yet. They needed money and fast. Veronica had thought she'd lost the scrap of paper with the number from the woman at the Black Forest restaurant, but she found it, washed and dried, in the pocket of her dress. She made a telephone call. "Hello, I'm try-ing to reach Mr. McDonnell," she said to the woman who'd picked up. It sounded like a home, not an office.

"What do you want with him?" the woman asked warily.

"I met his sister-in-law at the Black Forest in Santa Monica," Veronica explained. "I mentioned I was looking for a job, and she said he might have some typing he needed done. For the"—she checked the slip of paper—"Educational Services Bureau?"

The woman's voice changed. "Oh, that's my sister, Florence!" she said warmly. "Why didn't you say so right away? I'm Mrs. McDonnell, Donny's wife. You can type?"

"One hundred and twenty words a minute—plus shorthand. I'm also good at office organization. And make good strong coffee, if needed."

A long moment passed, while Veronica held her breath. Then she heard, "Sounds perfect! If Flo vouches for you . . . There's so much work to be done. Tell me, can you get to Fairfax?"

Veronica didn't know where in Los Angeles Fairfax was, but im-mediately said, "Yes, of course."

"That's wonderful! We're 444B North Poinsettia. How does to-morrow at ten work for you?"

"Ten sounds fantastic," Veronica said. "See you then."

*　*　*

VERONICA SLEPT UNEASILY that night, still not used to the new bed or the purring cat. She tossed and turned and woke at dawn, feeling off, a dark mood hovering over her. She went outside and sat on the back steps in her robe and bare feet, her hair in metal curlers. A dog barked in the distance. Seagulls glided in formation over the tops of palm trees, finches hopped in the roses, and sparrows pecked in the sparse grass. *You can do this,* she told herself. *It's what Martha Gellhorn would do.*

After coffee and toast, Veronica dressed in her favorite beige linen trousers, a green blouse worthy of Katharine Hepburn, and her resoled, polished shoes. She wore a touch of Elizabeth Arden's pink Printemps lipstick and a spritz of Blue Grass cologne. Her curls had turned out smooth and even. After taking the trolley and walking for blocks, allowing time for getting lost—which she did—and asking for directions at a gas station, she arrived at the McDonnells' house on North Poinsettia.

It was a modest Spanish bungalow, tidy and neat, with white walls and a red-tile roof, a tangle of scarlet roses blooming in the front garden.

"Come in, come in!" Mrs. McDonnell said, when she answered the front door. "You must be Veronica!" She was somewhere in her fifties, Veronica guessed, thin to the point of wiry, with platinum-blond hair that had just slightly grown out since its last coloring, revealing brown roots. "I called my sister, you know—to ask about you—and she told me you were blond and blue-eyed. But you're a real Rhine maiden, aren't you?"

"My—" Veronica didn't know what to say. "My mother's German," she managed. "Or, rather, her parents were German. But we just moved here from New York."

"How wonderful. I'd be so proud to be of German descent, but at least I'm Swedish and Donny's people are from Scotland. I've never been to Germany, although I'd love to go. It's so beautiful, so clean now, they say."

The hairs on the back of Veronica's neck stood up. "Hmm . . ." she managed.

"Let me take you to the office, or the 'War Room,' as Donny likes to call it." She led Veronica through a sunny living room, stocked with a full set of matching faux-Gothic department store furniture. Above the fireplace was the German coat of arms, the black Imperial Eagle with a red beak against a gold background. The air smelled of glass cleaner and floor polish, and everything was as tidy as a showroom. "Call me Harriet," she said confidentially. "Can I call you Veronica?"

Veronica smiled. "Of course."

Harriet knocked at a door to what appeared to be a recently built addition to the back of the house. "Donny?" she called. "Veronica's here to help with the typing."

There was the sound of footsteps and a man opened the door. He was small and fit, in his fifties, with ropy muscles and graying brown hair. He wore a red plaid cotton shirt, dungarees, and black western boots, and could have been the star of a cowboy movie with his wide grin and easygoing charm.

"This is the girl I was telling you about, hon," Harriet told him. "The one Flo found for us."

"Mighty pleased to meet you, Veronica," he said in a deep Texan drawl. "We won't hold New York against you." He winked. "Just me today, although there're plenty of others out there, working for the cause. What did Flo tell you about us?"

"That you need help typing?"

"Yes, yes—we've got to keep those names organized. A good mailing list's solid gold these days! Never know when we'll need to reach out."

"Is—is this your office?" Veronica asked, scanning the room. It was dimly lit, with low ceilings and closed and curtained windows. It was cluttered with papers, pamphlets, and books, plus reams of wrapping paper and rolls of twine. In one corner stood a battered black metal cabinet piled high with magazines and newspapers, and in another, a banner on the wall read AMERICA FOR AMERICANS. "You're an educational publisher?" Veronica said. "What grades?"

"Oh no, not that kind of education," he replied, chuckling. "Although Harriet and I are both teachers at North Hollywood High—where we met, about ten years ago." He gazed adoringly at his wife. "She teaches history, and I do math and the occasional science class. Woodshop, too."

"Oh," Veronica said, forcing herself not to shuffle her feet. "How nice for you both."

"But this"—he spread both hands wide—"is our *real* work. Wouldn't you say, honeybun?"

Harriet smiled broadly, her face transforming into prettiness. "It is!"

"We've got the mimeograph machine at her sister's next door, but all the writing, editing, and typesetting's done right here. And I know what I'm talking about—come by it honestly. Grew up in the Midwest, just outside Gary, Indiana. Went to college there. I was in the Army during the Great War—Army taught me aviation, and I was a pilot for Dixie Airlines in Texas ten years. Now I teach, but I'm also a captain in the National Guard."

"Oh," Veronica said, now warming to them both, "my father served in the war, too. He was a commander in the Navy, out of the Brooklyn Navy Yard. He died almost six years ago."

"Mighty sorry to hear," McDonnell said, placing a hand on his heart. "How's your mother feel about those cuts Roosevelt made to her widow's pension—to all of our military pensions?"

"I was younger when the cuts happened," Veronica admitted, "but I do remember her and the other Navy wives worrying about it. She's having a heck of a time getting her pension transferred right now."

"Aha!" he said, looking to his wife. "We have a kindred spirit here. And in your mama, too! Is she involved with any of the Navy wives' organizations? I'd love to share our work with her—and them."

"We just moved to town."

"Okay, gotcha." He grinned, revealing even white teeth. "Now look, I've been doing this type of work for about twenty years, but things are about to get big, really big."

Veronica was going to ask, "What kind of work, exactly?" but Harriet interrupted. "Oh, where are my manners?" she said to Veronica. "Would you like some lemonade? Or maybe an iced tea?"

"Oh, no—no thank you, Mrs., er, Harriet."

"All right, then—I'll let you two get to work!" she said as she left.

McDonnell handed Veronica a copy of *National American,* a tabloid-sized newspaper. "This is one of ours," he said. "We're publishing news for real, one hundred percent Americans here in Los Angeles. My brother's got a printing press at his place." Veronica glanced at the paper's subtitle, which urged, "*American Patriots! Rise up as one man and clean house politically and economically!*"

"You can get our paper at the Continental Bookstore, downtown," he volunteered. "Or the Aryan Bookstore at Deutsches Haus, you know—they've got a lot of good stuff there. They carry all our pamphlets," he added proudly.

Veronica had a bad feeling. "What . . . what kind of publishing company is this?" she asked.

"We're anti-interventionists. What Roosevelt and his crew call isolationists," he explained. "We want to keep America out of the war."

All right, Veronica thought. *Nothing wrong with that, just a difference of opinion.* "My mother's an isolationist, too," she told him.

McDonnell nodded approvingly and continued: "There's no reason for us Americans to get mixed up in that mess in Europe. I don't want to see my students used as cannon fodder. The German army's unbeatable, you know. There's no war between Germany and America, after all. We've got no problem with them." He gave her a hard look. "You're German—you get it."

German American, and we don't have to agree. "Why don't you tell me more about the job?"

"We're recruiting people. Educating them." He rubbed his hands together. "I want you to understand something. The printed word's the most powerful weapon in the world. With the right words, a war can be won—before it's even fought! We're here to meet people, then win over their hearts and minds."

Propaganda. "Oh" was all she could say.

"Come on," McDonnell told her. "I'll set you up in the back."

"I . . . have the job?"

"It's yours if you want it. You're just the right type—for typing!" He chuckled too hard at his own joke, adding, "But wear a dress next time, all right? I don't think it's right ladies should wear pants."

He led her to a small, dark room. Veronica sat down at a wooden desk with an old Corona Standard. She turned on the yellow banker's lamp, the light illuminating the dim room.

"What I want you to do," McDonnell told her, "is take these names and addresses we collected at the rally in Hindenburg Park and type them up on these index cards. Put them all in alphabetical order. Can you do that?"

Veronica nodded. *Rally in Hindenburg Park.* "What, uh, kind of a rally was it?"

"The Bund," McDonnell said. Veronica caught a whiff of his Aqua Velva aftershave. "The German American Bund. Some Silver Shirts. Copperheads. Friends from the KKK. A parade and a picnic, music, some speeches. That kind of thing."

Oh. "The KKK," Veronica ventured, hoping against hope she was wrong. "You mean . . . the Ku Klux Klan?"

"Oh, sure, they're big out here, didn't you know? People call Anaheim 'Klanaheim.'" He laughed. "You must be glad to get away from 'Jew York.'"

"I, er—" It was a small room. Veronica felt the walls press in.

But he kept talking, pleasantly, amiably. "They're out here, too, especially in the movie industry—running all those studios, brainwashing the American public. We hear they're making a film with Charlie Chaplin portraying Hitler as some kind of clown. Yet not one of them's been to Germany. Do you honestly think we should send our young men—our sons—to fight because of the Jews?" His eyes narrowed.

"W-well," Veronica stammered. "No one *wants* war, of course—"

"I gotta ask"—he looked hard at Veronica—"whose side are you on?"

"I'm—I'm on our side. America's side," she said truthfully.

"Good girl." McDonnell relaxed. "I can see you're one of us. So I'll tell you—our idea to keep America out of the war is to sell nationalism to the people first. It's easier that way. Once we sell it to the mob, the big boys'll swing around. You see, there're three groups that're conspiring to draw us into the war over there—the British, the Jews, and the Roosevelt administration."

This is nothing *like Mother's pacifism,* Veronica thought.

"Roosevelt's slowly been building up our military—soon he'll be manufacturing a series of 'incidents' to force us into the actual war."

"What about Britain?" she asked.

"Britain," he said, rubbing the stubble on his chin, "just might be able to hold out against the Germans. But even if they do, there's no way they could ever invade Europe and liberate France. You know," he added in confidential tones, "under normal circumstances the Brits would've made peace with the Germans long ago—but they're holding out to make the United States financially responsible for the war. While it's understandable Jewish Americans want war against Germany for what they're doing, if we do ever go to war . . . well, let's just say there'll be consequences."

She frowned. "What do you mean, 'consequences'?"

"The Jews—as you know, being German yourself—present a danger to our country. They own the papers, the movies, the radio, and our government—and use them for their own ends . . ."

On McDonnell's bookshelf, Veronica saw a copy of *The International Jew,* a collection of articles reprinted from Henry Ford's Michigan newspaper the *Dearborn Independent.* Shocked, she searched for something to say. "I remember reading about Ford's Peace Ship in the last war," she said. "Do you think he'll do something like that again?"

"Well, I was hoping Ford would run for president! Him or that Lindbergh fella. But we seem to be stuck with Willkie—no one's first pick." The election was just over three months away. "America must *not* fight a war in Europe, and it's our job to see she doesn't. Pretty soon I'm going to print up a lot of anti-war stuff and send it all over Los Angeles, and then the whole country. America *must* remain neutral. You see, we need your help, Veronica. We've all gotta help keep America out of the war."

"What about, you know," Veronica said evenly, "the electoral system?" She swallowed. "You know—democracy?"

"I love you think that'd work, kiddo, I really do. But we can't get it done that way. We need something faster—and more drastic. Nazism will allow us to get our country in order." Veronica recoiled in shock at the word. "Still, we're backing Willkie—we've got everyone out working for Willkie. But if Roosevelt wins . . ."

What about *if Roosevelt wins?* Veronica thought. *What are you saying?* But his voice trailed off.

"Come find me when you're done, and we'll get you paid. Cash, if that's all right," he said, with another wink. His muscular body was blocking the door.

I can't get out, Veronica realized. "That's—that's fine."

"Thought it would be. No reason to give the feds any more of our tax dollars, yeah? Let me know if you have any questions."

She was effectively trapped: the sour taste of fear was in her mouth, and her lips were dry. *I just need to get through this and never ever come back.* She did her best to smile. "Well, I'd better get to typing." Veronica looked at the huge pile, wondering how long it would take her to get through it, as McDonnell closed the door. She waited until he left to exhale.

Hours later, her hands and shoulders aching, she was finished. All she wanted was to leave. She exited the small room with palpable relief and went back into the main office. McDonnell took out his wallet and peeled off a few bills. "This should cover it, right?"

It was more than a fair amount of money for the time she'd put in. She didn't want to take it, but she couldn't risk offending him by turning it down. "Er, thank you." She looked at the newspapers on the table. "May I take one?" she asked. *At least this way I can show the police,* she thought.

"Of course!" McDonnell looked pleased. "Take a few! We're going to have another rally this coming weekend. Do you want to come in again on Monday—type up the new names?"

"Maybe." Veronica was backing away. *When hell freezes.* "I'll, uh, let you know." She reached the door and found it locked. She took a deep breath, told herself not to panic, and turned back to McDonnell. "The door . . . ?" she said, in what she hoped was a casual voice.

He laughed. "Oh, we have a special way of locking it," he said, pulling out a large key ring and opening it.

"Thanks. Goodbye," she murmured. A wave of relief flooded through her as she tried not to hurry through the house. Finally, out and onto the sidewalk, she could breathe again and began to run.

CHAPTER SEVEN

Back at home, Vi was cleaning, washing, and mending with efficiency, as her German mother had taught her, all the while talking to herself. *I married at twenty-two,* she reasoned, *right out of college. I was a Navy officer's wife, had three miscarriages, and raised a child. I have the right to go out into the world and earn my way like anyone else. And I'm sure I can learn new things as well. I may be having hot flashes, but I'm not dead, for heaven's sake. Not by a long shot.*

Finished, she washed and dressed carefully for her appointment with the Ingrid Scott Powell Employment Agency, wearing one of her own suits and a blouse hand-embroidered with tiny green apples.

The office was located downtown in a small suite facing an air shaft and smelled of fried ginger and garlic from the Chinese restaurant downstairs. Miss Powell was a plump pigeon of a woman, not much older than Vi, who chain-smoked. In the waiting room, she handed Vi a clipboard with an application and Vi filled it out neatly. *And I have good penmanship,* she thought. She filled in her age and nationality, as well as religion, education, and marital status. She listed "wife" and "mother" as her former jobs and gave Veronica and Walter as references.

She reached the real question: What type of work desired? *What can I do, really?* She looked out the window at the brick wall opposite and left that part blank. She turned to see Miss Powell waving her into her office.

Behind the desk, Miss Powell scanned the application, then placed it down on her desk and folded her plump hands. "You've never had a job?" she asked.

"I've worked all my life," Vi said.

"But you can't type, you can't take shorthand. You can't run a switchboard. You have no teaching certificates, no nursing skills. Not even first aid!"

Vi felt her heart sink. "I'm a fast learner, Miss Powell."

"No one wants to pay you to learn on the job." She leaned back in her chair and lit a fresh cigarette with her burning one. "At least you're white and Christian, but that's all you have going for you. It's not personal," she assured Vi, "but you just don't have what it takes. I can't send someone as unqualified as you out for interviews—it's my reputation on the line."

Maybe it was the heat of the day or maybe it was her shifting hormones, but Vi felt fiery hot, as though a small furnace burned in her chest. She knew her face was turning red, and she was sweating profusely. *This is a nightmare,* she thought, willing herself not to cry, ignoring the perspiration beading on her forehead. She bit the inside of her mouth until it bled, praying for the hot flash to pass.

She rose with as much dignity as she could muster and said, "My husband died knowing he was loved and cared for. I'm proud of the woman my daughter's become. My skills may not have earned money, but I wouldn't trade them for all the 'reputations' in the world." With a thundering heart, she walked out the door, turning to say, "Good day!" before she left.

* * *

VI NUMBLY MADE it back to Santa Monica on the trolley and walked to Ralph's grocery on Third, distracting herself by trying to think of what to pick up to make for dinner. She was still waiting on the pension to transfer, so she had to be careful with money, even more so than usual. *And now we have that damn cat to feed.*

She strolled numbly up and down the aisles, passing fresh produce stacked into towers. A sign reading WE'LL STILL ACCEPT YOUR FEDERAL FOOD STAMPS sat next to one declaring PRICE IS PER LB. The produce was all larger, fresher, and more colorful than what she could find in New York, even in the summer. The plums, nectarines, squash, and green beans were all in season and cheap, and she took advantage of the prices, weighing everything carefully.

She also got a chicken, a half carton of eggs, a loaf of bread, a stick of butter, a quart of milk, and coffee beans. *I'll make a chicken pot pie tonight,* she mused, and added an onion, carrots, and celery. *Veronica likes that. Makes the chicken go further—we can have leftovers tomorrow.* Vi glanced at a glass case full of layer cakes—apple, devil's food, red velvet—and pies—blackberry walnut, banana cream—then looked away. *You don't have the money,* she thought, *and you certainly* don't need the calories.

"Yoo-hoo!" a cigarette-burnished voice called from behind her. Vi tore her eyes from an apple pie with a lattice crust and looked up to see a well-dressed woman. She was hard and lean, face tanned, with a slash of red lipstick migrating past her lip line and iron-colored hair set in a helmet of the latest style. Up close, Vi realized she was weathered but chic, a sort of West Coast Coco Chanel.

"Hello?" Vi responded. *What on earth do you want?*

"I hope you don't mind my interrupting you, but I just *love* the embroidery on your blouse!" she said.

Vi felt a glow of pride; the blouse with the green apples was one of her favorite pieces. "Thank you," she said, smiling shyly. "I did it myself—it's my own design."

"Noooooo!" the woman exclaimed. "Oh, Dodie!" The iron-haired woman waved her hands at another woman pushing a cart; she was tall and suntanned, cottony hair pulled away from her face with two tortoiseshell barrettes. "Look at this! Isn't it wonderful? Dodie Tatum, meet—sorry, what did you say your name was?"

I didn't. "Vi—Violet—Grace. How do you do?"

"And I'm Ann Hunt."

"Pleasure to meet you," Dodie said, leaning in to inspect the delicate stitches on Vi's blouse. She wore a sharp lavender-scented perfume. "This is terrific work. It's almost like Elsa—"

"—Schiaparelli's!" Vi finished. "Yes! She's one of my inspirations. I mean, some of her designs are a little . . . odd . . . that lobster dress, you know. But the details are perfection."

Dodie looked up, taking in Vi's face for the first time. "What's the name of your atelier?"

"Oh." Vi smiled and turned pink at the very idea. "Nothing like that. I just make things for my daughter and me." Belatedly, she realized the opportunity. "I'm impeccable with my sewing. Not just the front, but the back, too. 'For the soul,' my grandmother used to say. And all my things are made to last."

"Do you ever make things for other people?" Dodie asked. "Would you be interested in making a blouse for me?"

"Oh, well—" *We need the money.* "I'm interested . . ."

"I'd like one just like yours. But instead of apples, I'd like flowers. Edelweiss is my favorite."

"Oh, I just love edelweiss," Vi said, her heart beating faster with excitement. *Maybe I* do *have skills after all.* "I remember picking them one summer when I was a little girl, on the mountains of *Zermatt.*" She pronounced it with a German accent.

"You're German?" Dodie smiled widely. Her teeth were pearly and white.

"I am," Vi replied. "Or, at least, my parents were."

"I'd like one, too," Ann said, raising a hand. "Astrological symbols. I'm a Leo. Say, I notice you have a bit of a twang—where're you from?"

"Just moved here from New York," Vi said. "I'm a widow," she added. "I'm living with my daughter."

Ann nodded, satisfied. "I'm the president of the Santa Monica Bay Woman's Club—we're hosting a talk at the Georgian Hotel on

Saturday with a woman named Nora Ingle. Why don't you come by for the lecture?" she said to Vi. "It's the turquoise deco place on Ocean Avenue. She's a pilot—*aviatrix,* she prefers—and has a lot to say about the state of the world."

"Oh yes, please come, Vi!" Dodie exclaimed. "It's always so interesting, and the other women are lovely. We have coffee and sandwiches and cookies—and talk and laugh and gossip."

"What time?" Vi asked, intrigued.

"Three," Ann told her. "You'll meet so many people. We can talk to them about your designs and how everyone can order. I bet a lot of the women there will want a bunch!"

"Thank you," Vi said, feeling a rush of pride in her skills. "Thank you—I'd like that very much." She smiled shyly. "See you then!"

* * *

VERONICA TOOK THE Red Car back to Santa Monica, reading McDonnell's paper from beginning to end, horrified by the anti-Semitic language and implied violence. When she arrived at the cabin, she found her mother taking a chicken pot pie with a flaky golden crust out of the oven and Uncle Walter with his jacket off and holding a hammer. "Mmm, smells delicious," he was telling Vi. Walter turned to Veronica. "Hey, kiddo! Just making a few more small repairs. The roof and the boiler are both fine, and that's what's really important."

"Another shutter fell while you were at work," Vi told Veronica.

Walter put the hammer back in the open toolbox on the kitchen counter. "Thank goodness no one was standing underneath."

"Could you set the table, sweetie?" Vi asked. "Dinner's almost ready."

After they sat at the kitchen table and Walter said grace over plates of steaming chicken pot pie and salad, Vi said casually, "So, I found a job today."

"What?" Walter and Veronica said in unison.

"Well, a potential job. Embroidering for some ladies. Very *rich* ladies."

"Ha!" Walter said, sprinkling salt over his food. "Good for you, little sis—already conquering Los Angeles!"

"Great," Veronica said quietly, spearing a lettuce leaf.

"So how did it go for you today?" Vi asked.

"How did what go?" Walter asked, through a bite of pot pie.

Vi blotted her lips, then took a sip of gin and lemonade. "Veronica had a typing job today in Fairfax," she told her brother.

"A job? Congratulations!"

"Thanks." Veronica frowned. "It was . . . strange." She told them about the McDonnells and her day with them. "The thing is"—Veronica lowered her voice—"I think . . . they're Nazis. I mean, they *are* Nazis."

"What?" Walter exclaimed.

"Just because they're against war doesn't mean they're Nazis," Vi told her. "If that were the case, *I'd* be considered one."

"Vi," Walter pronounced, "as your brother, I have to say, while you're good at many things, you'd make a lousy Nazi." Vi swatted her napkin at him.

Veronica laid her fork down on her plate. "Their publication's called the *National American,*" she told them. "It's virulently anti-Semitic."

"Well, you're not in New York anymore," Walter explained. "And New York certainly also has its own fair share of anti-Semites, I'm sorry to say."

"I know, but the people at this rally were from the German American Bund, the Silver Shirts, and the KKK. Those are the people whose names I was typing."

Walter and Vi looked at each other, then back to Veronica.

"You know as a journalist, I support the First Amendment," Veronica said. "Freedom of speech and freedom of the press, always. Always. Even when I don't personally like it. Perhaps especially then. But some of the things Mr. McDonnell said were . . .

disturbing," Veronica added. "Really disturbing. Anti-democratic. When I said something about the electoral system, he told me they wanted something 'faster and more drastic.' He said if Roosevelt wins, they're going to do . . . something. It didn't sound good."

"Well, that's the shadow that accompanies the light of democracy, sweetheart," Wally said, helping himself to more salad. "People are free to abuse their freedoms."

"True." Veronica pushed her plate away. "But there are still rules. Hate speech is disallowed if there's a 'clear and present danger.'"

"But you never heard a specific threat, right?"

"No, but—"

"Folks are within the law in writing, producing, and disseminating this material, as disgusting as it may be."

There was silence at the table. "These people could be dangerous." Veronica looked to Walter. "Do you really think we should just sit on our hands and do nothing?"

Vi looked up. "We could call the police?"

Walter gave a short, harsh laugh. "The LAPD isn't going to do anything."

"But *we* have to do something!" Veronica insisted. "They're threatening violence!" She got up and brought out the newspaper she'd taken from the McDonnells' house. "Read some of this—it's dangerous." She handed it to Walter, and Vi read over his shoulder.

"This is . . ." Vi searched for the word. "Vicious. He's inciting violence—and he's taking *pleasure* in it."

"Look," Veronica told her uncle. "I'm a journalist and support free speech, but writing like this—it pushes things into different, and dangerous, territory. There's reasonable ground to believe these American Nazis are inciting real violence. If we can stop something evil from happening—people being hurt, maybe even killed—shouldn't we do everything possible?"

"All right," Walter said finally. "I'll take it to the police." He raised a finger. "But I don't want either of you involved. We don't want him tracing anything back to you. He seems—well, let's just begin the list with 'unstable.'" He placed the paper on the counter. "Now, how about we walk to the pier and get ice cream? My treat."

"Ice cream's not going to solve anything, Wally," said Vi, beginning to clear the dishes. Veronica rose to help.

"Yes, but a little walk and some Rocky Road can never hurt, am I right?"

CHAPTER EIGHT

The next morning, Walter telephoned the bungalow. "I spoke to a friend of mine at the Pasadena Police Department," he told Veronica. "A detective, good man. I treated his wife a few years ago. She's made a wonderful recovery."

Veronica, in the kitchen, mouthed to Vi, *Uncle Wally*. "What did the detective say?" Vi stopped washing the breakfast dishes and came over to listen, wiping her hands on her apron.

"He was sorry—he truly was—but there's nothing the police can do. He said 'their hands are tied.'"

"But this is serious, Uncle Wally. There's a real chance these people could get violent, especially if Roosevelt wins."

"I know, I know . . . My buddy thinks it's terrible, too. But there's the First Amendment, of course—and they haven't actually *done* anything."

"That we know of!" Veronica ground her teeth. "And they're *planning* it! He could, you know, get someone to keep an eye on them, so nothing bad can happen."

"He told me all the LAPD resources are for catching communists. It's all about the Red threat, has been for years. He also told me—just between us—a lot of cops don't care about the Nazis and fascists, because at least they're against communism. 'The enemy of my enemy is my friend.' Some of them are KKK or Bund or Silver Shirts themselves."

"Ye gods and little fishes." Vi pulled the receiver over as Veronica rubbed her forehead. "Did you tell him about the newspaper? All of that anti-Semitic poison?"

"I did, I did! He agreed with me it's awful. But it's fairly common around town—and protected by the First Amendment." Veronica let out an exasperated sigh. "I know, Veronica, I know . . ."

"Thank you, Uncle Wally," Veronica said in a flat voice. "I hope we'll see you for dinner again soon." She hung up the receiver, then crossed her arms over her chest.

"That's ridiculous!" Vi exclaimed, going back to the sink and washing with a vengeance. "It's a credible threat of violence—they should follow up on it."

"When someone attacks Americans," Veronica said, "it's up to every other American to rally to defend them. I'm not letting this go." She picked up a striped dish towel and began to dry. "Do *you* want to let this go?"

"Absolutely not. But . . . what can we do?"

What would Martha Gellhorn do? Veronica thought. *Well, she wouldn't wait for an invitation, that's for sure. She was always interested in making her "tiny squeaking noise about the wrongness of things" and recording the stories of "the sufferers of history."*

Suddenly, the path forward was clear. "I'll tell you what we're going to do. We're getting dressed up, and we're going to the Los Angeles branch of the Federal Bureau of Investigation," Veronica announced, putting plates away in the cupboard with a resounding clatter. "If the police can't be bothered, we'll go straight to the FBI."

* * *

VERONICA AND VI took the Wilshire Avenue bus from Santa Monica to Westwood Village. When Vi saw the anonymous brick building, she was dubious. "Are you *sure* this is it?"

Veronica checked the scrap of paper she'd written the address on. "That's what the phone book said."

Outside, a man in his twenties with sandy hair, freckles, and no legs was begging. He used a plywood platform on wheels to move around, a wool blanket covering his stumps, his hands protected by thick leather gloves. As Vi and Veronica approached, he announced the day's headlines in a clear tenor voice: *"British fight off mass raids by swarms of Nazi planes!"* He took a deep breath. *"RAF bombs German bases! Roosevelt signs two-ocean Navy bill! Ambassador Bullitt says France is no fascist state!"* They waited until he'd finished, then dropped coins into his cigar box.

"Is this really the Los Angeles FBI office?" Veronica asked him.

"I know—doesn't look like much," he told her, "but it is. You ladies want the baseball scores now?"

"How'd the Dodgers do?" Vi asked.

"Get outta here!" he barked, waving them away with a leather-gloved hand, dismissing them. "You're in Los Angeles—you gotta root for the Angels here, even if they're minor league." He rolled away, muttering about the disgrace of Dodger fans in L.A.

The two women braced their shoulders and entered. Inside the front double doors was a sign: THE FEDERAL BUREAU OF INVESTIGA-TION, LOS ANGELES DIVISION. They went to the reception desk.

"Good morning. I'm Veronica Grace, and this is my mother, Mrs. Thomas Grace."

A young redhead looked up reluctantly from *Hollywood* magazine. "How can I help you?"

"We'd—we'd like to speak with an agent," Veronica said.

"What's this about?"

Veronica could see the woman was chewing a wad of gum; she smelled sweet, like Juicy Fruit.

"About something serious," Veronica told her.

The redhead stared, cracking her gum.

Vi added, "A planned attack—on American soil."

"Oh, okay." The woman had obviously heard it before. She

picked up a black Bakelite telephone receiver and dialed. "A Mrs. and Miss Grace to see you," she said. "Yeah, I'll send them in." She replaced the receiver in the handset and looked up. "Second floor, first door on the right. You'll be talking to Agent Doolin."

Both women nodded, and Veronica said, "Thank you." They went to the office; the door with its transom window was open. Agent Doolin was sitting behind his desk, broad-shouldered and muscled, with a brown leathery face and a full head of graying hair. He looked up from reading a memo with palpable annoyance, but said only, "Please sit down, ladies."

Veronica and Vi took the two seats opposite. "Thank you for seeing us without an appointment, Agent Doolin," Veronica began.

"Of course," he said patiently. Veronica saw he was missing two fingers. He followed her gaze. "Lost 'em in the first war. Navy. Just glad it wasn't the whole mitt."

"I'm sorry," Veronica said. "My father was in the Navy."

"God bless him," he said with genuine respect. "And God bless the U.S. Navy." His face relaxed and he looked a bit more hospitable. "Now, what brings you ladies here?"

Veronica cleared her throat. "I took a job, a typing job, for a man named Donald McDonnell. He works out of his house on North Poinsettia Drive in Fairfax for a small publishing company he runs, called the Educational Services Bureau. I worked for him on Tuesday, July twenty-third."

Doolin opened a notepad but didn't pick up a pen. "Okay."

"While I was typing for Mr. McDonnell, I realized his publication, *National American,* was virulently anti-Semitic."

He pushed the pad of paper away. "So?"

"He's working with the Bund, the Silver Shirts, the Copperheads, and the Klan."

"Unsavory people, in my opinion. But there's nothing illegal about that."

She told him about McDonnell's threat upon Roosevelt's possible election.

"Ah," he said. He leaned back in his chair and lit a cigarette. "I can see why you ladies would be disturbed by such an individual."

"We brought the paper he produces," Vi said, nudging Veronica, who took it from her bag and handed it across the desk. "If you read it through, you'll see he's inciting violence. Against Jews."

Veronica tried again. "Against *Americans*," she clarified, "who are Jewish."

Doolin leafed through the paper, then looked back at the women. "Ladies," he began, "I'm sorry you crossed paths with this individual. If it were up to me, I'd arrest him and the rest of his gang, knock their heads together, and put 'em all in jail."

"Yes!" Vi exclaimed.

He leaned forward, resting his elbows on his desk. "The thing is, everything you've told me is protected by free speech and the First Amendment. Now . . . has he actually done anything to anyone? Anything violent? Anything illegal?"

"I . . ." Veronica spluttered. "Not that I know of . . ."

"Well, see, I can't just have my men go arrest someone because you don't like his politics and because he's said some nasty things."

"This is more than nasty! He's—"

"I know. It's frustrating," he said, rising. "It's frustrating for us, too. We'd love to catch them all and put them away. But our hands are tied. We really can't do anything unless they break the law."

Veronica and Vi turned in their chairs and their eyes met. Veronica turned back to Doolin. "So, you're saying—until there's a dead body—or even a whole lot of dead bodies—you won't take it seriously?"

"Pretty much, ladies." He stood and walked to the door to show them out. "But thank you for coming in—we appreciate your civic mindedness."

* * *

"THAT PATRONIZING *ARSCHLOCH*!" Vi said through an angry bite of a tuna salad sandwich. They'd decided to get lunch at a nearby Automat before they went back to Santa Monica. It was one of a popular chain of cafeteria-style restaurants, where people purchased food and drinks from vending machines.

They sat at a table well away from the windows and other patrons. "I know you're really mad when you swear in German," Veronica said as she took a bite of her chicken club sandwich.

"My mother taught me well." Vi took a deep breath. "Well, this isn't over. Not yet, anyway. It can't be. Can it?"

Veronica looked out the window at a harried young mother, her raffia hat askew, pushing a baby carriage. "Who else can we talk to?" she said, selecting a potato chip. "J. Edgar Hoover?"

"No," Vi said. A bit of mayonnaise had dripped onto her chin. "But do you remember Daddy talking about his Navy friend on the West Coast? Commander Zabner?"

"Vaguely." Veronica took her paper napkin and wiped her mother's face.

"He was in Naval Intelligence in Washington, D.C., when Daddy knew him. He sent a beautiful wreath when your father died—white roses. The Navy transferred him to San Diego a few years ago. He's head of Naval Intelligence now. I can call him."

"Really?" Veronica raised an eyebrow. "Do you think he can do anything?" She took a sip of her Coca-Cola.

"I don't know." Vi shrugged. "I don't know anything anymore. But we've got to try. Right?"

"Right. Like Daddy used to say," Veronica began, *"Illegitimi—"*

"*—non carborundum,*" they finished together. "Don't let the bastards get you down."

* * *

"COMMANDER ZABNER," Vi began, twisting the metal telephone cord around her fingers nervously, "I'm not sure if you'll remember me. This is Mrs. Violet Grace . . ." She cringed inwardly at the uncomfortably long pause. *Of course he doesn't remember you, you goose.* "I'm Commander Thomas Grace's wife—widow, that is. You sent a beautiful wreath when Tom died." She was in the cabin's living room. Through the curtains, she could see her neighbor across the street out on his porch, mending fishing nets.

"Why, hello, Mrs. Grace," Ezra Zabner said without missing a beat. "How are you? It's been a while."

"Six years," she said. "My—my daughter, Veronica, and I are living in Santa Monica now. We just moved."

"Oh, I think you'll love it. Weather's beautiful here on the West Coast," he said easily, as though they chatted every week.

"Yes, but that's not why I'm calling," Vi said. She took a deep breath. "You see, I—I need your help."

"Help?" She heard his chair squeak and pictured him leaning forward. "What can I do for you, Mrs. Grace?"

"Well, Veronica took a typing job, and it turns out the man she worked for is a . . . Nazi."

Ezra sighed. "Yes, we have quite a few of those out here, unfortunately."

"The thing is, he publishes truly vicious propaganda," she said.

"The First Amendment . . ."

"He's calling for violence if Roosevelt wins." Vi had taken the time to read the entire paper on the trolley ride home. "His ultimate objective is, and I quote"—she picked up the paper and squinted to read—"'to foster a fascist form of government in the U.S.'"

"Did you talk to the police, Mrs. Grace?"

"My brother did. They were no help at all." She watched from the window as three neighborhood children on Flexy Racers—like snow sleds but on wheels—rode down the street face-first on their stomachs.

"Not surprised."

"Neither was the FBI when we talked to them."

"Not shocked, either." He cleared his throat. "Your daughter worked for this Nazi?" he asked. "What's his name—the man publishing the propaganda?"

"McDonnell. Donald McDonnell—I remember because it's so odd, the first and last name sounding alike."

"Does he want her back? To continue working for him?"

"Why, yes," Vi replied. "But of course Veronica wants nothing to do with him or his politics."

"Please tell her to keep her options open where he's concerned, all right?"

Vi was confused. "What do you mean?"

Ezra checked his desk calendar. "I can make it to Santa Monica by midday tomorrow. Would you have time to chat?"

"Of course, but . . ."

"Is one o'clock all right for you, Mrs. Grace? And your daughter? I'd like to speak with her, too."

"Yes . . ."

"What's your address?" She gave it to him.

"Thank you for calling me, Mrs. Grace. I look forward to speaking to you both tomorrow."

CHAPTER NINE

"We certainly didn't expect you to drive all the way from San Diego, Commander!" Vi exclaimed as she welcomed Ezra Zabner to their cabin. "Please, come in."

"Thank you." He took off his hat and stepped inside. He was a tall man, lean and graceful, with military bearing. His broad frame filled his blue double-breasted suit. "And this must be your daughter, Veronica! I remember how proud your father was of you," he told her. "He was a good man. A man of integrity."

Veronica didn't expect the wave of sadness that nearly crushed her, but grief was sneaky that way, she knew. "Thank you," she managed.

Ezra's brown hair was streaked with gray, and his dark hooded eyes turned down at the corners. He walked to the wedding picture on the fireplace mantel and picked it up, looking at it closely. "I have fond memories of your husband, ma'am." He put the photo back. "They don't make 'em like that anymore."

"No, they certainly don't," Vi replied. She beckoned to her daughter. "Veronica, please take Commander Zabner's hat, won't you, sweetie?" She turned back to Ezra. "Would you like a glass of water? Cup of coffee? Lemonade?"

"I'm fine, thank you. Call me Ezra."

"And I'm Vi. Why don't we sit down?" They did, with Veronica joining them.

"I hear you did some work for a man named Donald McDonnell, young lady," Ezra said to her. "What was that like?"

"It was . . . awful," she said. "I mean, at first it was fine. He and his wife were polite to me. Nice, even. But the newspaper he puts out—it's—" She handed him the paper. "Well, you can see for yourself."

Ezra paged through, skimming the contents. When he finished, he placed it on the wooden coffee table. "Veronica," he said, leaning forward, "can you tell me precisely what happened when you went to McDonnell's office?"

She nodded and related the entire visit, including the hints of violence.

"Is that a direct quote, or are you paraphrasing?"

"A direct quote. I'm—I used to be—still want to be—a journalist. So I'm careful to notice details and memorize things verbatim."

"I see," he said. "The German restaurant, plus the blond hair and blue eyes, probably made them think you'd be sympathetic to their cause."

"That's ridiculous!" Vi exploded. "Just because we're German American—and blond—doesn't mean we subscribe to any of this Nazi nonsense. In fact, it pains me deeply. I'm ashamed of Americans like them."

"What do you make of all this, Commander—I mean, Ezra," Veronica said. "Do you think there's a threat?"

"I'm going to talk to a friend later," he told them, "someone who knows a bit more about Nazi organizations in Los Angeles than I do. Would it be all right if I shared your story, Veronica?" he asked. "I won't use your name."

"Yes, of course."

Vi leaned toward him. "You don't think—you don't think they're dangerous, do you? That Veronica could be in any danger?"

"I just want to assure you I'll be careful about your privacy."

Vi nodded approvingly.

"Depending on what I hear, may I come back tomorrow morning?"

Vi and Veronica looked across the sofa at each other. "Of course," they answered simultaneously.

* * *

EZRA ZABNER MET Ari Lewis at Canter Bros. Delicatessen. It was on Brooklyn Avenue in Boyle Heights, on the east side of Los Angeles, and renowned for its pastrami, brisket, matzo ball soup, and black-and-white cookies.

The two men were old friends from their time serving in Naval Intelligence during the Great War, and Canter's was their favorite place to meet. They sat at their usual yellow Naugahyde booth in the back, both facing the door, able to watch everyone coming and going.

Ezra ordered a beef brisket with a beer, while Ari opted for a salad with smoked salmon and iced tea. "You're making me look bad," Ezra grumbled to his friend.

"I spend too much time in the office," Ari told him. "Can't exercise the way I used to." The waitress brought them glasses of water. "So, to what do I owe this honor?"

"Got a telephone call last night," Ezra said in a low voice. "From the widow of an old friend, Navy man." Ari nodded. "She said her daughter got a job doing some typing. Turns out it was for one of our interests, the one in North Hollywood."

Face blank, Ari reached for his water and took a sip. "What happened?"

"The daughter was appalled at some of the things our friend said, including some insinuations of violence if FDR's elected. She and the mother tried to report it to the police—"

"I can imagine how it went," Ari replied dryly.

The waitress came by with the beer and iced tea. When she was out of earshot, Ezra said, "Next they went to the FBI."

"And they were just as helpful, I'm sure."

"Exactly. That's when my friend's wife calls me—as a last resort, I'm guessing."

Ari cocked his head. "You think it's legit?"

"I drove down to Santa Monica and talked with them earlier today. The daughter's got an in—she typed up some names and addresses for them. They seem to like her and want her back."

"What are they like, these women?"

"Blond-haired, blue-eyed, German American . . ."

Ari nodded. *"Shikses."*

"In the best possible sense," Ezra clarified. "Most people just would have returned and forgotten all about it. But they felt compelled to pursue the matter."

The waitress returned with their plates. "Here ya go," she said. "Yours is hot," she warned Ezra.

Ari bowed his head over his plate to pray. *"Baruch atah, Adonai Eloheinu, Melech haolam, shehakol nihyeh bidvaro."*

"Always making me look bad." Ezra sighed and put his napkin in his lap. "I eat too much, I drink alcohol, *and* I'm a bad Jew." A confirmed bachelor, he never ever mentioned his private life. And Ari had never asked.

"There are many ways to be a Jew, my friend," Ari said amiably, as he cut into his salad. "You were saying?"

"The daughter's an aspiring journalist. She's got an eye for details and a good ear for conversation."

Ari looked up from his forkful of salmon. "Surely you're not suggesting . . ."

"Hear me out," Ezra countered. "You lost a man at Deutsches Haus recently. A real shame—I'm sorry. It's bound to be hard to replace him. They're onto us now, and they're going to be scrutinizing anyone we send around." Ezra cut a bite of steaming gravy-soaked brisket, then blew on it. "But if she plays her cards right, she can make it to Deutsches Haus. Replace our guy. Get in with the head honchos, and—" He took a bite. "Oh God—this is heaven!"

"And because she's a blond, blue-eyed female . . ."

"They'll never see her coming. She can hide in plain sight. Like Poe's 'Purloined Letter.'"

Ari nodded, pushing lettuce around his plate. "Have her and the mother come see me. The downtown office. I'll see what they're like. But you vouch for them?"

"I don't know them, really," Ezra admitted, "but the father was upstanding. A Navy man of real integrity."

"I'll meet with them. Tomorrow. Say, around noon?"

Ezra picked up his glass of beer. "I'll bring them by. And after, we'll get some of those French dip sandwiches at Cole's?"

"Yes." Ari chuckled with affection. "And after we'll get French dip sandwiches at Cole's."

* * *

OVER A DINNER of leftover chicken pot pie, Veronica was honest with her mother. "You know, I might have let this go. But you—you were unstoppable. I've never seen this side of you."

Vi smiled like the Mona Lisa.

"And I never knew you were a suffragette."

"No, no—those were the British women who fought for the vote," Vi clarified, sprinkling pepper on her meal. "I was a *suffragist,* that's what we called ourselves in the States. I know it probably doesn't seem like a momentous thing for you now, in 1940, but women have only been able to vote for twenty years."

"What did you do exactly?" Veronica asked, taking a bite of salad and looking at her mother's face and realizing there was more to the story. "How did you get involved?"

"Some friends and I from college believed—passionately—in the right of women to vote. We decided to march in Washington, D.C. In front of the White House."

"I've seen photographs of Alice Paul and her group," Veronica said.

"Yes, that was us!"

"You all wore white dresses."

"Yes, suffragist white. Purple was for loyalty to the cause, yellow was for hope, and white was for purity. But those dresses didn't stay white for long." Vi's face clouded and she set down her fork.

"What happened?"

"Our parade was considered 'unpatriotic,'" Vi told her daughter, as she blotted her lips with her napkin. "I wore a white dress, and I carried a sign that read 'Mr. President, how long must women wait for liberty?' They shouted at us, spat on us; men would . . . rub up against us. The police arrested us for 'disorderly conduct' and 'disrupting traffic.'"

"*You* went to jail?" Veronica's jaw dropped. *Who is this woman?*

"Yes, well, my big brother doesn't know everything." She took a sip of her gin and lemonade. "I went to jail—and from there to the Occoquan Workhouse in Virginia. We all decided to go on hunger strikes to protest our treatment."

My God. "What happened?"

"They force-fed us," Vi said in a flat voice. She pushed her plate away. "It doesn't sound that bad, maybe, but it was awful. They shoved tubes down our throats. It was painful and degrading. And dangerous."

Veronica had stopped eating as well. "How—how did you get home?"

"My father came to Washington. I don't know what he did, but he got me out. Those of us who got out started talking to the press. Once news of the mistreatment reached the papers, public sympathy swung to our side, and the others were released."

"The press, huh?" Veronica smiled. "And then what?"

"Ah, war had broken out. I met your father and fell in love, and we got married. And we had you. By the time *that* happened, I didn't feel it was right to risk myself—or to embarrass your father—by doing something so . . . public. Controversial. I was a wife, and a mother, and I had to take care of you both. But I did toast to Alice and the others when we finally got the vote—that was a good day." She nodded, remembering. "A *very* good day."

Veronica looked at her mother through new eyes. "I—I didn't know."

"I always meant to tell you. I still have a ring in my jewelry box—gold with tiny amethysts, peridots, and seed pearls. My suffragist ring. And I'm telling you now about what I did back then because I think it's important to have convictions. It's important to fight for what you think is right. I know you know, but I want to let you know *I* know it, too." Vi gave her a small smile before taking another sip. "And it wasn't just talk."

Veronica took a moment to process her astonishment and growing admiration. *My mother, a suffragist!* "I'm looking forward to speaking with Commander Zabner tomorrow," she said.

"So am I. And whatever you decide, I'll support you."

"I'm considering writing about it. What a story it would make, don't you think?"

"Absolutely. I'd be surprised if you didn't write about it."

Veronica frowned. "I worry it's my ego—that I want literary recognition and prizes and all the fuss."

"Do you want to stop these American Nazis?"

"Yes."

"Do you think an eventual book, telling your story, might help people understand what's happening here in America?"

"Yes. Yes, I do!" The words burst from her with unexpected passion. "We're so . . . content, aren't we? So pleased with ourselves. Especially all of us college graduates, with our fine speeches and big words. But what's it all for? The studying and the reading and the trying so hard to learn? The diploma? What are we supposed to do with it all? Surely not just stand by and watch. Not be passive while life happens all around us."

Since she wasn't working at *Mademoiselle,* Veronica had begun keeping a notebook of what she called her "Impressions"—essays based on the kinds she read in the newspapers and magazines by writers like E. B. White. They were made up of her observations of Los Angeles: She liked to watch strangers discreetly and observe the important details they inadvertently gave away. She wrote up her Impressions every night before going to sleep, as the cat purred from the bed. Writing was where her soul healed.

They cleared the table and moved to the living room, where Vi pulled out her embroidery hoop and Veronica her knitting. After their comedy program, Walter Winchell came on the air with his *rat-a-tat-tat* delivery. W.W., as they called him, the "Voice of America," was a link to their New York life. He'd labeled the German American Bund the "Ratzis" and "Bundits" and declared its national leader, Fritz Kuhn, a secret Nazi agent.

As Vi experimented with different stitches to make edelweiss flowers, they both listened to Winchell's staccato-style broadcast, with its underlying clacking telegraph sounds and Morse code. He began, words sounding like rapid-fire gunshots: *"Good evening, Mr. and Mrs. America and all the ships at sea . . ."*

As he spoke, Veronica couldn't help but think, *Will London streets be overtaken soon by tramping boots and thumping drums? Might Britain go the way of France? Japan already invaded and claimed most of China. Will it soon take French Indochina and make it part of its so-called Greater East Asia Co-Prosperity Sphere? Austria isn't even Austria anymore—it's just a part of "Greater Germany" now. It seems countries can just end and be lost,* she mused. *But that could never happen here.*

Could it?

CHAPTER TEN

The next morning, Ari Lewis opened the pebbled-glass door to his office. "Welcome! I'm Ari Lewis," he said to Veronica and Violet, nodding back to Ezra Zabner, who rose, hat in hand. "Please, come in." The office was illuminated by golden sunshine. On Ari's desk, in a cup for pens and pencils, was a small American flag.

"Coffee?" he offered. He was dressed in a dark blue linen suit complete with vest, and a silk striped bow tie. "Water?" Everyone demurred as they took seats around the small table in one corner. Overhead a fan whirled.

"So, we have a mutual friend in Commander Zabner," Ari said to the women. "Perhaps you can tell me why you called him?" Veronica found him unassuming and gentle, yet not someone who'd ever be pushed around.

Vi looked to Veronica and then back to Ari. "My daughter . . ."

"I can tell the story, Mother," Veronica said gently. She sketched out the same story she'd told Ezra, ending with: ". . . and that's when he said if Roosevelt *were* elected, he and some of his friends would resort to violence."

Ari nodded. "Did he say anything specific? When? What exactly they would do?"

"No," Veronica said. "But the look in his eyes . . . He was serious. I *know* he was serious."

Ari steepled his fingers. "Did you react?"

"I didn't," Veronica told him. "Just wanted to leave as soon as possible. I had a very bad feeling about the whole thing, especially when I saw his publication. It has some of the most vile and horrific anti-Semitic things I've ever read."

"And we're from New York," Vi added.

"I see," Ari responded. "Then what happened?"

Veronica told him about her uncle's call to the police and their visit to the FBI. Ari and Ezra shared a quick look. "That's when my mother"—she looked to Vi, who nodded—"called Commander Zabner. She told me he'd worked with my father and he's out here now, on the West Coast, in Naval Intelligence."

"You were right to contact Commander Zabner," Ari said. "He vouches for your late husband, Commander Grace. And the fact both of you were so disturbed by this man and his publication and his threats, and followed up so thoroughly, speaks well of you."

He leaned forward. "Donald McDonnell *is* a dangerous man. He's a suspected agent, working for German Nazis in L.A. Much of the propaganda he uses in his newspapers and pamphlets come from Joseph Goebbels himself. He's been active with the Bund and Silver Shirts, and has recently started a youth program, modeled after the Hitler Youth."

Vi swallowed. "So you know him."

"Know of him," Ari corrected. "Donald Pierce McDonnell is fifty-one, a high school teacher at North Hollywood High. Born in Texas, he's an Army vet, a former pilot, and is currently a National Guardsman. We believe he's taking orders from a man named Hermann Schwinn, a naturalized American from Germany."

He looked to Ezra, who nodded. "We have strong reasons to believe Schwinn's a German agent, working with the Nazis in Germany, organizing cells with McDonnell—groups of men—to infiltrate U.S. defense facilities on the West Coast."

"What—?" Veronica managed. "You mean sabotage?" *This is worse than we thought.*

Ezra nodded. "That's where I come in, with my position in the Navy. One of my jobs is to track down and arrest Japanese spies."

"*Japanese* spies?" Vi asked.

"Well . . . that's another story. But while I'm focused on the Japanese, Ari here's taken on the Germans."

"The men in these . . . cells," Veronica asked. "Who are they?"

"We suspect they're commercial pilots, aircraft mechanics, people involved in aviation—people who McDonnell befriends through his contacts," Ari told them. "McDonnell also has a boat and routinely tours San Pedro Harbor, taking photographs of the Navy's ships."

"And these are Americans, U.S. citizens?" Vi asked.

Ari nodded. "Mostly German Americans, members of the Bund."

"You think he's sending evidence of ship movements back to Germany?" Veronica asked.

"Yes," Ari said simply. "Yes, we do. And a whole lot more. But we don't know specifics, and we have no way to prove anything." Veronica nodded. "Which is why . . ." Ari said. His shadowed brown eyes were sincere. "Veronica, we'd like to ask you to keep working for McDonnell."

"No!" Vi interrupted, startling everyone with her outburst. "No," she repeated, softer this time, but just as vehement.

"Mother," Veronica said, laying a cotton-gloved hand on her mother's. "Let's hear the gentlemen out."

"What's there to hear out?" Vi snapped. "They want you to go back to this 'dangerous man' and work for him? I don't want you anywhere near those people!"

"*Mother,*" Veronica repeated, "let's just listen."

"Thank you," Ari said to both women. "I realize how enormous this request is, how huge the undertaking. But we believe there's a real threat to America from McDonnell and his cell. We've already discovered and thwarted a number of plots. For example, there was a German officer in Los Angeles who plotted to blow up U.S.-made airplanes bound for Canada—and ultimately for Britain—back in '39."

Vi's blue eyes were wide. "No!"

"What happened to him?" Veronica asked.

"He fled the country in December—never to be heard from again." He sighed. "There was also a plot to lynch twenty Jews and supporters—including Al Jolson, Charlie Chaplin, Eddie Cantor, Samuel Goldwyn, and Louis B. Mayer—but the authorities were tipped off before anything actually happened."

Ari stopped, looking out the window for a moment, the Venetian blinds casting bars of shadow across his face. "There's more, so much more. So, when you tell me McDonnell's saying these things, well, of course it might be just talk. But, then again, it might *not* be. It could be all too real. I feel we can't take the chance. No one believed Hitler's Brownshirts could seize control of Germany in 1933, but they did. And now look where they are! The window of opportunity to stop them without a major war was missed. But, at least in this country, we still have a fighting chance against our own Nazis."

Ezra cleared his throat. "When we spoke yesterday, I was impressed with your experience in journalism, Veronica. The qualities that make a good journalist also make for an excellent undercover agent."

"You mean spy," Vi said flatly.

"*Why* do you want to be a journalist?" Ari asked.

Veronica took a deep breath. "As Martha Gellhorn wrote to Max Perkins, 'If a writer has any guts he should write all the time, and the lousier the world the harder a writer should work. For if he can do nothing positive, to make the world more livable or less cruel or stupid, he can at least record truly, and that's something no one else will do, and it's a job that must be done.' She believed those words. She *lived* those words."

Vi recrossed her legs at the ankles. "What exactly *is* your organization, Mr. Lewis?" she asked. "This is a law office, yes?"

"I'm a lawyer, but my background is in Naval Intelligence—I served during the Great War. I'm one of a group of anonymous American citizens who was alarmed by the rise of Nazism in Germany, beginning in 1933. It's been paralleled by the rise of fascism in this country, particularly in Los Angeles. We're concerned German Nazi enemy agents have infiltrated Southern California and are turning American citizens against democracy."

"Pardon me for stating the obvious," Vi said, "but you're also Jewish, yes?"

Ari and Ezra glanced at each other. "Yes, we both are. And we're concerned about rising anti-Semitism, of course," Ezra replied.

"But we see this as an *American* problem," Ari continued. "We believe democracy itself is in danger. This isn't a Jewish war—it's an American war."

"Oh, please—" Vi began.

Ari looked her in the eye. "There's a real threat to our democracy, one that could—faster than you think—turn our country into a totalitarian dictatorship. In the Weimar Republic, in Germany, demagogues found recruits among the poor and the desperate. We have the same conditions here in the U.S. with the Depression."

"True." Vi nodded. "True."

"Mrs. Grace," Ari said, "there're rules to being Jewish. The first is to survive—which goes back to Exodus." He drew a breath. "But the second, just as important, is never to let ourselves or others become slaves. Because we as Jews know the bitterness of slavery. As the Rabbi Hillel said, 'If I am not for myself, who will be for me? If I am only for myself, what am I? If not now, when?'"

He turned his gaze to Veronica. "We're offering you a chance to do something important with your life. Do you consider yourself a patriot?"

"Of course," Veronica replied sincerely. "I love the United States of America with all my heart."

"If your country needed you to take a job, would you do it?"

"Yes."

"If your country needed you to serve in the military, would you do it?"

"Yes."

"Veronica!" Vi exclaimed.

"*You* went to prison to win women the right to vote," Veronica reminded her. The men's eyes widened in surprise.

"Yes, but—"

"But what? Because I'm your daughter?" She raised an eyebrow. "This is just as important. I'll fight like hell before I roll over and let something like that happen here." She turned back to Ari. "Sorry for swearing."

"Quite all right. If your country needed you to lie to your friends and family, would you do it?"

"Yes."

"If your country asked you to risk your life, would you do it?"

Veronica had not expected *that*. "What?" She remembered the conversation she and her mother and Walter had had at the Heidelberg after graduation. The United States was already at war, even if most people didn't realize it yet.

"This isn't hypothetical," Ari said, dark eyes solemn. "There's danger, real danger, with these people—the Bund, the Silver Shirts, the KKK, and the rest of them. They're violent. They're unpredictable. There's a real threat to anyone who works against them."

Ezra stated, "You attended the rally at Madison Square Garden undercover to write your story for the *Hunter Envoy*."

"What?" Veronica asked, shocked. "How do you know?"

"I made a few calls," he admitted.

"Ah." Veronica swallowed. "Yes—it was terrifying. But still, I'm glad I did it."

"So you know firsthand what worked-up American Nazis are like," Ari said.

"Yes."

"Would it surprise you to know it's even worse here in Los Angeles than New York?" he asked. "We don't have someone like Mayor La Guardia, who's aware of the issue, on our side. Our mayor is willfully ignorant. Our ports are open. Our police, as you found out, are only interested in chasing communists. The FBI, too. We're vulnerable here. That's why it's imperative my people keep tabs on what's going on. Document it. So we can build a case. Get the Germans deported. Arrest the American traitors and put them in jail. And, most important, make sure none of their violent plans turn into reality."

"We're going to be at war soon," Ezra added, "with the Germans, the Italians, and the Japanese. We need to know where the U.S.'s weaknesses are. How far these German Nazis have infiltrated, how many Americans have been duped into taking up their rallying cry. It's why we have agents posing as Nazis."

"I just want to say," Vi said, a hand to her throat, "*we're* German American, but we're not like that. Our German American friends back in Brooklyn aren't like that."

Ari gazed at her, seemingly aware of her conflicted feelings. "I understand, Mrs. Grace."

"How many agents do you have?" Veronica asked.

"I can't say, of course," Ari told her. "But they're German Americans, Christians—what you might call 'Gentiles.' A lot of them are veterans of the last war, doing their part for the upcoming one."

"But you—you're different," Ezra told them. "With your blue eyes and blond hair and being female. And so young! Not to mention the daughter of a Navy vet. You'd make the perfect spy. No one would *ever* suspect you."

"She's a child!" Vi snapped.

"Mother, I'm twenty-two. If I were a man, I'd be old enough to be drafted."

"Mrs. Grace," Ari explained, "Hitler's a psychopath, and he's infected an army of psychopaths here in America. Right now, we're at the same crossroads Germany faced in 1933—and we want to make sure we don't go down the same path here. Whatever the Nazis are doing, whatever they're planning, we need to know about it. To avert disaster." He looked to Veronica. "The U.S. needs you."

Ezra nodded in agreement. "She just doesn't know it yet."

Veronica thought back to the rally in Madison Square Garden—the contorted faces, the spittle coming out of their mouths as they shouted obscenities with glee: *"Death to Jews!" "Free America!"* She was angry.

"Your intelligence, your observational skills, your recall of detail—everything you used in journalism," Ari said. "You could use it to serve your country."

"Are you in or are you out?" Ezra asked, cutting to the point. "If you choose out, there's no harm, no foul. You'll never see us again."

Veronica felt an overwhelming sense of calling, even though she was woefully inexperienced and untrained. That somehow, life had brought her here, to this moment. Had put her in a position to serve. She might be young and female, but she loved her country and would do everything in her power to protect it.

"I want to do it," she said finally. "When people start threatening violence against my fellow Americans, you—I—need to stop talking and do something. I want to help."

"This sounds dangerous, sweetie."

"We can't live alone in this world, Mother," Veronica said. "We need to wake up. Take care of each other. Do what's right."

"We'll provide training," Ari told them.

Veronica sat upright. It would be a privilege to work for Ari, not a sacrifice. "When this—whatever work I do with you—is all over," Veronica said slowly, "I want to expose them. I want to write about my experiences. Like Martha Gellhorn. It might never be published, and maybe no one will ever read it, but I want to 'make an angry sound against injustice.' After all, it's our job as citizens to protest—and 'the price of freedom is eternal vigilance.'"

"When this is all over," Ari replied seriously, "really and truly over, I'll be the first in line to buy a copy of your book—and have you autograph it."

She nodded. "So . . . what is it you want me to do? Where do we go from here?"

"You're already in place. Make yourself indispensable to McDonnell to start. Gain his trust." Ari rose and went to his desk, opening a drawer. "Here," he said, handing her a book.

"*The Great Gatsby*?" Veronica said, confused. "I've already read it. More of a Hemingway fan."

"This is a special book," he told her. "A first edition."

Vi and Veronica looked at him blankly.

"We use it for code. Don't worry, my associate will go over everything in your training."

"So . . . what do I do now?" Veronica asked, looking up and accepting the book. Everything looked the same, but her life, she knew, had irrevocably changed.

"Go about your normal routine, go back and work for McDonnell—wait to be contacted. You'll be getting a message tonight. If you decide you're in, show up as directed. If you decide, after thinking about it, this isn't for you—just ignore it."

Veronica took a deep breath. "I understand."

"One more thing," Ari said as he rose. "Whatever you decide, you *must* burn the message after you read it. For your safety and for ours."

CHAPTER ELEVEN

The next morning, as directed by the missive she'd decoded using *The Great Gatsby*, utilizing the numbers and words as Ari had taught her, and then burned, Veronica walked down South Olive Street in the slanted sunlight, past a huge Hershey's chocolate bar billboard next to a watch repair shop. Car horns blared, trolley bells dinged, and a siren pulsed in the distance. Sunk in thought, she received a sharp blow to the shoulder as she collided with a man. He had a dour face with a bushy mustache. His lips twitched upward in an approximate smile. "Careful—you could get hurt."

"Sorry—so sorry!" She passed a diner, a pawn shop, a man selling fresh fruit from a cart, and a shoeshine boy on the corner. There was a clothing store next to an optometrist, next to a cigar shop. She took the bright orange cable car of the Angels Flight funicular train down the steep hill.

Veronica couldn't find the address. She looked again, and again, retracing her steps. The beginnings of panic fluttered through her belly. "No, no," she murmured, picturing the map in the atlas, going over the numbers she'd memorized. "It has to be here. It has to." *I can't fail even before I've started!* She checked the street. It was the correct one. Then the numbers again. No luck. *Did I memorize it wrong?* she thought. *Did I somehow transpose the numbers? I never should have burned the card . . .*

For a moment, she thought about leaving. Downtown, it felt even hotter and more sultry than Santa Monica and the ever-present sun was starting to blaze. Her blouse was sticking to her lower back.

It isn't here! It isn't here! Veronica started to panic as the address she'd been given didn't seem to exist. She felt a prickle run up the back of her neck. *What if this is a test?* She looked around. People on the street were passing by, impatient. She looked to the traffic: no one was slowing down. She scanned the parked cars: no one waiting. She looked up, to the windows of the buildings—up and across the street—and then, on the third floor, she spotted Ari Lewis, with his hangdog eyes, watching her intently. He stood next to another man, taller, darker, whom she didn't recognize. Her first impulse was to wave, but she stopped herself, not even allowing a smile—nothing that would alert anyone she'd seen anything.

Veronica went into an office supply store on the ground floor of the building and asked a sallow man with a toupee behind the counter about the entrance. He pointed to a dented metal door: it led to a cement stairwell in the back, the white paint yellowed and peeling in spots. She climbed the dusty, uneven stairs to the third floor, trying to remember which window it was and figure out which door it could be. Finally, when she was sure she'd found the office, she held her breath and knocked.

She heard a noise at the peephole, then several locks being undone. A man who wasn't Ari answered the door. "Took you long enough." He wasn't wearing a jacket or even a tie, but trousers and a rumpled white cotton shirt open at the neck, with blue-striped suspenders.

He stood stiffly, a faint frown creasing his forehead. Veronica looked up. He was in his late twenties, well over six feet tall, lean, and sinewy. His face was striking, with almond-shaped brown eyes, a high forehead, and sharp cheekbones. His affect was slightly off-center, and he gave Veronica the impression he was someone who didn't suffer fools easily. *And I'm pretty sure he thinks I'm one.*

What Veronica wanted to say was *Oh, stuff it up your nose!* But instead, she looked at her small gold wristwatch. "I'm two minutes late," she replied. "And I would have been early if you'd given me decent directions. I gave myself extra time—because if you're even part German, being late's considered a cardinal sin." She raised an eyebrow at him.

Smiling, Ari stepped over. He wore another three-piece linen suit and a blue polka-dotted bow tie. "Good to see you again, Miss Grace."

She walked in and extended her hand; Ari shook it. "Good to see you, too, Mr. Lewis."

"Please excuse my colleague, Jonah Rose. He can be a little . . . brusque. Have a seat."

She looked around the hotel room. It was worn, with a matted gray carpet, dingy chintz furniture, and smoke-stained wallpaper. There was an efficiency kitchen, a small sitting area, and, on the other side of the room, a sagging double bed. It smelled of must and brewed coffee.

As she took a seat, Jonah appraised her in a curious, almost clinical way—until their gazes met for a confusing second. Veronica looked away, then back, refusing to be intimidated. Ari sat, but Jonah remained standing.

"Apparently, you're an aspiring journalist. But your career was . . . cut short. And that's what brought you west." Jonah stood across from her, motionless, never moving his eyes from her.

Veronica forced herself to meet his face, to keep her hands still, to not smooth her hair or chew her lip. It was hot in the room, even with the window open; outside, she could see the orange Angels Flight cars pass on a diagonal.

"How would you phrase it?" he asked.

"I had a job and then I didn't," Veronica said simply. "And my mother and I decided to move to Los Angeles."

He rocked back on his heels. "Are you still a journalist?"

"Not a working one. Not right now, at least. I took a secretarial job to help pay the bills."

"For Donald Pierce McDonnell."

She folded her gloved hands. "Yes."

"There's an undercover movement going on in America right now, in Los Angeles," Jonah told her, beginning to pace. "McDonnell's a foot soldier, one among many. It's a nativist, nationalist, fascist movement, fed with money and propaganda by Nazi Germany. Normal, fine Americans are being indoctrinated, then going on to propagate the party line advanced by Hitler's agents here. Some of the American Nazis are truly horrific people, but others are doing it sincerely, for their country, to be good Americans.

"We want you to get beyond those people, the misguided, to find those with actual connections to Nazi Germany. Agents who are actively working against the U.S., attempting to subvert democracy."

"And not just for Jews," Ari added, "but for everyone. The attitude of our fellow citizens toward the Negro, the Japanese, the Chinese, the Mexican, is just as important to democracy as anti-Semitism. Now, we have a few questions for you, Miss Grace."

Veronica tucked one ankle behind the other. "Of course."

"Are you married?" Jonah asked.

"No."

"Engaged?"

"No."

"Boyfriend?" She shot him a look. "No, I'm not asking because I'm free next Saturday night," he snapped. "I'm asking because this is demanding, grueling, secretive work. It's better if you're not involved with anyone."

"Noted. No boyfriend."

"Do you love your country?"

"Yes, of course," Veronica replied.

"And what's true love of country to you?"

"It's . . ." She thought for a moment. "True love of country is a regard for *all* of the people of one's country," she said slowly. "We're all in this 'American experiment' together."

"And why do you want to do this?" Ari asked.

"If there's something, anything, I can do to help, I will. If I can play the smallest part in fighting the Nazis, I'll do it."

Jonah came to a stop in front of her. "Stand up," he said, and she did. He looked her up and down, not like most men did, but analytically, dispassionately. "Why did you choose this outfit?"

"It's . . . fashionable," Veronica told him, omitting the fact she'd been inspired by Lady Brett in Ernest Hemingway's *The Sun Also Rises*. Her mother had made her linen trousers and a blouse for her, and she'd styled her outfit with the backward-worn cotton cardigan so popular at Hunter, a green floral scarf in her hair, and chunky Bakelite bracelets. It was what she'd worn to class at Hunter, or when she went downtown to Café Society in the West Village, where she would smoke, drink Negronis, and listen to jazz with friends.

"Exactly," he retorted. "It's not what a girl flirting with fascism would wear."

"Woman," she corrected him. "But I see your point."

"Change your look," he ordered. "Grow your hair longer, color it blonder. Wear dresses and skirts. Lots of red and black." He considered. "Maybe a small cross necklace, some braids. Do you want to get married?"

"No, not really," Veronica replied. "Although, I suppose, you never know—"

"No!" Jonah stuck his hands in his pockets. "You—the you who's undercover—definitely want to be married. It's all you dream about. Your wedding dress, your handsome groom, walking down the aisle . . . Do you want children?"

Not particularly, Veronica thought. But she replied, "Er, yes?"

"How many children do you want?"

"One?" *One wouldn't be so bad.*

He shook his head. "At least four. At the very least. That's how many married women in Germany are expected to have. Why are you working?"

Veronica caught on. "I'm just doing a few secretarial jobs until I get married. I have no ambitions for a career, just hope to meet a nice Aryan man."

He nodded. "Do you cook?"

"Ha!" Veronica couldn't help herself; she was a terrible cook.

"You're learning to cook, then," Jonah told her. "Are you athletic?"

"Not especially."

"You'll need to be. For many reasons, including safety. We'll work on that."

Ari asked, "You covered the Bund in New York, the rally in '38?"

"Yes."

"It can be part of your cover story," Jonah said. "How you went and were converted."

Veronica nodded slowly.

"We'll meet after each encounter you have with them and debrief," Jonah told her. "I want you to relay everything—nothing is unimportant. We're counting on your eye for vivid detail. Can you reproduce conversations verbatim?"

"I can try."

"What were the last questions I asked?"

"Oh . . ." Veronica thought back, trying not to panic. "If I want to get married, if I want to have children, if I can cook, if I'm athletic. Then Mr. Lewis asked me if I covered the Bund."

"You'll have to do better than that, sister." Jonah turned to Ari. "I'm going to have to be Pygmalion with this one."

Sister? "I'm right here, you know," Veronica said tartly.

"Yes, yes, of course, Miss Grace. I want you to be sure about all this," Ari said. "This is your life. There is no obligation. You're free to walk away, forget you ever met us."

Veronica thought for a moment. *Mother would* love *that.* "I'm free. I *am* free. And that's why I have to do this."

"If you change your mind in the next twenty-four hours, let us know," Jonah said. He sounded cold, as if she were deliberately planning on wasting his time. "Otherwise, we'll proceed. You'll be reporting to me."

Veronica felt her heart sink. She liked the avuncular Ari much better.

"You'll continue your work with McDonnell. There's also a concert at Deutsches Haus this Friday. Beethoven, Blon, and Brahms. You need to go."

"And when I'm there?"

"Say you're new in town. You miss Yorkville. You miss German culture and music. You miss the people—Germans. Meanwhile, get to know them."

"Who specifically?"

"The McDonnells, to start. We'll go over more names at your training sessions." Jonah strode to the front door. "If you decide to proceed, tomorrow you'll come here without telling anyone. We'll let you know what time. I'll train you. And, if you're up to par, we'll hire you officially."

Ari and Veronica stood. "Thank you," she said. "I look forward to working with you both."

Jonah opened the door. "Don't go straight home from here," he told her. "Go to a diner or into a shop. Make sure no one's following you. There are two rules for staying safe—don't write down anything in public, and don't let them know where you live. Ever."

The parting felt dismissive, even rude. It wasn't that she was expecting gratitude, but perhaps some acknowledgment, a handshake, a thank-you. *You haven't actually done anything yet,* she reminded herself.

"We're offering you the opportunity to do something with your life, something important," Jonah told her. "But you'll be completely anonymous. You'll have to spend time with unsavory people and pretend to like them. You'll have to laugh at their jokes, nod along with all their propaganda. It all must be done in complete secrecy. This is not a way to break a story, even anonymously."

"I understand." She took a deep breath. "Are you always going to act like this, or are you going to lighten up?" For a moment, Jonah looked shocked, and Veronica wondered if he might actually smile.

But he folded his face back into a scowl. "We're professionals, Miss Grace," he said as he ushered her out. "Don't forget it. It may save your life someday."

CHAPTER TWELVE

Vi arrived at the Georgian Hotel, a turquoise-painted art deco skyscraper facing the ocean, known as "Santa Monica's First Lady." The Georgian was an oasis of luxury, as well as a former speakeasy. Inside, the air was cool; brilliant chandeliers glinted above a glossy marble floor.

She was wearing the ensemble she'd worn to Veronica's graduation, complete with her golden poppy–embroidered blouse. Her feet in their wedge heels were throbbing, but she put a smile on her face, determined to make sales. A sign on an easel next to a table with a huge bouquet of spiky orange birds-of-paradise and glossy leaves read:

NORA INGLE, AVIATRIX
PRESENTED BY THE AMERICA FIRST COMMITTEE,
WOMEN'S DIVISION
SAND DOLLAR BALLROOM
3 P.M.

She found the Sand Dollar Ballroom was already crowded, the air thick with cigarette smoke and perfume. Vi looked around and caught a woman's eye.

"You made it!" Dodie Tatum exclaimed. She was wearing a

black suit with red polka dots, her cottony blond hair rolled into two barrettes, a thick silver and marcasite choker around her neck. "Good for you! Oh, and what a *gorgeous* blouse! Even prettier than the apple one, I think."

"Thank you." Vi permitted herself a smile. "I made it myself— the suit as well."

"Stunning. Absolutely stunning. Now, what do you know about Nora Ingle?"

"Not much," Vi admitted. "But I've always loved the idea of a woman flying a plane. I've followed Anne Morrow Lindbergh's career closely."

Dodie's face creased. "So terrible about the baby."

"Tragic."

"But how wonderful they're back from Germany now! Lindbergh's involved with America First, you know!" Everyone knew Charles Lindbergh, the celebrated American aviator, world famous for his solo flight from New York to Paris.

"What is America First?" Vi asked, as Ann Hunt swanned over to join them. Like Dodie, she was also dressed in red and black, a plaid day dress with a shiny patent leather belt.

"The America First Committee," Ann explained. "We're going public in the fall."

"Sorry, girls," Dodie exclaimed. "Must keep moving!"

Ann rolled her eyes. "She's president now—thinks the world revolves around her."

Vi asked, "But what's it about? America first in . . . what exactly?"

"Oh, America First's a patriotic group for people all over the country," she replied. "We're against America entering the war in Europe—stopping Roosevelt and his cronies from sending those 'Lend-Lease' ships to England. Being the 'arsenal of democracy' is just going to lead to trouble."

She turned her scowl into a beaming smile. "But if you're a Lindbergh admirer, you'll fit in fine here," Ann added, taking Vi's arm. "We all just love the Lindberghs. We hope he might be president one day—fingers crossed! Now, let's get a seat."

I just want to make some sales, Vi thought, but she allowed herself to be led through the crowd.

The ballroom was set up with chairs facing a stage that had a podium with a microphone. Red, white, and blue banners were hung in graceful swags, surrounding a poster declaring: AMERICA FIRST! LET'S STAY OUT OF EUROPE'S WAR! KEEP AMERICAN BOYS SAFE!

They were able to find two seats in the back, near the aisle. As they settled their handbags in their laps, folded their hands, and crossed their ankles, Ann explained, "Nora Ingle's the heir to a tea fortune, can you imagine?"

Vi's lips twitched into a smile. "I suppose that's one way for her to afford a plane." The woman seated next to Vi was knitting, her needles clicking briskly. "Oh, what are you making?" Vi asked. She loved to knit, too.

The young brunette with vivid green eyes showed off her handiwork. "A sock," she said. "For charity."

"Bundles for Britain?" Bundles for Britain was an American effort to make and ship knitted items—socks, gloves, hats, sweaters, and scarves—overseas to help the war effort.

"Heavens, no!" the woman exclaimed. "These socks are going to our own Okies and Arkies. Let charity begin at home's what I say."

"Oh, look," Ann said as the lights dimmed, "it's starting."

A spotlight turned on to follow Dodie as she went up the steps to the stage, her necklace glinting. She tapped the microphone. "Can you hear me?" The women in the audience nodded.

"Well then—good afternoon, ladies! Welcome to the Women's Committee of America First." Applause filled the air. "Let me start by saying we believe in peace, not in war."

From her seat, Vi nodded in approval. "And while we deplore some of the things going on in Europe, we have enough to do here in America. My own sons're draft age, and you bet I'm doing everything I can to keep them—and all our sons—out of the European war. Let's not send our own young men over to be slaughtered for a war British boys should be fighting."

There was a ripple of approval through the audience and even a "Yes, ma'am!" from the back.

The woman continued: "I'm Mrs. Dodie Tatum, the organizer of this event, and I'm delighted to introduce our distinguished guest this afternoon." She picked up a small card and began to read. " 'Nora Ingle was born and raised in New York and studied music and languages in Paris and Vienna. She's worked not only as a secretary and a nurse, but also as a pianist *and* a vaudeville dancer.' " Dodie looked to the audience, who gave an appreciative chuckle.

" 'But then Mrs. Ingle found her true calling—aviation. She's set numerous records as a stunt pilot and achieved multiple firsts as an aviatrix, including a record of seven hundred and fourteen consecutive barrel rolls! A few years later, she earned an international award for a solo flight around South America.' Can you imagine?" she asked the audience. "I won't even drive to Santa Barbara on my own!" Another laugh from the crowd.

"And so, without further ado, the America First Committee is honored to present . . . Mrs. Nora Ingle!"

The aviatrix walked to the platform to warm applause and nodded. "Thank you, Dodie," she said into the microphone. She was tiny, trim, and immaculate, with a smart Chanel suit, sleekly coiffed dark hair, and hazel eyes, her neck wrapped in black onyx. "Thank you all for coming, ladies," she said to the women in the audience. Vi sat back and listened.

"I'm honored to be invited by the America First Committee— thank you so much for having me." The women of the committee, sitting in the front row, smiled; some raised their gloved hands in greeting.

"I'd like to talk to you a bit about my career in aviation and how, like Charles Lindbergh, I've been able to use it to promote our shared goal: keeping America out of the war." There was another, louder wave of applause. Violet clapped as well. *So far, so good,* she thought.

"Last September, I flew over Washington in my Lockheed Orion monoplane. And do you know what I did?" She scanned the audience, eyes wide. "Dropped anti-intervention pamphlets on the White House. That's right, direct delivery to the president and First Lady! My way of letting them know we don't want to be part of any foreign wars." There was louder clapping now. Violet continued to clap along. *Nothing wrong with that.*

"I was arrested for violating White House airspace," she told them. "But the police were so kind. They gave me coffee and doughnuts—delicious!—and let me go in just a few hours." She winked. "I think a few of them might be on our side!

"But things are much more serious now, especially since France fell and Britain is—sadly—determined to fight on. I personally went to my good friend, the baron Ulrich von Gienanth from the German embassy—who suggested I make a solo flight to Europe, where I would continue to work to keep America out of the war." She took the measure of the room. "But the baron asked me to stay in the United States. That's when he told me about a new group, the America First Committee. Let me tell you—I was honored, absolutely honored, to join.

"One of the aims of the America First Committee is to launch a petition to enforce the 1939 Neutrality Act. We *must* make President Franklin D. Roosevelt honor his pledge to keep America out of the war!" There was resounding applause, and a voice from the back of the room cried, "Yes, indeed!" Vi clapped even louder along with the others.

"We oppose the Lend-Lease bill, with all of our vigor. We are not the 'arsenal of democracy.' We oppose the convoying of ships, the Atlantic Charter. England is down on one knee, and when she's forced down on the other, she's going to shout for the United States to come in and save her. Again. But I don't believe we should.

We've barely come out of the Depression. We have enough problems here, in America!" Nodding, Violet sat up even straighter.

"Ladies, we *must* kick Roosevelt out of office this November. He's continually lied to the American people. I'd like you to look beyond the speeches and propaganda you're being fed, and instead look at who's writing the speeches and reports, who owns the papers, and who influences the speakers." She gave them a knowing look. *Wait,* Vi thought. *Who exactly is she talking about?*

"I don't know about you, but I'm tired of people who call 'Americanism for America' Nazism. I just believe we have enough work here to do in America. I am for America first. I believe in my friend and fellow aviator Colonel Lindbergh—the Patrick Henry of our time. He, I'm proud to say, has the courage to take a stand. He sees the trouble and he names it: 'pro-British imperialism.' He's not afraid to call out British interests and our pro-British government."

A few in the audience began to clap. "Lindbergh would rather see the United States enter the war on the side of Hitler than England." *Wait—no. No, no, no, no, no . . .* But a wave of *"Yes, yes!"* filled the ballroom.

Nora said, beaming, "To you all, I say, free America! Thank you so much!"

She exited to a standing ovation. Vi was slow to stand as she absorbed all she'd heard, clapping mechanically. *It's one thing to be anti-war. But pro-Hitler? No—a world of no.*

As the lights came up, Vi overheard snippets of conversation from the women around her: "One hundred percent for Lindbergh," "I'd like to burn the British flag," "We should impeach Roosevelt . . ."

"She's a marvelous speaker, isn't she?" Ann asked. "I just love how she says what everyone's thinking, but few dare to say in public."

Vi felt unnerved, but thought, *Surely, they can't all be like that. Right? They're just the loud ones? There must be some like me . . .*

There was coffee and lemonade on tables in the back, as well as small cucumber sandwiches and red raspberry Linzer cookies. Vi eyed the sweets, but resolved to eat nothing, instead getting a cup of black coffee from the silver urn.

"Vi, let me introduce you to some of the girls," Ann said, taking her by the arm. Vi put the speech behind her, allowed herself to be led to a small group of well-dressed women. "Here she is," Ann announced, "Mrs. Violet Grace, an artist with a needle. Look at the poppies on her blouse, ladies! Aren't they exquisite?"

The women all cooed in appreciation as introductions were made. "What else have you done?" one asked.

"Oh, every flower under the sun," Vi said, making her best sales pitch. "Fruit. Vines. Leaves. I can embroider anything, really. A lot of flowers have secret meanings, you know—bluebells for kindness, peonies for bashfulness, rosemary for remembrance . . ."

"I'd love a blouse with edelweiss," Nora Ingle chimed in as she fitted a cigarette into her mother-of-pearl holder and raised a pair of exquisitely plucked eyebrows. The women parted to let her through. "It's Herr Hitler's favorite flower."

"Oh, I'd love one, too," said Dodie, trailing behind Nora. "Maybe with swastikas? A bit of red?"

"Oh!" Vi said, overcome by shock and losing her voice. *It's one thing to be asked to a talk. It was another to embroider a swastika.* "Um . . ."

As the women clamored around her, Vi felt ill. *These women— they're so . . . nice,* she thought. So friendly, welcoming her into their circle. *And they're . . . Nazis.*

"Excuse me, ladies, please," she managed finally, clasping her hands together to disguise their trembling. "Where's the little girls' room?"

* * *

LOCKED IN A stall, she took deep breaths. *Dear God! What's wrong with these people?* She thought of Veronica and her reaction to McDonnell and his anti-Semitic tracts. She thought of Ari Lewis, his mission, and the work Veronica had committed to doing, and realized she was face-to-face with one of the biggest decisions of her life. Bigger than women's suffrage, bigger than going to jail. Bigger, even, than choosing to go on the hunger strike. At least she'd been one striker among many, arrested for a public protest, jailed with her friends who were on her side. What she was contemplating—the situation had stolen up on her and presented itself without warning—was something she hadn't trained for. She felt frozen, terrified. *But Veronica's doing it. Going undercover. Why can't I?*

At once, she was swarmed with negative thoughts. *I can't do it . . . Who am I? Just a housewife . . .* Leaning against the stall's door, she rested her forehead on her arm, then took a deep breath.

Well, why not me? All right, I'm fifty—and I may be a widow and have no real job experience—but maybe I can make a difference—like Veronica. After all, if no one would suspect her, surely no one would ever suspect me?

She drew herself up, let herself out, went to one of the sinks, and washed her hands with cold water. They were no longer trembling as she reapplied her lipstick, her war paint. Staring at her face in the mirror, she pressed her lips together and made a final, irrevocable decision. Housewife turned spy. *No one would ever believe it. Not in a hundred years.* She tried not to laugh.

She walked to the lobby, to a bank of telephone booths in the back. Looking around, to make sure no one from the lecture was close enough to hear anything, she took Ezra's card from her purse and dialed the number. She reached his answering service. "Yes, please tell Commander Zabner Mrs. Grace would like to speak to him again. Before he leaves Los Angeles. It's urgent, thank you."

Vi walked back to the Sand Dollar Ballroom with her shoulders squared and chin held high. She beamed as she approached the group, making color and style suggestions to the women. She would befriend them. She would listen to everything they said, remember it, then share it with Lewis and his men. And if there was anything important they knew, through their husbands or business associates—or Charles Lindbergh himself—she would find it out and report back.

As the women began chattering to her again, she felt a flash of resolve: *I went to prison and had a feeding tube shoved down my throat—I can beat you Nazi* hündinnen *at your own games.*

* * *

WHEN VERONICA RETURNED home, Vi was still out. Upstairs, she saw the tabby cat in the drawer and heard tiny smacking sounds with intermittent high-pitched mews. Looking closer, she saw a mass of damp furry bodies. It was Mama and three tiny tabby kittens, their eyes still closed, their tiny pink mouths opening and closing. "Oh!" she cooed, bending down. But before she got too close, Mama hissed a warning. "All right, all right! I won't touch. Good job, Mama, good job!" She got what she needed, then backed quietly out of the room. Mama's watchful eyes followed her until she left.

It was almost ten o'clock when Vi returned home. "Where have you been?" Veronica demanded. Usually, she was the one getting home late, and Vi was the one waiting up. She didn't like the change of roles. She quoted Vi exactly: "I was worried sick about you!"

"I know, sweetie, I'm sorry." Vi kissed her cheek. "We need to talk."

"All right," Veronica said, leading the way back to the kitchen, where she'd been sipping chamomile tea and reading the *Los Angeles Times*. They both sat at the table. "Where were you?"

"I was with Commander Zabner and Mr. Lewis."

Veronica's jaw dropped. "Why?" She felt confused, then annoyed. "It's all decided. I'm an adult now—what I choose to do is my business."

"Not everything's about you, sweetie," her mother said pointedly, and Veronica felt her cheeks grow hot. "The lecture I went to—it was really an America First meeting."

Veronica didn't understand. "America's first—in what?"

"The America First Committee," Vi explained. "It's a new organization. Putting America first over aid to other countries. They're isolationists—against the war. Supposedly Charles Lindbergh's involved."

"The pilot?"

"Exactly. But it's not just for isolationists or pacifists. Some of the women there, including the woman speaking, were . . . are . . . American Nazis."

Veronica made a face. "They grow like weeds out here."

"They want me to embroider blouses for them—with edelweiss and swastikas."

"Jesus H. Roosevelt Christ!"

"Veronica! Language!"

"Sorry, but what else am I supposed to say?" She rubbed her forehead as she absorbed this new turn of events.

"They were also anti-Semitic and anti–Roosevelt. Anti-democracy."

"So . . . you called Commander Zabner?"

Vi nodded. "Luckily, he hadn't gone back to San Diego yet. He and I talked to Mr. Lewis, at his office. And . . ." She took a deep breath. "Well, I've decided to work undercover for them as well."

Veronica snorted and began to laugh—her big, hearty guffaw. "What?" she asked in disbelief. "What? You? You're my *mother!*" Veronica said, trying to catch her breath. "You can't be a—a—*spy*—" She burst into spluttering laughter.

"I'm an American. I'm a citizen. I'm a widow. I'm a woman," Vi told her, with hurt in her voice. "I'm a lot of things, you know—not *just* a mother."

Veronica was still giggling. "Right, right—you were a suffragette."

"Suffra*gist,* Veronica. I don't know why you're laughing—I'll make the perfect spy. After all, who would ever suspect a middle-aged housewife?" She added, "Overlooked and underestimated people make the best spies, as Ari and Ezra told me today. And they were grateful for my help."

Veronica realized her mother was right. And that, together, they'd be unstoppable. She changed her tone. "Mother, how would you like to go to a concert?"

"A concert?"

"Yes, but not just any concert. A night of German music."

Vi reached for Veronica's tea mug and took a sip. "Sounds fun."

"At Deutsches Haus."

The name of the Bund's headquarters hung in the air, as the implications settled in. "All right," she said finally.

"Let's both go to Deutsches Haus and take down those Nazi bastards."

CHAPTER THIRTEEN

The night of the concert, Veronica took off her green-and-pink flowered cotton day dress and stripped naked to begin her transformation.

First she stepped into the dreaded girdle, then rolled up her stockings, inspected them for runs, attaching them to the garters. The belt dug into her waist like a medieval instrument of torture. She sighed and reached for her dress: red, with three knife pleats in the back. It was new, or at least looked it—her mother had recently dyed it in the kitchen sink, turning her hands bloody-looking in the process.

She removed the metal curlers from her hair and pinned up a section with a red silk rose barrette her mother had also dyed. Her good shoes, black leather and worn only for special occasions, were in fair shape, and she slipped them on. Surveying herself in the mirror, she smoothed Vaseline over her eyebrows and her eyelashes, powdered her nose and forehead, then dabbed on Elizabeth Arden's Coquette lipstick.

"My name's Veronica Grace," she said to the cat as she stroked her ears. Mama purred and regarded her through slit eyes; the tiny kittens were curled up against her belly, asleep. "I'm German American. In New York, I saw a lot of things, things that made me wonder what was really going on in this country . . . Now I'm in

Los Angeles, working for Mr. and Mrs. McDonnell. Only some people here seem to know what's *really* going on, and Mr. McDonnell and Mrs. McDonnell do. And I want to be one of them, too . . ." She felt her stomach clench at the lies. *But I need to believe it all tonight,* she thought.

She could hear Jonah's voice in her ear: *These are the men you need to know,* he'd told her during one of the week's training sessions, pointing at photographs. *Know their faces and their names. Those are the men you want to impress and ultimately to work for. Flatter them, bat your eyelashes, make them like you. Get close.*

"All right," she said, adding more lipstick at the last moment. She took a final look in the mirror. "You can do this." She turned to Mama. "Right?" But the tabby was already asleep.

When Veronica entered the living room and saw her mother, she gasped. Vi was Veronica's exact opposite—wearing the same dress, but dyed black, worn with red accessories. She'd been to the salon and her hair was freshly blond, lips and nails painted scarlet. She tried to smile, but it just didn't reach her eyes. *She's nervous,* Veronica realized, smelling her Arpège perfume. *Maybe even scared.* "Well, you're a fancy flapjack," she said, trying to tease a laugh from her mother.

Vi only turned. "Are the seams in my stockings straight?"

"Wunderbar," Veronica replied.

"Let's go, then."

Veronica nodded. She was scared, too—but she wasn't about to back down. Not like Chamberlain, with his "peace in our time." She remembered what her father used to say about his days in the Navy: *The only time you back down is when you're dead.*

* * *

DEUTSCHES HAUS, at 634 West Fifteenth at South Figueroa, was a two-story off-white stucco mansion. The entrance had broad steps and tall columns covered with climbing red roses. The wide terrace was covered with an ocher-striped awning, and a carved wooden sign on the right-hand side of the double doors read NO ADMITTANCE TO JEWS OR DOGS. A German cultural, social, and athletic center, it was home to the German American Bund as well as shops, a bar, a restaurant, a publishing house, a bookstore, and a gym. It was only a short walk from Lewis's offices in the Roosevelt Building, Veronica realized. *Small world,* she thought grimly.

Inside, the lobby was covered in marble and lit by brass chandeliers. It was crowded with well-dressed, pleasantly inebriated people leaving the restaurant, and heading to the auditorium for the concert. Their laughter was loud, and the air was thick with the smells of fried bratwurst, ladies' perfume, and cigar smoke. She heard conversations in both English and German, the thick and heavy dialect of the Bavarians mixing with the singsong of the Saxons and the softer accents of the Austrians.

As they entered, Veronica felt gazes taking them in—their blond hair and blue eyes, as well as their fashionable dresses, polished leather pumps, and immaculate gloves. A printed card on an easel to the side announced the program: Blon's *Sizilietta,* Brahms's "Sonntag," and Beethoven's String Quartet in C-sharp Minor. A sign outside the entrance to the Aryan Bookstore read:

WAKE UP PATRIOTIC AMERICANS!
A SECOND WORLD WAR IS BEING COOKED UP
FOR GENTILES TO FIGHT.
YOU ARE NOT ENLIGHTENED ON THE
JEWISH COMMUNIST MENACE IN AMERICA.
COME AND LEARN!

"Do you see Mr. and Mrs. McDonnell?" Vi asked as they walked into the auditorium, a great hall with rafters crossing high above them. At one end was a balcony, and at the other, a large stage.

Veronica hoisted a smile onto her face as she scanned the audience. "Not yet."

They took their seats as the lights dimmed. Members of the Deutsches Haus string quartet walked in to loud applause and took their places on the stage. Veronica and Vi sat up straight in their stiff wooden folding chairs, too nervous to hear the music. But Veronica couldn't help but notice the violin player, a young man with brilliantined platinum-blond hair. He had a blissful look on his face as he played. *A fellow music lover,* Veronica thought. *And handsome, too.*

The concert passed as if it were a dream, and then the lights flickered back on. As people stood, waiters pushed the chairs to the side to make room for a dance floor, and Veronica caught sight of Mr. and Mrs. McDonnell on the sidelines. She took Vi's arm and guided her over, saying, "Here we go," under her breath.

"Ah, Veronica!" Harriet said. "Glad you could make it. Wasn't the music wonderful?"

"It was," Veronica said truthfully. "I do love Beethoven. Mother, I'd like to introduce Mr. and Mrs. McDonnell, my new employers I've told you about. And this is my mother, Mrs. Violet Grace. Vi for short."

"Just first names here!" McDonnell admonished Veronica with one of his winning grins.

"Oh, so sorry," Veronica replied. "I'll get the hang of it soon, I promise."

"How do you do?" Vi said. "Veronica's told me so much about you." Veronica gave her mother a surreptitious poke in her back.

"Your daughter's a delight," Harriet gushed. "Such a hard worker—I could tell immediately she has good German blood."

"Thank you," Vi replied, giving Veronica a look and then swallowing. "She speaks highly of both of you."

The house orchestra was playing the sweet, lyrical ballad called "Adolf Hitler's Lieblingsblume ist das Schlichte Edelweiss." A soprano in a silver-sequined dress sang the words in German. Veronica translated them in her head:

Take this song through all the districts,
plant it forth from mouth to mouth,
take a piece of the German soul around the whole world.
Plant it in hearts for the leader to praise and cherish.
Adolf Hitler's favorite flower is the simple edelweiss . . .

A voice behind them called, "Vi!" It was Nora Ingle. She wore a black lace Chanel dress and yards and yards of pearls. "How wonderful to see you here!" She leaned in to kiss both Vi's cheeks, in the French manner. "What a beautiful evening, isn't it? Everything here's so clean, so white." Vi and Veronica looked at each other. *Surely, she wasn't saying . . .*

"Just how things should be," Harriet responded, nodding approvingly.

Nora clapped her gloved hands together. "I love it! No Jews, no Negroes, no Japs, no Chinks! No Mexicans! So *American!*" Vi gave a bland smile and a hum of agreement.

"Makes me want to *Heil Hitler!*" Nora continued. Then, sotto voce: "Although we're not supposed to do that anymore—at least, not since the FND became the Bund. It's all about appearing *American* now, and hiding our swastikas—although they're just like the Irish four-leaf clovers, really."

Vi made introductions, then Nora said, "Lovely to meet you—do you mind if I steal Vi away for a moment?"

"Of . . . of course not," Veronica said, eyes wide in surprise. She looked to her mother, who nodded, then smiled easily. *My goodness,* she thought. *Mother is . . . good at this!*

"There are some people I'd like to introduce you to," Nora said to Vi, taking her by the arm as they walked away.

The McDonnells looked on, impressed. "How does your mother know Nora Ingle?" Harriet asked Veronica.

This is good, Veronica thought. *This will help establish us in their eyes.* "They met last week at an America First lecture, actually."

"Is your mother a member?"

"Not yet."

The platinum-blond violinist approached, a tall man with sharp cheekbones. "McDonnell," he said with a lilting Viennese accent, clapping the shorter man on the back, "you lucky dog—surrounded by so many beautiful ladies."

"Wilhelm Wagner," McDonnell introduced him, pronouncing his last name like the German composer's. "Owner of the Continental Bookstore and chief distributor of German films on the West Coast."

Veronica felt his eyes travel over the contours of her dress, down her body, then up again to her face. She had noticed him earlier, as he performed. His powerful build and glowing tan made her think instantly of the countryside and vigorous sports performed in white. She guessed he was in his late twenties.

Wilhelm Wagner, she thought, remembering the picture Jonah had showed her. *Austrian. Writing a book on Hitler. Direct connections to Nazi Germany and now working with anti-Semitic isolationist groups to promote German propaganda films and literature.* "Oh, a bookstore, how wonderful!" Veronica offered.

"A political organization," Wagner replied smoothly. "Pro-American." As the orchestra segued into *The Skater's Waltz,* he extended a hand. "May I have this dance?" and before Veronica could even nod, he was leading her to the floor. "What did you think of the music?" he said as he took her into his arms.

"Lovely," Veronica said. "I enjoy Beethoven. You were excellent."

"Ah, you're passionate," he said, whirling her about. "I can tell. The Beethoven girls always are."

"I like music," she corrected him.

"Nothing like German music, though, yes?" She could smell his aftershave, lemony No. 4711.

Giddy with momentum from the sweeping turns, she momentarily forgot herself. "I like jazz, actually."

A shadow crossed his face. Before she could say anything more, he spun her around, and pulled her back in. "I like it, too, actually." He grinned like a naughty schoolboy. "Don't tell anyone, though."

"It will be our secret," she assured him. "How do you know the McDonnells?"

"I know them from Deutsches Haus. I carry some of his pamphlets in my bookstore," he told her. "How do *you* know them?"

"I just started working for them," she told him. "Secretarial things. Typing, mostly."

"Ah," he said. "So, in a way, you and I work together!"

She laughed; it sounded false to her ears and she cringed.

"Do you like movies?"

"I do," she said carefully.

"It would please me for you to be my guest to a German film sometime. I show many movies in various theaters around town. Next week's is at the Mason Opera House."

She forced herself to smile. "I'd like that." He was handsome, she had to admit. *But this isn't just any date.*

"Next Saturday?" He twirled her again. "A matinée and perhaps a good Viennese coffee and *apfelstrudel* afterward? I could pick you up?"

"Sounds wonderful." She remembered Jonah's advice from training: *Don't let them know where you live.* "Why don't I meet you there?"

* * *

WHILE VERONICA WAS dancing, Vi accompanied Nora to the bar. On the way, they passed a huge sign she'd missed on the way in, ten feet high and three feet wide, painted on canvas. She could see several names but couldn't read them without her glasses. It was a new affliction that had begun in her mid-forties, the increasing fuzziness of her eyesight. But she was too vain for eyeglasses, except when reading or sewing. *I hate getting older,* she thought. *Although it's better than the alternative.*

"Ah, our archenemies," Nora said, seeing the direction of Vi's gaze. "The worst of Los Angeles's meddling Jews. Come, let's get a drink and forget they even exist. Who knows? Maybe soon they won't."

At the bar, Vi ordered a gimlet. "Two, please," Nora told the bartender. "Hitler disapproves of women drinking giggle water, you know. But all those rules, they're for the rabble, the *volk*—not for us." She winked.

"I try to be good," Vi said as they clinked glasses. "But I'm not perfect." *I've earned this cocktail,* she thought as the icy liquid slid down her throat. *Goodness knows I'm still earning it.*

A young man stepped up next to them and ordered a beer. He was in his early twenties, Vi figured, Veronica's age, tall and thin, with round horn-rimmed glasses and curly brown hair in desperate need of a trim. His watery red-rimmed blue eyes reminded Vi of a rabbit's. He wore an old-fashioned suit vest with his shirtsleeves rolled up, but no jacket.

"Ah," Nora greeted him, "Marv! Good to see you here!" She turned to Vi. "This is Marvel Whiteside, our resident rocketeer. Marv, meet Vi."

"Rocketeer?" Vi said, taking another sip.

He ducked his head in bashful acknowledgment. "I just graduated from Caltech—physics major."

"That's wonderful," Vi said. "Congratulations! What're you doing now?"

"Well," he said, accepting his mug of beer from the bartender, "that's a big question mark. I want to make rockets—not like something from a comic book—but *real* rockets. Capable of reaching the moon!"

"The moon, huh?" Vi said. "You lack ambition, son."

He looked confused for a moment, then laughed. "And you'd think Caltech'd be interested in funding a rocket program—but no." He took a large gulp of beer, a bit of foam left on his upper lip.

"Marv here," Nora told Vi, "is pen pals with Wernher von Braun, in Germany."

Vi took another sip of her gimlet, waving away a waiter with a tray of hot pretzels. "I don't think I know him."

"Wernher von Braun's an aeronautics engineer who's pioneering rocket science in Berlin," Marvel told her. "They take rockets seriously over there, you know."

Nora put down her glass. "I keep telling Marv we must get him to Germany, to collaborate with von Braun."

Marv blushed. "I'd still like to make things work here, in the good old U.S." He looked to Nora. "Deutsches Haus has been generous in subsidizing my equipment and giving me a place to work until I can get real funding."

"Who would fund you?" Vi asked.

"Someone like Howard Hughes, ma'am. Or even the U.S. government."

Vi raised her glass. "Wonderful, Marv. To you and your rockets and the moon!"

As he moved into conversation with another group, she realized that while the Germans might not be interested in getting to the moon—yet—they certainly *would* be interested in rockets, loaded down with explosives, reaching Britain. And then, well, what would be next? Across the ocean? Rockets taking out New York City? Washington, D.C.? She shuddered.

Veronica showed up at the bar. "How are we doing, ladies?" she asked Vi and Nora.

"We're having such fun!" Vi said, while Nora smiled. "But I'm afraid it's past my bedtime."

Veronica had a bad feeling. "What are you drinking, Mother dear?" she whispered.

"A single gimlet, daughter dear," she replied. They both said their goodbyes to Mr. and Mrs. McDonnell, at the other end of the bar, before returning to the main hall.

"There's something I want to show you," Vi told Veronica. She nodded, indicating the painted canvas. "I don't have my glasses," she whispered. "Why don't you read that—so we can tell our friends."

Veronica tried to look casual. The sign read in full:

JEWISH AGENTS FOR PROSECUTION OF CHRISTIAN PATRIOTS ARE THE JEWISH ANTI-DEFAMATION LEAGUE OF THE B'NAI B'RITH, 660 ROOSEVELT BUILDING, AND THE HOLLYWOOD ANTI-NAZI LEAGUE, 6912 HOLLYWOOD BOULEVARD.

WE MUST DEMAND CONGRESSIONAL INVESTIGATION OF THEIR ALLIANCE WITH THE COMMUNIST PARTY.

TRACK DOWN THE HEAD AND SPONSORS OF THEIR AGENTS IN YOUR LOCALITY.

IN LOS ANGELES:

ERNST LUBITSCH

JUDGE ISAAC PACHT

EDDIE CANTOR

MENDEL SILBERBERG

And then, last:

ARI LEWIS

Her face must have given away her shock. "What? What does it say?" Vi asked.

Veronica didn't reply. "Let's get out of here. We can talk later."

* * *

THEY WALKED TO the Biltmore Hotel and had a drink at the bar, making sure they weren't followed. Later, upstairs in one of the suites, they had the debrief. Jonah didn't stand on ceremony as he let them in. "How was it?" he asked, pacing. Ari was also there, sitting in a blue-striped armchair. He stood to greet them and Veronica saw a glass of water, fizzing with antacids, next to him on a side table.

"Good, good," Vi told them, smiling. "The music was lovely."

"I don't mean the music," Jonah said through a clenched jaw. "I mean, who did you meet? What did they say? Tell us everything."

They filled the men in. Veronica ended with telling them about Willhelm Wagner. "He has a *backpfeifengesicht,*" she told them. It was a German word her grandmother had taught her that didn't exist in English, meaning "a face badly in need of a fist."

"The Mason Opera House?" Ari asked. Veronica nodded. "Shows all kinds of Nazi propaganda," he said. "He's writing a book, too—*Hitler: What Every American Should Know About the Man Whose Influence Is Felt the World Over.*"

Veronica blinked. "Awkward title."

"Maybe you can suggest your services as an editor, as a means to get closer to him?" Jonah suggested. "He's in close contact with a lot of Hitler's friends from Austria—we believe he's receiving money and propaganda." He turned to Vi: "All right, Mrs. Grace, please keep up your friendships with Nora Ingle and the rest of the ladies. Maybe ask them to lunch?"

Vi nodded. "I'm embroidering blouses for a few of the women. I'll deliver them to their homes and suggest coffee and a chat. Oh, and I almost forgot," she added, just as they were about to go. "I met a charming young man named Marvel Whiteside. Just graduated from Caltech with a degree in physics. Do you know him?"

"Physics?" Ari said. "What's his area of interest?"

"Rockets."

He and Jonah exchanged a look. "See if you can get to know him better," Ari told her. "Find out more about what he's working on."

"I'll type up the rest of the notes," Jonah said. "Call me if you think of anything else."

"There *is* one more thing," Veronica said, remembering. "There's a sign on the wall in the lobby of Deutsches Haus." She recited the text verbatim. Then, to Ari: "And—I'm sorry to say—there's your name as well."

Ari's face was a cipher. "Thank you for letting me know," he told both. "But I'm not at all surprised."

* * *

AFTER A NIGHTCAP at the Biltmore Hotel's bar, again making sure they weren't followed, they took the trolley home. As Vi set her purse in her lap and folded her hands, Veronica looked at her mother and gasped. "You're not wearing your wedding ring!"

"Took you long enough to notice," Vi said. She smiled and raised her hand to the light to display her ring finger, now sporting a gold band set with peridot and amethyst stones, along with tiny seed pearls.

"Is that your suffragist ring?" Veronica asked, grasping her mother's hand to inspect the ring closer.

"It is," Vi said. "I'm trying it out. It seems to fit this . . . new stage of life better. And it's a reminder to myself I'm just as strong—stronger—than the woman I was in my twenties."

"How wonderful, Mother," Veronica said. "You wear it well."

The two were silent, as the trolley passed a huge billboard for Van de Kamp's bakeries, its Dutch windmill illuminated by spot-lights.

"So . . . that's Jonah Rose."

"In all his grumpy glory," Veronica said, looking out the window at the lights twinkling in the darkness.

"He likes you," Violet said, smoothing her skirt.

"What?" Veronica turned.

Vi was undeterred. "You heard me."

"No . . . It's professional. Nothing more."

"And you like him, too."

"I do not!"

Several people turned to look.

"Veronica," Vi whispered, shushing her, "is it your 'lady time'?"

"Mother," Veronica hissed. *"Never* say the words 'lady time.' Ever. Ever."

* * *

WHEN HE'D FINISHED typing up the notes and locking them in a filing cabinet at the office, Jonah drove to his regular bar, the King Eddy, a hole-in-the-wall in Skid Row. He needed a drink. After walking down East Fifth, he pushed open the door and eased into the dark lair, dimly lit by fluorescent beer signs. The air was warm and smoky. The bartender grinned, recognizing Jonah. "The usual?"

The bourbon was strong. Jonah sat on an orange vinyl bench at a rickety wooden table against the wall. The bar was relatively quiet, with the radio giving the highlights of the day's baseball games. As the scores were announced, there were cheers and groans; bills changed hands.

Jonah sipped his drink and rubbed his head. Unbidden images of his trip to Berlin flashed before him. The parade down Unter den Linden and the black open Mercedes carrying Hitler, his face illuminated by glowing torches. The Brownshirts, reeking of beer and cursing. The Jewish man, out past curfew, taken into an unmarked van and shot, bullets blowing out the windows.

Once upon a time, people would have called the police. But in 1936, German people knew better. The police wouldn't come—or if they did, they'd just join in. People adapted, adjusted, changed in ways they never could have imagined. What would have been terrifying and perverse once was now commonplace—even normal. They turned over in their beds when they heard shrieks in the night, they ignored the sounds of their neighbors being arrested, they looked the other way at the ghettos. They ignored the rumors of the camps.

Little by little, small and regular acts of violence had escalated in Berlin, in Germany. The gradualness inoculated people. How long did it take before people would look the other way when a man was dragged screaming to a van and shot in L.A.? In the United States?

Three years, Jonah thought. *It only took three years in Germany. And only two more until Kristallnacht. Where is Los Angeles, the United States, on that timeline, rolling toward open fighting in the streets, people arrested in the middle of the night, shot in alleys?*

He thought about Veronica. A young woman—and now her mother—with open invitations to American Nazi meetings. It was perfect—what astonishing access they had! They could witness conversations, complaints, and confidences. They would have entry to social circles not even blue-eyed, blond-haired German men could penetrate.

And yet, he was concerned. Most of the men he'd run as spies had been U.S. Navy veterans. These were two women—brave, yes, but untried. The memory of Veronica's pretty, piercing blue eyes taking his measure rose before him. *If anything happens to her, I'd die from guilt,* he realized. *After killing whoever's responsible.*

It would be easy enough to befriend her—both her and her mother—as well. They were alone in a new city. Their new fascist acquaintances were false friends. They couldn't talk to anyone else about what was real. It was bound to be lonely for them.

Or are you talking about yourself? Are you the one who's feeling lonely? He swallowed the rest of his bourbon. *She's not even in yet,* he told himself, trying not to think of Adam Haber, of how one stupid mistake ended his life in Deutsches Haus's parking lot.

Let's see if she—they—can get anywhere with the Bund.

CHAPTER FOURTEEN

Veronica returned to the McDonnells' the following week. Harriet opened the door and smiled. "Come in, Veronica," she said warmly. "You're just in time—the gang's all here. Staff meeting."

A cold shadow passed through Veronica as she entered the house. In the living room, Veronica said hello to Mr. McDonnell and saw the woman she and her mother had met at the Black Forest. "Hello again, ma'am!" she called, plastering a huge smile on her face.

"Hello, Veronica. And please call me Florence—or Flo. I just *knew* you'd be a great fit here. Here're a few more of our crew." She gestured to three men.

"Such a pleasure to meet you all," Veronica managed. They were all in their forties and fifties, neatly dressed. Fear danced along her skin like something electric. She tried to slow her racing heart.

Harriet offered, "Veronica's our new typist, straight from New York."

Veronica took her time looking around the room, which she'd seen only in passing the last time she was here. On the mantel were vases with American and Nazi flags on wooden sticks, displayed like flowers, flanking a Meissen porcelain figurine of a Nazi storm trooper. Fearing she might say the wrong thing, or make a wrong move, she listened, intent on speaking as little as possible.

"New York's the old world—filled with rat peddlers—but Los Angeles's a place where man can live in the sun and spread his arms wide!" one of the men proclaimed. He had a thin mustache and hazel eyes.

"Manifest destiny," another said.

The third called out, *"Lebensraum!"*

"The *führer* looks here, to Los Angeles, and dreams, they say."

"Every meeting starts with a pledge to the flag," Florence told Veronica. "We used to sing the national anthem, but Harriet's a little tone-deaf."

"*You're* tone-deaf," Harriet replied, but with a smile.

Veronica realized she'd been holding her breath and consciously exhaled. After they stood and pledged, they all sat, Veronica on a rocking chair in a corner. Harriet went to the kitchen and brought back a tray with cups of coffee and a plate of warm cookies. They smelled buttery and delicious.

"Oh, chocolate chip?" McDonnell asked, taking one.

"Oatmeal raisin," Harriet told him.

"Now that's a mean trick to play on a man," McDonnell said. "They look just like chocolate chips—bait and switch!"

Veronica bit her tongue. *I'm a raisin,* she thought, fighting back hysterical laughter. *I'm a raisin disguised as a chocolate chip.*

"Raisins are good for you, Donny. They help with your constipation." She handed out fragrant cups of coffee.

He grinned. "But chocolate chips keep me . . . chipper!"

The assembled group groaned.

"He loves to make jokes," Harriet told Veronica. "Some of them land better than others."

"The bunch of us have known each other forever," McDonnell said. "We all started off as teachers at North Hollywood High about twenty years or so ago."

Veronica nodded and put her cup down, untouched. Her hand was shaking slightly, but she didn't think anyone noticed.

"We're just one of a lot of groups in Los Angeles, Santa Barbara, and San Diego," the man with the thin mustache told Veronica, "dedicated to keeping America out of the war and telling the truth about the Jews."

"And getting rid of them!" the second added with a chortle.

Veronica must have let something show on her face, for Harriet had the grace to look embarrassed. "We don't mean the poor Jews—you know, the butchers, bakers—"

"And the candlestick makers!" McDonnell chimed in.

"—those are all right," Harriet continued. "They serve their purpose. We mean the bigwig Jews, you know, the bankers and the Hollywood producers and the journalists—those puppet masters pulling all the strings—who're causing all the trouble." Veronica nodded and resolved to maintain a poker face.

"Well," McDonnell said, "if this is all new to you, you should start with the *Protocols*. It'll give you the truth on what's really going on today."

Veronica knew what he meant: *The Protocols of the Elders of Zion*, a hoax of a text. She'd read it in preparation for the Madison Square Garden rally. "Oh, I'm familiar with it," she told them truthfully, and they nodded approvingly.

As the group began to chat, Veronica tried to focus. But she hadn't slept the night before; she'd been too nervous. Her eyes were shadowed, and the multiple cups of coffee she'd had at breakfast were buzzing through her brain. She was in the middle of a real American Nazi meeting. What was she supposed to do? It was essential to act normal, she knew, but couldn't quite remember how. *You're a journalist. Blend in. Observe.* What did her adviser at Hunter tell her? *Make space for people with stories to tell—and then step back and listen to what they say.*

"So I went to a talk," McDonnell was saying. " 'Lend-Lease for the American Geese,' and I heard a joke."

Harriet smirked indulgently. "Oh, here we go . . ."

"Listen to this one!" He rubbed his tanned hands together. "Three ambassadors were making a flight across the ocean—a German, an Englishman, and a Greek. Over the middle of the ocean, something went wrong with the engine of the plane. The pilot said one would have to bail. So, the German says, *'Heil Hitler!'* and jumps."

The group chuckled, and the man with the mustache helped himself to another cookie.

"But the engine gets worse," McDonnell continued. "The pilot says someone else needs to jump. The Brit says, 'There will always be an England!' . . . and pushes the Greek out!"

Harriet shook her head as the assembled laughed. "This's what I have to live with . . ." she said to Veronica, who tried to smile in reply.

The man with the mustache's face was serious. "But the Limeys *would* turn on us in a second if they got the chance."

"Which is why we have to stop Lend–Lease before it starts," the second said.

The third declared, "If we do become the 'arsenal of democracy,' we should demand Canada as compensation!"

"It's only fair, after all," said Flo, finishing her cookie and reaching for another.

"We should get *all* of Canada!" McDonnell declared. "A new frontier! 'Go north, young man!'"

"Amen," intoned Harriet.

They're all insane, Veronica thought. She felt so overwhelmed she reached for her coffee cup as a cover—and knocked it over with her shaking hands. She looked on in horror as the brown liquid spread through the carpet. "I'm so sorry," she said to Harriet, jumping up. "Let me get a cloth . . ."

"It's all right," Harriet told her. "We'll go to the kitchen, hon."

Veronica took the cup, unbroken, and followed her. The kitchen was small and cozy, still smelling of freshly baked cookies. Harriet took a clean dish towel from a hook and ran it under the faucet. "Just dab with this, dear," she told Veronica. "It'll just blend right in. Nothing the rest of them haven't done before."

"Thank you," Veronica said, unexpectedly touched by the woman's kindness. *She's a Nazi,* her brain screamed. And yet, when Harriet put a gentle hand on her shoulder, she felt a rush of gratitude.

"I get nervous around new people, too," Harriet told the younger woman. "It's all right. I know Donny and his buddies can be intense sometimes, but we're a good-natured gang overall. And we love to take picnics to Hindenburg Park and go to concerts at Deutsches Haus. You'll see. It'll be fun—and you can meet some other nice young people. I know you're new in town," she said, the lines between her eyebrows creasing. "That must be hard."

"It's all right," Veronica said, thinking of Ari Lewis and Jonah Rose. *If Harriet only knew . . .*

"There's a picnic on Sunday at Hindenburg Park," she said. "You should come! There's music and games and lots of beer and grilled wurst. There're a few handsome single men," she added confidentially as she led Veronica back to the living room. "Although you seemed to hit it off with Will Wagner at the concert."

"Yes, we're going to a movie on Saturday," Veronica told her. "Thank you for the invitation, Harriet. It's all right if my mother comes, too?"

"Oh, of course! Donny and I both loved meeting her. The more the merrier!"

As Veronica knelt and blotted the rug with the damp towel, the man with the mustache asked, "So you're from New York?"

"*Jew* York," another snickered.

"Yes, from Brooklyn," Veronica said, keeping her face hidden. "Near the Brooklyn Navy Yard. But my mother's from Yorkville, originally. Her parents were German."

"From where?" he asked quickly, as though trying to catch Veronica in a lie.

"Munich."

"When did they come over?"

"They came to the U.S. in the 1880s."

Harriet chided gently, "Veronica's a guest."

"What?" he said. "She *could* be a Jew."

Flo laughed. "With those eyes and that hair? Heaven forbid."

But he was undeterred. "Where were you baptized?"

Veronica stopped and looked him in the eye. "At the Church of the Epiphany," she told him, "on the Upper East Side."

"The Church of the Epiphany? What kinda place is that?"

"Episcopalian. My father's religion."

Another cut in: "What's your favorite passage from the New Testament?"

Veronica thought for a moment. "'I give you a new commandment,'" she recited. "'That you love one another.'" *Ironic,* she thought, but it had popped into her mind.

He nodded, content now, but McDonnell snorted. "Real Nazis aren't Christian," he told them. "In Germany, they've realized Christianity is nothing but Jewish propaganda. My religion," he said proudly, "is National Socialism. It's the only religion I believe in. Christianity is bunk."

"Herr Hitler's a Christian," Harriet told him.

"Hitler believes in the laws of nature—red in tooth and claw," he countered. "The Jews want us to go to war because they hate Hitler. They say he's the worst man who ever lived, he's a monster—we should all hate him, etcetera. But he took away a false money and profit system, and in return he gave Germany social reform and jobs for everyone. He put the people to work and fed everyone. Meanwhile, we've got people going hungry right here in the city of Los Angeles. Hooverville. Many of them veterans! It's a disgrace! How can you hate a man who takes care of his people? I think instead of hating him, we should take a closer look at what he's doing and give it a try here."

Cole nodded. "Huey Long did the same for the people."

"Well, *I'm* Christian," Harriet told them. "And *we* are a Christian family, despite what His Nibs says." Veronica realized this was an ongoing disagreement between them.

"Eat your cookie, honeybun," Harriet told her husband as she went to a bookshelf and took down a folder. "Here's today's sheet." She drew out a piece of paper with writing in German Fraktur calligraphy. "We just need to make copies."

"Veronica," Flo asked with a smile, "have you ever seen a snowstorm?"

"A snowstorm?" *In Los Angeles? In summer, even? Are they nuts? Crazier than nuts?* "Uh, sure, in New York, we had them every winter." She saw them smile the way adults did when a small child says something unintentionally adorable.

"Well, we're planning one, a big one." McDonnell winked. "You'll see." He rose. "Come on, I'm ready and rarin' to get back to the office, eh, Veronica? Got a lot of new names to type up!"

* * *

IN MCDONNELL'S OFFICE, a small fan recycled the stale air. Veronica went to work, adding more names from the latest rally at Hindenburg Park. While she typed, he stuck BUY GENTILE stickers on some of his pamphlets. "I got 'em made, but the post office won't let us put them in the mail," he told her. "Might as well get some use out of them."

"Mm-hmm." She was less uncomfortable than she'd been earlier, but still wary.

McDonnell was chatty; he told her he was getting orders for his literature from all over the nation, particularly from Florida, Philadelphia, and Chicago, and a certain "nationalist" actor in Hollywood was organizing a force and "getting ready for the revolution."

"A revolution?" Veronica asked.

"We call it *der Tag*."

The Day. "And . . . when is it?"

"If I tell you, I'd have to kill you!" he laughed and slapped his thigh before returning to his stickers, then dug out a letter from the Franklin Institute of the State of Pennsylvania, which insinuated that the anti-Semitic statements attributed to Benjamin Franklin were forgeries. "That letter's fake," McDonnell told her. "It's lies! Stick around with us, Veronica, and you'll find out all about the lies of these people."

During the afternoon shift, they went next door to Flo's and mimeographed papers in her spare bedroom. As the machine hummed, McDonnell mentioned how proud he was of his youth group. "The Bund's doing all the things with young people— marching, shooting, hunting—but what about the little ones? That's why I have them out every Sunday afternoon, marching and saluting."

"You'll see them in their uniforms if you come to the park on Sunday. We just *love* children," Harriet said to Veronica as they consolidated papers into bundles. "God didn't see fit to bless us with any of our own kids—but now I see maybe he wanted us to take these young ones from the Bund in hand."

"Get them while they're young!" McDonnell exclaimed. "You've got to get them while they're young!"

Back at the McDonnells', Veronica mentioned how delicious the cookies were, even though she hadn't eaten any before. When McDonnell took the hint and went to the kitchen to get them more, she surreptitiously went through his dented black filing cabinets. Veronica discovered a large part of the propaganda material written in English came directly from the Nazis' U. Bodung-Verlag, courtesy of Joseph Goebbels.

There was also a news bulletin called "World Service," published by a Lieutenant Colonel Ulrich Fleischhauer, which defamed Jews and democracy; it bore the imprint Deutscher Fichte-Bund, from Hamburg, Germany, which called itself "a union for world veracity." She also found shipments from the Terramare Office, the Reichsdruckerei, and the Amerika Institut. She wished she could write down all the names but forced herself to memorize them.

On McDonnell's desk was a faux-leather calendar showing upcoming trips to Long Beach, San Diego, and Santa Barbara. Veronica closed her eyes and committed them to memory as well.

When McDonnell returned with a plate stacked high with cookies, Veronica nervously began chatting about the picnic. To her surprise, McDonnell had criticisms of the German club. "They've changed," he told her, taking a bite of cookie, then brushing crumbs from his shirt. "Back when Deutsches Haus was the FND—Friends of the New Germany—they handled themselves the right way—with swastikas, military uniforms, and *Heil Hitlers!*" He saluted.

"But when we started getting bad publicity, they dropped all that, renamed themselves the German American Bund, kicked all the German nationals out of leadership positions—although they're all still there, just working behind the scenes. Darned shame." He pushed the plate in her direction. "Oh, come on," he cajoled. "Take one! You just said how much you liked them!"

"I'm sorry," she said, thinking quickly. "I just remembered—there's a special dress I want to wear for my date with Will Wagner, and I have to be sure it still fits." She gave him what she hoped was a winsome smile.

"Women!" McDonnell laughed and selected another cookie for himself. "I'll *never* understand women!"

Veronica laughed along with him. But all the while, she was taking mental notes.

CHAPTER FIFTEEN

When Veronica boarded the bus to the Red Car going back to Santa Monica, she was surprised to see Jonah in the very last row, reading the *Los Angeles Times*. She made her way down the aisle and sat one seat away. "I thought we were going to meet tomorrow, at your charming hotel," she said in a hushed voice. The sunlight illuminated his ears, which stuck out a bit, daring to suggest he'd once been a cute little boy.

"I realize while most of our 'friends' can come and go in that neighborhood, a young woman like you might attract too much attention," he replied without raising his head.

"Ah," she said. "I don't scare easily, you know."

"You should. Who was there today?" Veronica told him the salient details of the meeting. "What else?"

"He has propaganda from Germany . . . getting it directly from Germany. From Goebbels."

"We know McDonnell's taking orders from Hermann Schwinn, a Nazi agent."

"And he's planning trips to Long Beach, Santa Barbara, and San Diego in the next few weeks." She gave him the specific dates. "Those are port cities," she said, realizing. He nodded. "The Navy . . ."

Jonah looked out the window at the houses covered in red bougainvillea. "Commander Zabner will arrange for a group of naval officers—our men—to be 'converted' by McDonnell. We'll have eyes on the inside."

Veronica was thinking. "McDonnell has a boat, doesn't he?"

"He does, in San Pedro Harbor, Port of Los Angeles."

"He could be spying on Navy facilities—on Schwinn's behalf."

"Which is why you need to listen carefully if Schwinn's name comes up—and keep a careful record of all conversations with everyone. Anything else?"

"They seemed so . . ." Veronica searched for the word. ". . . normal—more or less. They were high school teachers, for heaven's sake. I just wasn't expecting that. There were freshly baked cookies. Harriet seemed interested in my making friends here, maybe even finding someone to date. I spilled coffee, and she didn't even seem to mind. They were charming, warm, and friendly. And yet, the things they said, especially about . . . Well, you know . . ."

"They *are* nice people," Jonah told her. "To their own. It's one of the things that's appealing about the group—when you join, you have a purpose, friends, a social life. They become a tribe who love you and protect you—based on who you all hate."

He looked back at her. "But don't be fooled. If they ever find out who you really are and what you're doing, they won't be so 'nice.' Believe me, content and secure people don't go Nazi.

"And their patriotism isn't false, either, to the extent that they see the United States as an expression of specifically white, Christian values. They're also well aware of their constitutional rights, especially the right of free speech. But they have no interest in democracy and no loyalty to the United States as such—only to their vision of the United States as a white and Christian nation."

"People can be awful—but if you look at them as a writer, an observer, it helps."

"You did well," he said in a gentler voice.

"It's hard to believe any of this will make a difference." She tried to crack a smile. "If only Hitler had become a housepainter."

"Have you ever seen a Georges Seurat painting?"

Veronica nodded. "*Circus Sideshow* at the Metropolitan Museum."

"It's the details—all the tiny dots, taken together—that make a picture. You've just provided another dot. Another few, really." He added, "And it's not naive to think tiny, particular acts of bravery are ultimately going to swing the balance."

Veronica felt a small thrill of pride and quickly chided herself: *This isn't about you.* She knew she was still an apprentice; it would take time for her to earn her way, to prove herself.

As Jonah sat back, Veronica considered his profile. "What's *your* story?" she asked.

His face was closed and impenetrable, monk-like. "We're not supposed to talk about that."

"We're not supposed to be meeting on a bus," Veronica pointed out. "Yet here we are."

He sighed. "My father's a Jewish academic—teaches history at the University of Chicago."

Makes sense, Veronica thought. *There's something professorial about him.*

"My mother's Italian, from Campania originally. She's an opera singer, mezzo soprano. Catholic, too."

"What about you?"

"I grew up in Buffalo, a smart aleck."

"Eating matzo parmesan?"

His mouth twitched in a smile. "Moved to Chicago for high school when my father got a job there. Went to college there, and journalism school." He looked at billboards for Wrigley's Spearmint gum, Ovaltine, and Al-Caroid antacids. "I wanted to change the world."

Really? Just like me, she thought. "So how did you end up here, doing this?"

"I was covering the Olympics in Berlin in '36 for the *Tribune* and saw how screwed the world really is." He looked over to her, eyes dark. "I checked on your story," he admitted. "Read your piece on the rally in New York City." A long pause. "It was good."

She was aware of how much that simple *good* meant, coming from him. "Thank you."

"You were supposed to work at *Mademoiselle*."

It was not a question. *How did—oh, never mind.* "Yes, I was supposed to work for *Mademoiselle*."

"And the editor found out you'd been with—"

"That's private!" Veronica was angry. A woman a few rows in front of them looked up from her knitting.

"Shh . . ." Jonah stared straight ahead. "I don't care, I'm not the morality police," he said in lower tones. "I just had to make sure you are who you say you are. With what we do, we can't be too careful."

Veronica turned to see small white stucco houses with red clay roofs. Overhead, the sky was a hot blue. It was open and felt so big. *A universe away from Brooklyn.*

"I'm sorry," he said finally. "I know it's an invasion of your privacy. I should have told you how much I know."

"It's all right. I understand."

"What's your favorite movie?" he said finally.

She pulled a face. "What, you didn't find out in your research?"

"Okay, I deserve that," he admitted. "But no, you didn't write any movie reviews."

Veronica thought back to one of their other conversations, about how she should have the interests of a simple, marriage-minded German girl. "What do you think my favorite movie should be?" She said in a high-pitched, breathless voice: "Oh, I know, anything and everything with Shirley Temple. Because she's absolutely *adorable*—and I want to have five babies just like her."

"Those babies should be boys, so they can grow up and fight for their country," he said mildly. "But that's the right idea. But what's *really* your favorite movie?"

"*His Girl Friday.*"

"Ah, with Cary Grant as the editor and Rosalind Russell as his ex-wife and ace reporter."

"How about yours?"

"*The Grand Illusion.*"

Veronica had never seen it, but she knew it was a French war film, directed by Jean Renoir, about French prisoners of war during World War I. "Lots of singing and dancing in that one, I hear," she joked. "Okay, what's your favorite *fun* movie."

"Fun?" He said the word as if it were foreign. "All right—*The Adventures of Robin Hood.*"

"You relate to the outlaws of Sherwood Forest?"

He cracked a smile. "Maybe a little." It was his true smile, Veronica realized, one that lit up his face and opened up a chink in the armor of his control—a glimpse of the real man inside.

"What was it like," she asked, "covering a story in Berlin?"

"It was . . . intense," he said. "I was covering the 1936 Olympics. It was a spectacle. It was dramatic, theatrical, cinematic. I remember it almost as white and black, like a film, with red torches and flames against the night sky and spotlights illuminating red Nazi banners. So many people looking up, their faces lit by those flames. Their expressions were almost childlike, full of awe. As if Hitler were casting a spell over them. A group burned the flag of the Weimar Republic in front of the French embassy, and then they sang '*Siegreich wollen wir Frankreich schlagen.*'"

"*We will defeat France.*"

"This mob of Brownshirts began shouting and stamping in an almost religious fervor. It was rage, salvation, and vengeance all wrapped up together. It was . . ." Unable to speak, he looked out the window at a firehouse, men in overalls outside in the hot sun washing the red trucks, a dalmatian chasing the arcs of water from the hose. ". . . terrifying. The most horrible thing I've ever witnessed." His eyes were unblinking, as if he'd been transported back in time.

"Do you really think the war's coming to America?"

He turned back to her, eyes haunted. "I do."

"There are so many things to love about Germany," she said. "Rilke, Bach." She thought some more. "Dachshunds."

"Dachshunds?" he asked as a man in the front of the bus lit a hand-rolled cigarette.

"They're adorable." Then, "When do you think war's coming?"

"We're already at war. Most people just don't know it yet. The upcoming election's going to be a tipping point. Most people can't see it—don't want to see it. And a few really determined, unscrupulous men can exploit this stupidity and apathy."

"But that sort of thing—what you saw in Berlin—it can't happen here," she said. "Can it?"

"It's already happening," Jonah told her. He pulled on the metal cord to ring the bell.

"You're leaving?"

"I have some things to do." The bus slowed. "Just remember when you're with them, 'nice' isn't the same as good." He tipped his hat, his face shuttered once again. "Good luck with your 'date.'"

CHAPTER SIXTEEN

That Saturday, Veronica met Will Wagner at the Continental Bookstore, on Seventh and South Coronado downtown. From the outside, it looked innocuous, sandwiched between a barbershop and a stationery store. Upon closer inspection, she could see the display windows were charming, with Ludwig Hohlwein's colorful German travel posters of castles lining the walls. On a child's-eye level was an arrangement of *Grimm's Fairy Tales* in translation, along with a cardboard gingerbread house covered in painted candies and white icing, fit for Hansel and Gretel.

She pushed open the front door and went inside. A stiff raffia hat was set jauntily to one side of her head, and soft blond curls reached her shoulders. She wore a red dress with a modest scoop neckline and carried a straw purse embroidered with colorful flowers. There were long tables of books in both German and English; a selection of German folk song records; a table heaped with chocolates, marzipan, and lebkuchen; and another with wooden toys and painted dolls.

There was also a community bulletin board with notices and flyers: pistol target practice on Sunday afternoons at the Murphy Ranch, in the Pacific Palisades. The *sportabteilung* was looking for more men at Deutsches Haus, and there were various cards for German language lessons.

The walls were hung with art of Greek and Roman gods. One

that caught Veronica's attention was a graceful charcoal sketch of Bernini's sculpture *The Rape of Proserpina*. The goddess of spring and daughter of the goddess Ceres was picking flowers when Pluto, god of the underworld, abducted her, forcing her away from nature and toward the underworld.

"Do you like it?" said a voice behind her. Veronica spun around, startled. Will had walked up behind her as she'd been looking. "I drew it," he said with shy pride. "And some of these others."

"They're well done," she replied. "You capture light and shadow beautifully."

He grinned, and she realized he was, in fact, handsome, as well as literate, musical, and charming. He checked his watch. "You're five minutes early. I like that," he noted with pleasure. "We have some beautiful leather-bound volumes of Goethe and Schiller."

Veronica perused the shelves, reassured by the familiar titles: poetry by Johann Wolfgang von Goethe next to Werner Beumelburg's novels. In the back of the store was another section filled with political books: Hans Grimm's *People Without Space,* Alfred Hesselbein's *Hitler Is Right,* and *Mein Kampf* in German and English. Below was a wooden table piled high with pamphlets. Looking through them, Veronica saw McDonnell's pamphlets next to copies of Father Coughlin's *Social Justice* and William Dudley Pelley's *Liberation*. She felt dirty. No matter how handsome and charming, Will was working for Nazis, and she couldn't ever forget it.

When Will gave final instructions in German to the woman at the cash register, Veronica walked over. "Are you ready?" he asked her.

She plastered a bright smile on her face. "Let's go!"

* * *

"I LEASE SEVERAL theaters around Los Angeles," Will told her, as they entered the Mason Opera House on South Broadway, "including this one." A sign outside read:

BOX OFFICE OPENS AT 12:30 p.m.
Performances start at 1 and are continuous
until midnight.
See films plus the latest newsreels from Germany—
2½ hours of Cultural Entertainment!
You don't need to understand German
to enjoy this program!

Inside was dim and cool. A poster for *Jud Süß* was displayed on an easel in front of the concession stand; Süss's demonic face, with a large, hooked nose and yellow eyes, peered out from the darkness. Her stomach churned. "It's a beautiful theater," Veronica said. *At least that's honest.*

"Would you like anything?" he asked. "Chocolate? Candy?"

Veronica looked at the colorful sweets displayed behind the glass, but felt nauseated. "No—no, thank you."

"Ah, good," he said. "I hate popcorn—in Austria we only feed corn to the pigs. It's unheard of for people to eat."

They entered the theater. It was grand, with orchestra seating and two balconies; Veronica estimated it could hold at least eight hundred people, and it was nearly full. The theater was crowded with respectable-looking men in suits and women in straw hats with ribbons and flowers, chatting, laughing, and smoking.

"*Jud Süß* is one of Goebbels's favorite films," Will told her as they took their red velvet seats. "We were able to get this copy a bit early." He grinned modestly. "I have connections."

"Really?"

"Oh yes—you must have them to succeed in the import business."

Veronica realized it felt strange to be in a theater again. Since she'd moved to Los Angeles and begun working for Ari and Jonah, she hadn't been to a single movie. She'd missed *Pride and Prejudice* with Laurence Olivier and Greer Garson, and would have much preferred to see Hitchcock's *Foreign Correspondent,* about an American reporter in London who exposes undercover German agents. *Can't imagine that would go over well with Will, though,* she thought, and swallowed a hysterical giggle.

"Although the Jews don't want these movies shown," he told her. "They don't like us showing German pictures to Americans. They've been trying to shut us down at the Pacific Electric Theater and the Criterion, too."

"Isn't that against free speech?" she asked, knowing the Jew he was referring to was Lewis.

"You'd think!" He gazed approvingly at her. "My films show Germany in a good light, of course. So, these Jews, they go to my landlords at the various theaters and threaten them with boycotts if they don't kick me out. Now, every time I try to sign a new lease, some damn Jew intervenes." He looked momentarily embarrassed. "My apologies for the language."

"But you're able to show films here, at this theater?"

"For now," he replied. "And I'll fight to keep showing these films. This is America! We have the First Amendment here!"

"You work with UFA?" she asked. Jonah had schooled her in Goebbels's film company and propaganda.

He looked down at her, impressed. "Yes, their Continental Films division."

"Look who has contacts in high places!" she said, trying to flatter him.

"UFA's keen to show people in the U.S. the best of Germany." As Veronica looked up at the ceiling, covered with gilt panels, he continued, "I'm angry how movies in America depict Hitler—as a clown, a buffoon. There's a film coming out this fall, *The Great Dictator,* with Charlie Chaplin—a mockery! Disgraceful! It's the Jewish influence, of course—the new production code Joseph Breen forced through—"

"I read about it," she said, frowning.

"Germany isn't the natural enemy of the United States—there are too many here with German and Nordic blood. Like you and your mother."

She knew what she had to say. "Exactly!"

A man approached Will. "Excuse me," he said, rising. "I must introduce the film."

As Will walked out onto the stage, a spotlight followed him, and the house lights dimmed. The curtains opened to reveal a picture of Hitler on the screen. Will greeted the audience, thanked them for coming, encouraging them to rise to sing the "Horst Wessel Song," the Nazis' unofficial anthem. Extending their arms in a Nazi salute, the enthusiastic crowd ended the song with rounds of *"Heil Hitler!"* and *"Sieg heil!"*

The auditorium hummed and buzzed like a kicked beehive, a heady mix of anger and adrenaline. When he returned to his seat, she was thoroughly horrified. *I'm just an ordinary girl,* she thought over and over again, forcing herself to lean her head against his broad shoulder. *An ordinary girl, spending the afternoon at the movies with a handsome, successful, literate man,* she told herself. *Just an ordinary girl . . .* She tried to slow her racing heart. *An ordinary girl who's been brought down to the underworld, as the special guest of Hades.*

First came the newsreels, a trumpet fanfare and the black-and-white spinning globe of the *Die Deutsche Wochenschau:* *"Blitzkrieg im Westen"*—"Blitzkrieg in the West"—that showed the American audience the relentless Nazi war machine demolishing Allied tanks, trapping British troops at Dunkirk, and engaging in door-to-door combat in which no Germans were killed. She couldn't help herself—she pulled away from him as the silvery pictures flickered.

"Light and shade" was a journalistic technique Veronica was familiar with, and she realized the compilers of the newsreel were using it, mixing in trivial items with the heavy news. The next story concerned a Hitler Youth marching band in Bremen that had won a national competition.

But as the film began, she felt Will's muscled thigh press against hers. She moved her leg away and his followed, warm through the linen of his trousers. *Breathe,* she told herself. *Breathe.*

But the air was filled with the lemony scent of his cologne and the film was abhorrent, with Süss portrayed as a worldly grasping moneylender and rapist. She felt ill when Will placed his hand on her thigh, rubbing up and down, then playing with the buckle of her garter. *Hitchcock's "foreign correspondent" never had to deal with this kind of thing, I bet.* She repressed the urge to run but waited, as the hand began to inch upward.

She placed her hand over his, interlacing their fingers. That stopped him for the moment, and their connection remained innocent until the lights went on again. When they did, she pulled away with what she hoped was an impression of regret. "I'm a good German girl," she told him in what she hoped was a teasing tone, even though she felt ill. "I don't do things like that at the movies."

"I see," he said, looking even more interested, as though he just realized his prey might be capable of giving more of a chase than he'd anticipated. "You must let me take you for coffee now," he was saying as they walked through the lobby. "Perhaps a pastry? There's a good Viennese café not far from here."

"I'm sorry," she said truthfully, "but I'm not feeling well."

He studied her. "You do look pale," he admitted. "Perhaps this film was too much for your delicate sensibilities."

"A rain check?"

"I'd like that." At the trolley stop, he leaned down to kiss her, but she turned her head at the last minute, so he only got her cheek. She looked up at him, torn. *He's smart. An excellent musician. Knowledgeable about literature and film. A fine artist. Certainly easy on the eyes. What went wrong?* she wondered. *What happened to him, to make him so sophisticated and urbane in some areas of life, but so ugly in others?*

"Feel better," he told her as the Red Car pulled up, bells clanging. "Dinner next Saturday?" he said, as passengers exited. "Pacific Dining Car? Shall we say seven?"

She forced herself to smile; it felt painful. "Sure," she said, heading for the trolley stairs. Before she got in, she turned and forced herself to wave and blow him a kiss.

*   *   *

AFTER TAKING THE Red Car a few stops, ducking off unexpectedly, and heading to a café for a ginger ale to settle her stomach and see if she was being followed, Veronica set out once again, taking the bus to Westlake Park. She walked down a palm-lined allée, looking behind her using her compact mirror.

She was a little surprised to find Jonah already waiting for her, sitting on a bench overlooking the lake, shaded by oak trees and perfumed with the scent of eucalyptus. A brass band played a jazzy version of "Pop Goes the Weasel" in the distance. In the shadows, the lines and planes of his face were even more severe. He stared off into the distance, mysterious as a sphinx.

"It was horrible," Veronica said without preamble as she sat next to him. She could still feel Will's lips on her cheek.

Jonah murmured without looking at her, "You're sure you weren't followed?"

"I wasn't followed," Veronica assured him, watching sailboats glide by, outpacing the rowboats and canoes. *It's peaceful, even serene here,* Veronica realized, *while in London, planes are battling in the skies overhead.*

She knew that despite the sunny skies, the threat of war was growing closer. Roosevelt was calling for reinstating the draft as well as cutting off shipments of scrap iron, steel, and aviation fuel to Japan. Lockheed had just received a huge rush order from the government to build more planes. The moment seemed surreal, knowing what was happening in other parts of the world: the boats on the lake, the children's laughter, the puffy white clouds in a brilliant blue sky. *Peace is fragile.*

"You're early," Jonah observed. "I thought you were going for coffee and dessert after the movie."

"I couldn't do it," Veronica said. "He was . . . odious. The film . . ."

"You *canceled*?" He sounded incredulous.

"I said I wasn't feeling well. Which was true."

"That was . . . *unprofessional*!" Jonah flung out the word like a gauntlet. "He likes you, obviously," he said, a curious expression on his face. "You can use that, don't you see? We can all benefit from your having a close relationship with him."

"You mean *you* can use it. *You* can benefit. You don't have to have a letch running his hand up your thigh in a dark movie theater!"

Jonah swallowed. "What if he'd been a source for a story that could win you the Pulitzer?" he asked, turning back to the lake. "Would you have left early then?"

"Well, I'd never sleep with a source!"

"I don't like the idea of him with you either, if you must know," Jonah said finally. "But here we are. This is the job." They sat in silence as a young man in a rowboat, holding a bottle in a paper bag, stood up to sing. He lost his balance and fell into the water, to the amusement of his friends on shore.

"I'm seeing him again," Veronica offered finally. "We're having dinner."

"Where?"

"Pacific Dining Car. Next Saturday."

Jonah rose. "Good." He walked away, hands in his pockets, hat pulled down low.

Veronica watched him go, furious and, to her surprise, hurt as well, that he'd allow—no, *encourage*—her to sleep with a Nazi. *Don't be ridiculous,* she told herself. *This is a job. Nothing more.*

Remember, honey—you're tough. You're from Brooklyn. Don't forget it.

CHAPTER SEVENTEEN

Spying was a lonely business, Veronica discovered. She'd never experienced such intensity; it was like living with her heart constantly in her throat, a constant hum of tension. And yet she kept a bland smile on her face, typing endlessly, dating Will and evading his advances, pretending to be friends with people she'd rather see in jail.

Training with Jonah, Veronica learned basic surveillance skills. To listen for the click on the telephone line that indicated it might be tapped. How to vary her route to and from work. How to recognize patterns and when they changed. "Think before speaking," he'd say, as they hiked the trails near the Griffith Observatory.

Yeah, no kidding, she thought.

"Keep your face neutral. Never relax. Avoid attention. Never ever underestimate the savagery of these thugs." His face softened for a moment. "And, as my father always said, 'Know the exits and make sure you're closer than the Cossacks.'" He'd grinned, which made him look younger, more boyish, even mischievous.

Veronica snort-laughed, which turned into a loud guffaw. She had never met anyone like him. He was blunt and impolite at times, yet also direct and true. He had no practiced weariness, no ennui, no cynicism—just a quiet self-confidence, his eyes seeming to look at something just beyond, at something most people couldn't yet see.

One day, as they broke for lunch—ham and cheese sandwiches wrapped in brown paper and two root beers from the diner below—Veronica couldn't help but ask, "You don't keep kosher?"

Jonah flashed his rare smile. "During Passover, I eat bacon on matzo."

Veronica looked horrified, and he laughed.

"I'm half-Jewish, half-Catholic, and completely atheist—which means I get to eat what I want."

They proceeded to chew in silence, the small rusty fan whirring, the clock ticking. "What did you think of Churchill's speech?" Veronica asked. She did her best to imitate Winston Churchill's plummy tones: " 'Never in the field of human conflict was so much owed by so many to so few . . .' "

"It was excellent," Jonah admitted. "But the real battle for Britain is only about to begin—and 'the few' will unfortunately soon become fewer."

Veronica nodded, taking a sip of root beer. "But even though you have to take everything coming from Britain with a grain of salt—because of the censorship and keeping up morale and whatnot—it's pretty clear the battle for Britain wasn't going to be the fast smash and grab the Germans thought it would be, especially after France."

"You follow those things?" Jonah asked, eyebrows raised, looking for all the world like a surprised vulture.

"Of *course* I follow these things," she replied. "By the way, would it kill you to say 'good job' once in a while?"

He looked at her, eyes inscrutable. "I will when you've earned it."

"Just let me at the bastards," she told him. "Then you'll see."

* * *

SOMETIMES, IN THE middle of coffee and cookies in the McDonnells' living room, Veronica wanted to scream from the pain of the
split between pretense and reality. With each newspaper she read,
the stakes seemed higher: the Battle of Britain raged, the Warsaw
ghetto was opened in Poland, the Italians were encroaching in
Egypt, and Japan's army and navy threatened Indochina.

Veronica was almost manically cheerful in the company of
"them," but when left on her own she was lethargic and despairing.
She'd lost eight pounds because she couldn't quite swallow food,
enervated by the dull and repulsive people—"nice" as they were—
yet keenly aware of the constant threat of possible danger.

In the evenings, she listened to the radio with her mother, her
head filled with pictures of the men and women, the children, who
were being shot and burned and bombed the world over. *Slaughtered,* was all Veronica could think.

"I don't want to get out of bed in the morning anymore,
Mother," Veronica said, pulling out a row of stockinette stitches
she'd knitted wrong as they listened to Walter Winchell on the
radio. "It's like I've slipped into a life that belongs to someone else.
It's a war with nerves, and I'm about to go stark dingo."

"This is what we signed up for, sweetie," Vi told her, glasses on
and using satin stitch and French knots to embroider edelweiss and
swastikas for the ladies of America First. She, on the other hand,
was gaining weight from the stress of constant pretense. Her only
outlet was the garden, which she'd dug up and planted with rows of
vegetables: carrots, lettuce, cucumbers, tomatoes. Spending time
outdoors, with the plants, soothed her as nothing else could in
these days. She would sometimes pray as she worked with her hands
in the soil. "And besides, we're both making progress—you have
access to so much more information. But still . . ."

"What?"

"Will Wagner." Vi jabbed a hole into the fabric with her needle.

"What about him?"

She made a knot to secure the stitch and bit off the thread. "I don't like him."

Veronica gave a harsh laugh and put down her knitting. "You're not *supposed* to like him, Mother."

"Just be careful—that's all I'm saying." She hastened to add, "I'm on your side, you know that. I trust you." Her face darkened. "But I don't trust him."

"I know you're on my side," Veronica said. She met her mother's blue eyes with her own. "Just like I'm always on yours. You're my North Star." She grasped her mother's hands. "It'll be okay."

Vi smiled sadly. "I think I'm the one who's supposed to say that to you."

* * *

AT WORK, VERONICA had let it "slip" she knew shorthand. And so McDonnell had asked her to take notes for him at meetings, then type them up. The first time had been on the sixteenth of September, in his dim garage, the hot air lit by one lone electric bulb.

The space had been cleaned out and metal folding chairs set in rows, although the dark oil stains on the concrete remained. A black garden hose was coiled on a hook on one wall, and a few dented trash cans were lined up against another. A woman's bicycle with a straw basket hung from a hook in the ceiling, along with flypaper dotted with dead insects.

Veronica had arrived early and was sitting in the corner on a squeaky folding chair in the garage's far back corner with the new shorthand notebook Harriet had given her, along with two freshly sharpened yellow no. 2 pencils. Her hands were sweaty, but she was trying to look natural—a quiet, conscientious stenographer, silent and respectful—even as chalk-faced men gathered, talking and laughing and smoking.

The last of the men to arrive was led in by McDonnell himself.

The guest was small and slim, with dark hair touched with gray, eyes hidden behind round silver spectacles, and a Hitleresque mustache. He was well groomed and dapper, wearing a double-breasted suit, his leather shoes polished to a gleam. Veronica started and her stomach flopped—she recognized him from the Bund rally in New York, as well as from photographs Jonah had showed her. She dropped her pencil, then bent to pick it up, taking the moment to breathe deeply and collect herself.

"Afternoon, gents," McDonnell said, facing the group. The men quieted. He was smiling, the lines on his leathery bronzed face crinkling, and looking every inch a movie-star cowboy. "Good to see you all again." He raised his hand in salute. *"Heil Hitler!"*

They all returned the greeting, except for Veronica, whose hands she deliberately kept occupied with the pad and pencil.

"Please, have a seat," he said. "Thanks so much for coming— I appreciate your being here, some of you all the way from Long Beach, Santa Barbara, and San Diego. Well, I'd like to introduce our special guest—Captain Hermann Schwinn."

He gestured to the man in the double-breasted suit. Veronica had had nightmares about him: the western region leader of the German American Bund. The man Ari and Jonah had specifically told her to watch for. *Well, here he is,* she thought. *In the flesh.*

"Captain Schwinn spent years working on the *führer's* staff as his personal military adjutant, even marching into Prague with him in 1939."

Veronica forced herself to look at him. He seemed so mild, so forgettable, so . . . ordinary.

McDonnell couldn't hide his excitement. "He was Hitler's superior officer in the Great War—even saved the future *führer's* life by pulling him out of the rubble of a building that collapsed under heavy bombardment! And now he's here, as Herr Hitler's trusted personal emissary, the Nazis' main man on the West Coast."

Schwinn looked over the group without smiling, taking the men's measure. They all tried to sit up even straighter. He pointed straight to Veronica. "Who is she?" he asked in a heavy German accent.

"My personal secretary," McDonnell said proudly. "She's going to be taking down the minutes of today's meeting." Veronica felt cold but tried to smile as she clutched her pencil tightly.

"I don't like it," Schwinn said.

"My wife and I vouch for her, Captain Schwinn," McDonnell was quick to say. "Her mother, too. Both decent, honorable Aryans. Her mother's part of America First and even knows Nora Ingle."

Schwinn looked somewhat mollified. "Are you willing to take the oath?" he asked Veronica. She looked to McDonnell, questioning.

"He means the secret oath, required of all initiates," McDonnell explained.

"Yes," Veronica said in a small voice. "Of course."

"Stand. Raise your right hand. Repeat after me," Schwinn ordered. She stood, putting the notepad and pencil on her chair.

"I am prepared to enter the League of Friends of the New Germany," he said.

"I am prepared to enter the League of Friends of the New Germany," she echoed.

"The aims and purposes of the league are known to me, and I pledge myself to support them without any reservation whatsoever."

She swallowed and said the words.

"I acknowledge unconditionally the leadership principle upon which the league is formed. I belong to no Semitic organization. I am of Aryan stock and have neither Jewish nor colored blood in me."

She recited the lines quickly, stumbling twice. When she had finished, Schwinn nodded, satisfied. McDonnell gave her the thumbs-up. Shaking and feeling ill, she took her seat.

"Her mother's the widow of a Navy officer, badly affected by

Roosevelt's pension mess," McDonnell offered. "They're helping us reach out to other dissatisfied veterans in the area."

"Good, good," Schwinn said, nodding. "Follow up with that." He refocused his attention on the men. "Now, let's get down to business." Veronica's hand was sweaty and shaking, but she managed to keep up with her Pitman squiggles.

"We've coordinated a 'snowstorm' throughout your areas," Schwinn was saying.

What the heck's this "snowstorm"? Veronica thought.

"We've held off on the time and place because of security concerns. But tomorrow is the day—high noon. You each have your cities to cover."

She had to do more than keep up; she had to take notes to type up for McDonnell and surreptitiously take a second set of notes on a later page, more complete, one she would smuggle out for Jonah and Ari. McDonnell had told her he'd be collecting the pad at the end of the meeting, so she couldn't take the original notes with her.

As she marked down the symbols and abbreviations in her notepad, she began to realize what was at stake with the meeting. The group was large—and coordinating activities. The men assembled in McDonnell's garage were all heads of their own cells—small groups of men, *paramilitary groups*—each in his own part of coastal Southern California.

All these men, Veronica realized, *as well as the men they represent, are connected to Nazi Germany through Captain Schwinn. Through him, they're taking direction from Berlin.* She forced herself to concentrate only on the words spoken and getting everything, every detail, down on paper.

The next order of business was an upcoming recruiting trip to San Pedro Harbor. "Charlie," McDonnell called. "Come on up."

Charles Schroder, one of the cell leaders, was short and sturdy, a grizzled man with a full head of gray hair, a mustache, and a beard. He wore a faded plaid shirt and patched dungarees. Veronica knew he was the owner of the City Water Taxi Company, a franchise with seven boats running from Long Beach to Catalina Island. He was also a decades-long member of the Ku Klux Klan.

Charlie came to the front with a pronounced bow-legged walk. Schwinn put a hand on his shoulder and said solemnly, "I hereby promote you to *Kreis Führer*, in command of all the cells in Orange County and Long Beach." Charlie broke out into a toothy grin as the other men applauded.

Schwinn drew a badge from his breast pocket and held it out. "This will open the doors to all German secret agents in friendly circles." Charlie accepted it with reverence.

"Never show it to anyone unless they present theirs first," the captain warned. "And we are adding to your list of duties. We need you to provide even more detailed information about American military preparations along the Pacific Coast," he said. "Especially if any mines have been placed and their locations."

When the meeting was over, McDonnell gave the boat captain a friendly clap on the back. "Congratulations, buddy. I'll be heading the snowstorm in San Diego tomorrow," he told Charlie.

Veronica raised a hand. "May I ask—what's a 'snowstorm'?"

"Oh, you'll see," Charlie said. "Nothing so beautiful as snow in Southern California."

Still doesn't answer my question.

McDonnell grasped Charlie by the shoulder. "Want to stay over tonight and ride with me in the morning?"

"Anything you need, boss man," Charlie replied, grinning widely.

"Henry!" McDonnell called to one of the other men. "Henry Allen! Get yourself over here!" He introduced Charlie. "This here's Henry Allen from Pasadena—head of the American White Guard."

Veronica noted Allen was small and thin, with a high forehead and sunken cheeks. He was carrying an overstuffed black leather briefcase embossed with a gold eagle as well as two golden swastikas. Attached to it was an oak club with a leather strap, over a foot long and two inches thick.

"Say, what's that?" Charlie asked, pointing at the club.

"Kike killer," Allen told them. "You wrap it around your wrist, then use it to poke him in the stomach. When he doubles over in pain, ya hit him over the head with it."

Veronica winced. McDonnell caught sight of her, hanging back. "Got any boyfriends getting too frisky?" he asked, pointing to the club.

"Will Wagner and I are going to hear the orchestra at the Biltmore this weekend," Veronica told him. "But I think I'll be okay."

"Will?" Allen raised an eyebrow. "Will Wagner?" He shook his head. "You're on your own with that one, honey," he said, as he, McDonnell, and Schroder laughed.

So much for "nice," Veronica thought.

* * *

AS THE MEN dispersed, Veronica went back to the office. Assured she was alone, she ripped off the duplicate pages she'd made for her own notes, folded the pieces, and hid them in her brassiere. By the time McDonnell entered, she was already typing up the minutes. "You get everything?" he asked her.

She looked up. "Yes, thank you."

"I'm sorry to do this, Veronica, but I'm going to need your pad." She handed it to him, and he flipped through it. There were still bits of paper where she'd ripped off her own notes. "What's this?" he asked, pointing to the shreds.

Scheisse! Veronica kept typing without missing a beat. "That's how it was when Mrs. McDonnell gave it to me," she lied, her voice even.

"Ah, okay. Her and her recipes." He paced a bit, still excited from the meeting. "You just finish that up, then let yourself out," he told her. "I'm going to take a walk." He grinned. "Big day tomorrow!"

She nodded. "Big day."

He started to head to the door, stopped, and turned. "Say, Veronica, what about coming with us to San Diego? We could use an extra pair of hands. You can see where all those photostats you make really go."

This—this could be big, Veronica realized. *I've got to tell Ari and Jonah.* "I'd—I'd be honored. Thank you, Mr. McDonnell."

"You're doing a great job for us, Veronica," he said with almost fatherly pride. "You've earned yourself a field trip."

CHAPTER EIGHTEEN

After the meeting at the McDonnells', Veronica met Jonah at the Griffith Park Zoo in Los Feliz, built on the site of Griffith J. Griffith's defunct ostrich farm. It was late afternoon, and although it wasn't crowded, people enjoyed the sunshine. Children ran and played; Veronica passed one little girl who was in tears because her scoop of pink strawberry ice cream had fallen off the cone.

Jonah was waiting for Veronica in front of the lion cage, holding a brochure. "A lot of the animals kept here were in the movies," he told her. "Apparently, the gorillas were in *Tarzan*."

"I don't like zoos," she told him, avoiding the lion's gaze. "I don't like seeing animals locked up in cages."

"Neither do I, actually. Let's take a walk."

They took a gravel path away from the cages and sat down at a painted wooden picnic table in the shade. People had left their marks in the brown paint: Veronica saw BENNY LOVES ANN in a heart cut with a pocketknife, as well as a few profanities and a single swastika. They were alone.

"The meeting . . . it was bad," Veronica told him.

"Tell me everything." She did, reaching into her bra and handing him the sheets she'd taken down in shorthand.

He looked shocked. "This is dangerous," he told her. "It's risky to put anything in writing. We had this one agent—"

"No one noticed," she told him. "There were a lot of details I wanted to get down. And none of them can read shorthand."

"You can't be absolutely sure of that." He put the notes in the pocket of his leather jacket. "But thank you. It'll be useful."

"He made me take an oath," she admitted finally, feeling tarnished. Stained.

"Who did?"

"Schwinn."

"Schwinn . . . that cut-rate Boris Karloff?" he said, making her guffaw. "And did you?"

"I did." She watched as a purple finch flew into the branches of a walnut tree. It opened its beak and warbled, the sound mixing with the wind in the trees and the distant sounds of children shouting and laughing. "McDonnell also told them about my mother being a Navy widow—and she could introduce them to recruits."

Jonah watched as the finch flew away. "Could be good for us," he said. "Do you think she'd be interested?"

"You'd have to ask her, but yes, I'm sure she'd do it." She pulled at her cotton skirt. "I'm also working tomorrow," she told him.

"More typing?"

"No, McDonnell asked me to help out with a 'snowstorm.' It's in San Diego—noon at the U.S. Grant Hotel. What on earth's a 'snowstorm'?"

"It's when a group makes mimeographed sheets of propaganda, then drops them en masse from high windows or balconies. The falling papers look like a blizzard—certainly gets everyone's attention. Who else's going?"

Ah, okay then. "McDonnell's giving Charlie a ride, so he's part of it. Also, a man named Henry Allen."

Jonah's eyes narrowed. "Did he have his briefcase with him?"

"He did," Veronica told him, remembering how it had embossed swastikas. "Along with what he calls his . . ." She didn't want to say the words out loud. ". . . club." She rubbed at her arms.

Jonah nodded, unflinching. "Good. It's good you're going. Just go along with everything. Trust me. We'll have your back—even in San Diego." The afternoon light had slowly changed, becoming thicker and more golden. "I have something for you." He reached into his shirt pocket and pulled out a newspaper clipping.

"A comic?" Veronica asked, accepting it.

"It's a new one—*Brenda Starr*."

Veronica looked closer and smiled. "She's a reporter!"

"From the Chicago Tribune Syndicate," he told her. "And written by a woman, too."

"Thank you!" *My days of journalism seem long ago and far away.* She refolded it and slid it in her purse. "You know, I used to put out a family newsletter when I was little, with everything spelled wrong and little drawings. My mother still has a few, I think."

"Was it writing the story or getting the credit that made you happier?"

"Both, I think," she said. "Although I realized early on reporting had nothing to do with being liked. If you're doing your job right, you're impartial—and whoever you're reporting on may very well be mad you didn't take their side."

"Good training for undercover work," he said with a half smile.

"Why are you smiling?" His unfamiliar expression had taken her off guard.

"I can just imagine you as a small girl, investigating your neighborhood."

"The neighborhood cats were of particular interest," she told him. "I wrote fascinating exposés about the calico who lived next door, the birth of her litter, and speculation on who the father might be, based on who I'd spotted in their backyard. When the kittens turned out to be the colors of all the toms in the neighborhood, I realized there was actually more than one father. Meanwhile, all the neighbor moms were *scandalized*—not that it happened, but that I'd written about it. But it was *true*."

Jonah leaned back suddenly and laughed—a loud guffaw—then looked at her with an expression of . . . well, something she couldn't quite place. The sun dipped lower. "What was it like, growing up in Brooklyn? Was it idyllic?"

Veronica paused. "Sometimes." Her youth was like a painting, ripped through the middle by her father's death. When she thought about the past, images flashed before her: her grandmother teaching her to make German cookies. Their brownstone with the front garden covered in pink climbing roses, which her mother would tend. Their quiet, tree-lined street, where the kids all played stickball and people would sit out on the stoops. Trips on summer weekends to Amagansett, where they escaped the heat of the city and swam in the briny waves.

He broke her reverie. "How are things with Wagner?"

"All right," she said. "No real information. And I've been putting him off. The last time we went out, I made a show of eating raw oysters—and going to vomit in the ladies' room."

"Did you actually throw up?"

She gave a lopsided smile. "I stuck my finger down my throat, and made sure to get some of it on the front of my dress. Believe me, he was in no mood to tarry afterward!"

"Smart," he said, "but you're not getting all you can out of him."

"You sound like my pimp," she snapped. *Isn't it enough I'm having dinner with him?* she thought. *I have to let him stick his tongue down my throat, too?*

"I know," he said, shamefaced. "And I hate it. I really do."

"We need a better place to meet," she told him. "You should come out to Santa Monica."

"Where's a good place?"

"I can pick?"

"You know what the requirements are."

"The pier, after dark." She grimaced. "We'll need to debrief tomorrow night—after I get back from San Diego."

"By the way," he said, "you're doing a good job." He looked as though he was going to say something more.

She imagined Jonah kissing her, running his hands over her

dress, feeling the warmth of his body as they embraced. She could smell the washed cotton of his shirt, mixed with Bay Rum aftershave and sweat.

But as she looked up at him, his face shuttered. "Until next time," he said, rising from the picnic table. He tipped his hat, then walked away without a backward glance.

＊ ＊ ＊

AS VERONICA MADE her way back to Santa Monica on the trolley, Jonah drove to the Hollywood office. Inside, Ari was already at his desk, listening to the radio. He put a finger to his lips as Jonah entered. A plummy British voice from the BBC was saying, *"Today, one of the greatest munitions disasters ever recorded tore the heart out of the Hercules Powder Company, a munitions plant in Roxbury, New Jersey."* Jonah leaned against the doorframe to listen.

"The explosions have been going on all afternoon and are projected to go into the night. Already, fifty have been proclaimed dead, two hundred injured, with an estimated two hundred million dollars in property damage. The cause of the explosion is under investigation . . ." Ari quirked an eyebrow as the newscaster ended with *". . . but sabotage is suspected."*

"Our friends on the East Coast are getting busier," the lawyer said, turning the dial off. His face was grim.

"What's the FBI saying?" Jonah sat at his desk. "Anything?"

"Nothing official—and my source can't get anything yet. But regardless, Martin Dies—head of the committee for investigating 'un-American' activities—is going to put the feds on warning for Nazis, not just communists."

Ari's face twisted. "You know, everyone laughed when witnesses testified before the committee about the plans to blow up the Hercules Company. And now it's happened *exactly* the way they said it would." Ari slammed his fist down on his desk. *"Damn* it! This attack was preventable!"

"The FBI's whole approach has to be changed radically," Jonah said. "German agents need to be identified and exposed before they can do any more harm."

Ari rolled his eyes. "Mark my words, even with this attack on American soil, Hoover's still going to be too busy battling the Reds to care about Nazis."

"I met with Veronica today," Jonah told him, putting his feet up on his desk and crossing his long legs. "West Coast may be next."

"Tell me."

"I'll type up her shorthand and give you a copy of the details, but the immediate concern is she, McDonnell, Charlie, and Allen are going to San Diego tomorrow. There's going to be a snowstorm."

"Allen?" Ari asked. "Really?" Jonah nodded. Ari said, "Did she happen to notice . . ."

"His briefcase? Yes, she confirmed he had it with him."

"Are you thinking what I'm thinking?" Jonah nodded. Ari picked up the telephone receiver, put it to his ear, and dialed some numbers. "Ari Lewis for Commander Zabner," he said into the receiver.

"Yeah, it's me. Storm's on the way. We need to talk."

CHAPTER NINETEEN

The next morning, the trunk of McDonnell's old wood-paneled station wagon was crammed with luggage—suitcases and valises. But instead of being full of clothes, they contained stacks of photostats for the "snowstorm." Veronica had met the men at the house in East Hollywood; she wore a red linen skirt, a floral blouse with a scalloped collar, and a small pearl necklace. As they sped south on the Pacific Coast Highway, Veronica was silent, pretending to look at the spectacular views of the ocean out the window, but listening intently. They passed road signs—HUNTINGTON BEACH, LAGUNA BEACH, DANA POINT HARBOR—with the men discussing everything from mulching tips to Texas versus Memphis barbecue to baseball.

By the time they passed San Clemente, Veronica was pretending to nap. McDonnell asked Charlie about Count Ernst Ulrich von Bülow: "I heard you had dinner with him last week," he said, as he changed lanes and the car swayed. "At his house. Do you call him 'Count'?"

"He's asked me to call him Ernst," Charlie replied modestly. "He has a beautiful house up in the hills."

"Up in the hills, huh?" Allen pressed. He was sitting next to Veronica in the backseat, his briefcase and the club at his feet. "Must be a great view of the shoreline."

"Fantastic view," Charlie replied. "*Strategic,* you might say—he can see every move made by the Navy."

McDonnell changed lanes again. "He's with the German government?"

"Who knows?" Charlie replied. "He's not specific about stuff like that. But he's definitely *connected,* if you know what I mean."

McDonnell grunted his approval. "What're you doing for him?"

"Let's just say I do some groundwork that enhances his 'view.' You know, when I take folks from Long Beach to Catalina for the bands, I can see Navy operations. Sometimes I give people special tours of the harbors, and I can get a good look at the new fortifications, power lines put in, what's being shipped in and out, that kind of thing. Snap a few pictures. You know, of the 'sunsets.'" He chuckled.

"Ah, yes." Allen chuckled. "Those 'sunsets.'"

"And now I'm on the lookout for any new mines. You know about the German subs, right?"

"There're Nazi subs out there?" said McDonnell. "Jap subs—now that I'd believe."

"Nah, not here," Charlie said. "But in Mexican waters, just over the border, there're Nazi subs for sure. They're just waiting. Sometimes Bülow takes a boat out at night and meets with them."

Allen said, "You're sure this one's all right?" Veronica started, but forced herself to keep her eyes closed and her breathing even.

"Yeah, she's a good egg," McDonnell said.

"Amen."

* * *

FINALLY, THEY REACHED San Diego. "Wake up, Sleeping Beauty!" McDonnell called to Veronica. He parked on Fourth Avenue at B Street in the Stingaree district. He opened the car door and proclaimed, "We're gonna make it snow!"

McDonnell opened the trunk, and they took two suitcases each, stuffed with papers. They were heavy. "Why the U.S. Grant Hotel?" Veronica asked, noting Allen took the oak staff, slipping it up his suit sleeve, but left his briefcase in the trunk.

"Judge Howzer's speaking today to some high-hat San Diego Jews," McDonnell told her. "We want to let them know they're not welcome."

"Plus, it has great balconies," Allen added.

"Hey, you okay?" Schroder asked Veronica. She'd had to put the heavy suitcases down for a moment and shake out her hands.

"I've got it, thanks," she told him, gritting her teeth, and picking them up again.

"Attagirl!" Veronica could hear the pride in his voice and for a moment warmed to it—before she remembered who he was and what they were planning.

Inside the U.S. Grant Hotel, the tallest building in the city, the enormous marble lobby was lit by crystal chandeliers. The air was cool, and the room was filled with chattering tourists coming and going alongside well-heeled businessmen in fine suits headed to the restaurant for lunch. Veronica looked at the grandfather clock: it was five to noon.

"Up there," Schroder told her, indicating the second floor with its balcony overlooking the lobby. They went upstairs and put their suitcases down on the floor, then opened them.

"Do what I do," McDonnell whispered to Veronica. They placed stacks of papers on the ledges, all around the three sides. "When I give the signal, push them off," he told them. "Then take the fire doors back down to the lobby." Veronica took her place as McDonnell, Charlie, and Allen manned theirs.

"Ready?" McDonnell asked. They all nodded. "On three . . . One, two, *three*!"

The papers fell slowly, spinning, white as snow. People looked up to see what was happening, their faces lit with shock, dismay, or delight. They grabbed them from the air, or picked them up from the floor, and started reading. Veronica and McDonnell watched,

MOTHER DAUGHTER TRAITOR SPY 181

but Charlie looked anxious. "Come on, let's get out of here," he said.

"This is amazing!" McDonnell said, gazing around him in joy and wonder. "It never gets old! Now you see what we're doing— right, Veronica?"

She forced herself to giggle. "Incredible!"

As they rushed down the stairs with their empty suitcases and back to the lobby, three police officers had arrived. "Stop! You're under arrest!"

McDonnell turned red and looked furious. "For what?"

"Illegal posting."

"One of our undercovers saw you push those flyers off," one of the officers said. "Sir, hand me the suitcase."

McDonnell's hands were clenched. "You got a search warrant, buddy?" His face was mottled with anger; Veronica could see the pupils of his eyes constricting. He cleared his throat a few times, as if to keep himself from saying anything incendiary.

An officer gave him a shove, and McDonnell stumbled back, catching himself, but he dropped the suitcases. Another officer opened them. "Empty," he said. "Now why would tourists be hauling around empty luggage?"

Veronica found her voice. "We dropped off our things at a laundry," she told them. "They're going to wash everything, then deliver it back here later today."

"You were upstairs," the officer said. "Why would you take your suitcases up the stairs? Why not take the elevator straight to your rooms?"

"I had to use the restroom," Veronica told them. She could sense people in the lobby staring, and she could feel her face turn hot.

"There's one on the first floor, no stairs required," the first officer told them. "Eh, we're going to the station. You can tell us the full story there." He began to cuff them, none too gently.

"Get your hands off me!" McDonnell growled.

"Nah, buddy—you're coming with us."

* * *

AT THE STATION, they all presented their identification. "Veronica Rose Grace," the cop read. "Twenty-two years old." He turned to the men. "You make little girls do your dirty work?"

"No one makes me do anything," she said, watching McDonnell's eyes. He nodded at her with approval.

"We'll need to write you all up."

Another officer brought in the handbills for evidence. "Here's what they were dropping," he said to the officer filling out the forms, turning over a stack of flyers.

" 'Our duty in America is to preserve Americanism and Christianity,' " he read aloud. " 'And to build an America along the pattern created by our great *führer,* Adolf Hitler, and to battle until the country is purged of communists and Jews.' " He looked up. "Hey, this is good stuff! They told us you were *communists.*"

"No, we're *fighting* the commies," McDonnell told them.

"This's a hell of a good note," another of the arresting officers said.

"Yeah, too bad we had to pinch folks *fighting* commies," the first said in a genial tone. "I'm gonna take one of these home to the wife and kids."

Another nodded. "My boys are teenagers. Don't want them fighting some Limey war for Jews and Reds."

"They oughta give you folks medals instead of arresting you!"

A man walked in, and the officers all straightened and the arresting officer said, "Sergeant Whitney, sir!" The men saluted.

"We'll do the girl separately," he told them.

Veronica wasn't expecting this. "Wait—what?"

"You're coming with me. Different laws for women."

The sergeant led her down the hall and opened a wooden door. There, in the office, were Ari and Jonah. Veronica's eyes widened. "Where did they park?" Jonah asked without preamble.

In an instant, she knew why they were there: Allen's briefcase. "Fourth and B," she told them. "It's in the trunk."

The sergeant inclined his head. "Thank you, miss." He looked to Ari and Jonah. "I'll get my men on it." He left, closing the door.

"Here," Ari told Veronica. "Sit. I brought you some lunch." Veronica sat, grateful to be off her suddenly wobbly legs. So much had happened so fast. "Eat something," he urged. "You'll feel better."

Numbly, Veronica unwrapped a sandwich, liverwurst on dark pumpernickel.

"I hope you like liverwurst. My aunt made it."

"My favorite," she told him, realizing she was ravenous. "My grandmother and I used to have liverwurst sandwiches and dill pickles for lunch and listen to the radio when I was little."

Ari opened a bottle of ginger ale for her and poured it into a glass. "And this might help settle your stomach."

"How did you know my stomach was upset?"

He clasped her shoulder. "I'd be shocked if it isn't."

Jonah had been watching her with his best Easter Island statue expression. "I'm going to assume you figured what we're doing."

Veronica nodded as she chewed and swallowed. "You're arresting them for illegal distribution of handbills on private property. They can get even more time for Allen's carrying the . . . you know, the stick—his weapon. While they're all in jail, you're going to make copies of what's in the briefcase." She took a sip of ginger ale.

"Not bad," Jonah said.

"And you couldn't tell me," she continued, taking another bite, "because you wanted me to act surprised."

Ari nodded. "I do apologize, Miss Grace."

"Is it possible—" She needed to talk to her mother.

"I've taken the liberty of telling Mrs. Grace what's happening."

"Thank you." She took another bite. "May I help with the copies?"

"We were just going to ask," Ari said, "if you'd lend us a hand."

"Is this"—she looked to Ari—"on the up-and-up? I know you're a lawyer and everything, but . . . aren't the papers Allen's property?"

"Before we do anything, we'll wait for the state district attorney. Commander Zabner called him," he reassured her. "Everything we do will be by the books."

* * *

THEY MET WITH Ezra at the Naval Base. "Heard you had a rough time of it, Miss Grace," he said to Veronica.

She shrugged. "Hard to complain when England's getting bombed every night."

When District Attorney James B. Abbey arrived and gave his approval for them to photostat the documents in Allen's briefcase, Jonah removed the documents and Ari began to copy them, with Veronica collating the documents and returning the originals.

"My God," Jonah said as he showed one of the pages to Ari and Veronica. "We hit the jackpot!"

Allen was a collector, with every memorandum and letter carefully preserved—even those that bore the inscription DESTROY IMMEDIATELY UPON READING.

They found the names and addresses of nearly a hundred Nazi agents in Southern California, as well as the names of their contacts in Germany. There was correspondence between Allen and all the well-known American pro-Nazi organizations, as well as the Mexican Gold Shirts.

There were blueprints for setting up nationwide secret military organizations, letters discussing the purchase of arms and ammunition, and grandiose plots to overthrow American democracy. There were all the carbon copies of Allen's own reports, as well as maps, diaries, and calendars, including reports of his secret meetings with foreign spies and embassy officials from Germany, Austria, Hungary, Egypt, and Mexico.

Despite her fatigue, Veronica was energized by the adrenaline of such a massive scoop. "Why would he be dragging so much important information around with him?" she said as she copied a memo marked TOP SECRET with a handwritten scribble "Destroy immedi-ately!"

"Ego," Jonah told her. "It's ego, pure and simple. And thank God for it—otherwise we'd never have found these."

They also discovered the code names for various correspon-dents. Allen himself used "Rosenthal," while Schwinn went by "Auntie." Nazis were referred to as "Arabs," Japan as "Alaska," and Jews as "Garlics."

"Wait a minute," Veronica said, reading over a particular set of papers. She held it up. "Did you know about this? Is this *der Tag*?"

It was correspondence from the leaders of the American Na-tionalist Confederation, a coalition of several militant Christian groups, describing their plan to overthrow the American govern-ment if Roosevelt won the 1940 election.

Ari put on his glasses, read the letters, then nodded. "We've only heard unsubstantiated rumors," he said, passing them to Jonah. "Nothing like this, though—actual written memos, with specific details we can collaborate. This is . . ."

Jonah spread his arms wide, like the wings of an ecstatic vulture. "Truly fantastic. Intelligence with concrete evidence of espionage and treason by Nazis and fascists we haven't been able to obtain on our own."

"Until now," Ari added, slapping Jonah on the back.

"Until now."

They copied into the night. Veronica was particularly struck by one missive, from Clayton F. Ingle, the husband of Vi's "friend" Nora Ingle: a blueprint for a fascist military organization and the names and addresses of hundreds of coup leaders and subleaders scattered across the country. They were organizing their military cadre into "cells of thirteen each, consisting of four Nazis from the German Bund, Italians with Fascist connections, White Russians and three Americans who 'believe in the Cause.'"

As they took a coffee break, with a plate of pink-glazed dough-nuts, Veronica's mind reeled with all the information they'd discovered. After the planned government takeover, citizens who refused to surrender peacefully—and Jews and communists—would be shot on the spot. Coup leaders, Ingle insisted, must not "flinch from issuing orders to mow down without hesitation the great Communist front."

"Where's Mr. Ingle planning on getting the weapons?" she asked Ari, drinking her coffee. It was bitter, but hot.

"Ingle's working with the National Rifle Association in Washington, D.C. Also some Nazis down in Mexico with access to guns."

"Do they have enough money to pull something like this off?" Veronica asked.

"They have the might of Nazi Germany behind them," Jonah said grimly. "And its bankroll."

"Have you called the FBI?" she asked. "About"—her arms flailed—"all of this?"

"We have," Jonah replied. "And the State Department." From his seat in the corner, the watching DA nodded.

"We're giving them copies of everything," Ari told her. "Don't know what they'll do, though."

Veronica finished her coffee, silent, shocked. *A group of Americans plotting treason against their own government,* she thought. *With Nazis assisting them. If I didn't see it for myself, I'd never believe it.*

The last few months had been difficult, stressful, sometimes frightening, generally unpleasant, and often lonely. But here it was: payoff, finally. In her mind, Veronica wrote and rewrote how she'd later describe the scene. She felt as though the world had risen to shake the complacency out of her, insisting she rise, too, somehow. That she finally wake up and open her eyes to what was really going on. To change, completely and irrevocably, into someone new, someone she never would have been if she'd stayed in New York.

Veronica knew this night was her moment of transformation. Who cared about Max Feldman or *Mademoiselle* magazine or the Barbizon? She was witnessing history. No, she was *part* of history.

And someday she'd write the story of everything she'd seen and done.

She looked up and realized Jonah was watching her. "You okay?" he asked. "Do you need to take a rest?"

"Take five," Ari told them. "You've earned it."

Veronica and Jonah went to the dark parking lot and sat on the curb. They brushed hands, then held them. They leaned in for a kiss. But despite the current of attraction, Veronica also sensed resistance. Jonah pulled his lips away, but kept holding her hand. "Sorry," he began.

Her blood was still racing. "There's nothing to be sorry about."

"I should have stopped myself."

In her best Brooklyn accent, she replied, "I wasn't exactly objecting!"

"All the same. That can't happen again."

Why? But she knew the answer: it was unprofessional. All the atoms inside her were still vibrating for his touch. But instead, she pulled her hand away and said lightly, "We should get back."

Inside, they got back to work, avoiding each other's gaze. Ari told her he'd reached her mother and updated her. "How mad is she?" Veronica asked.

Ari smiled. "About as mad as my wife."

"And how mad is your wife?"

"Let's just say—I'm glad to be out of town tonight."

* * *

BY FOUR IN the morning, they were done; all the papers were copied and the originals returned to Allen's briefcase. The sergeant took Veronica back to the women's holding cell. She sat on a hard wooden bench between a prostitute and a self-proclaimed poisoner, smiling to herself.

"Whatcha on?" the prostitute asked, her kohl-lined eyes red and watery. "Got any more?"

"Sorry," Veronica said. "Just happy."

"Woo! Must be some good stuff," the poisoner muttered, shaking her head. Hours later, she was released with McDonnell, Schroder, and Allen.

"You, young lady," the judge said, "I'm letting off with a warning, as this is your first offense. Don't ever let me see you back here."

"Yes, Your Honor," she replied, willing herself to tear up and look appropriately chastened. Meanwhile, McDonnell and Charlie each had to pay a three-dollar fine and Allen a six-dollar one.

"Sure am sorry, Veronica," McDonnell said as they walked to the car. "Your mother's gonna kill me."

"Not your fault," she told him, trying to downplay her joy. She yawned widely, unable to stop.

"Well, you're definitely one of us now," Charlie crowed, giving her a gentle punch on the arm. "I may have had my doubts at first, but you're a good egg, Veronica."

McDonnell grinned. "*Egg*-zactly!"

"I just need to make sure my briefcase is safe," Allen said nervously.

Veronica's heart was in her throat, worried they hadn't gotten everything back in order. At the car, Allen fidgeted until McDonnell got the trunk open. He riffled through the briefcase, pulling out documents at random while Veronica held her breath. But, finally, he closed the case with a sigh of relief. "Thank God," he muttered, taking it with him to the backseat.

Indeed, Veronica thought, able to breathe once again.

Once they were all settled, McDonnell asked, "Anybody want to get some breakfast? I know a little place not too far that has great corned beef hash."

Veronica caught his glance in the rearview mirror. "If you don't mind, Mr. McDonnell, I'd really like to get back to Los Angeles. I—" her voice broke. "I really want to see my mother."

CHAPTER TWENTY

Word got around Deutsches Haus about the snowstorm in San Diego and the night in jail, and suddenly Veronica was a hero—and her shorthand skills were in demand. She was appointed secretary to several executive committees and made privy to multiple inner-circle meetings.

Vi was becoming increasingly popular as well. As Nora Ingle, Dodie Tatum, and Ann Hunt began wearing their edelweiss-embroidered blouses to various events, demand for her work grew. She became more involved with America First. The women started dining at Deutsches Haus together regularly, or sometimes Veronica with Will and Vi with Nora.

Veronica's interactions with Will had progressed into something approaching a relationship. But although he'd invited her time and again to his apartment after whatever movie or restaurant they went to, she always declined. Veronica held on to her good-girl persona—she didn't drink, smoke, swear, or wear obvious makeup.

And as far as Will knew, she was a virgin, saving herself for her husband. She would tell him, with a straight face, she didn't believe in sex before marriage, as she wanted to be "true to my husband always" and keep her body "pure for our eventual children." He grumbled, but it seemed to make him both want and respect her even more, although she often wondered where exactly he went, and with whom, after their dates.

* * *

WHEN HERMANN SCHWINN himself invited Vi and Veronica to a small, exclusive party at his house in Brentwood, they jumped at the chance. They dressed carefully in their best and splurged on a taxi. Schwinn's house was the Hollywood version of a castle, with crenellations and a turret, shrouded by lofty trees.

The entrance hall was filled with the scents of pine needles and candle wax, and the ceiling glittered with chandeliers. It had been transformed into a palace of the occult. The stone walls were draped with tapestries and decorated to look like a pagan temple, with Egyptian and Babylonian and astrological symbols, the evil eye, and countless swastikas. Hors d'oeuvres—bloody beef tartare on small rounds of brown bread and tiny bratwursts wrapped in salt-flecked pretzels—were served on silver trays by waiters in black knee breeches.

Many of the male guests were in uniform, while the women wore satin and silk gowns topped with ropes of pearls and jewels. Nubile "priestesses" in diaphanous veils carried trays of sparkling *sekt,* while snake handlers intermixed with guests, and a woman in a purple turban, wearing thick eyeliner, read palms in a shadowy corner. Music was playing—a classical piece that sounded Wagnerian to Veronica.

The floor was covered in billowing fog from dry ice, and everything was lit by the glow of an inordinate number of red candles. A signed portrait of Adolf Hitler was proudly displayed on the grand piano, and there were so many flowers—red roses, white lilies, and the inescapable edelweiss—it smelled like a funeral parlor.

Veronica and Vi shared a look. "Shall we get a drink?" Veronica asked her mother. She wore an elegant garnet-colored backless silk dress Vi had made especially for the occasion. Vi's dress was similar, but black, and with a higher back and longer sleeves. They both sported long white kid gloves.

"Oh, this definitely calls for a cocktail," Vi murmured as a waiter passed, serving cheese straws twisted into swastikas. She took Veronica's arm and they headed into what must have been Schwinn's library, turned into a candlelit cocktail lair.

A group of men standing at the bar, including Will, was holding old-fashioned tumblers filled with brown liquor. Their voices were loud and boozy. "Did you hear the Luftwaffe bombed London?" one was saying. "Not just the East End docks—but the City and the West End."

"Cost of doing business," replied another dismissively.

Tell that to all the dead and grieving, Veronica thought. *Tell it to the people without homes.* She tried to imagine the bombers screaming out of the stillness of an autumn morning, the terror of the people fleeing as they were strafed from the air.

She pictured the same happening in New York, with the Luftwaffe raining its deadly payload on the Statue of Liberty, the Navy Yard, the Empire State Building. On St. Patrick's Cathedral, and Central Park, and the Metropolitan Museum of Art. She imagined the air-raid sirens, the women and children hurrying out of their houses, the fighter planes diving low to finish off those stumbling figures who had escaped the incendiaries. She shook her head to dispel the vision.

"Churchill's going to milk this for all the sympathy he can— wait and see," a man leaning on the bar was saying, swirling the liquor in his glass. "Roosevelt'll get suckered. We've got to be on our guard when the Jews start their teeth-gnashing and crocodile tears . . ."

Will looked up from the conversation and spotted Vi and Veronica. He smiled. "Ladies!" He walked over, bowed, kissed Vi's gloved hand and Veronica's cheek. He wrapped an arm around her, and she gazed up at him in fake adoration. He smelled of scotch and No. 4711 cologne. There was an impatience about the flare of his nostrils and the brief glance he cast toward the door, which said that as far as he was concerned, this party couldn't end soon enough.

In the corner a woman was giving astrology readings. "Do you know Hitler has his horoscope read every day?" he asked.

"I do!" Vi replied. "And many of the women of Los Angeles as well, it seems. I've been embroidering any number of astrological symbols on blouses."

A gong sounded: the snake charmers and priestesses beckoned for them to follow into an enormous candlelit dining room. On the wall hung a tapestry bearing a pronouncement from Hitler, stitched in elaborate Gothic letters in black thread: WOMAN'S WORLD IS HER HUSBAND, HER FAMILY, HER CHILDREN, AND HER HOME. WE DO NOT FIND IT RIGHT WHEN SHE PRESSES INTO THE WORLD OF MEN.

Veronica and Vi hung back. There was a long table in the middle of the room, covered by a cloth with Masonic symbols and swastikas. At the head of the table was a "medium," a woman in her thirties dressed in brocade and wearing heavy jewels, her hair piled under a dark veil. Schwinn sat with his wife, who looked ridiculously young next to him, younger than Veronica. Several other prominent Nazi couples were already at the table, one bald man gnawing on a giant cigar, his wife chomping on a wad of spearmint gum. An elderly woman with a purple orchid corsage and even more purple marcelled hair was fighting sleep.

"I bet the young Frau Schwinn's drinking Shirley Temples," Vi whispered to Veronica.

Veronica whispered back, "I'd put money on Yoo-hoo."

"Friends and travelers from occult lands," the medium intoned in a rich, sonorous voice as the lights lowered, "tonight we are privileged to glimpse into the future. We may see signs and portents of events that could change the world!" There was a chorus of oohs and aahs. "Now we must all join hands." Those at the table did, their laughter quieting.

Suddenly, Veronica couldn't stand any more. What kind of party was it, where you detested everyone and felt too ill to eat or drink? What a life this was, mixing with people whose views she loathed, associating with a regime that stood for everything she hated: intimidation, violence, brutality. Befriending people who represented a version of America she didn't recognize—or want to recognize. The strain of being constantly on her guard, of laughing and chatting and dissembling, of never putting a wrong foot forward, was soul-killing. She had to escape, if only for a moment.

She drifted onto the terrace as though in search of fresh air and moved away from the French windows so the chatter of the party receded. After easing herself into the shadow at the edge of the house, she stood quietly, listening to the calls of the night birds in the garden and, farther off, the hum of traffic. A large fountain splashed; in the outdoor lights, Veronica could see at its center was a bearded, muscular Neptune, a trident in one hand and a conch shell in the other, surrounded by dolphins spitting arcs of water.

She realized she wasn't alone: Will had followed her. "I see we have the same idea," he said, and his hand traveled around her waist and downward. Veronica's flesh crawled, but she closed her eyes, braced herself, and allowed herself to be kissed. He tasted of smoke and whiskey. When she couldn't bear it anymore, she pulled away.

"Someone might see," she told him, batting her eyes.

"Oh, let them look." But at least for the moment, he was done. "I was thinking maybe sometime soon, we could take a trip," he told Veronica, tracing a finger down her neck. She steeled herself not to pull away.

"A trip?"

"A friend of mine has a house near Santa Barbara. Very quiet, very private, on a little hill, with a view of the beach and the ocean."

"Santa Barbara, hmm?" she said in what she hoped was a teasing voice. "I don't think Mother would approve."

"Your mother adores me."

"She does!" *At least she puts on a good act.*

"And she knows I'm a gentleman."

As Will leaned in for another kiss, Veronica realized she might have to commit to the weekend and all it entailed. "What about next weekend?" she asked, nuzzling his neck. She knew they had plans with Uncle Walter, so she could always cancel with Wagner, saying she'd forgotten and couldn't get out of them.

"Ha!" He drew back, looking at her with an amused expression.

Veronica was confused. "What's so funny? It's Columbus Day weekend."

"*Schatzi,*" he said in his Austrian accent, drawing her in close. "It's the one weekend I have to work."

"You have to work on Columbus Day?" Veronica asked. "You know it's a national holiday."

"I can't tell you," he said, kissing the top of her head. "But it's going to be a big weekend for me—for us. How about the next one? Are you free? Don't tell me McDonnell's insisting you type for him—I'll challenge him to a duel . . ."

But all Veronica could think was, *Columbus Day. What's being planned for Columbus Day?*

*   *   *

AFTER THE SÉANCE, Vi found herself chatting with a man with a black satin eye patch, a downy puff of white hair, and tufted side-burns. "Where's your husband, ma'am?" he asked, glancing at the wedding ring she wore over her kidskin glove. "And how could he possibly leave a delightful young woman such as yourself on your own?"

"Oh, I'm widowed," she told him through the haze of alcohol. "And hardly young."

He smiled too widely. "May I get you another drink?"

"I'd love a gimlet, thank you." *And a balcony to jump off.* She turned and spotted Nora and her husband, Clayton Ingle, approaching them slowly, Nora carefully, in her heels.

"What did you think?" Nora asked Vi. By now, Vi knew all the women truly believed in their horoscopes, their star signs, their love signs, and any other occult offerings that could possibly be read to their advantage.

"It's all very . . . *mysterious,* isn't it?" Vi said diplomatically, glad not to be talking about the Nuremberg Laws. In truth, she thought all the occult business was hogwash.

Nora took Vi's hand and led her away to a quiet corner. "I was just wondering," she said, "if you have any plans for Columbus Day weekend?"

Vi forced herself to focus. "My brother's coming for a picnic. Nothing fancy. Why?"

"Just—" She looked around, making sure no one could hear her. "Just make sure you have plenty of fresh water and canned food. Candles and matches, too."

"What?" Vi wasn't sure she caught what Nora was saying.

But Nora trilled, "Oh, that's Mr. and Mrs. Decker, I simply must say hello!" and sashayed off, leaving Vi openmouthed with shock.

The man with the tufted sideburns reappeared. "Your gimlet, madam." She took it from him wordlessly and took a deep sip.

* * *

EXCUSING HERSELF TO powder her nose, Veronica ignored the first-floor lavatory, venturing up the back servants' stairs to the shadowy second floor. Her pulse quickened. Upstairs, her eyes adjusted to the darkness, and she walked quietly down the corridor, opening doors until she finally found Schwinn's study. She turned on a light.

Tall windows overlooked the fountain in the back garden, and she could hear the gurgle of water and the faint sounds of music from the party. The walls were decorated with the skulls of dead animals. A large map of Europe hung on one wall, covered with medieval-style writing. She felt a strong temptation to turn tail and slip away, but forced herself to remain.

When she looked closer at the map, she noticed Germany was colored in red, as well as the Sudetenland, Austria, Poland, Belgium, Holland, Luxembourg, and France. And Britain as well, even though the battle for Britain was still ongoing. *Those cocky bastards,* she thought, looking at the British Isles, which were already assumed conquered. *They're being more than a little presumptuous about their win.*

After ten minutes had passed with no sound of footsteps, she walked slowly, quietly, toward the massive mahogany desk. *Pulitzer,* she thought as she took silent steps, fear creeping up her spine. *P-u-l-i-t-z-e-r, Pulitzer.*

She kept one eye on the door while searching the enormous desk. The desktop was immaculate, the blotter clear, the pencils all sharpened to the same length. There was an SS–issue Olympia typewriter, specially fitted with its double lightning bolt key. A journal, a brass reading lamp, and a glass paperweight heavy enough to kill someone filled out the desktop.

Hands shaking, she paged through his leather-bound appointment journal, looking for Columbus Day weekend. The only thing entered on that Monday was a huge black X. She heard someone in the hall and shut the book.

As the door swung open, Veronica started. It was Charlie Schroder, looking awkward in an ill-fitting dinner jacket. "Jumping Jehoshaphat!" he cried. "What are *you* doing in here?"

Her heart was hammering in her chest. "Oh, I was looking for the bathroom," she covered, smiling brightly while wanting to sink through the floor. Her mouth tasted of acid.

"Well, it's not in here." His usually jovial face was shocked.

"What are you doing in here?" she asked, turning the tables.

"I saw the light on from the back garden and wondered who was up here."

"Honestly, Charlie?" she said in a light tone, throwing herself into Schwinn's leather desk chair. "I just needed some time away from the party. I mean, I love parties—and people—but sometimes it's all just . . . a bit much, you know?" She spun herself around in the chair to turn her face away. "I just needed a minute to myself before heading back into the fray." *Too much?* she asked herself before turning back and trying to read his face.

"This isn't the best place. I don't think Captain Schwinn would be too happy to find anyone here."

"You're right, of course," Veronica said, rising and smoothing her skirt with sweaty hands. "Should we go downstairs and get some of those plum dumplings before they're all gone?" she asked, forcing a bantering tone to cover her fear. "My grandmother used to make them—they're absolutely delicious."

* * *

VI SIPPED HER gimlet and chatted with some of the ladies about the Windsors: a recent article in *Vogue* magazine detailed their move to Nassau's Government House in the Bahamas. But while Vi went through the motions of gossiping, she was really trying to listen to the men's conversation behind them. She picked up they were talking about the Douglas Aircraft plant and noted bits and pieces of their conversation, like "Canada," "loose bolts," and "fall out of the sky." She looked at the ladies speaking, their mouths moving, and just wished for all the world they would shut up so she could focus on what was going on behind her. But she'd heard enough to make her blood curdle. *They're talking about sabotage.*

As Vi went to get another cocktail, she recognized Marvel Whiteside moving through the crowd, looking lonely and out of place. "Marv!" she called to him from the bar.

His face brightened when he recognized her. "So lovely to see you," he said. She realized his jacket was old and several sizes too big for him.

"And you!" She accepted another gimlet from the bartender. "How are the rockets? Ready to fly to the moon?"

"Not quite." He shuffled his feet. "Need to do a lot more testing."

"How do they work?" she asked. "Can you tell me in layman's terms?"

"You're familiar with Newton's third law of motion?" Vi wasn't but nodded anyway. "Well, you burn some kinda fuel in the chamber, and the gases the combustion produces shoot out the only exit available. The gases go one way, the rocket another."

"So it's 'hoist by its own petard,'" Vi joked, taking a sip.

"Yes," he said, nodding seriously. "There's a part of the rocket that's in control, and another that's trying to burst free."

"Marv," she said, extracting a small pad of paper and pencil from her beaded purse and scribbling. "Here's my address and phone number." She knew she shouldn't be giving out her home information, it was against all of Ari's directives, but he just looked so sad and lost, like an abandoned puppy. "If you ever need a listening ear and a decent hot meal, just give me a ring, all right?" She handed it to him, and he stuck it in his jacket's breast pocket.

He looked up at her and grinned. "Thanks, Mrs. Grace," he said. "I just may take you up on your offer someday."

* * *

AS THEY HAD arranged, Jonah arrived at midnight, driving a rented limousine; ten minutes later, Veronica and Vi made their escape into the wide leather backseat.

"Columbus Day," Veronica told him breathlessly as he shifted gears and pulled out to the quiet street. He was wearing a chauffeur's cap pulled down low over his face.

"What about it?"

"Whatever they're planning—sabotage of the factories—is happening on Columbus Day."

Jonah looked at her in the rearview mirror. "How do you know?"

"Because Will invited me for a romantic weekend in Santa Barbara. And when I said, 'What about Columbus Day?' he said he couldn't, he was working. But it's a holiday."

"Will invited you away for the weekend?" Vi asked. "You didn't tell me that."

"We just got in the car, Mother."

"Would you go?"

"I can't exactly put him off forever," she said, looking at the back of Jonah's head in the light from the streetlamps. His ears stuck out in the shadows as he made a few twists and turns to make sure they weren't being followed. "I'm practically doing jujitsu with him as it is."

"But he couldn't make it that weekend?" Jonah prodded.

"No, and he was odd about it, like he had a big secret. He said, 'It's going to be a big weekend for me—for us.'"

"Nora said something curious about Columbus Day weekend to me, too," Vi said. "She told me to have water and candles and matches on hand. I was able to hear bits and pieces of a talk some of the upper-level men were having. I couldn't get much, but I did hear 'Douglas Aircraft,' 'Canada,' and 'loose bolts.'" She bit her lower lip.

"The U.S. sends planes to Canada, which they then send on to the British," Jonah told them. "If those bolts are loose . . ." They were silent, realizing.

"I also got upstairs and got a look at Schwinn's appointment book," Veronica told them. "On Columbus Day, there was a big black X. Think about it: most people will be off for the three-day weekend, celebrating. With fewer people and less security, it would be the perfect time for sabotage."

Jonah nodded. "Let's swing by the Hollywood office now for a debrief, if you don't mind," he said. "I'd rather it didn't wait."

* * *

ONCE THEY WERE safely inside the office, Vi busied herself making a pot of coffee for all of them in the tiny kitchen, while Veronica kicked off her heels. "I hope you don't mind," she said, sitting down and rubbing at the red welts on her toes. "My feet are killing me."

Ari was already there, at his desk, nearly hidden by stacks of papers. When Jonah and the women filled him in on everything that had happened, he sighed. "Another letter to the FBI . . ."

Jonah rolled his eyes. Vi brought coffee and mugs to the table, and they all came over.

"I don't suppose there's any food?" Veronica asked.

Jonah looked shocked. "Didn't you just come from a fancy party?"

"Couldn't eat anything there," she said. "Too nervous."

"Well, no—sorry," he said with just the slightest hint of embarrassment.

"What kind of a spy operation is this?" she joked, as Vi poured steaming coffee into the mugs. "No snacks?"

Ari went back to his desk and opened the bottom drawer, pulling out a brown paper bag. Jonah's eyes widened. "You've been holding out on me, old man?"

"Just some chocolate-covered pomegranate seeds," he said. "My *tanta* put them in my briefcase today. She gets them at the Farmers Market on Fairfax."

"Aren't you supposed to wait for Rosh Hashanah?" Jonah asked. He held up his hands. "I mean, not that this half-goy atheist is judging, but that's what I recall Pops saying."

Ari pulled out a bowl and poured in the chocolate pomegranate seeds. "She says when you're in your eighties, you don't buy green bananas. She doesn't wait for anything."

Veronica reached out a hand and dug in. "Thanks, Ari," she said, as she crunched down. The seeds were delicious, sweet and intense, and she felt a pulse of pure pleasure as she took another, and another.

"What we need to do is give the FBI the names of our suspected fifth columnists working in the aviation industry and the power and water plants," Jonah said. "Then they'd have something to go on."

"We need to warn the security agents at all the major plants of potential sabotage," Ari said, taking off his glasses and slipping them into his shirt pocket. "As well as Army and Navy Intelligence."

"My father used to say, 'Army Intelligence is an oxymoron,'" Veronica joked.

"You're going to talk to Commander Zabner?" Vi asked.

"He's my first call when we get done here," Ari told her.

Jonah turned to Veronica, eyes sparkling. "Want to help write an article?"

"An—an . . . *article*?" she asked. It had been months. She didn't even know if she remembered how. "For what?"

"Do you know Drew Pearson and Sam Allen?" he asked. "Walter Winchell?"

"Yes, of course," she replied impatiently. "*Everybody* knows them."

"Well, I write a weekly newsletter, the *News Research Service,* which contains information culled from operatives, including both of you," Jonah said, looking to the women. "It's a few thousand copies a week—exposés of Nazi activities, of anti-Semitic activities, of un-American activities. And I send it to opinion molders, like Winchell. We reach millions every week because of the 'pickup.' I never ever say anything I can't prove and do a lot of documentation. It's a way to provide news organizations with the detailed intelligence reports we collect."

Veronica's mouth hung open. "You never thought to mention this?"

"We've established it as a public relations campaign to alert Americans to the Nazi threat," Ari explained. "We send copies to government agencies, national and local newspapers, magazines, and influential political columnists to expose the Nazi groups we're investigating."

"Is that wise?" Vi asked.

"We might not catch them red-handed—but we believe it's best to never allow a Nazi plot to develop past the planning stage," Ari explained.

"I'm writer, editor, proofreader, cook, and chief bottle washer of *News Research Service*," Jonah told them. "What we're hoping for, with something like this, is for it to make it into 'Merry-Go-Round.' You're familiar with that?"

"Um, yes," Veronica said. "Of course."

"Well, they have tens of thousands of readers," Jonah told her. "And what we need for this issue of the newsletter is a piece detailing the vulnerabilities of West Coast defense, power, and water plants—although you can't use any names in the article. We need to write something so good they'll pick it up—let people know the nation's biggest 'danger spot' isn't on the East Coast but in Southern California. And if we mention Columbus Day, it'll force the FBI, the police, everyone, to take the threat seriously."

"I think after the disaster at the New Jersey factory, they'll pick up the story," Ari added.

"So, what do you say, Ace?" Jonah asked Veronica. "Ready to take a pass on a first draft?"

Veronica's jaw dropped, and she squealed in joy. "I've been waiting for this my whole life!"

"Well, let's not dance the hora just yet," Jonah told her, even as his lips twitched in a smile. "We still have a lot of work to do."

* * *

BY DAWN, THEY had the article finished, using reports from multiple undercover agents.

Despite the hour, Veronica was awake and feeling more alive than she had since she'd left New York. Even when they were done, she still had so much energy humming through her she felt she could go out dancing. While Vi catnapped on the worn sofa and Ari stayed behind his stacks of papers, Veronica was suddenly aware of how well she and Jonah worked together. *It's been . . . fun,* she realized. Her face flushed and she felt light-headed. She focused on proofreading the piece one more time, so she could turn away.

And she suspected Jonah felt it, too, because his face was also flushed as he pushed his chair back and stood, saying in a too-loud voice, "Who's hungry? Should I go over to the diner and bring back some eggs and pancakes?"

As they all gave their orders, Veronica went back to the pomegranate seeds.

CHAPTER TWENTY-ONE

Agent Doolin didn't look up from his metal desk at the Los Angeles FBI office when his secretary knocked. "What now?" It wasn't a good morning: he'd already spilled his coffee over important papers, and grease from his fried egg, bacon, and cheese breakfast sandwich had stained his favorite tie.

The calendar on his wall featured a nubile Miss October in a skimpy yellow-and-red bathing suit. Only a day and a half to go until the long weekend: Doolin had a fishing trip to Lake Tahoe planned with some of his war buddies and was looking forward to drinking beer and maybe even catching a few mackinaws.

"Mail," the redhead told him, placing a large envelope in his inbox. She snapped her gum. "You're welcome."

"Sorry, yeah . . . thanks," he told her. "Please close the door on your way—" But it had already shut.

With a resigned sigh, he picked up the envelope. No return address. He knew exactly who sent it—the two Jews who played at being spymasters. He put on his glasses and began reading.

After the first few lines, he sat up. "Captain Hermann Schwinn . . . orders from Berlin . . . sabotage . . . Pacific coast . . . Columbus Day . . ." "Shit," he muttered.

According to the report, the Bund had more than eight hundred trusted men working in airplane plants, shipyards, oil refineries, auto factories, and other key defense industries, all with instructions to attempt sabotage without violence. If that failed, Schwinn's plan was for pilots in private planes to bomb the plants. They would start in Seattle and work their way down the coast, with a second contingent of planes starting from Mexico and working north.

In the event both plans failed, Schwinn had ordered local Bundists working in the defense plants to persuade employees to stop production—by any means necessary. Attached was a handwritten warning from Rose: *"Keep this information top secret for the safety of our agents."*

"Shit," Doolin muttered, pinching the bridge of his nose. "Shit, shit, shit." He picked up the telephone receiver and started to dial. "Yeah, it's Doolin," he said. "You really got all those names, crossreferenced and everything?" He listened. "I'll be by today."

Doolin hung up, walked to the door, and opened it. "Hey!" he called. "Get me through to FBI offices in Seattle, Portland, San Francisco, and San Diego—and then Army and Navy Intelligence." The redhead looked up just as she was peeling back the foil on a fresh stick of Juicy Fruit gum.

"And Mr. Hoover, too."

* * *

ON COLUMBUS DAY, Vi opened her eyes warily, letting the golden blue dawn wash over her. From outside came the song of a mockingbird, the shout of children's voices, and the bells of the knife-sharpening van. She could hear her next-door neighbor singing something in French. From the sounds of water running and the clatter of pots and pans, it sounded like she was making breakfast. Everywhere up and down the West Coast, she knew, people were waking, dressing, and preparing for another ordinary day—a vacation day, even—with no hint of the shattering events that might be unfolding.

Vi knew that all along the West Coast, the saboteurs would be putting the final preparations in place. She imagined the click of guns being loaded, the shuffling of boots, the final cigarettes, and the last nervous coughs among the plotters. Her head was throbbing from stress and lack of sleep. She made her way to the bathroom, blinked in the harsh light at the pallid face staring back at her from the mirror, then swallowed a couple of aspirin. She used more makeup than usual, brushing rouge across her pale cheeks and smoothing lipstick on her bloodless lips. Then she dressed quickly in a khaki linen skirt and pale green blouse.

After going downstairs and making coffee, Vi welcomed her brother to the house. "Howdy, stranger!" she said, forcing a smile and accepting the box of See's chocolates he'd brought. She called up the stairs, "Veronica, Uncle Wally's here!" She wondered what was going through Veronica's head.

"Down in a minute!"

"Picnic's all ready," Vi told him as they walked into the kitchen. "I've got fried chicken, potato salad, fruit salad, bread-and-butter pickles, and brownies," she told him. "And some beer."

She'd had the radio on, terrified of hearing about any explosions or attacks. But so far, the only news was the president had signed the Nationality Act into law and was giving a speech later about Christopher Columbus. Aimee Semple McPherson, better known as Sister Aimee, famous for founding the Foursquare Gospel Church, came on. *"Brothers and sisters, it's our sacred duty to spread the Good Word far and wide, all over this great nation of ours . . . I see unhappiness and strife and aching hearts crying out for the embrace of their loving father . . ."*

"What kind of sister is she?" Vi said, twisting the knob to change the station to a Bach cantata. "Is it some kind of cult?"

"They grow like weeds out here," Walter told her. "Hey, can we talk?" he asked, sitting at the table.

"Sure," Vi said, bringing him a cup of coffee. She bustled about, taking items out of the icebox and placing them in a straw basket.

"Sit down, sis."

"Uh-oh, this sounds serious," she said, taking off her apron and sitting. She folded her hands in front of her, so she wouldn't twist her ring.

"A few of my patients tell me you're involved with that America First group," he said.

"Oh, them!" She laughed nervously. "No, I've just used the meetings to reach out to ladies who want to buy my blouses. You'd be amazed at how many I've been commissioned to embroider! If it keeps going like this, I'm seriously thinking about getting a few women in to help me keep up with the orders." She looked out the open window. "Maybe even open my own shop in town one day. Picture it: *Visions by Violet*."

"They—they're not nice people, Vi. I know Lindbergh and his wife are involved, so it seems on the up-and-up, but they're anti-Roosevelt."

"You *know* I'm an isolationist, Walter, even if you and Veronica aren't."

"There are isolationists—and there are Nazis."

"What?" She held back a sarcastic *I know!*

"They've also seen you and Veronica at Deutsches Haus. That's a snake pit, you know."

"They have very good schnitzel," she told him. "And, again, it's how I can reach out to women to buy my blouses." She swallowed. "Veronica and I like their music program as well."

"Some of them like schnitzel more than apple pie, if you get my meaning."

"Walter—"

"Look," he told her. "I just don't want to see you getting involved with these people."

"Who?" She laughed to cover her nerves. She knew she could never tell Walter what she was really doing. "Germans? German Americans?"

"*Nazis,*" he told her. "While some may be misguided, others are dangerous."

Veronica burst into the room, a floral cotton dress over her bathing suit, a huge smile on her face to break the tension. "Uncle Walter!" she said, going over to give him a hug. "Why so glum? Let's take all this food down to the beach! We need to go early to get a good spot."

Walter grumbled but picked up the heaviest of the bags. They walked down to the beach and put up their canvas umbrella, spreading their blanket on the sand. Veronica rubbed on suntan lotion, while Vi unpacked the food, keeping up a steady stream of chatter as sandpipers pecked nearby.

They each went for occasional dips in the glassy blue swells. In the distance, bronzed surfers with longboards rode the larger waves. Vi watched as a tanned lifeguard in faded pink shorts and sunglasses blew his whistle up in his tower, causing a group of children to scatter. But under her facade, she worried. She knew Veronica was worried, too. What if the authorities hadn't listened? What if a lone cell was able to cause serious damage?

* * *

WHEN THEY RETURNED home, sunburned and sandy, eating pulled saltwater taffy, they did their best not to rush Walter off, tried not to babble. When he finally left with a large basket of leftovers, Vi pounced on the radio. She twisted the dial through static until she reached KECA.

Veronica and Vi held each other's hands as the honey-voiced announcer went through the day's headlines: *"Charles Lindbergh attacks the Roosevelt administration's record and appeals for the election of leaders 'whose promises we can trust' . . . Japan establishes the Imperial Rule Assistance Association, merging all political parties into a single totalitarian ruling party . . . Wendell Willkie is campaigning in New York, Pennsylvania, Illinois, and Ohio . . . And fourteen-year-old Princess Elizabeth made her first radio address, to the children displaced by the bombing in London and sent to the British countryside . . ."*

As the station cut to the princess's speech, the two women looked at each other, then embraced tightly in relief. The plan had been for the attack to happen during daylight hours. "We're not out of the woods yet," Violet said, going to the cupboard for her bottle of gin.

"You're right," Veronica said. "Let's give it until midnight. And why don't you pour me one, too?"

* * *

THE NEXT MORNING, Veronica met Jonah at St. Augustine by-the-Sea, a white-painted wooden church on Fourth Street in Santa Monica. Morning Mass was over and the church was empty, except for a janitor walking by, pushing a mop, and an organist, practicing "For Those in Peril on the Sea" in the choir loft. The air smelled of floor polish and beeswax candles.

"What happened?" Veronica whispered as Jonah took off his hat and sat next to her on the hard wooden pew.

"We got a break." He drew a newspaper from his leather jacket. "Reactions to the 'Merry-Go-Round' piece, inspired by our work in the *News Research Service*."

Veronica took the paper, folded to the letters to the editor section. One man, a war veteran from Mississippi, had written: "What's the U.S. government waiting on anyway, Mr. Hoover? Why does this government not take out this old traitor, Schwinn, and shoot him at sunrise? Is the FBI doing everything in its power to destroy this subversive activity?"

Veronica looked up. "What's the FBI doing? Anything?"

"Yes! Apparently, there's been enough public outcry to make them pay attention for once. Just heard from Doolin, at the Los Angeles Bureau. Hoover called and asked him what he had on Schwinn . . . and it's nothing. Nothing on the Bund or any of the other American fascist groups, either. So now they're asking for our information."

Veronica shook her head in exasperation. "It's a little late, isn't it?"

"Better late than never," he told her. "And don't blame Doolin. Turns out he's been following up on all the information we've been sending him. It's Hoover who told him to lay off on Schwinn and the Bund—and put all their effort into stopping the Reds."

"Do the feds have all the information on the Nazis now?" Veronica asked.

"Yes, and not only that, they're going after Schwinn."

"For the sabotage? It never happened! They don't have anything."

"No, there's a loophole. Schwinn's German, not an American citizen. It seems there are issues with his immigration status—it might have been illegally obtained."

"Which means they can deport him?"

Jonah grinned. "Which means they can *arrest* and deport him."

He put his hand over hers, as the light from the stained-glass windows shifted, illuminating their faces in rainbows. She could feel the warmth of his hand through her cotton glove. Veronica squeezed his hand and looked up at the altar. "Thank God."

"I've got to go."

Veronica nodded, pulling her hand away. "There's a meeting this afternoon."

"They're going to be angry. If you need anything . . ."

Veronica swallowed. "I think I'll stay a few minutes longer and say a prayer."

CHAPTER TWENTY-TWO

That afternoon, Violet and Veronica attended an emergency meeting at the upstairs conference room in Deutsches Haus—Vi as a member, and Veronica now as Schwinn's secretary, taking down the minutes of the meeting with a shaking hand. They glanced at each other. *Is the gig up? Is this the end?*

"Someone's betrayed us!" Schwinn ranted. Veronica sat quietly, her pencil flying. "We have a mole—a rat—or maybe even a few!"

Veronica swallowed, forcing herself not to look at her mother. In the audience, Will raised a hand, then stood. "I'm sure Ari Lewis's somehow behind this. There must be someone here who reports to him."

There was grumbling from the assembled; Schwinn raised his hand for silence. "There is." He looked searchingly through the audience, taking his time, letting his gaze linger. "And we've found one," he said. Veronica did her best not to shudder. "Charles Schroder. You all may know him better as Charlie."

There was a collective gasp. Veronica felt her stomach drop. *Charlie? Charlie's also a spy? Working for Ari and Jonah? Charlie Schroder?* Veronica remembered how he'd appeared in Schwinn's office the night of the séance. He said he'd seen the light in the window and came to check—but had he been on a mission of his own?

"We've begun the process of having him liquidated."

At that, whispers broke out. *What did it mean?* Veronica thought. *He can't be talking about . . .*

Schwinn gestured for silence. "In the meantime," he said in a more neutral voice, "we have the upcoming election to be concerned with. We have to make certain Wendell Willkie wins on November fourth." There was a groan from the audience. "Yes, I know we'd prefer Charles Lindbergh—or even Taft or Dewey—but Willkie is the nominee, whether we like it or not."

"Should have been Lindbergh!" one man shouted from the back. The aviator's recent speech in Des Moines had sparked a firestorm.

In it, Lindbergh had blamed Jews for the outbreak of the war in Europe, and intimated they were in control of the Roosevelt administration. The very same claims being made by Adolf Hitler and his fellow Nazis in Berlin. In Veronica's opinion, Lindbergh was wrong—so wrong—to use the religion and race of a group in the discussion of domestic and foreign policy. And even America First had put out a statement after Lindbergh's remarks, asserting the organization was not anti-Semitic. However, they blamed the interventionists for inserting "the race issue" into the "discussion of war or peace."

A murmur of approval ran through the audience. "And if Roosevelt wins?" Nora Ingle called out. "Maybe this time we could . . . make some *real* changes?" She lifted her chin.

"Don't worry, my dear," he told her. "All in good time."

✻ ✻ ✻

AT SEASIDE HOSPITAL in Long Beach, Charlie Schroder was dying. His room faced west, catching golden sunlight through the gauzy curtains, illuminating the narrow enamel bed and IV bag. Ari Lewis sat at his bedside, wearing his yarmulke, murmuring the *Mi Sheberach,* the Jewish prayer for the sick. He finished with a soft "Amen."

Charlie blinked up at him. "Thanks for coming to my big send-off, boss." He grimaced. "But you could have been saying anything," he joked in a weak voice. "I bet you were listing what you're going to pick up from the grocery on your way home."

"Shh, save your energy," Ari told the man.

Charlie had felt stomach pains early that morning; thinking nothing of them, he continued with his work, until he was so ill he took to his bed in the late morning. His wife had called an ambulance, and he'd been admitted to the Seaside Hospital before noon. Blood tests showed he'd been poisoned; the doctors thought he had only a few more days to live.

"We're an odd pair, aren't we?" Charlie said, looking out the window.

"I'll say," Ari said, straightening the gray hospital blanket. "KKK member no. 31712!"

"It was only because I hated communism," Charlie told him. "And I was young. Stupid. But I'll defy with my last breath anyone who tells me the Jews are connected to the communist movement. Or that the coloreds or Orientals are in any way inferior." His voice gave out.

"Sometimes saints come in unexpected forms," Ari told him softly. "Sometimes they seem like just the opposite." He noticed Charlie's lips were dry. "Water?"

Charlie nodded. Ari held the glass and Charlie took a small sip. "It's my fault, not yours," he said. "They got me on my spending. Steamed open my bills, found out that I was investing in the stock market." He shook his head. "I thought my money would be safe there, but they found it. When they saw the money you guys pay me, they knew . . ." He was unable to say more.

"It's all right," Ari told him. "You're a hero, Charlie. A true patriot."

As Charlie fell into a labored sleep, his wife appeared at the door. She looked exhausted, her dress wrinkled and makeup mussed. "Who are you?" she asked, suspicious.

"A friend," Ari told her, his eyes sad. He stood. "Your husband's a good man."

She nodded, then walked to the seat Ari had left empty, picking up and holding her husband's hand. Ari turned and walked out, pulling his hat down low over his face.

*   *   *

VERONICA AND JONAH met that evening on the bluff at the northern end of Palisades Park, near a totem pole carved and painted with a raven, fish, bear, and wolf. They overlooked the highway and the Santa Monica pier to the south, the mountains to the north. The cool breeze was tinged with salt.

Veronica could see the blue-green waves with foaming white-caps and hear their rhythmic crash on the beach. "Charlie Schroder's being 'liquidated,'" she told him. "He may already be dead."

"I know," Jonah said. "We know. Ari called me from the hospital earlier." Pigeons and seagulls flew in formations; like Messerschmitts and Spitfires, they hunted in packs.

Veronica took in the news of Charlie's imminent death as she stared over the horizon. She felt tears come to her eyes and blinked them away. It seemed clear enough one could almost see the Hawaiian Islands. "Schwinn used the word *liquidated*"—she stumbled over it this time—"in the meeting. When I asked him later, he said something about Charlie having a stomach bug?"

Jonah's face was impassive. "We believe Charlie was compromised and poisoned."

Veronica watched as yellow- and red-painted buoys bobbed in the water. "Was Charlie really a spy? One of us?"

Jonah sighed. "Yes."

"And you couldn't have mentioned that?" They both stopped talking as a small boy, with a yellow Labrador puppy on a leash, ran past them and the carved totem pole.

"It would have endangered both of you."

Veronica sat, staring out at the ocean, as screaming seagulls hovered and dove for a fish. In the distance, she spotted a red boat making its way to shore. "I'm so sorry. Charlie was . . . nice. I always thought he was funny." Then, "That could have been my mother, killed. Murdered." She began again: "It could have been me."

"It could have, but it wasn't. But we need to be careful."

"Do you think it's satisfied them? The blood sacrifice?"

Jonah sighed. "They're definitely on high alert, especially with the election coming up. Anything else mentioned in the meeting?"

"More things are going unsaid. My fear is that if the election goes for Roosevelt—and it's looking like it will—they'll plan something big in response. May already be planning it. Nora Ingle and Will Wagner seemed to intimate they wanted something to happen."

"How is Wagner?" Jonah asked.

"Fine," she said carefully. "Number two at Deutsches Haus now, just behind Schwinn."

"What's he been talking about?"

"Besides the usual? He's thinking of buying a motorbike. Or he's bought a motorcycle, I'm not sure. It seems . . . out of character."

Jonah considered. "Any of his friends getting motorcycles?"

"Yes, and they're planning some sort of trip to Lake Tahoe, which I find hard to imagine, as I can't believe he'd ever let a helmet muss that perfectly lacquered hair."

"Armed motorcycle brigade would be a way to spread terror," Jonah said. "And they could protect marchers. It's something we saw being done in Germany."

"I'll keep an ear to the ground."

"Is he still . . . interested?"

"Yes."

"Well," Jonah said, also looking out to the horizon, "keep him interested."

"Of course." They both fell silent as a young man and woman passed, holding hands. How simple and easy it must be for them, Veronica thought, feeling wistful. She looked at Jonah's hands, his long and tapered fingers. The strangeness of their situation brought them a peculiar intimacy.

The sun was sinking lower in the sky and the wind picked up. A group of lean young men ran into the water with their surf-boards, paddling out to catch the last waves. "Why don't we ever talk about you, Jonah?"

"I'm not the spy."

"You could be. You have the poker face for it." She stuck out her neck and hunched her shoulders, pulling a long and serious face. "I'm Jonah Rose," she said, doing her best Jonah impression, scowling and dropping her voice down into the bass register. "I wear a leather jacket. I'm too cool for you. By the way, were you followed?"

He couldn't help it; he laughed. It was a big laugh, hearty and genuine. She laughed along with him, relieved to see his façade crack. She noticed that when he laughed, he looked boyish, hand-some, even.

"All right, you got me," he said finally, pushing his hair out of his eyes. "I'm doing my job. We—I—can't complicate things."

"What does that mean?" *Is he having "complicated" thoughts about me as well?*

"It means we're strictly professional. We have a . . . unique rela-tionship," he admitted. "It's intimate. But still professional—"

"It's a bond," Veronica finished.

Jonah swallowed. "If Wagner does make . . . demands . . . on you, you'll have to decide how to proceed."

She felt nauseated. "I'm not going to sleep with him, if that's what you're thinking!" *Is he crazy?*

"If you and he break up, he could be a dangerous enemy. And—" He swallowed. "If you do sleep with him, it . . . would allow you to become more intimate. He might tell you information we can use. Like if they're planning something for after the election. The more we know, the more lives may be saved."

The wind picked up. "So, you want me to fuck him for democracy? Lie back and think of George Washington?"

"Hey!"

"Well, that's what you're saying, isn't it?"

Jonah reddened. "It's your decision, of course."

She felt ill. "I could always tell him I have my period," she said. "Although it's only going to work once a month." She half joked to hide her hurt feelings.

"Everything you're doing is tremendously important, okay?"

"Right. I deserve a goddamned medal."

Jonah leaned forward, his elbows to his knees. "We can't play by the rules," he said quietly.

"There's a difference between breaking rules and . . . sleeping with someone."

"Well, you don't actually have to sleep with him." He looked uncomfortable. "Like I said, it's your decision."

"Damn right it is." Two ravens flew overhead, settling in a nearby cypress tree, preening.

"Veronica . . ." Jonah reached for her hand, but she pulled away.

"How would you feel?" she asked him. "If I slept with him? If I allowed his . . . demands?"

"I'd feel terrible," he said honestly. "If you want to quit now, you can. I'll understand. Ari will understand, too. Especially in light of . . . Charlie."

She suddenly understood he didn't like this at all. But it was war. This was the job. And it was his job to ask her. And her job to fight.

"I'm not quitting," she told him. She rose and brushed off her skirt, feeling hurt and somehow ashamed, even though she'd done nothing wrong. Without saying goodbye, she began walking back toward Santa Monica.

* * *

LATER THAT EVENING, at the beer garden outside Deutsches Haus, Vi and Veronica sipped gimlets with Nora Ingle. "You know all of Deutsches Haus is bugged by the FBI now?" Nora was telling them. "Schwinn told me. There are clicks on the lines, so everyone knows to be careful about what they say. You can't trust anyone. Jewsevelt doesn't care about our privacy. Hoover either." She stabbed at the table with a scarlet-painted nail. "We have rights!"

"Do you really think so?" Vi asked. "I mean, the clicks could just be operators on the line, putting the calls through."

Nora sniffed. "Those FBI agents are no better than schoolboys," she said with contempt. "One of them's parked outside—with a visible wire going from Schwinn's office to his car below! I mean, can you believe?" She shook her head. "The fools."

Veronica and Vi exchanged looks. "That seems . . . amateurish," Veronica offered finally.

"It's almost adorable—like the Keystone Cops." Nora laughed. "Apparently, they had so much trouble disconnecting the wire, Schwinn gave them extra time when he left his office last night." Another giggle. "He wanted to give them enough time to follow him, which I think is sporting of him."

Veronica took a slice of lemon and squeezed it over the fried schnitzel she'd ordered. "Absolutely."

"Ah, I miss eating whatever I want and staying slim," Nora said wistfully. She and Vi had cucumber salads. "When I was in my early twenties, I loved ice cream. Ate it all the time. Now I can't touch it."

"Oh, I understand, believe me," Vi said, nodding.

"By the way," Nora offered, spearing a round of cucumber. "You're both suspected of being spies as well."

Veronica almost dropped her fork. "What?" Next to her, Vi blanched.

Nora didn't seem to notice. "Yes, but everyone's being considered. I'm even being considered. I wouldn't worry about it." She lowered her voice. "But I can't believe our Charlie was the mole.

Still," she said, smiling coldly, "you'll want to watch out . . . People have been saying some very unkind things about you."

Veronica forced herself not to clench her jaw. "Who?"

"Sorry—can't say. But I'd advise you to be careful." The effort of trying not to scream as she processed Nora's revelation was almost beyond Veronica.

When they could leave, Veronica and Violet got on the first trolley they found. As the car swayed under them, Veronica realized anew how the smallest inconsistency, the tiniest slip, could cause their entire, carefully fabricated existence to unravel, just like an embroidered cherry blossom.

CHAPTER TWENTY-THREE

"Where are we going?" Veronica asked. Will had picked her up from Tommy's Diner in his freshly waxed and polished BMW convertible, roof down, and they were driving north along the Pacific Coast Highway. Above them, the hot blue sky was dusted with high cirrus clouds. She was wearing round tortoiseshell sunglasses, and her hair was covered by a floral silk scarf tied tightly under the chin. If she'd been with anyone else, it would have been a glorious day out. But despite her sunny expression, her jaw was clenched.

"Somebody has been saying some very unkind things about you." For days, Nora's comment had been haunting Veronica. *What did she mean? Is it just gossip, or am I being watched, suspected?* She decided she'd find out.

"I really shouldn't show you—but I can't resist!" Will turned to her and winked. He was wearing an off-white linen suit and a red pocket square, his white-blond hair shining in the sun. When he caught her staring, she forced herself to smile. "The sea air agrees with you."

"You as well." He picked up her hand and kissed it. "We're going to have such fun!"

They turned right onto a small, dusty unmarked road, and Veronica's skin prickled. "Where are we going?" she asked again.

"You'll see!" She tried to slow her beating heart by admiring the tall sycamore trees. They came to black iron gates with two guards in armbands, who nodded to Will and opened them, waving both in. She couldn't stop the dread seeping into her, moving like ice water through her veins. "Are we visiting someone?"

"Not exactly." They passed a large wooden sign with MURPHY RANCH in carved Germanic letters. They pulled into a circular gravel driveway, up to an enormous house. *It's more like a mansion,* Veronica thought as she took the scarf off her hair. The car came to a stop.

"Here we are!" Will said as he came around to open her door and help her out. "The perfect place for a picnic."

A small gathering was already under way: women in sundresses and straw hats were setting out plates of food, while men in dungarees and plaid shirts lit firecrackers in the pollen-flecked sunlight. Birds warbled in the surrounding circle of sycamores, oaks, and eucalypti and tangled thickets of wild grapes. There were picnic tables and chairs set up, large barbecue grills with the coals already smoking. Small children played tagalong with a good-natured German shepherd. A group of teenage girls had spread a blanket beneath a tree and were braiding each other's hair. A little ways away, their male counterparts shot guns at targets.

"That's the *jungend* shooting," he said, pointing to the boys. "Practice for *der Tag.*"

What day? Which *day?* Veronica thought, but said nothing.

Everything shimmered. "The sunlight's extraordinary here, isn't it?" Will commented. "I want to bring my paints and easel someday."

Veronica breathed in the warm air, even as the hairs on her forearms stood on end. "I . . . don't think it's quite finished," she said, looking up at the ranch.

"Oh, it will be soon," Will told her.

In the distance, Veronica saw McDonnell overseeing the boys' shooting practice.

"There are meetings every week for boys and girls—two hours of political instruction and sport every Saturday afternoon. Fifty-mile hikes on the weekends. Camping over the holidays," Will told her.

"Is it just open on weekends?"

"During the week there are all kinds of things going on here for the *sportabteilung*—target practice, drills in street fighting, hand-to-hand combat, knives, jujitsu, you name it."

Veronica saw old cans riddled with bullet holes. *Live ammunition,* she realized. *This is a paramilitary training camp.* "Do they keep the guns here?" she asked, as they strolled toward the house and its massive front double door.

"Ah, that's not something a pretty girl needs to know." He patted her hand. "But rest assured," he told her, "when *der Tag* comes, we'll be prepared. We have brigades in New York, Boston, and the South. Vancouver and Toronto, too."

"Goodness." She wanted to keep him talking. "Where do they even get the weapons to practice with? Can't be easy, can it?"

"Well, it's difficult to smuggle weapons into the United States on ships," he admitted. "They have to go through the Panama Canal, where their cargo's checked. Most of our guns come from Mexico and Canada. Of course, a lot of the men have their personal weapons. The climate's dry here, so it won't affect ammunition, but we're building a special temperature-controlled storage unit, just to make sure." He smiled as he opened the front door and let her in.

Veronica nodded. "What's happening on '*der Tag*'?"

"At some point, the Red Revolution will lead to a Nazi seizure of the American government—'*der Tag*.' Our goal's to take out Roosevelt and install a temporary dictatorship—to eliminate the communists and Jews. Then we'll go back to democracy—but with only white men voting."

Oh, scheisse. "And these men are from Deutsches Haus? The Bund?" she asked carefully.

"Yes—but also the Silver Shirts, Copperheads, KKK, you name it. Some police and FBI agents as well. Politicians." He was gleeful. "All of us."

Veronica nodded. "Of course."

"We're using the cell system used by Hitler in the twenties— preparing for the day when physical violence will be necessary to rescue our country." He took her hand and led her through the shell of a soaring atrium. The floor was covered in sawdust and smelled of raw wood.

"Well, this will be grand when it's finally done," Veronica offered. She swallowed.

"It should be grand—for the *führer*."

Veronica's mind stopped working for a moment, then resumed. "For whom?" She was sure she'd heard wrong.

"For Herr Hitler—when he comes to the West Coast."

"Why . . . would he come to the West Coast of the United States of America?"

"It's an excellent halfway point between Germany and Japan," Will told her. In one of the main rooms, there was a huge stone fireplace. "Someday this will be a house for Hitler and his men. Twenty-two bedrooms! And it's all self-sustaining—there's a water storage tank, power station, and oil tank. There will be orchards and fields for crops and animals."

"I see," she said gently, as though talking to someone mentally unstable. *Which, I suppose, he is.* "And when is Herr Hitler arriving?"

"After he wins the war, of course. Now you see why it's so important to keep the U.S. out of it."

"Yes, of course," Veronica said in soothing tones. "Tell me more about this place."

"First, I want to show you something." He led her through unfinished room after unfinished room, the floors covered in sawdust, until they reached the kitchen.

"Almost there!" he told her, as they went to the back garden. From there, they took a newly made path down the side of a ravine.

"You should have told me to wear flats!" Veronica said, almost tripping on a tree root. *Where the hell are we going?* she kept thinking. *And what's going to happen when we get there?* She feared the worst. *Does Will suspect anything?*

She heard men's voices; they came to a sandy patch of open land with a shed made from wood and corrugated sheet metal. Veronica recognized a few of the men from Deutsches Haus, as well as Schwinn in a gray linen suit. They were clustered around a young man her own age, his shirtsleeves rolled up, revealing skinny fore-arms. *Marv Whiteside.*

"It's good you're here!" Schwinn called to them. "We're almost ready!"

"What is this?" Veronica asked. She saw a wall of sandbags, as well as something that looked like one of those rocket ships on the cover of *Amazing Stories,* a magazine devoted to Jules Verne– and H. G. Wells–inspired fantasy stories about space flight, with huge guns, antigravity devices, and occult rays. She remembered its motto: "Extravagant Fiction Today—Cold Fact Tomorrow."

Will gestured grandly. "The future."

"Is that . . ." Veronica began. *No, it couldn't be.*

He leaned in, and she caught the whiff of starched linen and brilliantine and felt his breath warm in her ear. "Just wait."

* * *

VIOLET GRACE WAS on her knees. At Nora Ingle's house in the Pacific Palisades, the two women were in the dressing room and Vi was taking up the hem of Nora's new dress. "I can't thank you enough, Vi," Nora was saying. "It's Chanel, you know—from her new collection. I couldn't let just anyone touch it."

Vi, mouth full of pins, managed an "Mm-hmm." The room was small and intimate, with gold Chinese screens, glossy black surfaces, and a sitting area with a silver suede sofa.

As Nora looked down, she smiled. "We need to get you your own shop, Vi. Your own atelier!"

When all the pins had been inserted, Vi sat back on her heels. "You're all set. Please take it off, and I'll do the sewing tonight."

"You're a doll! An absolute doll!"

As Nora went into the enormous marble bathroom to change, Vi had a chance to look around the dressing room. It was impeccably organized, with clothes on matching wooden hangers, all ordered by color, from simple day dresses to silk and chiffon evening gowns. There were shelves of leather and satin shoes, as well as crocodile and alligator bags on display. On an ebony-and-bone dresser were photographs—Nora and her husband on their wedding day; Nora with Hitler and a tall, glamorous blonde somewhere with an incredible view of the Alps—as well as tarot cards and a cloisonné pillbox. A mirrored tray held bottles of Chanel's No. 5, Schiaparelli's Shocking, and Tabu.

"You'll need a shop in Berlin, too, of course," Nora was saying through the door. "I've been thinking if things go south here, after the election, I'll take a little trip to Germany. Would you like to come with me? I'd adore some company."

"Go to . . . Berlin?" Vi had no illusions of actual friendship. She knew she was being picked up, like a shiny penny. In all their time together, Nora had never asked her where she lived, about her late husband, about her family—anything about herself. She existed simply to make beautiful clothes and provide an admiring glance and sympathetic ear. *Which is all you need as a spy,* Vi reassured herself. "That's quite a generous offer. But I do have Veronica to take care of."

"Veronica's a grown woman," Nora told her, stepping out from the bathroom in a black silk robe festooned with red dragons. She saw Vi looking at the photos. "Oh, that's Clara Hess," she said, pointing to the blonde in the photograph. "She'd just adore you! I'll introduce you two in Berlin."

"I'm not sure what Veronica and I'll do if Roosevelt wins," Vi mused, returning the tomato-and-strawberry pincushion back to her sewing box.

"Well, things seem to be going swimmingly for Veronica and Will."

"He's . . . a bit older than she is."

"He's established," Nora countered, settling in on the sofa. From a side table, she found a pack of gold-tipped cigarettes and lit a Sobranie. "What a handsome couple they make. Surely wedding bells can't be too far in the future?"

"When exactly is this trip to Berlin?" Vi asked, perching delicately on the sofa's edge.

Nora picked a stray piece of tobacco off her tongue with one hand, tapping the ashes impatiently into a Waterford ashtray. "Well, it all depends on the election, of course."

"What do you think's going to happen?"

Nora's face shuttered. "I think Willkie's going to win," she said, her face hard. "But if he doesn't, we have plans, big plans, for if and when that happens." She smiled. "You'll see!"

* * *

IN THE CLEARING in the Pacific Palisades, Veronica and Will waited behind the wall of sandbags for Whiteside to begin. She could see tanks, pipes, and other equipment she didn't recognize. At the center was what she could only assume was a rocket attached to a tall stand with a motor connected by four hoses and spidery wires.

Veronica could feel the anticipation in the air as the rest of the men moved behind the sandbags. She watched as Whiteside connected and tightened the lines, checked valves and meters and pressure gauges. "Welcome to the testing of the prototype of my new rocket motor," he said to them. "I'm calling her the Hermes, after the Greek god of flight—and I have to thank Captain Hermann Schwinn and so many people at Deutsches Haus for the funding to

build her. It's great to be taken seriously here, especially after getting laughed at by those eggheads at Caltech."

He rubbed sweat from his face. "Despite what you may have
heard, rocketry's a legitimate science. It deserves respect and
support—and I'm so grateful to have found it here, with you." He
grinned, turning some of the valve wheels, then rushed back behind the sandbags to turn a few more gauges.

"Here we go!" he shouted over the hissing. "Three, two,
one . . ."

He lit a wooden match and touched it to the fuse, which ran to
the rocket. An orange-and-blue flame burned and pushed up into
a column as the pressure gauges strained. Veronica watched as the
red needles of the gauges recorded the pressure—rising, rising,
rising—until the glass coverings broke.

"Thrust is two hundred pounds!" Whiteside crowed. "Enough
thrust to reach the ionosphere!"

She realized the rocket wasn't meant to lift at this point—but if
the pressure was that high, who knew how high and far it could go.
*Could a rocket from Germany reach Britain? Could it someday reach the
United States?*

There was a wave of applause, and Whiteside blushed. Schwinn
popped open a bottle of Champagne as one of the men passed out
glasses. "To the moon!" Whiteside toasted when each glass was
filled.

"To the moon!" Veronica toasted, still overwhelmed by the
implications. *What if this really does work? What would the Nazis do
with it?*

"Your fellow 'rocketeer' in Peenemünde, Wernher von Braun,
will be pleased to hear of your success here," Schwinn said. He
raised his glass high. "To weapons!"

"Oh, but I'm not political," Whiteside clarified. "I'm a scientist."

"Well, then—to science!" Schwinn said, clapping him on the
back. "But with military application."

Veronica felt her blood run cold, but she looked him in the eye, smiled, raised her glass and drank, then again looked Schwinn in the eye in an old-fashioned German way. "To science!"

* * *

LATER THAT AFTERNOON, back at the ranch, Will had procured another bottle of Champagne and led her up to one of the ranch's bedrooms. She made herself take a sip, although she couldn't taste it at all. She hadn't eaten and felt the acid plummet to her stomach.

He looked her dead in the eye as he sat on the bed's bare mattress. *"Prost."*

"Prost," she echoed.

"People have been warning me you might be a spy," he said after they each took another sip.

She swallowed calmly, even though she felt an explosion of panic in her heart. "Who?" she said, setting her glass down on the floor so he wouldn't see her hand shake. "Who would say such a thing?"

"Doesn't matter," he told her. "But I know you're not. That's why I brought you here. To see everything. To see the ranch, to see the rocket. Come, sit," he said, patting the spot next to him.

Veronica forced herself to sit next to him and not tense. She forced her shoulders to lower. But it was impossible to shake the tension in her clenched stomach. He put an arm around her, kissed her gently, then again with more force, running a hand down to her breast.

"As long as you're with me, you're protected." He lowered her down on the bed and shoved a thigh between her legs. She rolled onto her back, looking up at the unfinished ceiling. *It's a job,* she thought. Outside, she could hear the low hum of people's voices and a few men singing a German drinking song. "Wait!" she cried out finally. "Do you have a condom?"

He pushed back his white-blond hair. "Oh, that's so bourgeois."

"Well, bourgeois or not, I'm not about to get knocked up."

He tried kissing her neck. "Hitler wants us to have as many Aryan babies as possible . . ."

"Hitler," she stated firmly, "is not going to have to face my mother when I tell her I'm pregnant out of wedlock."

"Fine," he said. "Do this—" He took her hand and guided it to his fly. He made her rub up and down, then let go. She gritted her teeth and continued, pulling the zipper down.

It was all over quicker than she expected. "Sorry." His face was red, his brow sweaty. "You made me wait too long."

Veronica wiped her hand on the mattress, then took a long gulp of Champagne. "So . . ." she said, doing her best to smile even though she felt ill. "Tell me more about *der Tag*? When will Hitler come? Will there be a big party? And will we be invited?"

"Of course, *schatzi*," he told her, kissing her full on the lips. "But for now, let's go down and join in the fun."

* * *

BACK AT THE house that evening, in the shower, Veronica scrubbed herself with scalding water, trying to wash away the feeling of his meaty hands and sour wine mouth.

All that Will had told her, all the weaponry, the rocket, the idea of Hitler in Los Angeles, the idea people thought she was a spy for the Jews—it all swept over her. The Champagne, bitter and acidic, came up as she was racked with sobs.

When there was nothing left inside her, she turned off the water and slid down to the floor, numb with shock. She felt her two worlds crash into each other. She stayed there for minutes, maybe hours, until finally Vi returned.

Seeing Veronica on the floor, she knelt and wiped Veronica's mouth, gave her a glass of water, pressed a cold washcloth to her forehead. Veronica curled up into her lap as best she could, as though she were still a little girl.

"It's all right, sweetie, it's all right," Vi told Veronica, and held her as she cried. When Veronica was too tired to sob anymore, Vi helped her upstairs and into her twin bed, where she crawled in beside her, stroking her hair until she finally fell asleep.

CHAPTER TWENTY-FOUR

In Deutsches Haus's beer garden the next day, Donald and Harriet McDonnell were sitting at a small iron table with Hermann Schwinn. For lunch, they'd been served mugs of frothing beer and plates of "heaven and hell"—baked apples and clouds of mashed potato—alongside *blutwurst,* blood sausage.

"How're our *jugend* coming along?" Schwinn asked.

"Excellent!" McDonnell took a sip of beer. "Those boys are fantastic marksmen now, even moving targets at a great distance. They're also tougher, leaner, harder," he said proudly. "Just like their counterparts in the Reich. They'll be ready."

As Schwinn nodded, Harriet couldn't contain herself. "Our Band of German American Maidens are coming along as well." Modeled after the Nazi's Bund Deutscher Mädel, the group's goal was to groom young women for marriage, motherhood, and domestic life, with a strong dose of "racial hygiene."

Schwinn took a bite of *blutwurst.* "Well, they're looking into my citizenship status."

"But everything's all right, isn't it?" Harriet asked. "I mean, you're German—surely all the *i*'s are dotted and *t*'s are crossed?"

"Yes, but the feds have gotten the Immigration and Naturalization Service to build a case against me," Schwinn said. "They want me deported. Of course I'll fight them in court."

"Make sure you've got an Aryan judge." McDonnell wiped his lips on his red-checked napkin. "First thing we do when we're in power is stock the courts with good, solid Americans we can depend on."

"The thing is," Schwinn admitted, "when I first signed my naturalization papers, back in '32, I may have . . . stretched the truth a bit. I told them I'd been in L.A. since '26 instead of '27—because that would have left me three months shy of residency here."

"Three months?" Harriet said, outraged. "What's three months? Pfft! That's nothing!"

"They're saying it was 'illegally procured,'" he said, putting down his fork and pushing his plate away. "I also failed to 'disclose,' as they say, my Nazi activities in Germany and here—another strike against me."

"Why should you have to be ashamed of your Nazi background?" McDonnell asked.

"Exactly! This is America! But the bad news is, now the court appearances are taking up all my time. I know Wagner's stepped up." Schwinn looked to McDonnell. "I'm counting on you, too, my friend."

"Of course," McDonnell answered solemnly. Harriet glowed with pride. "You know you can count on me."

"We all heard what happened with Charlie Schroder," Harriet said, toying with her half-pint glass of beer. "Do you really think you've cleared out all the spies?"

"What are you saying?" Schwinn asked.

McDonnell groaned. "Not this again . . ."

"He has a right to know," Harriet insisted.

Schwinn's eyes narrowed. "Know what?"

McDonnell sighed. "Harriet has a bee in her bonnet about the Grace girls, Veronica and Vi."

"There's something fishy about them, I know it," she said. "They came in too fast, got too friendly with too many people. Now they're accepted and respected, and they've only been here, what, four months?"

Schwinn took a sip of beer. "Do you really think women could be spies?"

"Look at what I'm doing for our cause, what my sister's doing!" Harriet exclaimed. "Look at what Nora Ingle is doing! Yes, I'd say women can be spies and government infiltrators—just as they can be patriots."

"Government infiltrator I can understand, at least. But working for Jews? Like Lewis?" He shook his head. "That's a step too far."

McDonnell raised his hand to indicate to a waitress he wanted another beer.

"Do you have any proof? Because they're obviously not Jewish," Schwinn said.

"They came from New York . . ." Harriet said ominously.

"They knew the Bund in Yorkville!" McDonnell countered.

She raised an eyebrow. "Did they really?"

"But they're obviously fine specimens of Aryan woman-hood . . ." Schwinn said.

"Are they?" Harriet questioned. "And Veronica uses my note-pads for stenography and I've noticed that some of the pages have been ripped out."

"Really?" McDonnell said. "She said you were using the papers for your recipes."

"I would do no such thing with your meeting notepads!" she exclaimed.

"Well, why don't you do some looking around then, Harriet," Schwinn told her, his tone patronizing, as he motioned for the check. "See what you come up with, hmm?"

"Well," Harriet said with a tight smile. "Maybe I will."

* * *

THE STREAMLINED, MODERNE-STYLE Aero Theatre, its name a tribute to the aerospace industry, was located on Montana Avenue in Santa Monica. It had originally opened in 1939 as a twenty-four-hour movie theater for round-the-clock Douglas Aircraft Company workers. It was not, Veronica knew, one of the ones Will had dealings with. There was one screen, playing *'Til We Meet Again,* a romance with Merle Oberon and George Brent as star-crossed lovers.

Veronica realized the theater was new when she walked in, pocketing her ticket—everything was shiny and sparkling. There were only a few people in the theater, which smelled of buttered popcorn and cigarette smoke. She made a swift head count of the audience, as well as the four exits, before taking her seat. But before the film started, there were newsreels from Pathé. Veronica watched as Hitler, Churchill, Mussolini, Pétain, Heydrich, Gandhi, King George, and Pope Pius flashed across the screen—newspaper head-lines come to life.

Although Veronica loved words, she could understand how a picture could be worth a thousand of them. As she watched RAF fighters and Messerschmidts being blown up over the skies of Lon-don, she was aware of a figure sliding in next to her: Jonah, long and lanky, a wary look in his eyes, wearing khaki trousers and a white shirt and tie, his battered leather jacket draped over his arm. He pulled out a paper-wrapped tinfoil roll. "Life Saver?" he whis-pered.

"What flavor?"

"Cryst-O-Mint."

"Okay." She accepted one and popped it in her mouth. The mint was almost painfully strong. He took one as well. On screen, *Movietone News,* narrated by Lowell Thomas, played "The Battle of Britain."

They both turned their eyes to the screen. *"From the chalk cliffs of Dover, Britain's famous ramparts, they see a convoy of ships and squad-rons of Nazi warplanes swooping to the attack. The Straits of Dover is the hot spot of the English Channel."* Veronica turned to look at Jonah, his high cheekbones accentuated in the silvery light, so he looked al-most alien.

"The Royal Air Force goes into swift action, speeding to the attack. The British fighting planes engage the enemy in an air battle. Scenes like this are witnessed again and again . . ."

They watched as barrage balloons were attacked and shot down. They witnessed a hit—incendiary bullets setting a Messerschmidt on fire. It spiraled, finally crashing to the ground in a burst of flames, one more wreckage of a German plane strewn along the coast of Dover to a trumpet fanfare.

So different from the newsclips Will was showing at the Continental theater, she thought, realizing how powerful images were. *But that's over there,* Veronica thought. *Here, in a dark theater, people are sitting on velvet seats, watching while eating candy and popcorn.* As horrible as it was to see, it was still not reality. Not in Los Angeles. Not yet.

"You look terrible," he told her.

"Trouble sleeping last night." She was glad she didn't have to make eye contact. She gave him a completely factual and unemotional summary of everything she'd learned at the Murphy Ranch, including extensive details about Whiteside's rocket and the fact the Nazis were funding him and sharing his findings with Wernher von Braun.

"You haven't said anything about Wagner," Jonah said finally.

Veronica swallowed. "Do you want every little detail? Would that make you happy? The wine we drank? How I'd rate his performance?" She wanted to tell him everything, to unburden herself, almost as much as she wanted to keep everything bottled up, secret.

He looked at her. "Do you think I want you to sleep with him? I don't even want you to be in the same room with him! It makes me sick."

"Do I make you sick?" she asked. "Now that I've . . . touched him?"

"No," he told her, bringing his face close to hers. "Never."

Her shame melted away. She both wanted to tell him every sordid detail and pretend it never happened. A man a few rows in front of them had looked back a couple of times while they'd been speaking. He looked again and this time got up and made his way up the aisle.

Suddenly, Jonah brushed back Veronica's hair and kissed her on the mouth. The connection between them made the heat rise to the surface of her skin and her mind churn with possibilities. *He tastes like mint,* she thought in shock. He used his hands to hide her face. When the man had left, Jonah released her. They kissed again, as if a floodgate had been opened. Yet even as she did, a part of her still held back. Sensing it, he drew away.

How she felt about him was mixed up with everything happening around her. Britain was holding on for dear life as they watched on, helpless. Los Angeles was filled with Nazis and fascist-leaning Americans. But out of the horror came the opportunity to work with Jonah—and the feeling of being seen and understood. Of making a difference, no matter how small. There might be no future between them, no future at all, but time seemed to have slowed down for a moment. *This is the work we're doing; this is now. No matter what else happens going forward, Jonah and Los Angeles and the war are forever tangled up together inside of me.*

Finally, she drew back and looked at him, wondering how she ever found his eyes enigmatic, because now she could read them clearly. She reached for his face and traced a line down his chin. "Want to get a drink?" he asked.

Is he nuts? "Where could we possibly go and get a drink?"

"I'm going to leave now," he told her. "Meet me in twenty minutes on the corner of Euclid Court and Alta Avenue. I'll be driving a navy blue Plymouth."

* * *

JONAH BROUGHT THE car to a stop on Mulholland. The sun was setting in a burst of crimson over the horizon, illuminating the Hollywoodland sign. They watched as the light faded from the horizon and the city and car lights turned on, dotting the vista like fireflies greeting the night. They regarded each other in the dim light. Veronica was suddenly aware of the stubble on Jonah's face.

"I hate him, you know," Veronica said without preamble. "He makes me sick."

Jonah nodded. "If it makes you feel any better, I hate him, too."

As the indigo sky turned black, they kissed in the growing darkness, claiming each other. Softly at first, then with increasing passion, as if together they could erase Will's touch. Veronica helped him take off his jacket, pulling him on top of her. Beneath him, she felt the length of his body. Dizzy and reckless, she wondered if she might be falling in love with him—or if he was just the only person in the world who could understand her and what she was going through. But whether it was the mission or Jonah or just her needing comfort, did it really matter?

Afterward, as they caught their breath, Jonah opened the glove compartment and pulled out a silver flask. "Bourbon?" he asked, handing it to her. "I did promise you a drink."

She took it. "Thanks." The liquid burned her throat.

Jonah turned on the radio, and Tommy Dorsey's orchestra began to play.

"What are you going to do about Marv and his rockets?" she asked. "I've heard a lot of talk and a lot of chatter about *der Tag,* but this—an unmanned long-range missile—this could change the course of the war. It's all I could think about when we watched those newsreels—what if Germany could reach Britain? The fight would be over before it even began. And then what? Who will they bomb? They could launch them off ships to hit New York and Washington . . ."

"I know," he said, taking her hand. "You did well in getting the information. Now we need to tell Ari."

CHAPTER TWENTY-FIVE

Vi knew it was coming, but she was shocked to hear a commotion when she was eating lunch with Nora Ingle at the restaurant at Deutsches Haus. They both left their meals and peeked into the lobby to see Agent Doolin, along with four additional agents, enter. Doolin flashed his badge and a warrant, that said he had reasonable grounds to suspect that Hermann Schwinn had violated United States law, to the woman at the front desk and asked for the captain.

Vi realized Doolin most likely wanted to make the arrest in public, so Schwinn couldn't charge the FBI with any sort of abuse. The woman at the front desk blanched when she saw his identification, then picked up the telephone receiver and dialed a few numbers.

"Please tell Captain Schwinn he has a guest—a gentleman from the FBI." She hung up the receiver. "He'll be with you shortly."

Vi spotted Schwinn at the top of the stairs, legs wide, fists on his hips. "Captain Schwinn?" Doolin called. Schwinn glared. "We're going to need you to come with us."

Everyone in the lobby turned to stare.

"And why on earth should I do that?" Schwinn said, his eyes darting around the lobby.

Doolin pulled out an envelope from his suit's breast pocket. "Because we have a warrant for your arrest."

"Ridiculous," Schwinn taunted, not moving. "I don't believe you."

"You can tell us about your naturalization papers all you'd like back at the Bureau office," Doolin told him in a measured voice. All conversation had ceased, and his voice echoed on the marble. "Don't make us come up there, Captain Schwinn."

"This is just some wire-pulling by that Jew, Ari Lewis," Schwinn reassured people as he walked down the stairs. Vi cringed when she heard the name and forced herself to keep a blank expression. One of the agents handcuffed Schwinn, and two others escorted him out, with Doolin bringing up the rear.

Veronica had come out from the upstairs secretaries' area and was watching from the balcony with a few others, including Will Wagner. He watched Schwinn and the officers leave, then snapped, "Meeting! Conference room! Now!" He gestured to Veronica. "I'll need you to take notes."

Veronica and her mother exchanged glances. *Be careful,* Vi communicated with her eyes. Veronica nodded back.

*   *   *

IN THE CONFERENCE room, Will paced. "I smell a rat! A Jewish rat. Another one at Deutsches Haus!" He looked around the table at the assembled men and women. "One of you here is working for Ari Lewis. And as we did with Charlie Schroder," he said, "we'll be liquidating those working against us." He looked around the room. "Anyone found working with Lewis will be liquidated, too."

McDonnell sat back in his chair and looked around. "Who'd want Schwinn out of the way?" he asked the room. Veronica stopped writing for a brief second, but forced her frozen fingers to keep moving. McDonnell stared at Will. "Who'd want the number one top dog job?"

Will's face was mottled with rage, but he spoke calmly. "Are you accusing me of anything, McDonnell?"

"I can also think of another person here—Veronica Grace." Veronica felt her blood turn cold and heard a high-pitched ringing sound. She forced herself to stare him full in the face.

"You heard me," McDonnell told her. "You were there for the snowstorm in San Diego. That's when things started to go haywire. Then the mess on Columbus Day. Maybe you're helping your boyfriend?"

Veronica looked to Will. If she were to get out of this, he needed to take her side.

"How dare you accuse Miss Grace of anything except patriotism?" Will said through clenched teeth.

"We've got a rat here—or more than one—and it brings up questions. And she and her mother are new."

"I was in San Diego, if you recall," she said. "I was arrested!" Veronica forced herself to stand and face McDonnell. "Is there something you want to ask me? Because go ahead and I'll answer."

"Yeah, thanks to my wife, I've been doing a little research on you, Veronica—your life back in New York. It sounds like you're all hat and no cattle. How come you never mentioned you went to Hunter College?" To the others: "In case you don't know, it's a school for girl kikes and coloreds."

"It was affordable and provided an excellent education," Veronica said calmly. "I hated I had to attend class with those people. But I never socialized with them."

McDonnell bent down to his bag, taking out a yellowed newspaper. "And there's this article—from the school paper, the *Hunter Envoy,*" he said, slamming it on the table. Harriet looked on approvingly. "You went undercover to the Nazi rally at Madison Square Garden." He narrowed his eyes. "Just like you're undercover now?"

"No!" *Oh, scheisse . . .*

"Let me see that." Will picked it up and scanned the piece. "Veronica," he said, his face falling, "did you write this?"

Veronica swallowed. "I—I did," she said, and there was a collective gasp in the room. Will looked like a kicked puppy. "But I'm not proud of it. Not now."

"Help me understand," Will said.

"I'll tell you what happened," Veronica said, her mind whirling. "I'll tell you—I was supposed to work for *Mademoiselle* magazine, it's a women's fashion magazine, very prestigious. But a man— a Jew—took advantage of me." She burned with remembered shame, real and scalding.

One of the women gasped. She saw Veronica's distress and reached a comforting hand to her arm. *"Er war ein Jude,"* she said in soothing tones. *He was a Jew.* As if that explained everything.

"Yes," Veronica continued, warming to her subject. "He was a journalist with the *New York Times*—of course. When I won a prize for the article, he said he would mentor me, but instead . . ." She left it up to their imaginations.

"His wife found out. Not only is she a Jew as well, but she comes from one of those big Jewish publishing families. The Feld-mans." She looked around the room, ending with Will. "Maybe you've heard of them. He ruined me, and she took my job and told me I'd be permanently blackballed in New York publishing. Be-cause they can do that, the Jews!" Her voice rang with conviction.

She took a shuddering breath. "Well, that happened, and I started to wise up to how the world worked. I began to realize my view of the rally at the Garden was all wrong. I'd gotten it back-ward."

Harriet also stood and went to Veronica, putting her arm around her. "Oh, you poor girl," she said, patting her back. "You poor thing." She glared at her husband.

Veronica's eyes began to tear. "I didn't want anyone to know. I'm so ashamed." She hid her face in Harriet's shoulder and the woman stroked her hair.

"You have nothing to be ashamed of," Harriet told her in sooth-ing tones. "I'm sorry I was suspicious—but we just didn't know . . ."

Veronica sniffled, and one of the men handed her a handkerchief. "It disgusts me to even think about it," she said. "About him. And them. When people say the Jews control the media—well, they aren't kidding. I learned firsthand."

"Of course," Harriet said, visibly relieved. "It all makes sense now. I knew Veronica and her mom were okay."

"Now do you see?" Veronica cried, her face tear-streaked, eyes flashing. "I'm not your rat! I'm in your corner, cheering you on— us on—doing everything I can for the cause!"

"There is a trait in the Jewish character that's seductive and does provoke animosity and rancor," Will said, considering. "Hitler doesn't just pick on them for no reason at all, you know." He looked at her, his eyes gentle. "No wonder you wanted to wait . . . You'd been hurt, abused . . . Of course. It all makes sense now."

In a lightning-flash moment, Veronica realized on some level, she'd told the truth. Max was a much older, much more experienced man. He held a high position in a profession she wanted to be part of. He'd used her—just as he used so many other young women. His wife, unable to blame him, punished her and who knew how many others instead. *The filthy Jews!* she thought. It felt so right. *Max defiled me—and his wife used all the power she had in the media to tarnish me. Jews!*

For a moment, Veronica was able to hold on to her persona's thought at the same time as her own, superimposed on each other. She could see the world the way the Nazis did. Everything had shifted for her. How much danger the white race was in! How bright the future could be if the Jews and coloreds and immigrants were stopped! *I am special. We are special. And we're also victims of the Jews, persecuted for their very superiority* . . .

She excused herself when the meeting was over and went to the telephone booth in the parking lot. "I need to get out of here," she told Jonah. "I'm not okay. It's not safe. Meet me at Wallichs."

✳ ✳ ✳

WALLICHS MUSIC CITY on Sunset and Vine was the place for records, sealed and displayed on racks, as well as concert tickets, sheet music, and musical instruments. The walls were plastered with concert posters, mostly the big bands—led by Glenn Miller, Cab Calloway, and Tommy Dorsey—but also for Walt Disney's upcoming *Fantasia,* the Andrews Sisters, and Ella Fitzgerald and Her Famous Orchestra. In the back of the store were doors to tiny listening rooms: for a small fee, customers could preview records in privacy.

Jonah was waiting, a Woody Guthrie album on the phonograph, playing "Worried Man Blues." "You're a Guthrie fan?" Veronica said, putting her purse down on the table and sitting next to him in the booth. She was pale.

"I own *Dust Bowl Ballads,*" he told her. "As great as Steinbeck's *Grapes of Wrath,* in my opinion. But from the way you sounded on the telephone, I don't think we're here for the music."

"I don't think I can do this anymore," she told him. "McDonnell accused me and my mother of being spies. In public. In a meeting with Will."

Jonah's face shuttered. "What happened?"

Veronica told him everything, even her confusion with viewpoints. "You look into the abyss," she said, "and eventually the abyss is going to look back."

"I think it was a brilliant move." Jonah regarded her. "Did they buy it?"

"Will did, I think. Harriet, too. McDonnell—I'm not so sure."

"Is that why you're upset? Because you may have been made?"

"I'm upset," Veronica told him, "because I let my emotions get out of control. In the moment, I believed what I said. I hated Max. I hated Evelyn. I hated their family. Everything that happened—it was so easy to make it their fault. And the fact they're Jewish just made it all seem . . ."

"Like everything they've been saying is true. Veronica," Jonah said knowingly, "you've been working undercover for months now. You've been hearing that poison almost nonstop. You don't have a 'normal' life with 'normal' friends. Everything you do, and your mother does, is at Deutsches Haus, with those people."

"Sometimes," Veronica admitted, remembering how Harriet had comforted her, "they aren't horrible. Or, at least, they're not horrible to me."

"Of course they're not horrible to you. It's great to be one of them! The camaraderie, the music, the food . . . If there weren't wonderful, seductive parts, no one would join—and no one would stay."

She needed to tell him. She needed him to know. "For that moment, though—I was furious with Max, with his wife . . . with the Jews. I could feel it, running through my blood. I felt powerful in the moment. I loved how everyone in the room supported me, took my side." She took a ragged breath. "But now—I'm appalled that happened. Horrified." She shuddered. "And I'm still confused by it."

"You go, you observe, and you come and debrief. Your feelings, in this case, don't matter. You came to me. You're telling me everything."

"I didn't think it would be so hard," Veronica said. "Like I'm betraying them. Harriet—she's an American. She's . . . nice. Once I told them . . . she took my side."

"Here's the thing, Veronica," he said, "nice isn't good."

She took a moment to let it sink in. "It's normal to feel like that when you're undercover, to like them. It's good—it means you're in character. You must allow yourself to fall under their spell while you're there—and then put it all away after. Can you do that?"

"It just got blurred there, for a moment."

"If you were actually anti-Semitic, you wouldn't be doing this work."

"I know."

"You're doing great, Veronica. And you're right, they're not bad people. They're misinformed. Poorly educated. Ignorant. There aren't actually white hats and black hats in this scenario. Sure, Hitler and Goebbels are monsters. Schwinn and Wagner, too, on a smaller scale. But the common man and woman, like the McDonnells? There's a lot of gray."

"I like cowboy movies, where there're white hats and black hats."

"Don't we all." Jonah looked at her. "How serious do you think McDonnell is? Do you think your story put him off?"

"I don't know. He put a lot of work into digging up my past. I think I bought some time, but . . ." Veronica looked up at him. "I don't want to die."

"Well," he said gently, "that's not the plan."

"And I'm going nuts—I can't be someone else every day. I've been doing it for months. I can't do it anymore. I've had enough."

"Look at all you've done! We saved the air industry! Schwinn's been arrested!" He looked at her seriously. "You can quit now, of course. But if you do, we won't have any information on *der Tag.*"

"When are you going to have enough to take them down?"

"We still need actual specifics, not just talk."

She froze, her body completely still. "They're going to kill me, is that what you want? Is that what you're waiting for?"

"We're building a case. It takes time. You know that."

"Something's wrong. I can feel it. Something's wrong. I got out this time, but . . ."

"Hang in there, just a little while longer, can you?" He took her into his arms as Guthrie sang on. "We're so close."

He kissed the top of her head, and for the briefest moment she could hear her father's voice: *Illegitimi non carborundum! The only time you back down's when you're dead!* She realized she needed to see the job through. *What would Martha Gellhorn do?*

It came to her. "I have an idea," she said, pulling away.

Jonah glanced out the window, then picked the needle off the record, replaced it in the holder, and switched off the turntable.

"We've stayed here long enough." He put the disk in its white paper sleeve, slipping it back into the cardboard album cover.

"I'll go to the bowling alley on Vine and get a soda there. There's a back exit. Pull up in an hour and I'll jump in." Veronica added: "I'll explain everything on the way."

"The way where?"

"You'll see."

CHAPTER TWENTY-SIX

Tuesday, November 5, 1940, was Election Day. Speakers at the
restaurant and bar of Deutsches Haus blasted the radio broadcast's live coverage. Veronica, sitting next to Will at a red-checked
cloth covered table, pictured radios on in every house and apartment in America, every bar and restaurant across the country.

"Roosevelt shouldn't even be running," Will was saying as he
took a swig of beer. "Two terms are enough."

Veronica nodded, pretending to agree.

The nearest speaker was blaring an ad for Alka-Seltzer, said to
relieve heartburn and indigestion. *They certainly know their audience,*
Veronica thought, her own stomach churning. While the numbers
coming in for Roosevelt looked good, anything could still happen.

Vi and Nora returned from the bar with fresh gimlets. *"The re-
turns from all over the country are pouring in,"* the announcer was saying
in a deep, sonorous voice. *"It's a landslide for Roosevelt! A Roosevelt
sweep! A Roosevelt triumph!"*

There were groans from those assembled as well as a few audible
protests and words of profanity. Over the radio, they heard Roosevelt, speaking from Hyde Park: *"We define our values in opposition to
totalitarian regimes—placing civil liberties, religious pluralism, and tolera-
tion at the center of the national creed. Americans will not be scared or
threatened in the ways the dictators want us to follow—because we believe*

we shall be all for one and one for all . . ." The words were greeted with
a chorus of boos.

"Oh, democracy," Nora said, swigging her gimlet. "It's as old-
fashioned as a horse and buggy! When will we be done with it
here?" She looked up and saw Marv Whiteside holding a mug of
beer in one hand and a bratwurst on a roll in the other. "Ah, here
comes your admirer," she said to Vi.

"I'm only trying to help the poor boy—I don't think he even
has enough money to eat," Vi replied, patting the empty chair next
to her. "Quite a night, huh?" she said to him.

He took a huge bite of brat. "So good!" he exclaimed. "I don't
really follow politics."

"You don't follow politics?" Veronica echoed, aghast. Then she
thought with relief, *At least he isn't a Nazi.*

He shook his head while he chewed and swallowed. "I'm a scientist," he told them. "A dreamer. I just want to go to the moon."

Will stood; he made eye contact with a few of the men with
grim faces who were also standing. He leaned down to kiss Veronica on the cheek.

"Where are you going?" she asked, noticing the men heading
for the doors. She could smell the tension. They had something
planned and she swore she heard someone say "American *Kristallnacht.*" *Kristallnacht,* the "Night of Broken Glass"—that sinister, poetic name was inspired by the shards from the shattered windows of
Jewish-owned stores. During *Kristallnacht* in Germany, synagogues
were burned, Jewish homes and shops demolished, and thousands
of Jews arrested all over Germany. *It could never happen here,* Veronica thought. But then she realized, *Of course it could. And it can happen sooner than we think.*

"Off to practice our 'freedom of assembly,'" he said, clicking his
heels together and giving a low bow. "Good night, ladies."

Veronica and Violet exchanged glances. They knew Ari and
Jonah were aware of potential violence on election night—they had

alerted the police and the FBI to the threat. *But just how bad,* Veronica worried, *is it going to be?*

* * *

A CELEBRATION WAS going on downtown, in Pershing Square. Percussive swing music was playing over the same loudspeakers that had announced Roosevelt's victory. Men in suits and women in bright dresses were dancing, while others drank bottles of beer hidden in paper sacks. Will and his men on motorcycles began to circle the square as others from Deutsches Haus infiltrated the crowd. "Heil Hitler!" came a voice. "Heil Hitler!" more responded.

"You lost, ya dumb Nazis!" one of the men in a bright blue zoot suit called back. "Get over it!"

One of the men on motorcycles jumped the curb and advanced into the crowd. People dove out of the way, as others pushed the rider off. He moaned from the sidewalk, clutching a bloody leg. Someone pushed someone else, a fistfight broke out, and there was the sound of breaking glass bottles. The music ceased as the speakers were overturned. Will's men threw rocks at the streetlights, plunging the square into darkness as Will threw himself into a fistfight. As people screamed and tried to run, more men with motorcycles blocked their way. A roar began, the chants of "Blood and soil! Blood and soil!" growing louder and echoing through the park as the police watched.

Thirty-one people were injured, no arrests were made, and the incident was never covered in any of the papers.

CHAPTER TWENTY-SEVEN

Despite the reelection of Roosevelt, and the disappointment and anger of those at Deutsches Haus, the annual Christmas party was still an extravagant affair. In the lobby, a brass band played carols by an enormous fir tree covered in tinsel and painted tin decorations, as people dressed in their holiday best milled about. The stair's handrails were wrapped in evergreen and twinkling lights. Wooden German smokers, carved in the shape of Santa, exhaled ginger-scented fumes.

Inside the auditorium, a traditional German Christmas fair had been set up. There was a huge mural of snowy Alps displayed on the walls. A group of storm troopers in civilian clothes sang German carols, accompanied by the storm trooper band. Food stalls sold *Christstollen*—braided fruitcakes made of almonds, rum, and candied lemon and orange peels—and *lebkuchen*—iced gingerbread men. There were also mountains of marzipan in the shapes of fruit and vegetables, brightly painted and sprinkled with colored sugars.

Waiters with tea towels folded over their arms ensured everyone's cup was filled with steaming, fragrant *glühwein,* as people shopped for wooden nutcrackers, carved Nativity scenes, and glass tree decorations. And employees from the Aryan Bookstore passed out leaflets: *Christmas Greetings,* allegedly written by a prominent rabbi, which contained sacrilegious statements about Jesus, Mary, and the Nativity.

Veronica and Vi entered Deutsches Haus knowing full well that while some people supported them and stood firmly behind them, others did not. The women had done their best in the past weeks to use it to their advantage, to sow dissent among the members: gossiping with Nora and the ladies about those who were treating them with suspicion. They were careful not to be anywhere alone and to make sure they weren't being tailed.

Vi had her own booth at the market set up in the auditorium, with Christmas stockings embroidered with candy canes, bells, and ribbons. Veronica was helping Vi, making sales, wrapping the stockings in red tissue paper, and ringing them up. As a girl, Veronica had learned to sing *"Stille Nacht"* from her grandmother, bake *stutenkerl,* little men made of sweet, spiced dough, and made lunch of goose and red cabbage. "Grandmother . . ." Veronica began.

"Would have loved this," Vi said with a warning look.

Will showed up with two cups of mulled wine for the ladies; his broken nose from election night was almost healed, although it was still bandaged and his eyes had residual bruising.

"Oh, you angel!" Vi exclaimed, accepting her cup.

Veronica kissed his cheek. "Thank you." She put her arms around him and held him close. "Thank you for everything these past few weeks."

"Of course, *schatzi,*" he told her. "And tonight, we go to Lake Arrowhead!" A friend of his had lent them his cabin, and the idea was for them to spend a romantic weekend together.

Veronica smiled, showing all her teeth. "Can't wait!"

There was a noise from the lobby. *"Was ist . . ."* Will said, looking up.

A group of men, led by Agent Doolin, burst into the auditorium. The brass band stopped playing and Doolin flashed his badge.

"FBI!" he shouted. "We're looking for Mrs. Violet Grace and Miss Veronica Grace!"

"What?" Veronica said, clutching Will's arm as Vi put a hand to her heart and whispered, "No . . ."

"Ladies, you're under arrest," he said loudly, placing handcuffs on both. Everyone turned to watch.

"Why?" Veronica cried.

Vi's eyes flashed. "What did we do?"

"We're taking you in for questioning," he told them in the lobby, his voice echoing off the marble.

"About what?" Veronica asked indignantly.

"Writing anonymous threatening letters to President Roosevelt, for one," Doolin told them.

"That's our First Amendment right!" Vi cried.

"You're on a list of prominent anti-Semites being passed around Hollywood," another agent said.

"I consider it a compliment!" Veronica called out to a burst of spontaneous applause.

"I'm calling my lawyers," Nora told them, following them through the lobby. "Don't you worry about a thing, either of you!"

"We'll talk about everything down at the station," Doolin said. He pushed Veronica's shoulder, causing her to stumble as they paraded through the lobby. "Now move."

* * *

THEY WERE TAKEN to the police station. After they'd been booked, photographed, and fingerprinted, Veronica and Vi were left in the interrogation room with Agent Doolin, Ari, and Jonah. "Do you think they bought it?" Veronica asked.

"I'll say!" Doolin told them. "You gals wanna give up spying, you should try Hollywood!" Veronica laughed her deep, guttural laugh.

"Just as long as it gets them off the scent," Vi said.

"You were great," Doolin told her. "You, with your 'That's our First Amendment right!'"

Vi didn't hide the pride on her face, and Veronica saw her mother's cheeks flush pink. "Just doing my job."

Ari looked at them thoughtfully. "Well, this should buy you some time, at least."

"As we were leaving, Nora Ingle said she'd have her lawyer telephone us. So we've got to smooth things over in case she does call," Veronica told him.

Doolin nodded. "I'll take care of that." He smiled at Violet. "Can I get you ladies anything? Coffee? One of my buddies here has a box of Fig Newtons stashed in his desk."

"No, no, thank you," Vi told him, as Veronica folded her arms over her chest.

"Agent Doolin," she said, "you don't recognize us, do you?"

"Er, should I?" He looked to Ari and Jonah, confused.

"We both came to your office in July, to tell you about Mr. McDonnell and his plans."

Doolin did a double take. "Oh, right," he said as Ari and Jonah looked on. "Right! Well, we had a different mandate from Mr. Hoover back then." He cleared his throat. "The serious threat to the aircraft factories changed his mind, and fast." To Ari and Jonah: "You know I was always on your side—but my hands were tied."

"We know," Ari told him. "We've always known we'd be hard-pressed to find viable political or legal grounds to fight. The Constitution protects the Bund in its right to denounce American Jews, no matter how vile the language. There's nothing illegal in the group's front organizations or the ways its Americanized Nazi symbols and ideas into community events. The only legal tactic available to us is to catch individual Bund members actually breaking the law."

"So," Veronica said, only slightly mollified, "are we going to have to stay in jail tonight? What do we have to do to make this thing look real?"

"We'll keep you until tonight," Doolin said. "But then I can drive you home."

"No," Vi said. "We should take the trolley. In case anyone's watching."

"Good point," Doolin said, and Vi flushed pink again. Ari, who was watching, smiled.

"But just pretend to be shaken up by the whole experience when you go back to Deutsches Haus," Jonah told them.

Doolin nodded to the women. "You know, you two ever want a job here—"

"They're ours," Jonah told him flatly.

"It's up to you," Ari told Vi and Veronica.

"I'm happy to coordinate with you, of course, Agent Doolin," Veronica said, reaching for Vi's hand.

"But I think we're going to 'dance with the ones who brung us,' as they say," Vi replied, gripping her daughter's hand back tightly. She blushed. "But I do look forward to working with you, Agent Doolin."

"All right, I'm going to send someone to the diner to bring back some food." Taking out a pad of paper and a pencil, Doolin asked, "What's everyone want?" He grinned. "It's on Mr. Hoover."

* * *

AFTER THEY FINISHED eating—a hamburger, fries, and Coca-Cola for Veronica, and a Cobb salad for Vi—they stayed in the interrogation room. Vi picked at the remains of her salad, while Veronica finished her soda. "Well, that was really . . . something," Vi offered finally.

"It was."

"Your second arrest now," Violet noted, and clicked her tongue. "Seem old hat?"

"Hardly," Veronica said, hunting for the last french fry. "At least I knew this one was coming."

"Can you believe we're doing all this?" she asked. "I mean, look at the two of us—living in Los Angeles. Under fake arrest. Making it look good so a bunch of American Nazis believe we support them. It's like something from a movie. But it's our lives now." She started to laugh. Veronica joined in, and they both laughed until tears ran down their faces and Vi gave a loud hiccup.

My daughter's a spy, Vi thought, the actual word seeming like something from a film. *Unreal* was the word she kept thinking. *Spy. Unreal.* She remembered the last spy film she'd seen in Brooklyn, *Confessions of a Nazi Spy,* with Edward G. Robinson. She'd gone with Veronica, to the Gem Theatre on Fulton. They'd had popcorn and Red Hots, watching a film based on the Rumrich Nazi spy case. *What was the last line?* Vi tried to remember: *"When our basic liberties are threatened, we wake up."*

Veronica kissed Vi's powdered cheek. "Daddy would be proud."

"He would." Vi's face grew serious again. "It's different, isn't it?" she said. "Seeing things the way they really are. Seeing these things for yourself. I'd forgotten what it was like. Being in the middle of things."

"It's what journalism's all about," Veronica said.

"Being involved—*really* involved—can change the way you feel. It did once for me. And now I'm changing again." She looked to her daughter. "Do you feel like you've changed?"

"Absolutely." Veronica considered. "Not always for the better. But definitely changed. And I do think we're doing good in the world, even though it doesn't always feel like it." She laughed bitterly. "Sometimes, what started off as a shining adventure just feels like an endurance contest. If we're being honest, I'm feeling pretty soggy and deflated."

"Where did we go, you and I?" Vi wondered aloud. "I feel so grim most of the time these days, too. It's hard to remember there's still light out there in the world."

"There is, Mother," Veronica said. "You're still my North Star and always will be." She looked at her mother. "What's your heart telling you to do?" She cracked a grin. "Should we get out while the getting's good?"

"We must stay the course," Vi said, putting down her fork and pushing the salad away. "We've got to fight." She looked at her suffragist ring, the purple amethysts and green peridots sparkling in the light. "What was it Daddy used to say?"

Veronica looked at her mother proudly. *"Illegitimi non carborundum."*

"Then *illegitimi non carborundum,* sweetie."

CHAPTER TWENTY-EIGHT

It was the Graces' first winter in Los Angeles, and they were shocked by how cold it felt, despite temperatures that would seem warm in New York in January. When they'd moved in, they thought the fireplace was just for show, but now they pulled their chairs close in the evenings, for warmth as well as cheer. Occasionally, they'd drag each other out for walks. To the pier, usually, the La Monica Ballroom at the very end. They walked slowly, arm in arm in the sharp breeze, as though seeing the Pacific could somehow ward off upcoming evil. "The waiting's worse for those of us who remember the last war," Vi remarked. "But I'm grateful for the sheer beauty of this place—the mountains and ocean. And the sun."

The day of Roosevelt's inauguration passed with the president giving a speech about the "Four Freedoms"—and they both breathed a sigh of relief. Veronica visited Schwinn in prison, in the Federal Correctional Institution on Terminal Island in Los Angeles Harbor, hoping to gain something, anything, that might help glean more information about *der Tag*. "I'm sorry I missed Al Capone," Schwinn said of one of the more famous inmates, when Veronica visited him.

"I hear he had good bootleg gin," she joked.

"They found my trunks, didn't they?" She nodded; when the FBI had searched Schwinn's house, they'd found two trunks filled with incriminating information, including detailed maps, short-wave radio broadcasting sets, photographs, stacks of bundled American money, and reams of Nazi propaganda. His family, friends, and colleagues were all being questioned by the FBI.

"Can't be helped now . . ." He sighed.

They were in the prison's meeting room. As it was a low-security facility, they were face-to-face across a small table, sitting on metal folding chairs. Outside the window, the sky was blue, and Veronica could see the browning fronds of a palm tree through the bars.

He smiled. "I'm glad you and your mother are all right after all that nonsense."

"Oh, we're fine," she told him. "Just dandy."

"You've added much to the movement, my child. I'm—we're—eternally grateful. You must continue your good work. I hear Carson's been using your excellent secretarial services?"

"He has." One of the aftereffects of the arrest was her shorthand was in more demand than ever. She'd been taking dictation for Samuel Carson, a slick man in his thirties with the charm of Jimmy Stewart, being also prone to saying things such as "oh dear," "geez," and "for cryin' out loud."

There was no denying the force of this man, Veronica realized. She'd never experienced anyone, anything, like it. *Being in his orbit must be like being in Charles Lindbergh's,* she thought. There was a dazzle of danger in his gaze, the hypnotic promise of power. It was exhilarating. Narcotic. And terrifying. *Führer Kontakt,* it was called with Hitler—an intense magnetism that could make people believe, in that moment, they were the only one in the room, the center of the universe. It made them willing to follow him anywhere.

And she was afraid of him. Willkie had lost the election and Lindbergh was focusing on opposing Lend-Lease. But Carson might just be the man to unite all the American fascist organizations and lead them.

He'd dictated sentences to her, such as: "Blood will flow on the streets of the United States." She had the horrible feeling the changes were coming slowly before they came suddenly. There were many things she wasn't privy to, but she did know that as winter turned into spring, *der Tag*, an American version of *Kristallnacht,* was being planned to pave the way for an American dictator.

Veronica looked at Schwinn. She knew he had a wife and a teenage daughter back in Brentwood; his daughter had made friends in the United States and was terrified they'd all be sent back to Germany. As Schwinn chatted on about the horrible food, the lack of a library, the poor living conditions, he let slip details about his childhood, his strict upbringing, his authoritarian father and terrified mother, hinting at the violence that had gone on.

She observed him as he spoke, taking mental notes. *What will I write about him? His beliefs and his behaviors are abhorrent—but there's also pain. So much pain.*

* * *

BUT AS SPRING turned to summer, Veronica was hard-pressed to find anything decent about Samuel Carson. A controversial radio personality in the thirties, he'd headed the "Ham and Eggs" old-age pension scam before founding the Friends of Progress. Angry after the election, he was furious when the U.S. House of Representatives voted 265–165 in favor of the Lend-Lease bill, giving Churchill "the tools to finish the job."

Carson's answer to the United States being the "arsenal of democracy" was to plan a public mock impeachment trial of Roosevelt for the fall. "We need to create an American party—truly American—that's openly anti-alien, anti-Semitic, and anti all the mud people," he told Veronica, pulling out a piece of thick cream-colored stationery. "We've received a wonderful letter from the

Reich Ministry of Public Enlightenment and Propaganda. They've proclaimed my work, and I quote, 'truly American and truly patriotic'!" Veronica made herself smile and nod.

"Thanks to Lindbergh, we've been able to take groups from the margins of society and move them to the mainstream by protesting Roosevelt's policies. We associate Jews with treachery—with treason—and then implicitly encourage people to take matters into their own hands. Brilliant!" He leaned back, beaming. "The American Rangers and the Royal Order of American Defenders are already calling for death to Jews!"

"But when are we really going to see something done?" Veronica asked, although her voice was tight. "What's everyone waiting for?"

Carson raised a finger. "Patience, my girl—leave that to the men. But I promise you, when *der Tag* comes, you and your mother will be very, very pleased and proud. Now!" He clapped his hands. "Back to planning the impeachment trial!"

* * *

UP ABOVE THE city, on the observation deck of city hall, Veronica had a 360-degree view of Los Angeles, from the mountains to the ocean. The Santa Ana winds were blowing, hot and strong, and she was the only person on her side of the deck. There was the sound of wind in her ears and the faint muffled noises of traffic from below.

Jonah came up behind her and she jumped. "Nervous?" he asked.

"Always."

He was wearing his leather jacket and brushed his wind-blown hair out of his eyes. He looked more tense than usual, his hands rammed in his pockets. They had reached an unspoken agreement they would not speak of Will, at least of her being with Will. The roses he sent, the dinners at Pacific Dining Car, the jewelry, the weekends in Catalina, their intimacies.

He'd also been busier since Schwinn's arrest and more distracted, for which Veronica was grateful.

"The first part of the trial's scheduled at the Embassy Auditorium, third week of November," she told him.

"Not Deutsches Haus?"

"They're expecting an even bigger crowd than they could accommodate there. They're taking out advertisements in the papers, hoping to bring in new people, the folks put off by Roosevelt's Lend-Lease." She sighed. "The tagline for the event is '*If Congress Won't Impeach the President, the People Will.*'"

He looked to her. "What are you up to?"

"Mostly taking down Carson's memos and speeches in shorthand, making arrangements for the hall, the food, the music. The swastika bunting and flags . . . Did I mention the wax effigy of Roosevelt they want to burn when it's all over." As she rolled her eyes again, Jonah nodded, looking out over the vista to the mountains. "It's going to start with open 'hearings,' where people will be able to hear the 'House' debate and then vote on impeachment."

"What's Carson's role?"

"He's playing a California congressman, presenting the prosecution's case."

"And what's that, in his mind?"

"According to Carson, when Roosevelt was elected in '32, he promised to cut taxes, reduce unemployment, and make government more efficient—and he's failed at all three. The other prong of his argument is 'certain groups that control the media' are, with Roosevelt, pushing us toward war. And 'great Americans like Charles Lindbergh' are being prevented from speaking out against Lend-Lease and isolationism."

"Have you heard any calls for violence?"

"Not specifically. But they're bringing more guns up to the

Murphy Ranch. They're still friendly with Marv Whiteside, the rocketeer. I wonder . . ." Her voice was taken by a gust of wind.

"Wonder what?"

"I wonder if Whiteside could be building a bomb for them. Or some other kind of weapon. I don't think he's a Nazi—but I do think he's desperate for money. Is there any way the U.S. government could pay him for his work instead? Even if they think rockets are science fiction, it would keep him away from the Bund and America First."

"Why don't you go back to the ranch? Take another look around? See what they have?" They both knew Will would have to take her.

"I'll . . . see what I can do."

"Your mother—she's friends with Whiteside, right? Maybe she could have a one-on-one conversation with him about his work. Find out what's going on."

"You want to get out of here?" she asked suddenly, clapping a hand down on her hat so not to lose it.

Finally, he smiled. "Absolutely."

* * *

THEY MET AT a hotel room near Angels Flight, each using a different entrance. Inside, Jonah left the lights off and pulled the curtains. Veronica leaned against him, feeling the length of his body as they kissed. Finally undressed, they fell onto the bed, which creaked in protest. It was hard and lumpy, seemingly made from rocks and wire springs. They didn't care. They were more practiced now, more confident with each other's bodies. In those fleeting moments, Veronica allowed herself the luxury of not thinking. Veronica made love to him as though she wanted him to cleanse all memories of Will from her. In those moments at least, he did—and she was grateful.

Afterward, they lay on the twisted sheets and watched the ceiling fan rotate, squeaking a bit with each turn. Outside, through the chink in the curtain, she could see the orange Angels Flight cars crisscross. "I feel like something big's going to happen." Jonah turned on the radio.

"Nooooo!" Veronica groaned, pulling the sheet over her head. "Five more minutes!"

"I know," he said, stretching. "But now we've got the ships and planes heading to England . . ."

She peeked out. "That's not it—people can't keep living like this, so on edge."

"People can live with it—and quite a bit more," he assured her as he pulled on his pants.

"No," she told him, her voice rising in annoyance. "Not people—not 'my' people. They've been preparing for war and coups and insurrection and *der Tag* for so long, I'm not sure how much longer they'll hold the line." He sat back down on the edge of the bed.

"No, I don't have any specific evidence," she told him. "And I feel like I'm being kept more at arm's length than ever, even after the fake arrest."

"Keep looking," he told her. "You'll figure it out."

"But what if it's too late?"

CHAPTER TWENTY-NINE

The debates to "impeach" President Roosevelt were being held at Embassy Auditorium, downtown on the corner of Ninth Street and Grand Avenue. The evening's event, the first debate, hosted by America First, was presented by the German American Bund and the Silver Shirts.

Posters for the "impeachment" were plastered everywhere, alongside those declaring NO WAR and the image of a heart pierced by an arrow, with the caption: ADOLF LOVES LINDY. On the corner of Ninth, protesters had congregated. There were almost fifty of them, with hand-painted signs reading NO NAZIS IN AMERICA and HITLER'S NOT WELCOME HERE.

A line of police officers kept close watch on both the protesters and those entering to hear the mock impeachment. Veronica, walking arm in arm with her mother, felt a wave of shame as she passed the protesters. *We're on your side!* she wanted to cry out, but couldn't.

"Make no mistake!" a grizzled man standing on a wooden orange crate shouted into the crowd. "We're in a brutal, no-holds-barred battle for the soul of our nation!"

Yeah, no kidding, buddy, Veronica thought.

Inside the Beaux Arts building's high-ceilinged lobby, the air was thick and hazy with cigarette smoke. *Hell is empty and all the devils are here.* Veronica could hear men and women speaking in both English and German. There were tables selling specialty news-papers: Julius Streicher's *Der Stürmer,* Joseph Goebbels's *Der Angriff,* and the local California publication *Staats-Zeitung,* along with pa-pers and pamphlets, including the McDonnells'. A smiling young woman with a middle part and blond Gretchen-style braids passed out big buttons reading KEEP AMERICA OUT OF THE JEWISH WAR!

Inside, the cavernous auditorium was filled with a crowd of more than a thousand. The space had a sloped floor, balconies on three sides, and a massive ceiling dome with a stained-glass medal-lion at its center. The atmosphere was electric, an edgy cocktail of victimization and rage and pride. Nerves flashed and shorted, like the orange sparks above the Red Cars; people were pumped up and jittery as a dog being forced to fight.

Onstage, young boys in lederhosen sang in sweet treble voices: *"Vorwärts! Vorwärts! Schmettern die hellen fanfaren"*—the Hitler Youth marching song. Men in the different uniforms of the Bund, the Silver Shirts, and the Copperheads—the military arm of America First—looked on and saluted their leaders with extended right arms.

"Yoo-hoo!" trilled a high, feminine voice. Veronica and Vi turned to see Nora in one of the seats, waving a lace-gloved hand.

Veronica said hello, while Vi added, "How wonderful you look tonight!" Nora was dressed in a red crepe jacket and skirt with a small black fascinator—and smelled as though she'd bathed in Cha-nel No. 5.

They sat next to her as they all looked up at the stage: a massive full-length portrait of George Washington was flanked by both American and Bund flags with swastikas. Veronica could hear ex-changes of *"Heil Hitler!"* and *"Heil Mussolini!"* among those around her from Deutsches Haus. It felt like a flashback to the rally at Madison Square Garden.

As the boys' choir stopped singing and filed offstage, footlights flashed on and "The Star-Spangled Banner" began to play. On dis-play was patriotism, to be sure, but a vulgar patriotism, Veronica thought. *Patriotism sold in a can, a jar, a carton—good for all that ails you. Only fifteen cents and available everywhere!* Vi and Veronica, as well as everyone else in the audience, stood and applauded as Samuel Carson strode onto the platform, followed by a bright spotlight, his manner friendly and engaging.

"Heil Hitler!" he cried into the tall microphone, his arm flung out in front of him. His handsome face with its chiseled jaw broke into a smile.

"Heil Hitler!" the crowd responded in kind, jumping to their feet and saluting. Veronica and Vi mouthed the words.

"Heil Mussolini!"

"Heil Mussolini!" the crowd echoed.

"Free America!"

"Free America!"

Carson gestured for the audience to sit, dark eyes flashing. "Some of you may be surprised to see me using this hand signal." He demonstrated, once again, a salute with the right hand extended from the shoulder and palm down in an elevated position. "If you remember, we decided not to use that a few years ago, when the Friends of the New Germany changed its name to the German American Bund.

"However," he told them, lowering his arm, "this's not the so-called Nazi salute—no sir—but a form of greeting devised by the old Romans." He winked, pointing to the Bund's flag with its swastika, next to the Stars and Stripes. "Just like the swastika's not just for Germans and Germany, but for all Gentiles, in all countries—including us, here in the United States of America!" This remark was met with fervent applause.

"Our flags, the bunting, our uniforms, are all made in this country. They're American uniforms. The swastika is not foreign but one hundred percent American. And our salute," he told them, "is the symbol of free men everywhere.

"But tonight, my friends, we're here for a trial—the impeachment trial of President Franklin D. Roosevelt." He paused for applause. "In my 'role' as a California congressman, I will argue Roosevelt's playing into the hands of the perfidious British, the Jews worldwide, and, particularly, the Jews in this country," he said, taking the microphone from the stand and beginning to pace. "These Jews should realize in the event of war, they'll be among the first to feel its consequences." In the audience, there was a smattering of applause, as well as a few whistles and hoots.

"Fellow Americans," he intoned, "we need to rise and stop these forces who would lead us into war. Our battle cry is for Christianity and the Constitution. Our objective is to rid America of subversive influences that could destroy the Constitution of our forefathers. We'll unify the fifty scattered German American organizations of Southern California—and their one hundred fifty thousand members—into a single body. Hitlerism *will* succeed in the United States," he said in an ecstatic voice, "if Aryans here all support the cause. Let's begin the trial!"

At the thunderous applause, Veronica felt her stomach clench and her breath sour. She took out a package of Life Savers, offering the pineapple one to Vi, before taking the lime for herself. As the band played a rousing version of "The Battle Hymn of the Republic," the stage's curtains opened to reveal the set of a courtroom, complete with a wax-faced effigy of Roosevelt. The men playing congressmen and senators took their seats as the "trial" began.

The crowd's applause and cheers as Carson made his legal points had lust for violence rumbling just beneath the surface. Veronica was afraid of what could happen and she knew her mother was as well. It seemed anything was possible, especially after the first section of the trial concluded on a high note for the prosecutors, anger rippling through the crowd.

The two women made their way out after the frenzied ovation. Veronica's limbs were heavy from sitting so long, but her heart was heavier still. *How did we get here?* she thought, even as she smiled and waved at people she knew. *How is this happening in the United States of America?* But she knew all too well.

In the lobby, they met up with Will. "Ladies!" he greeted them, kissing both their hands. "The trial's off to a wonderful start!"

"It is," Veronica gushed, trying to break the wave of terror that threatened to engulf her.

"May I offer you a ride to Deutsches Haus? There's going to be a party to celebrate the first day of the impeachment trial."

Vi smiled up at him. "Wouldn't miss it for the world!"

* * *

AT THE BAR at Deutsches Haus, everyone was drinking. Carson, still high from his performance in the trial, led the crowd in singing the national anthem and the "Horst Wessel Song." As Carson stepped up onto the stage, the brass band made room for him. He stood there for a long moment, his face grim, his lower lip curled with contempt. The crowd waited, hushed.

"All those present are here by invitation," Carson cried. "This meeting's for Americans—one hundred percent white Christian patriotic Americans!"

Veronica saw Nora Ingle cheer, her red lipstick, so perfect before the trial, now mostly chewed off. She threw her hands into the air in savage joy, her long fingernails the same red as her lips.

"In such a room as this the Boston Tea Party met. Wake up, Christians! Look around you! See what's happening to America! The whole country is overrun with foreigners, Negroes, Jews . . . Is this the America of our fathers? Is this a land of Christian patriots? Or of bloodsucking communists?"

There was an answering roar from the mob. Veronica and Vi exchanged glances. Were things about to get violent? Veronica felt her body become even more rigid, her shoulders near her ears, her hands sweaty and clenched.

Carson glared at the crowd. "This country's been stolen—and what are we going to do about it?"

The crowd went wild. A man in front of Vi and Veronica was

on his feet, his face twisted with rage. "We'll go to work on the Jews. That's what we'll do!"

There was an answering chant of "Kill the Jews!" and "Hang them from lampposts!"

Veronica looked at Will. His face was livid. "Hang the Jews!" he cried, fist in the air. She had to look away.

A plump woman in a tight red suit cried, "Send them back in leaky boats!" Her eyes were wild, and her voice rang with fanatical passion.

On all sides people were on their feet, screaming. Behind them, a woman shouted, "There's foreigners everywhere. My son can't get a job, but the coloreds and Mexicans sure can!"

"Free America!" came a few voices from the back. A few tables in front of them, a little bald man turned around, his visage distorted with hatred. "Let's wipe every Jew off the face of the earth. Let's show 'em real Christian power!"

The crowd screamed approval until Carson finally quieted them. "Nationalism is Americanism," he said. "It was the Americanism of Washington and Lincoln. What was good enough for them is good enough for us. No one's going to deny us our rights!"

"Free America!"

"To hell with everybody else!"

"Democracy, democracy, democracy!" Carson howled. "They throw it in our faces. You hear it on all sides till you're sick of it. What is this democracy? It's a rotten form of weakness. I say—to hell with democracy and up with nationalism! America for the white Christian Americans!" He raised his arms in triumph as cheers rang out.

"We have several more weeks of the impeachment trial," he told them, "but I'm sure we all know which way it's going to go—"

"Guilty!"

Veronica summoned the strength to thrust her fist into the air. "When is *der Tag*?" she called out.

"The last night of the impeachment will be *der Tag*!" Carson confirmed to thunderous applause. "The night we impeach Roosevelt will be the night we free America!"

Veronica and Vi looked at each other. Finally—a specific date.

Nora leaned in and told them, "We've acquired explosives, Springfield rifles, thousands of rounds of ammunition, and other small arms. The plan's to blow up bridges, seize power plants and telephone networks, and take control of the Federal Reserve. We'll set up our own leadership, similar to Hitler's, seizing the reins of government in this country as he did in Germany."

"But . . . that's revolution," Veronica managed. "A coup."

Nora nodded. "Exactly."

Surely they don't have the arms and manpower for that, Veronica thought, itching to tell Jonah and Ari, but still . . . The fact a plan was in motion, a plan with a real end date, was chilling. *But what if they can get the police and Army and National Guard on their side, too? Or at least get them out of the way?*

The speech ended with a rousing rendition of America First's anthem:

The skies are bright, and we're all right,
In our Yankee Doodle way,
But it's up to us, ev'ry one of us,
To stand right up and say:
AMERICA FIRST! AMERICA FIRST! AMERICA FIRST,
*   LAST, AND ALWAYS!*

As the evening devolved into more shouting, Veronica left the auditorium and cornered Will in the lobby. "Is this it?" she asked him. "Will it really be *der Tag*?"

He put an arm around her. "We've laid the groundwork, *shatzi*. Come!"

Veronica clung to Will as he went upstairs, to a back room filled with men, including McDonnell. There she heard plans for the bombings of homes of prominent Jews, such as film producers

Louis B. Mayer and Samuel Goldwyn, using pipe bombs filled with dynamite, shrapnel, iron fillings, and soap. One man called for using machine guns to kill the Jewish residents of Boyle Heights, using tape to cover up their cars' license plates.

Another proposed bombing gas stations in Jewish neighborhoods and using slingshots and steel balls to break the plate glass windows of Jewish-owned stores. Yet another revealed his idea for a fake fumigation company, which would surreptitiously kill Jewish families using poison gas.

They also had plans to blow up the power grid, to blow up a munitions plant in San Diego, and to destroy docks and warehouses all along the coast. A doctor was working with a chemist to make needles tipped with poison that could be shot into Jews with a blow gun.

A lynching of kidnapped prominent Jews in a grove was planned, with four men to attend to each victim. "Hemp rope's better," one declared, while another said, "I'll be glad to see those sons of bitches on the ends of ropes, and the sooner the better. And the rest of the country should take note!"

Veronica couldn't take anything down in shorthand, but she knew she'd remember—the words were burned into her brain.

"We'll all have alibis prepared, of course. And afterward, we'll meet back at Murphy Ranch," Will told them. "Our West Coast fortress for Herr Hitler—we must have it ready for him after our ultimate takeover of the U.S. government."

As the others reacted, Will breathed in her ear: "How about we go back to my place after all this—celebrate, just the two of us?"

Veronica couldn't help it. She didn't have time to think, just emptied the contents of her stomach all over his polished black shoes. "I think," she said, wiping her mouth with the back of her hand, looking up at his shocked expression, "I think I'd better take a rain check."

* * *

WHEN VI SAW the stain on Veronica's dress, she took it as an opportunity. "Oh, sweetie, let's get you home and cleaned up." She smiled up to Will. "Let the menfolk have their fun." They walked to a diner on North Spring, made sure they weren't being followed, then took a cab to their prearranged meeting at the Biltmore Hotel.

Inside one of the rooms, with a view of Pershing Square, Veronica and Vi unburdened themselves to Jonah and Ari. Veronica finished with: "It's fashionable these days to call Hitler's regime hell. But it really is. And Los Angeles is the fifth ring."

Ari sighed as Jonah poured them all bourbon in mismatched glasses. "You're going to need this," Ari warned, raising his glass.

"I'm now going to tell you something the public doesn't know," he continued. "Over the fall, the Germans have deported approximately twenty thousand Jews from western and central Europe to the Łódź ghetto—Jews from Berlin, Vienna, and Prague. Many of them are elderly and sick. More than three thousand of them died before they even reached their destination." He took a sip of bourbon. "The Nazi leaders are cleaning their cities of Jews. The deportations to the Łódź ghetto are the first step in this process."

Vi swallowed her bourbon in one gulp. "What 'process'?" Ari was silent as he poured her another.

"What? What's going on?" Veronica asked.

"They're killing the Jews," Jonah told them.

"Yes, we know," Veronica said. "The ghettos, the firing squads. The mass graves."

"No," Jonah told her. "This is something new. From Łódź, they're taking them to camps farther east. There's one in particular—it's called Auschwitz."

Vi downed her second bourbon in one go. "Another?" Ari asked.

"No," she said in a tight voice. "That's enough. Because if I start drinking, really drinking, I don't think I'd ever, ever stop."

Veronica couldn't get her head around it. She felt numb, a

numbness slowly and painfully melting into growing horror. "Why?" she whispered finally.

"*Ani mamash lo yodea,*" Ari said sadly.

"It means 'There is no answer,'" Jonah told the women. "But, thanks to both of you, we now have concrete evidence of an attack being planned on American soil. In our own small corner of the world, we can fight. And so," he said, "you ladies are done. We thank you for your service."

"Wait—what?" Veronica said, standing, her horror giving way to anger. "We give you the biggest scoop of this war so far, and you're kicking us out?"

"What are you going to do? You're not going to fight them after the impeachment. You could be killed," Jonah told her. "This is where we turn everything over to the FBI. Doolin and his men are on it. They have full backing from Hoover."

Veronica couldn't process it. "I can get more detailed information!"

Jonah stood in front of her. "You can't stop them."

"But I can do *something*." Veronica forced herself not to cry from anger and frustration. "I can help."

"You are helping—but if you stay too long at the party, you'll just be one more dead spy."

"Veronica," Vi said gently, "Jonah's right."

"Don't talk to me like that! I'm not a child!"

"Veronica," Ari said in his kindest voice, "I'm going to set up a meeting first thing tomorrow with Agent Doolin, so you and your mother can tell him everything you told us. Then you'll be done. Finished. Kaput. You got me?"

Veronica arranged a carefully calibrated neutral expression on her face. *Like hell.*

"So when's the final day of the so-called impeachment trial?" Jonah asked.

Veronica took a deep breath. "The evening of Saturday, December sixth."

CHAPTER THIRTY

The evening of the verdict of Carson's impeachment trial, Veronica was in the living room of the Santa Monica bungalow, playing with the young cats as Mama C looked on approvingly from a floral pillow, her eyes half closed.

"What are their names again?" Walter asked. He'd come over and stayed for dinner, since Vi and Veronica weren't going to the trial. Veronica had gotten Jonah, Ari, and Doolin a list of weapons stored at Murphy Ranch and as much information on the plots as she could. Now it was up to the FBI and the police.

"Pomegranate, Avocado, and Lemon," she told him, pointing to each cat, as they scampered after a scrap of tinfoil crumpled into a ball. "After the trees in the backyard. Mama C's full name is Mama Cornucopia."

"You're welcome to all three of them," Vi told him as she put on her glasses.

"Not the mama cat, too?" he asked, feigning shock while Veronica snickered.

"She, at least, has manners," Vi said, threading a needle. "Doesn't go after my embroidery while I'm working."

"And . . ." Veronica prodded.

"And she's rather nice on one's lap in the evening when it gets colder," Vi admitted. As the cats continued to play, Vi teared up.

"It's sweet, isn't it?" she told Mama C. "And a little overwhelming. Seeing your kittens grown up." The two mothers eyed each other with mutual respect.

"Aha! I told you she'd come around," Walter told Veronica.

The broadcast of Leopold Stokowski conducting the NBC Symphony Orchestra in Verdi's *La forza del destino* finished, and an announcer broke in to say President Franklin Roosevelt "had sent or was sending a message to Emperor Hirohito."

Veronica shook her head. "Japan's refusing to withdraw from China, and threatening Thailand, Malaya, and the Dutch East Indies. This isn't good."

Walter grimaced. "War's inevitable at this point."

It was true; through the fall, tensions between the United States and Japan had risen to a dangerous level. Roosevelt had sent multiple warnings to the Japanese emperor that the United States would "take steps" if Japan attacked neighboring countries. And Japan had volleyed warnings back, saying it would be forced to take steps of its own if the United States wouldn't let up on its economic sanctions.

Walter picked up the tinfoil ball to throw it again. "Thank goodness the president's moved the Pacific Fleet and all those bombers to Pearl Harbor."

"Unbelievable," Vi said, using small scissors to cut the floss. She looked over the top of her glasses. "Another war. We're not healed from the last one."

"I'm sorry, Vi." He looked up from the tangle of cats. "I'd love another cup of java, if you have one."

"We do, but I'm afraid we've used the last of the milk."

"Oh, I'll run out and pick up a pint. That should last us until the next delivery," Veronica said, standing and brushing cat hair off her trousers.

"Isn't it a bit late?" Walter said.

"We'll need it for breakfast anyway." But before she could leave, there was a knock at the door. She opened it to see Marv Whiteside. His face was pale. "Marv!" Veronica said. *How does he know where we live?* "This is unexpected."

"Is your mom here?" he asked, shuffling his feet.

"Marv," Vi called, "is that you?"

"Mind if I come in, Mrs. Vi?"

"Of course," Vi replied, as Veronica poked her head out the door and looked up and down the street to see if he'd been followed.

When she saw no one, Veronica opened the door wider. "Please, come in."

Mama C and the young cats raced upstairs as Whiteside took off his hat and held it in his hands. "Marv," Vi said, putting down her embroidery and standing. "Is everything all right?"

Walter stood as well. "Who's this, Vi?"

"Walter, this is Marv Whiteside, Caltech graduate and rocketeer. Marv—my brother, Dr. Walter Engle."

Whiteside nodded as he walked in. He looked terrible, with dark circles under his eyes.

"How'd you get our address?" Veronica asked as they all sat. *Don't let them know where you live* was one of Ari and Jonah's cardinal rules.

"Your mom gave me her telephone number and address one night. Said I could always come over if I needed to."

"Oh, she did, did she?" Veronica said, glaring at her mother. "Was she on her third gimlet at the time?"

"I was worried about the poor boy!" Vi exclaimed. To Whiteside: "You always look like you don't have enough to eat, putting every penny toward those rockets . . ."

"With all due respect, Mrs. Vi," he said, "I was at the impeachment trial—things are blowing up, getting nuts. There's talk about an attack on Wilshire Boulevard Temple."

"What?" Veronica asked, heart pounding.

"And they want to put me on a plane to Berlin. I don't think it's optional anymore. So I gave them the slip on Wilshire and took a cab here."

"*Scheisse!*" Veronica exclaimed.

Vi twisted her hands. "Do you want a cup of coffee, Marv? Some hot cocoa?"

"He's on the run, Mother—this isn't exactly the time for snacks."

"No, thank you." He exhaled. "I know you're friends with the folks at Deutsches Haus, but you always seemed nice. Motherly, even," he said to Vi, clasping his hands tightly. "I didn't feel safe going home."

"It's good you came here," Vi told him as Veronica went to the telephone.

"I'm calling Ari and Jonah," Veronica said, raising the receiver. "Let them know . . ."

Walter kept looking from face to face. "I don't understand!" He looked to Vi. "You know this kid from Deutsches Haus? What did I tell you about going there? That's a viper nest of Nazis!"

"It's not what you think, Walter," Vi told him.

"I just wanted money for my rockets," Whiteside said. "I didn't want to get involved in politics . . . But I told them about another idea I had—about explosions using plutonium—and they began talking about getting me out of the U.S." He looked up. "I've never been out of California, let alone out of the United States. I don't want to go to Germany—"

"Shh . . ." Violet said, sitting next to him. "No one's going to make you go anywhere you don't want to go . . ."

"Plutonium?" Veronica placed the telephone receiver back in the cradle.

"A fission weapon," Whiteside explained. "Incredibly powerful."

Walter began to pace. "Vi, what on earth do you and Veronica have to do with Nazis and rockets—and weapons?"

"Nothing, you *dummkopf,*" Vi told her brother. "And we're not

Nazis. We've been working with a group to take the Nazis down. Which is why we can't let them get to Marv and ship him over to Germany . . ."

As Vi was speaking, Whiteside stood and went to the front window, where he pulled open the curtains. The living room's lamplight spilled out into the darkness.

"What are you—?" was all Veronica could manage before Will and his group burst in, most holding guns, and two with cloths reeking of sickly sweet chloroform.

*　*　*

"GUTEN ABEND!" Will said cheerfully when he saw Veronica's eyes flutter open. At first she was confused. *Why does my head feel like it's been split apart? Why's my mouth so dry? What's that sickly sweet smell?* And then, as she looked around, *Where am I?*

"Will?" she croaked as his white-blond hair came into focus. She realized she was tied to a chair. The room was lit by a lone hanging bulb; it was too dark to see much around her, but the air felt cool and damp, like in a basement. Like Hades's realm. She looked around: her mother was tied up next to her, and also Uncle Walter. They were both still unconscious. "What time is it?" Her body was stiff and sore and she felt as though hours had passed.

"Why weren't you at the impeachment trial?" Will asked, pleasantly, as though they were enjoying Viennese coffee and pastries at a café.

"I—I wasn't feeling well."

"Is it because of your work for the Jews?"

"What?" Veronica's mind whirled. "What Jews?"

He stepped to her and slapped her across the face, hard. "Ari Lewis."

Veronica's face stung and her ears rang. She felt real cold fear run through her, like a fist to the stomach. "I don't know what you mean." She smiled weakly. "Will, this is silly. Please untie me and then . . ."

He went to a wooden table and picked up a folder, filled with photographs. "I've had you and your mother followed," he told her. "Here you are," he said, holding up a photo of her, coming from the office, the one at the hotel near Angels Flight. He dropped it to the cement floor. "Here you are at the movies, with one of his Jew associates." She recognized Jonah. He dropped that photo to the floor as well, as though it burned his fingers. "And here you both are at the Pacific Palisades. You make a lovely couple, I must say."

"It's not—it's not what you think," Veronica managed. She struggled at the ropes tying her wrists. "Please, Will—let me out of this. Let us go."

"All in good time."

Red. The floor is red. And then she realized, *This is a basement. There's a drain in the middle of the floor. He could kill us here and no one would ever know.*

"I took your side when people whispered you weren't loyal to the Bund. That you may in fact be a spy for the Jews."

Stay calm, Veronica thought. *Don't react.* "That's an outrageous accusation—it's insulting." *Indignation and fear are the only correct response. The response of the innocent.*

"I'm glad you see it like that," Will said. "I feel the same. But we found this." With a flourish, he reached beneath the desk and pulled out a book, which Veronica recognized as her copy of *The Great Gatsby,* the one she used to break coded messages. She bit her lip.

"When you were accused of being a spy, I didn't believe it," Will said, putting the book, along with the photos, on the table. "But I had to be certain. So I had you followed. And, just to make absolutely sure, I had Marv Whiteside come to your house and ask for asylum."

"You shouldn't believe any of this!" Veronica felt herself starting to cry and only forced herself to stop by focusing on the drain in the center of the room. *Think, you need to think.*

"You can say anything you want, but I know the truth now. What did you tell them? What did you tell the Jews about us?"

"Nothing! This is all a misunderstanding!" Veronica could feel his eyes on her, calculating and wary.

He slapped her again, harder this time. "Don't insult me. And it's worse—because you're not even a Jew. You're an Aryan. You're supposed to be one of us." His lip curled. "You're a race traitor!"

Veronica's heart stopped beating for a moment. "What about my mother?"

Will laughed. "What about her?"

"She's innocent—and my uncle is as well. Let them go."

"Your mother's hardly innocent! As for your uncle, it's unfortunate because we know he's not involved, but he was at the wrong place at the wrong time tonight." His lips twisted. "How long do you think it will take your Jew friends to get here? If they have the guts to come, that is."

"I'm not going to be your bait!" She looked around. "Where are we?"

"Oh, you don't recognize it? Perhaps it's because you've only seen the upstairs."

Veronica understood. "The Murphy Ranch."

"Yes, I realized you'd tipped the FBI off to our plans. But that didn't stop us from celebrating Roosevelt's impeachment here. Oh, Veronica, you should see it! We have a burning swastika outside, and German music, and food—it's quite the party! Everything we organized for Deutsches Haus is here!"

"I'd love to see it! Untie me and let's go upstairs," Veronica cajoled.

"Oh, no, *schatzi*. We're going to have our own party—down here."

* * *

ARI WAS AT the Graces' house with Jonah. "Where the hell are they?" Jonah kept saying, looking in the kitchen, then upstairs. Ari looked around at the overturned furniture and the untended fire, as Jonah came down the stairs. "No one," Jonah said. "Nothing."

"Got in Himmel," Ari whispered.

Jonah was thinking out loud. "Will Wagner's place's too small. Deutsches Haus is watched by the FBI . . ."

"If I were . . . kidnapping people, I'd take them to Murphy Ranch. It's quiet there, far from anything, anyone. Plenty of room."

"It would be easier to kill them there," Jonah said, his face bleak. "Hide the bodies."

Ari held up his hands, palms out. "I didn't say that."

"You didn't have to. Look," Jonah said, "Veronica's given me the location and schematics of the place. We'll go, you'll stay in the car, and I'll get her."

Ari gave a strangled laugh. "You and what army?"

"General Marshall trained me himself," Jonah reminded him. "Come on!"

* * *

"OH, I'M SUCH a mean Nazi," Will was saying in a singsong voice. "What you all must think of me . . ."

Vi and Walter had come to. "I do feel sorry for you," Vi said truthfully.

Veronica nodded. "Those things you told me—about your father, the way he treated you? It's horrible. I can't imagine a child coming through that unscathed." She knew Will's mother had committed suicide. He'd lost all his security and was left with only a grandmother who put him to work on the family farm and treated him like a hired hand, not even providing enough to eat. No wonder he poured all his passion and loyalty into that other family, his adopted Nazi family—the family who would never betray him.

"Although it's still no excuse. You're a man now, and as a man, you're responsible for your actions."

Will looked at her, his eyes bright with what she suspected might be tears. "I actually cared for you, Veronica," he told her. "I thought about marrying you—what a good wife you'd make, what beautiful children we'd have."

"I doubt you could ever really care for anyone besides your-self . . . I do wonder, if all the Jews are gone, who will you all find to hate then?"

"Den! Mund! Halten!"

The New Yorker urge to mouth off rose instinctively, but she kept the *Why don't you shut your trap, arschloch?* behind her teeth and instead looked to her mother, who shook her head, indicating they should keep quiet.

Mother—my North Star, she thought, *my moral compass . . .* Ve-ronica suddenly felt protective of Vi, protective as her mother must have been of her as an infant. She wished for anything to be able suddenly to sprout enormous bulletproof feathered wings and wrap them about her mother tightly, enveloping her and keeping her safe.

"Now," Will said, going to a metal tray covered in equipment and selecting a pair of pliers. "Let's start again."

* * *

JONAH AND ARI drove down a dirt road to the place Veronica had said the front gates were. They were exactly where she described, tall and black in the car's headlights. A guard with a red armband with a swastika was keeping watch. "Hey, this is private property!" he said. He was short, brown-haired, and plump—the exact op-posite of the Aryan ideal. And he was carrying a rifle.

"Sorry," Jonah said, getting out of the car. The sentry raised his gun. "We're lost—trying to get to Malibu." Jonah, smiling and hands up, walked to the gatehouse. "Big party at Frank Capra's place."

"Stop!"

"Here, I'll show you my driver's license." He was a foot away when he reached into the pocket of his leather jacket. "Damn it, I just had it! Must be back in the car."

He gestured to the vehicle then swiftly turned back. In one fluid motion, Jonah clamped his hands over both of the sentry's and twisted the rifle around, breaking the man's trigger finger while pulling the rifle away. He jammed the weapon's butt into the sentry's stomach. As the man doubled over in pain, Jonah slammed it down on his head.

He made sure the man still had a pulse and then, keeping the rifle, opened the black gates wide before getting back in the car. The road was long, but they could see the ranch house lit up by a twenty-foot burning swastika. Ari pulled over, near some scraggly bushes, and parked. He turned off the engine and got out. They stared at the flickering red flames in silence. *"Heylike drek,"* he managed finally.

"*Holy shit* is right," Jonah said. "Let's go."

They approached the house in the gray just before dawn, keeping to the trees on the side of the road, their ears strained for the sound of danger approaching. As they moved closer, they could hear music playing from a portable radio, laughter, dogs barking, and gunshots, and smelled smoke and charred meat. Fires burned in metal trash cans, illuminating teenage boys using their pistols for target practice, and in the shadows, couples gyrated in various stages of undress. "It looks like a Hieronymus Bosch painting," Ari whispered.

Jonah motioned they should go around to the back of the ranch.

"Who's there?" Another man, also with a red swastika armband, was sitting on a rock, eating a sausage roll; his gun lay beside him. "Hey!" he said, hearing something in the underbrush. "Someone there?"

As the man turned, Jonah came up from behind, placed the rifle across his neck and his knee against his back, and pulled. "Get the keys," Jonah whispered to Ari. He held on as the man began to gasp, his hands clawing and flailing as he tried to free himself.

Ari went through the man's pockets. "Got 'em."

But the man pulled a knife from a side holster. He stabbed it into Ari's abdomen.

"No!" Jonah released the man, swinging the rifle like a baseball bat, catching him in the face with a sick thud. He fell to the ground, blood spurting from his nose.

"I'm fine," Ari said, sinking to the ground.

Jonah's face was inscrutable. "You're not fine."

"Go and get them—come back for me later."

"I'm not going to leave you—"

"It's superficial," Ari said, taking off his jacket and applying pressure. "Just go!"

"Yes, sir," Jonah said reluctantly, and ran toward the house.

Ari whispered the proverb "Walk straight and you will not fail," before losing consciousness.

CHAPTER THIRTY-ONE

Alone, Jonah reached the back door, the servants' entrance to the ranch. The door was locked, but he opened it using the keys from the guard.

He froze in the large kitchen when he heard loud, drunken voices. A man staggered in, went to the icebox, and pulled the door open. He took out a bottle of beer and then noticed Jonah. "Hey!"

Jonah charged him. The man smashed the beer bottle on the edge of the counter and brandished the broken bottle as a weapon. Jonah stopped just before running into it. As the man stabbed forward, Jonah sidestepped, grabbing the man's wrist and pivoting. Jonah pushed down hard, and the man's wrist audibly cracked as it broke. He screamed in pain, but Jonah landed a solid punch to his face, knocking him out. The unconscious body landed with a thud on the tiles of the kitchen floor.

Jonah heard a creak. Looking over, he noticed the basement door slightly ajar. As he approached the door, it flew open, and a fist met his face. He staggered back from the blow as Will grabbed him by the shirt collar, spun him around, and punched him again. Jonah was in a daze when Will raised his foot, kicking him square in the chest. He tumbled backward, falling down the stairs.

In the basement, Veronica gasped and looked on with disbelief. Will shouted, "Get up! Hands up!"

Jonah, kneeling, raised his palms. "I'm the Jew you want. Take me." He looked to Veronica. "Let her go." His eyes widened as he saw Vi and Walter. "Let them all go."

"I know who you are," Will said. "You're working with Lewis. You bring shame to the Italian side of your family."

"You don't have to do this," Veronica said to Will.

"It won't make you feel any better," Jonah offered. "And it will probably make you feel worse. You'll have to live with whatever you do for the rest of your life."

"I regret nothing!" Will shouted.

"Then what?" Vi said. "What's next? Who's next? What if you run out of people to blame—what then?"

"You think all this is worth it?" Veronica asked.

"I do, you know I do," Will replied. "When we clean out the Jewish scum—"

"You're a small, small man, Will," Veronica told him sadly, "if you need to inflict pain on others to make yourself feel good."

"I know you both hate me—just as I hate you." His eyes were bloodshot, and his usually immaculate clothing was crumpled and sweat-stained.

Her pulse beat so loud in her ears she was sure he could hear it. "But I don't, Will," Veronica told him. "I don't hate you. I never hated you. I tried to understand you. You're educated and well-spoken. You're a wonderful musician, and painter, and orator. You're a mastermind at organization. We both love Beethoven."

She shook her head. "You told me a little about your family, and from what you've said, you have every reason to hate your father—"

"Shut up!"

"Sounds like she struck a nerve," Jonah noted.

"But the thing I've realized," Veronica continued, "is that—ultimately—it doesn't matter where the hate comes from. You know, I've spent so long trying to figure it out, trying to intellectualize it."

She drew a deep breath. "Yes, of course there are always 'reasons.' The violent father, the authoritarian mother, poverty, abuse, war—but at the end of the day, who cares? Let's just stop it. Stop hating each other. We need to transcend the hate, the chaos. We need to move past it."

Will twisted to face her. "You're a foolish woman. You know nothing!"

Jonah, still on his knees, spread his arms wide. "Do it," he said. "Kill me."

Will leaned down and pointed his gun at Jonah's head. Jonah began reciting a prayer in Hebrew. Will snarled, "Shut up!"

At that, Jonah turned his head away from the gun and grabbed Will's hands. The gun dropped to the floor. Will clenched his fist and punched Jonah in the eye, then wrapped his hands around his neck, slamming Jonah's head to the floor.

With his last breath, Jonah pushed off with one arm, causing them to both fall on their sides. As Will's grip loosened, Jonah grabbed his upper arm, twisted, and pulled, dislocating Will's shoulder. He howled in pain as Jonah grabbed him by his white-blond hair and slammed his forehead to the ground. It was over.

Jonah, on his hands and knees, was coughing. Finally, he stood, and staggered over to untie Veronica. "You all right?" he asked quietly.

"Just dandy," she said shakily, and helped untie Vi and Walter. "Now, let's get out of here."

But Will was slowly reaching for his fallen gun. He picked it up and aimed. "Die, *Juden*." They all turned to stare at him in the frozen horror between breaths.

Noise filled the room. Veronica closed her eyes in shock, fearing the worst. But the bullet never landed, although she felt drops of hot blood rain across her face and the air smelled of burning gunpowder.

When she opened her eyes, she realized Vi was still alive and safe, and so was Walter. She looked to Jonah. But he was all right, too, just breathing heavily. Finally, her gaze settled on Will. He looked surprised and staggered a step before jerking sideways and falling to the floor. Veronica could see his skull had been shattered, splattering bone and brain on the basement wall. As the blood began to trickle down the wall, she looked up from Will's body to see Ari, his face white and covered in droplets of Will's blood. He was leaning on the stair railing, holding a gun, his arm shaking.

"'Rejoice not at thine enemy's fall,'" he said, lowering the gun. He tried to smile. "But, then again, don't be in a big hurry to pick him up either."

Jonah exclaimed, "You own a gun?"

"I get death threats from Nazis all the time," Ari told him, tucking the gun into the waistband of his pants. "Of course I own a gun."

* * *

VERONICA AND JONAH, each supporting Ari, climbed up from the basement. They were followed by Vi and Walter. By this time, it was midday, but instead of a sunny blue sky, all they could see was hellish black smoke through the kitchen windows.

They headed for the back door and then outside. Sparks from the huge burning swastika, blown by the Santa Ana winds, had caught fire in the sage and umber landscape—the dry desert shrubs and the brittle underbrush. The dry land had turned into an inferno.

The radio was still on. The station had switched from music to news: *"Hello, NBC, hello, NBC,"* a male voice said over static. *"This is KGU in Honolulu, Hawaii. I'm speaking from the roof of the Advertiser Publishing Company building."*

As they hid in the tree line behind the house, Veronica whispered, "Wait!"

"No time," Jonah whispered to her as the fire burned closer.

Veronica was transfixed. "Shh . . . listen."

"We've witnessed this morning a distant view of a brief, full battle of Pearl Harbor and the severe bombing of Pearl Harbor by enemy planes, undoubtedly Japanese."

"Oh, God," Ari gasped. "It's happening."

"The city of Honolulu has also been attacked and considerable damage done . . . It's no joke—this is really war."

✳ ✳ ✳

AS THEY REACHED the car, parked near the gate, they realized the FBI, police, and firemen had arrived. "What are you doing here?" Doolin said to the group, then saw the blood on Ari's shirt and Veronica's face. "We need to get you to the hospital!"

"What are you doing here?" Ari countered weakly.

He choked a little from the smoke. "We're at war with Japan now. On Hoover's orders, we're taking Will Wagner, Samuel Carson, and the others into custody—also seizing whatever arms and ammunition they have."

"What about Marv Whiteside?" Vi asked in a trembling voice.

"Yeah, got him, too."

"Wagner's dead," Veronica told Doolin. She had begun to shake violently, a delayed reaction to the tension. One of the firemen noticed and found a blanket to wrap around her. "His body's in the basement."

"I killed him," Ari stated as he sat down on a nearby rock. Another fireman rushed over to attend to his wound.

Doolin looked at Ari's bloody shirt. "I assume in self-defense?"

"Veronica, Vi, and the uncle were kidnapped," Ari told him, his voice weak. "Jonah and I came to help."

"You didn't call me?"

"You were saving Boyle Heights." Ari hesitated. "How—how is everything?"

"It's all right now," Doolin said. "Your warning gave us an edge when it came to picking them up. It was ugly for a while—with plans to blow up defense installations and seize munitions from the National Guard—but we got them before they could do any real damage."

"Thank heavens," Vi said.

Doolin told them, "We're also hearing Japan attacked the Philippines, Guam, Malaya, Singapore, Hong Kong, and Wake Island."

"So many lives lost," Veronica said, shaking her head.

"You know," Jonah said as they all made their way to the car, "years from now people will ask us, 'Where were you when you heard the news Pearl Harbor was bombed? When war began in the United States?'"

Veronica reached for his hand. "And we were at Hitler's Los Angeles bunker."

Jonah cracked a half smile. When they were all in the car, he turned the key in the ignition. Doolin gave the vehicle a final pat on the roof, and they drove away from the fire, following the ambulance carrying Ari to the hospital.

As they passed back through Murphy Ranch's black iron gates, Veronica kept her eyes forward. "And we can never say—because no one will ever believe us." As they drove away on the dirt road, heading for the Pacific Coast Highway, the winds from the ocean cleared the dark smoke. She added, "I feel like we're leaving the underworld."

She laughed her huge laugh, just slightly tinged with the edge of hysteria. "Whatever you do, don't look back."

CHAPTER THIRTY-TWO

For Ari and Jonah, this was the endgame.

President Roosevelt proclaimed the Japanese attack on Pearl Harbor, which killed more than 2,400 Americans and damaged or destroyed 8 battleships and 300 airplanes, "a day which will live in infamy" on his radio broadcast. Congress passed a declaration of war against Japan. Germany and Italy declared war on the United States, and the United States responded in kind.

Los Angeles and the entire West Coast were braced for anticipated attacks, and a state of emergency was declared. Antiaircraft crews and National Guardsmen were rushed in to protect airports and factories. The Navy secured the harbors. Military camps were set up in Exposition Park near the University of Southern California, as heavily armed soldiers in Army trucks and Jeeps barreled down Hollywood Boulevard. All bridges, tunnels, gas lines, and telephone lines were placed under twenty-four-hour surveillance. Stores were ordered closed at 4:30 P.M. and a blackout was imposed.

More pertinent to their specific work, local FBI agents moved with incredible speed and efficiency to round up suspected German spies, according to the detailed information Ari and Jonah had sent to the Justice Department.

A week after the attack, the four—Veronica, Vi, Jonah, and Ari—met at the Hollywood office.

"I brought food," Vi announced, carrying a basket of egg salad sandwiches and chocolate chip cookies, "because I know you don't have any. And it's kosher—or at least it doesn't mix meat and dairy. Honestly, I still don't know how that all works."

"It's perfect," Ari said, taking off his glasses and rising from his desk as the women entered. "Thank you. May I get you ladies anything? Water? Coffee?"

"Why don't you let me do everything?" Vi told him. "I'm surprised you're already up and around after everything you went through. By the way, what did you tell your family?"

"That I tripped holding a letter opener."

Vi raised an eyebrow but didn't comment as she went to the kitchenette.

"We're still calming Uncle Walter down," Veronica told them, as she set her purse on Jonah's desk. "But at least he's relieved we're not Nazis."

"And how are you?" Ari asked with concern.

"Oh, fine—fine," she said, hurrying to help her mother with the sandwiches.

The truth was, she was still exhausted and sore from the ordeal at the ranch, and felt as if her entire body and soul were bruised.

Jonah cleared his throat. "Hello? Am I chopped liver?"

"Yes, hello," she said affectionately, stopping to kiss his cheek. "I like chopped liver."

"Well, let's sit and eat," Ari said, gingerly making his way to the table.

"You've got to fill us in!" Veronica insisted while her mother got out plates and started making a pot of coffee. "What's happened with the FBI?"

"The U.S. attorney general authorized the L.A. FBI to apprehend people believed by the Bureau to be dangerous," Jonah told them, picking up half of a sandwich. "Hoover sent Doolin a teletype ordering the arrest of all German and Italian aliens who posed a threat."

He looked to Ari, who continued: "On Hoover's orders,

Deutsches Haus was raided by the FBI on December eighth. They seized ten thousand pro-Nazi circulars prepped for another snowstorm operation. The police chief warned them any future attempts to distribute hate-filled materials would result in prosecution under the California State Criminal Syndicalism Act."

Jonah picked up his coffee mug. "They also found all of the Bund's registration files and membership lists. And a whole lot of propaganda—straight from Goebbels in Germany."

"What about Schwinn?" Veronica asked.

"Schwinn was on Hoover's list, too. Considering the attack on Pearl Harbor," Ari told them, "the judge's moved up the date of his citizenship trial."

Veronica blotted her lips with a napkin. "Do you think he'll be deported?"

Jonah nodded. "It's looking good. They found all kinds of additional incriminating evidence at Deutsches Haus, including more shortwave radios, maps, photos, and cash. Schwinn's now facing federal charges."

"Well, good riddance!" said Vi.

"He's being held on Terminal Island with some of the others, awaiting trial."

"What about the McDonnells?" Veronica ventured.

"It seems they've gone underground, along with the sister—cutting ties with Deutsches Haus."

Veronica shook her head. "It's not going to stop them from their work. Or at least, for long."

"No, it won't. But at least they won't be getting money and propaganda from Nazi Germany anymore," Jonah said. "Which should slow them down."

"And Marv?" Vi asked.

"He was also arrested." Ari and Jonah exchanged a glance.

"What?" Vi said. "What aren't you telling us?"

"The government seized his research—and they're going to use it," Ari told her. "They're in talks with him."

Vi pushed her plate away, sandwich untouched. "They want to work with him now?"

Ari nodded. "They have several ongoing projects with rockets and nuclear fission, and they think he'll be of use."

"Weapons," Veronica said, realizing. "Nuclear weapons."

"We're at war," Jonah told her. "All's fair, as they say."

"They better keep a close eye on him," Vi muttered. "By the way"—she took a deep breath—"his coming to our house—that was my fault," she admitted quietly. "I gave him our address. I never should have done that."

"You were just trying to be kind," Ari reassured her.

"I had one too many gimlets," Vi admitted.

Veronica asked, "And what about Samuel Carson?"

"If you can believe," Ari began, "he's been released from jail—and continuing the Roosevelt impeachment trial. He's allegedly going to argue Japan didn't actually attack the United States—because Hawaii's not a legitimate U.S. possession."

Jonah rolled his eyes as Vi exclaimed, "Oh, that's rich!"

"He'll be arrested again soon, this time for sedition," Jonah said darkly.

Veronica grimaced. "Yes, but who knows if the charges'll stick?"

"It's been a revolving door around here," Ari said proudly, "with all the FBI agents needing our files."

"As well as the Army and Navy," Jonah added.

"Don't be so modest," Ari chided him. "Jonah's not telling you—J. Edgar Hoover himself called to thank Jonah for his service."

Veronica and Vi both exclaimed, "Congratulations!"

"I've been asked to serve as an unofficial agent for the FBI," Jonah said, cheeks pink. "Recommended by Walter Winchell himself!"

"Well done!" Veronica told him, placing her hand on his arm. "Well done."

"But what about you?" Vi asked Ari.

Ari shrugged. "What's important is the work. We're doing everything we can to help the government."

Jonah added, "We're sending our weekly summaries directly to Hoover now."

"Well, finally," Vi said. "I hope he appreciates everything you've done and continue to do."

"So, for the most part, the Los Angeles Bund is dead," Ari said. "Although I doubt they're not planning a retaliatory strike."

"They still have Murphy Ranch," Veronica pointed out.

"No," Ari said. "I'm pleased to say most of it burned to the ground in the fire. Whatever remained was seized as evidence. And everyone there was taken into custody."

Jonah told them, "As far as the authorities are concerned, Will Wagner died in the fire."

"And . . . where does that leave us?" Veronica asked.

"What do you want to do?" Jonah asked, eyes serious.

"Well, it's not over, is it?" Veronica said. "I mean, the war—it's just beginning for the United States."

"You'll both probably be called to testify in the state and federal trials," Ari said. "I'm focusing on organizing the information for the prosecution for the hearings in Sacramento and Washington, D.C. All the agents who worked with us will most likely be called."

"I'd be delighted to testify against those sons of bitches," Veronica said.

"Veronica!" Vi objected. "Language!"

"Sorry—those Nazi sons of bitches."

"Well, that's more accurate, at least." Vi took a tentative bite of sandwich. "And I'll testify, too, of course."

"You could write your book now, if you wanted," Jonah told Veronica, as he rose to refill his coffee mug. "You've gone to hell and back—no one would think less of you if you wanted to get out."

"But the story's not over yet!"

"It could be, for us," Vi told her daughter, placing a hand over hers. "We could go back to normal."

"I don't even know what 'normal' is anymore." Veronica snorted. "What if I stayed undercover?"

Ari and Jonah looked at each other. "You could visit the men in prison," Jonah said. "Schwinn and the rest of them. As far as they know, you're still loyal. You weren't seen by anyone at the Murphy Ranch—besides Will Wagner. And he's dead."

"Don't forget Marv," Vi added.

"Marv's not in any position to talk," Ari assured them.

"I'll think seriously about seeing it through," Veronica said. "It'd be hard to close Pandora's box now—even if we do have reason for hope."

Jonah gazed at her. "Someday, though, you'll find a new story. And you'll have to follow it where it leads. That's the job of the journalist."

"I'll worry about it when it happens."

"Vi?" Ari asked.

"What happened to Nora Ingle and her husband?" Vi asked, taking a sip of coffee.

"Immediately after the Pearl Harbor attack, they left for Washington," Ari told her. "We've just received word they've been arrested. It seems they've been taking money from the Nazis, and Nora never registered as a paid Nazi agent, in violation of the Foreign Agents Registration Act of 1938. They're most likely going to jail."

"Oh, thank goodness!" She chuckled. "Maybe I could embroider Nora's prison uniform. But I want out," she confessed. "I'll do my duty and testify if I'm asked, of course. But this has all been . . . unbelievably stressful.

"While I'm happy to help with the war effort, I also think it's time for me to do something for myself. There's a little shop on Third Avenue in Santa Monica that's been empty for a while. I spoke with the owner and the rent's not too much." She swallowed. "I don't think I can bear to embroider any more edelweiss and swastikas, if I'm honest. It just might be time for Visions by Violet."

"Wait, you never mentioned that!" Veronica exclaimed.

"I wanted to get my business plan together first and see about the rent."

" 'Visions by Violet'?"

"My shop," she said proudly. "My *atelier.*"

Veronica grinned at Ari. "What my mother also hasn't mentioned is . . . Agent Doolin's been calling."

"Veronica!" Vi blushed.

Ari raised his eyebrows. "Really?"

"He doesn't have much time, of course, because of, well, everything," Vi said. "But he's sent flowers to say thank you—and asked me to dinner when things calm down." She reached for Veronica's hand and held it. "If they ever calm down."

"And he knows about Daddy?" Veronica asked.

"Of course he knows about your father. And I have my wedding band in my jewelry box," Vi admitted. "But I do think—especially after coming so close to dying—it's time for me to start living my life again. I'm an entirely different woman from the one who first arrived in Los Angeles, you know. I've hated so much of what we had to do. But now I'm creating a business for myself. A new life. And, you know, maybe going on a date or two."

"And you fought Nazis," Veronica said with a smile.

"*We* fought Nazis." She squeezed Veronica's hand. "Not bad for a widowed middle-aged housewife going through 'the change,' right?"

"We owe you a debt of gratitude," Ari told them both, raising his coffee mug in salute.

"You owe us nothing," Vi told him. "We're all Americans. We're all fighting for a better America. As flawed as it is, those are the scars of a democracy worth fighting for."

Ari nodded. "Not everyone sees us"—he looked to Jonah—"as

real Americans, you know. But we are. And lots of other people here are as well."

Vi nodded and took a sip of coffee. "Amen."

"The thing is," Veronica said, "it's not just the Nazis like Schwinn and Will. It's the McDonnells as well, and Carlson. They're the most obvious, but there are so many more who agree. Good people. Decent people. People who laugh and bake oatmeal cookies and go to picnics and concerts. A lot of Americans have lost our way."

"What do you suggest we do?" Ari asked.

"Stop the spread of lies that feed their fears." She looked up. "We can handle the truth here in America. It's the lies that put us all in danger."

Vi twisted her suffragist ring, then removed it. "I want to give this to you," she said to Veronica.

"Oh, Mother, I couldn't—"

"You can and you will," Vi said, slipping it on Veronica's ring finger. It fit perfectly.

Veronica held it up to the light, where the amethyst and peridot stones sparkled. "It's beautiful," she murmured.

"It's yours now. I hope it reminds you of how strong you are."

Veronica kissed Vi's cheek. "Strong like you, my North Star."

Later, in the kitchenette, Jonah approached Veronica, helping herself to a chocolate chip cookie. *Not oatmeal raisin,* she thought, and forced herself not to giggle.

"So . . . maybe I could take you to dinner sometime?" he asked. "Even if it's in the car? I know a great place to park and watch the sunset."

Veronica smiled wickedly. "I just bet you do."

* * *

ALMOST AS SOON as she and Vi returned from the Hollywood office, Veronica went upstairs to her bedroom, sat down at her desk, turned on the light, and began to write. She'd held off until now, but the dam was breaking, and she wanted to get everything down on paper while it was still vivid. To speak her truth about what she had seen. The cats slept, curled up on the bed as Veronica worked. Mama C watched over them all with slow-blinking eyes, as Veronica's pencil scratched the notepaper.

Veronica wasn't sure what would come. She started with small moments, impressions: The sound of McDonnell's voice, so warm and pleasant, as he called for killing Jews. The incongruity of Harriet's generosity and hospitality with her bloodlust. The scent of Will's No. 4711 cologne and how beautifully he played the violin. How he'd spoken of his family, especially his father, and the beatings he'd endured. Schwinn's idea of an Aryan Renaissance—and how white Christians were more important than anyone else. How he believed democracy was dangerous. How he impressed upon the McDonnells and the like that they were the "real" Americans. How they thought nothing—nothing—of using violence against their fellow citizens to get what they wanted.

She remembered a particular moment when Will told her he'd realized a childhood friend of his was Jewish. He didn't hate his friend, he'd told her—he was just terribly sad the friend had been unlucky enough to be born that way. She worked to flesh out snippets of conversations and impressions. She wrote and wrote and then put it away. Tomorrow, she'd pull it out and write again. Who were they? Why had they acted in this way? Why had it all happened?

I believe in this country, Veronica thought, looking out the window at the pomegranate tree. *I love this country. I believe in democracy. And I want to speak the truth about what I saw.*

Night after night, she'd remember ever-darker things she'd witnessed, while still realizing her piece of human suffering was small, a minuscule part of what was going on in the United States, in the world. One sentence after another, writing out the accumulated rage and grief she felt at her fellow citizens' betrayal of the United

States's democratic ideals. Writing became not just an act of faith, but also a way to save her sanity.

One night near Christmas, at their bungalow, Veronica asked Jonah how his work was going.

"Everything's quiet right now," he told her, placing takeout from the diner on the kitchen table. "The FBI's taken over everything. Deutsches Haus is closed except on the weekends. It's a shell of its former self."

"Well, that's good, isn't it?" She took a bite of french fry with ketchup. "Or do you think they're just staying quiet—until the time is right?"

"What do you think?"

"They've taken a blow, for sure. The war'll keep Hoover and the FBI's sights on them. But they're still out there. Even if it's just people like the McDonnells having coffee and cookies with his sister and their neighbors and talking about killing Jews. It'll continue."

"It will," he agreed.

"And it's getting worse. There's so much hate for the Japanese now, too. Hate for the young Chicano men who wear zoot suits. Hate for the colored families coming here to work in the aviation industry. Hate for the women going to work in the factories, too."

Jonah nodded.

"I'm third-generation German and my mother is second. And yet, we're in no real danger—even though we also trace our roots to an Axis country. But because of the way we look, people assume we're good and loyal Americans."

"Being blond and blue-eyed helps."

"I know." Veronica nodded slowly. "I also know there's already anti-Japanese hysteria gripping Los Angeles—and running up and down the coast. Probably all over the country. Of course we have to guard against fifth columnists, but by the same token, we can't punish the innocent for the crimes of the guilty in lands from which they came and long since disassociated themselves."

Jonah pushed back his hair. "I'm absolutely sick at all the ignorant things people are saying—in private and in public. We can't dismiss it, because underneath that rage is fear—and below that, pain. Letting go of the rage means facing the fear and the pain. And that's not going to happen any time soon—if ever."

Veronica took a deep breath. "I've been writing," she told him.

"Good for you!"

"But I don't think I'm done with spying."

"What do you mean?"

"I've been thinking about what you and Ari said, about visiting Schwinn and the rest in jail. Maybe they'd tell me something."

Jonah was still. "You could also walk away."

"I know," she said. "But maybe I don't want to. Not yet, at least. Maybe not until the trials are over."

"So, keep spying. And writing—and do a bang-up job at it."

"Oh, I plan to!" she assured him. "I want to help people to see what it's like—what it's *really* like—in the thick of it here. Writing truthfully could wake minds to what's really happening in the United States." She took a deep breath. "'This should have been a noble creature: he / Hath all the energy which would have made / A goodly frame of glorious elements, / Had they been wisely mingled.'"

Jonah looked at her. "'As it is, it is an awful chaos—light and darkness, / And mind and dust, and passions and pure thoughts / Mix'd and contending without end or order, / All dormant or destructive.'"

"Ah, I should have known you'd be a Byron fan."

He smiled modestly. "I do read, you know."

"The thing is, there's so much lost potential. What good could they have done—for themselves and the country—if they hadn't been focused on hate?"

"That's why you did so well—you never saw them as monsters. You saw them as humans, humans who'd gone terribly wrong."

"They wanted purpose, companionship, a sense of identity and community. As people who need to see themselves as superior and yet also as victims. People who want to lash out and hurt the way they've been hurt. If I can hold up a mirror, maybe people can see themselves. Maybe not make the same mistakes we've all been making, myself included, over and over again." She gave a short laugh.

She remembered her moment thinking of Max and the Feldmans, how easy it was to extrapolate from one person and situation into hate of the many. *It's just so easy,* she thought, feeling guilt and knowing she'd have to include that part as well. It wasn't about writing for a prestigious paper or winning literary prizes anymore. She wanted to do it because it was her story, and it was important to her. *It's all too easy for us to fall into hate. For any of us. For all of us. I used to think, "It could never happen here"—and it not only could have, but almost did. And there's every reason to believe it could happen again in the future.*

"As Martha Gellhorn said, 'The only way I can pay back for what fate and society have handed me is to try to make an angry sound against injustice.' Maybe someday I light out for Europe, like Martha—a crazy girl war correspondent—running straight into the burning building."

"I wouldn't bet against you." Jonah looked at her with shining eyes and took her hand. "If you want to do this, you will. Write what you saw, what you felt. The words will come—and it'll be a wiz of a book. Just start."

"Thank you," Veronica said. And when he finally left, she went upstairs to her desk, picked up her pencil, and resumed writing.

AFTERWORD

VERONICA GRACE is loosely based on real-life secretary Sylvia Comfort. Comfort really did begin working for William Pierce Williams and his wife, who were publishing anti-Semitic materials in 1940. Like Veronica, she was horrified and reported them. Ultimately, Sylvia was introduced to the spy Leon L. Lewis and began to work undercover. Like her fictional counterpart, Comfort was accused of spying by many at Deutsches Haus, and to protect her, the FBI made a fake arrest of both her and her mother. Comfort continued to work as a spy after Pearl Harbor, and testified against many of the people she worked for in the sedition trials in Sacramento and Washington, D.C. She then moved to Washington, D.C., working as a secretary to Los Angeles congressman Gordon McDonough. Little is known about her personal life.

VIOLET "VI" GRACE is based on the real-life Grace Comfort, the mother of Sylvia Comfort and the widow of a Navy commander. She primarily worked behind the scenes with Navy veterans and their wives.

ARI LEWIS is based on the real-life spymaster Leon L. Lewis. Lewis's often thankless work resulted in the successful expulsion of Nazi Germans from the United States and prosecution of multiple American Nazis. Lewis continued to fight for civil rights—for Black Americans, Asian Americans, and Mexican Americans, as well as Jewish Americans—all his life. He served as executive director of the Community Relations Committee of the Jewish Federation Council of Greater Los Angeles for seventeen years, after which he returned to his law practice.

JONAH ROSE is roughly based on Joseph Roos, Leon L. Lewis's assistant in the lead-up to World War II. Roos eventually succeeded Lewis as executive director of the Community Relations Committee of the Jewish Federation Council of Greater Los Angeles. He was involved with social and political issues in Southern California such as school busing, discrimination, and prayer in schools. Roos was a prolific writer and also formed his own public relations business.

DONALD PIERCE MCDONNELL and HARRIET MCDONNELL are inspired by East Hollywood High School teachers William Pierce Williams and his wife, Hannah Williams. Williams was involved with various plots, including one to sabotage the West Coast's aircraft factories. They really did live on Poinsettia Drive next door to Williams's sister-in-law, who owned the mimeograph machine that printed their anti-Semitic and anti-democratic pamphlets and flyers. Sylvia Comfort did secretarial work for them, and she and her mother did become friends with the couple, who introduced them to people at Deutsches Haus. In 1948, Williams shot his wife, then himself. His suicide note read: "Collapsed nerves. Returning to the Creator."

COMMANDER EZRA ZABNER is inspired by Commander Ellis M. Zacharias. The Navy commander was friends with Lewis; his focus was on targeting Japanese spies in the United States, and sometimes their worlds overlapped. When the Japanese attacked Pearl Harbor on December 7, 1941, Zacharias was on USS *Salt Lake City*, escorting the aircraft carrier USS *Enterprise* between Wake Island and Pearl Harbor. After the war, Zacharias was appointed to the Office of Naval Intelligence, where he developed plans to restructure and centralize military intelligence, ultimately resulting in the Defense Intelligence Agency, established in 1961. The television series *Behind Closed Doors* was based on Zacharias's wartime experiences.

CHARLIE SCHRODER was another undercover agent who worked for Lewis and Roos; his real-life counterpart is Charles "Chuck" Slocomb. The Long Beach water taxi driver, who belonged to the German American Bund and the Silver Shirts, really had been a member of the KKK for decades, which gave him the perfect cover. The real Slocomb did not die by poison; fictional Charlie Schroder's death was inspired by another real-life spy for Lewis and Roos named John Schmidt, who was allegedly poisoned by the Nazis.

HERMANN SCHWINN (his real name) was a Nazi spy in Los Angeles. German-born Schwinn was head of Friends of the New Germany, which became the West Coast German American Bund. Schwinn was in contact with high-ranking Nazis in Germany and a constant presence at Deutsches Haus, where Sylvia Comfort did secretarial work for him. He also had his U.S. citizenship revoked on a technicality, was tried for sedition, and was held as an enemy alien. In 1948, he went to Buenos Aires, Argentina, and returned to the United States in 1952, living out his life in San Antonio, Florida.

WILHELM "WILL" WAGNER is based on the Austrian Franz Ferenz. He was an active Nazi agent in the United States, as well as a distributor of German films on the West Coast. He was the owner of the Continental Bookstore in downtown Los Angeles, which distributed anti-Semitic propaganda, and the author of a biography of Hitler. He was close with both Sylvia and Grace Comfort. But unlike the fictional Will Wagner, Ferenz lived. He was arrested and imprisoned for violating state anti-subversion laws in 1942 and released in 1945 after an appeals court ruled there was insufficient evidence that he had ever advocated a violent overthrow of the government. He returned to working at his bookstore.

SAMUEL CARSON'S real-life model is Robert Noble, an American anti-Semite and member of the Friends of Progress. Ultimately, he was charged with conspiracy to violate the sedition law of the United States and found guilty of sedition and conspiracy. He was imprisoned, but his conviction was reversed after the suspicious death of the presiding judge and a mistrial, and he returned to Los Angeles.

ADAM HABER (from the prologue) is based on Julius Sicius, another real-life spy for Lewis and Roos who was caught taking down license plate numbers in the Deutsches Haus parking lot. He died in mysterious circumstances not long after, and the spymasters believed he'd been murdered, along with several other of their undercover agents who'd also been "made" and found dead in shadowy circumstances.

NORA INGLE is inspired by the aviatrix Laura Ingalls (a distant relative of the *Little House on the Prairie* author). Ingalls and her husband, Clayton F. Ingalls, worked closely with George Edward Deatherage, the leader of a fascist military organization planning a coup. Laura Ingalls was close with Grace Comfort and did invite her to Berlin.

Ingalls was charged with failing to register with the government as a paid Nazi agent, in violation of the Foreign Agents Registration Act of 1938. She was arrested, convicted, and sentenced, serving time at the U.S. federal women's prison in Alderson, West Virginia. She was released in 1943. However, she was arrested at the Mexican border in 1945 for smuggling seditious materials, including notes she had made of Japanese and German shortwave radio broadcasts. She was never charged and ultimately returned to Burbank, California.

MARV WHITESIDE is inspired by real-life rocketeer Jack Parsons, who was born Marvel Whiteside Parsons. He was an American rocket engineer, chemist, and Thelemite occultist who was corresponding with the German rocket scientist Wernher von Braun. Associated with the California Institute of Technology, Parsons was one of the principal founders of the Jet Propulsion Laboratory (JPL) and the Aerojet Engineering Corporation. Parsons, however, believed in democracy and was never tempted by Nazi financing.

THE MURPHY RANCH—"Hitler's White House"—was built by Winona and Norman Stevens, members of the anti-Semitic white supremacist Silver Shirts organization, in the Pacific Palisades. After the attack on Pearl Harbor, the unfinished ranch was taken over by the FBI and LAPD. A few cement buildings, now covered in graffiti, remain to this day.

ACKNOWLEDGMENTS

Radicalized hate groups. Propaganda. Calls to violence. Conspiracies to overthrow the U.S. government. Spymasters and undercover agents. These elements are part of a little-known story that took place more than ninety years ago in Los Angeles.

I'm profoundly grateful for the opportunity to write about this overlooked chapter of U.S. history. This novel is about American Nazism, yes, and a look at the United States's complicated past—but to me it's much more about the promise of the United States of America, as well as the courage, love, and hope of its citizens, including women.

Thank you to Noel MacNeal, who found Steven J. Ross's book *Hitler in Los Angeles* and got it for me, the reason this book exists. And Matthew MacNeal, who's always (always!) patient and supportive.

This book would not exist without the Special Collections at the California State University Northridge Library. I'd like to thank librarian David N. Siegler, Reading Room Supervisor for the Special Collections & Archives in particular. He was an absolute hero to photocopy and email the contents of boxes of Leon Lewis's and Sylvia Comfort's papers to me during the pandemic.

I'd also like to thank Michaela Ullmann, Exile Studies Librarian at the Special Collections of Doheny Memorial Library at the University of Southern California, for allowing me access to Joseph Roos's papers.

Thank you to Victoria Skurnick at Levine Greenberg Rosten Literary Agency, and Elana Seplow-Jolly, Kim Hovey, Jenny Chen, Sarah Breivogel, Allison Schuster, and Mae Martinez at Penguin Random House for their support and good cheer throughout this journey. Jenny, you took on this book and author without warning—I'm so grateful for your sensitive reads and thoughtful comments. And thank you to all the unsung heroes of publishing—the copy editors, designers, production team, copywriters, and sales reps as well. I appreciate you.

A special thank-you to Idria Barone Knecht, fellow novelists Kim Fay and Mariah Fredericks, and Martha Gellhorn expert Janet Somerville. Thanks to proud Hunter graduate Lauren Marchisotto. As always, I'm also grateful to the historian I'm lucky enough to call a friend, Ronald Granieri. I'm grateful for lawyer Amanda C. Aubrey, and her legal knowledge about the First Amendment and Nazism in California in 1940.

Thanks to Liz Hara, Jennifer Serchia, Kim Fay, Naomi Hirahara, Bruce Lanoil, and Laura Urstein Lanoil for helping me and hanging out with me during my time doing research in Los Angeles.

Thanks to Michael Pieck, Heather Beckman, and Alexa and Kaia Pieck for their love and support—and generous offers of space for me to write and edit. And journalist (and fellow Wellesley alum) Lynn Sherr, for talking about her experiences as a young journalist and *Mademoiselle* guest editor, her love of Brenda Starr, and her podcast, *She Votes!* with Ellen Godman, about women's suffrage in the U.S. A lot of the podcast inspired Vi's background. Speaking of Wellesley alums, thanks, as always, to Dr. Merideth Norris, for making sure the medical details were correct.

And special thanks to Melanie Koski, for allowing me to read her 1998 California State, Northridge, college thesis, *Sylvia and Grace Comfort: Informants for the CRC.*

SOURCES

First and foremost, I must again credit Steven J. Ross's *Hitler in Los Angeles: How Jews Foiled Nazi Plots Against Hollywood and America.*

I also immersed myself in John Roy Carlson's *Under Cover: My Four Years in the Nazi Underworld of America—the Amazing Revelation of How Axis Agents and Our Enemies Within Are Now Plotting to Destroy the United States.* It's the actual story of Carlson's journey as a spy in a New York Nazi organization, and provided an incredible insider's perspective. It's out of print now, but copies are available at secondhand bookstores.

Ross's *Hitler in Los Angeles* led me to the Special Collections University Library at University of California, Northridge, where I was able (with Reading Room Supervisor David N. Siegler's patient and expert assistance) to read box upon box of Leon Lewis's original papers, as well as Sylvia Comfort's memos and reports. Access to the Special Collections Library made history come alive for me and I can't thank the staff enough.

Below is a list of other sources I used.

BOOKS

Dinnerstein, Leonard, *Antisemitism in America,* Oxford University Press.

Evanosky, Dennis, and Kos, Eric J., *Lost Los Angeles,* Pavilion Books.

Federal Writers Project of the Works Progress Administration, *Los Angeles in the 1930s: The WPA Guide to the City of Angels (WPA Guides),* University of California Press.

Friedrich, Otto, *City of Nets: A Portrait of Hollywood in the 1940's*, Harper Perennial.

Gabriel Louise B., and Santa Monica Historical Society Museum, *Early Santa Monica*, Arcadia Publishing.

Hart, Bradley W., *Hitler's American Friends: The Third Reich's Supporters in the United States*, Thomas Dunne Books.

Jeansonne, Glen, *Women of the Far Right*, University of Chicago Press.

Kipen, David, ed., *Dear Los Angeles: The City in Diaries and Letters, 1542 to 2018*, Modern Library.

Klingaman, William K., *The Darkest Year: The American Home Front, 1941–1942*, St. Martin's Press.

Littleton, C. Scott, *2500 Strand: Growing Up in Hermosa Beach, California, During World War II*, Red Pill Press.

Lotchin, Roger W., *The Way We Really Were: The Golden State in the Second Great War*, University of Illinois Press.

Marquez, Ernest, *Santa Monica Beach: A Collector's Pictorial History*, Angel City Press.

Medoff, Rafael, *The Jews Should Keep Quiet: Franklin D. Roosevelt, Rabbi Stephen S. Wise, and the Holocaust*, University of Nebraska Press.

Murphy, Michael, *Santa Monica: A Look Back to 1902 from Today*, America Through Time.

Nagorski, Andrew, *Hitlerland: American Eyewitnesses to the Nazi Rise to Power*, Simon & Schuster.

Olson, Lynne, *Those Angry Days: Roosevelt, Lindbergh, and America's Fight Over World War II, 1939–1941*, Random House.

Rice, Christina, ed., *How We Worked, How We Played: Herman Schultheis and Los Angeles of the 1930s*, Photo Friends.

Rosenzweig, Laura B., *Hollywood's Spies: The Undercover Surveillance of Nazis in Los Angeles*, NYU Press.

Somerville, Janet, *Yours, for Probably Always: Martha Gellhorn's Letters of Love and War, 1930–1949*, Firefly Books.

Stanley, Jason, *How Fascism Works: The Politics of Us and Them,* Random House.

Stephenson, Elaine, *My Life Above the Carousel in Santa Monica,* Laneybee Publishing.

Wallach, Ruth, et al, *Los Angeles in World War II,* Arcadia Publishing.

White, E. B., *On Democracy,* HarperCollins.

Whitman, James Q., *Hitler's American Model: The United States and the Making of Nazi Race Law,* Princeton University Press.

Williams, Joan M., *Hunter College: The College History Series,* Arcadia Publishing.

VIDEOS

Hollywoodism: Jews, Movies, and the American Dream. A&E.

Nazi Compound in L.A.—What Remains of Murphy Ranch. AOL. YouTube.

A Night at the Garden. Marshall Curry Productions.

Walter Winchell: The Power of Gossip. PBS.

DIGITAL

California State University, Northridge, *In Our Own Backyard: Resisting Nazi Propaganda in Southern California 1933–1945,* https://digital -library.csun.edu/in-our-own-backyard/historical-context.

THESIS

Koski, Melanie, *Sylvia and Grace Comfort: Informants for the CRC,* thesis for CSU Northridge, 1998.

HISTORICAL NOTES

When I read Steven J. Ross's *Hitler in Los Angeles* to research the tenth Maggie Hope novel, *The Hollywood Spy* (with Ari Lewis as a supporting character and Veronica making an appearance), I couldn't help but note Professor Ross's mention of two women, a mother-and-daughter team. Sylvia and Grace Comfort worked for Ari Lewis and Joseph Roos in the '40s: the two women went undercover, posing as Nazi sympathizers, to infiltrate Los Angeles's German American Bund and German and American Nazis. They were footnotes to a footnote of American history.

What did I know at this point? Not much, really: that Grace Comfort was a Navy commander's widow, and that she and her daughter had moved from San Diego to Los Angeles for financial reasons. That's pretty much it.

My characters, however, are from Brooklyn. I decided to make this change because I wanted Veronica to graduate from Hunter College, a diverse (then) women's college in New York City. And I wanted her to have experienced the Nazi rally at Madison Square Garden.

Veronica's a journalist (which Sylvia was not), because I wanted her to have an eye for "reporting" what was going on. I also wanted her to know of and admire female journalists of the time, particularly Martha Gellhorn (inspired by Janet Somerville's excellent *Yours, for Probably Always: Martha Gellhorn's Letters of Love and War, 1930–1949*).

Nothing is known about Grace Comfort except for the dates of her birth, death, and marriage. I filled in her work with the suffragist movement and her embroidery skills.

From then on, the story follows Grace and Sylvia Comfort's more closely, with a random recommendation for a job that ended up being for the American Nazis William Pierce Williams and his wife, Harriet Williams. Sylvia was troubled by the material they were producing, and she and Grace contacted a friend of their late father's in Naval Intelligence, Commander Ellis Zacharias. Zacharias, who was spying on the Japanese in Southern California, introduced the Comforts to Leon Lewis and his assistant Joseph Roos.

Much of the plot is true, meaning factual—these things actually happened. At times, however, the timeline is compressed, and some plots other agents were involved with were given to the fictional Veronica and Violet.

America First was a real organization, with Charles Lindbergh as a prominent member. The German American Bund was real, as well. Deutsches Haus in Los Angeles was real. Actual Nazis, from Germany, were working with the Bund and America First to influence German Americans—providing a positive view of Nazism and encouraging the U.S. to stay out of foreign wars. This is fact, not fiction.

Now let's address some of the major plot points. There really was a scheme to lynch prominent actors and Hollywood figures, including Al Jolson, Eddie Cantor, Charlie Chaplin, Louis B. Mayer, and Samuel Goldwin.

There was a plan to drive through Boyle Heights and machine-gun as many Jewish people as possible.

There was a strategy to fumigate Jewish homes with cyanide (in an uncanny foreshadowing of the Nazi concentration and extermination camps).

There were actual plans to sabotage Southern California aviation plants—explosives were found at Lockheed. Nazi Hermann Schwinn really did have a plot to destroy the airplane factories on

Memorial Day of 1941. Lewis and Roos and their agents discovered the plans and the FBI intervened before anything could happen.

Henry Allen really did have a briefcase filled with incriminating documents. And, during a "snowstorm," Lewis, Roos, and Zacharias got hold of it while Allen and his men were imprisoned. A number of early readers noted no one would be stupid enough to carry around that much incriminating information. But Allen was and he did. It's true.

The Hercules Powder Plant in New Jersey was sabotaged on September 12, 1940, with groundwork laid by Nazi Germany and the IRA.

Yes, spies discovered by the Bund were called on to be "liquidated," and many died in strange and suspicious circumstances—although none were ever legally proved to be murdered. This includes Julius Sicius, who'd been spotted taking down license plate numbers at Deutsches Haus. The coroner's report states he "fell." John Schmidt, Leon Lewis's first spy, died under suspicious circumstances; his wife believed he'd been poisoned.

Laura Ingalls was an aviatrix, and she was close with the Comforts and really did invite Grace Comfort to accompany her to Germany.

Hermann Schwinn did have issues with his citizenship and was eventually arrested for that reason.

Robert Noble was an anti-Semite and isolationist who hosted and participated in a "for show" impeachment trial of Roosevelt.

Yes, there was a plot to overthrow the U.S. government after the election of Roosevelt in 1940, headed by Clayton F. Ingalls, husband of Laura Ingalls, and George Deatherage (yes, his real name).

They did indeed have a blueprint for "a fascist military organization and the names and addresses of hundreds of coup leaders and subleaders scattered across the country." Ingalls was planning to "equip them with weapons from the National Rifle Association" (Ross, *Hitler in Los Angeles*). This coup would "rid the nation of

'Jewish Imperialism and Judeo-Communism'" (Ibid.) There were also plans to blow up defense installations and seize munitions from the National Guard.

Lastly, there was a showdown with the Bund's Nazis and the FBI at the Murphy Ranch the day after the attack on Pearl Harbor— but there are no records of what actually happened.

The ruins of the ranch can be found in the Pacific Palisades to this day—you can hike to the remains that are left and covered in graffiti—and take pictures of the site of what was supposed to be Hitler's West Coast Bunker.

ABOUT THE AUTHOR

SUSAN ELIA MACNEAL is the *New York Times, Washington Post,* and *USA Today* bestselling author of the Maggie Hope mystery series. She has won the Barry Award and has been nominated for the Edgar, Macavity, Agatha, Left Coast Crime, Dilys, ITW Thriller, and Nero awards. She lives in Brooklyn, New York, with her husband and son.

susaneliamacneal.com
Facebook.com/MrChurchillsSecretary
Twitter: @susanmacneal
Instagram: @susaneliamacneal

ABOUT THE TYPE

This book was set in Bembo, a typeface based on an old-style Roman face that was used for Cardinal Pietro Bembo's tract *De Aetna* in 1495. Bembo was cut by Francesco Griffo (1450–1518) in the early sixteenth century for Italian Renaissance printer and publisher Aldus Manutius (1449–1515). The Lanston Monotype Company of Philadelphia brought the well-proportioned letterforms of Bembo to the United States in the 1930s.